CRA...

Includes new stories ...

JIM DEFELICE

New York Times *bestselling co-author of the Dale Brown's Dreamland series*

"Former U.S. Air Force Captain Brown . . . and DeFelice are in fine form here." —*Publishers Weekly*

JAMES H. COBB

National bestselling author of the Commander Garrett thrillers, Sea Fighter, Sea Strike, *and* Target Lock

"Garrett is an original." —*USA Today*

"The best naval hero since Tom Clancy's Jack Ryan." —*Murder Ink*

BRENDAN DUBOIS

Award-winning author of Resurrection Day

"Grabs you by the sheer power of its storytelling, a thriller with punch." —*The Denver Post*

R. J. PINEIRO

Acclaimed author of Conspiracy.Com *and* Firewall

"Move over, Tom Clancy, there is a new kid on the block." —*Library Journal*

WILIAM H. KEITH, JR.

Acclaimed author of Bolo Strike

"His combat scenes work superbly." —*Starlog*

JOHN HELFERS *Coeditor of* Villains Victorious, Warrior Fantastic, *and* The Valdemar Companion

TONY GERAGHTY *Respected author of the military non-fiction books,* Who Dare Wins *and* March or Die

JEAN RABE *Author of the Dragonlance novels,* Downfall, Betrayal, *and* Redemption

DOUG ALLYN *Edgar Award–winning author of short mystery fiction*

Titles in the First to Fight Series

FIRST TO FIGHT
FIRST TO FIGHT II
CRASH DIVE

CRASH DIVE

Edited by

MARTIN H. GREENBERG

JOVE BOOKS, NEW YORK

CRASH DIVE

A Jove Book / published by arrangement with Martin H. Greenberg
c/o Tekno Books

PRINTING HISTORY
Jove edition / July 2003

CONTENTS

CRASH DIVE

Cat Bag Bay

JAMES H. COBB

James Cobb lives in the Pacific Northwest, where he writes both the Amanda Garrett techno-thriller series and the Kevin Pulaski fifties suspense mysteries, not to mention the occasional odd bit of historical and science fiction. When not so involved, he enjoys long road trips, collecting classic military firearms, and learning the legends and lore of the great American hot rod. He may also be found frequently and shamelessly pandering to the whims of "Lisette," his classic 1960 Ford Thunderbird.

**April 1943
The Philippine Sea, Somewhere South
of Parece Vela**

TO AN OBSERVER somehow transported to the wastes of the Central Pacific she would have been a sliver of moon shadow flowing effortlessly across the starlit waters.

A bull-nosed bow, low riding and sharply raked, scissored with deliberation through the hunchbacked ocean swells, spray arcing from the cutwater. A long stretch of sea-washed hull followed, foam sifting through the latticed teak of the decking. Then came the first massive six-inch mount on its low gun platform and the great looming ax blade of a conning tower with man shapes silhouetted along its upper rim. A second six-incher aft and another trailing expanse of deck haunted by the writhing silver plumes of diesel exhaust.

Sweeping past, the sea roiled with the beat of her propellers. Then she merged once more with the night, her wake healing itself with a fading hiss.

At 371 feet in length and with a submerged displacement of nearly 4,000 tons, the USS *Niobe* was a giant of her breed, the last and best of the experimental V-class "sub cruisers" built by the United States between the two world wars.

When her keel had been laid in the late 1920's, she and her sisters, the *Nautilus* and the *Narwhale*, had been the largest and most powerful units of the navy's undersea fleet. They were the largest still, but now they were worn and sea-weary mammoths. Built to match the parameters of an obsolete battle doctrine, they had been superceded on the patrol line by the stream of new and deadly Gato- and Balao-class fleet boats pouring off the wartime slipways.

Still, America stood at arms and there was use for every seaworthy hull. *Niobe* and her kin had been gathered into the exotic fold of SPYRON, the Pacific Fleet Submarine Force's Special Operations Squadron. There, tasks were found uniquely suited to the great size and range of the sub cruisers: a marine raider force to be carried deep into enemy territory, an arms shipment to be delivered to a resistance movement, an allied agent to be spirited off a hostile beach.

Or, as on this night, a payload of aviation gasoline to be delivered to an isolated atoll.

As continued

Your current "patrol" fruitcake is still lasting, Amy. I'm having my one slice a day with my breakfast coffee. As usual, a lot of good thoughts of you and home come with it.

We'll be arriving shortly at our objective. Naturally enough I can't put in writing where it is or what we intend to do once we get there. That'll have to wait for when this war isn't important anymore. I can say that things are coming along about as well as can be expected. Good Lord willing, this shouldn't be a shooting job. Or at least that's how it looks for now . . .

A submarine relies heavily on the water flow over its bow and stern diving planes for depth and angle control. Submerging vertically in place like a descending elevator is not a task routinely or casually undertaken. It demands both a finicky management of the trim tanks plus a diving officer with a near supernatural ability to project what his boat was going to do even before she began to do it. *Niobe*'s Lieutenant Clancy was indeed that good, but the sub cruiser's bulk mandated an even more radical methodology.

"Crew's Quarter's," Clancy's voice roared over the 1-MC circuit. "I want six men into the forward torpedo room! On the double!"

Through the open 'tween decks hatch those in the conning tower could hear the living ballast racing from the crews quarters amidships, through the control room below, and on toward the bow, knob-toed safety shoes clattering on the linoleum decking.

Leaning forward, Commander Cullen Perry studied the curving glass tubes of the inclinometers, nodding with approval as the bubbles recentered, erasing the first trace of an up angle. Stocky, solid, and balding with a face sea-weathered beyond his thirty-seven years, Perry held the intercom mike cradled ready in his palm.

"Forward torpedo room, this is the captain."

"Forward torpedo, aye."

"Verify that the sound heads are rigged in."

"Sound heads are inboard and secure, sir."

"Very good." There was a friendly bear mildness to Perry's baritone growl, enhanced by a South-coast Texas drawl. "Diving officer, verify all Kelson valves are closed and secured for bottoming."

"All ballast tank and hull valves are closed and secure, sir." Clancy yelled his reply up through the control room hatch.

Across the polished brass and white-painted steel confines of the conn, Lieutenant Daniel Mercurio, *Niobe*'s dark and youthful exec, looked up from the master depth gauge. "Dropping through seventy feet, sir," he announced.

"Good enough, Danny." Perry switched the intercom to the all ship's squawk box. "All hands, stand by to bottom the boat."

There was a protracted moment of silence, then coral rasped against steel. The keel thudded down and *Niobe*'s frames creaked softly as the big sub settled into her bed on the lagoon floor. Her decks tilted slightly and her crew noted infinitesimal change from motion to nonmotion. They had arrived at the "objective."

Perry turned to the forwardmost of the two silver shafts that pierced the center of the conning tower from the deck to the overhead. "Up scope," he commanded, sinking down to his knees beside the periscope well.

The electric hoist motor hummed and the periscope shaft shimmered as it slithered upward. Catching and snapping open the handgrips with practiced ease, Perry nestled his face into the worn rubber eyepiece as it emerged, allowing the periscope to lift him to a standing posture.

Given the depth of the lagoon floor, the slim lens head of the attack scope just barely pierced the surface. Wavelets broke across the glass, intermittently blurring Perry's view as he made the first instinctive fast sweep around the horizon. With no immediate threats visible, his second rotation was more deliberate, a point-by-point study of the local environment.

Little had changed topside since they had crept through the narrow entry channel at first light. There was little to change.

The searing sun had crawled higher in a tropic azure sky and the marching mid-Pacific rollers continued their stubborn beat against the low wind- and sea-scoured islets that made up the lagoon's perimeter, their spray flashing white against the old bone color of the dead surface coral.

A passing windjammer captain in the eighteenth century had discovered the atoll, naming it "January," after the month of its sighting, and listing it on his charts only as a potential hazard to navigation.

January was a flyspeck on the ocean, a remnant of a prehistoric undersea volcano that had pushed through to the surface at the western edge of the Great West Mariana submarine basin. Scrubbed bare by numberless typhoons, its reefs lifted only a few meager inches above the sea. It supported no human habitation, nor had it ever. There was no water uncontaminated by salt. No plant life. No animal population save for the occasional resting seabird.

There was nothing of value on January for any passing mariner ... save possibly for the four or five square miles of sheltered anchorage within its curving barrier reef, and that was valid only in a moderate sea.

And yet the dictates of war had suddenly made this little patch of still water a treasure briefly beyond price.

That was why Cullen Perry had nursed his command through the bristling Japanese defense line of the Marianas barrier and why he had brought *Niobe* to this dubious haven on the lagoon floor.

Perry hesitated in his march around the horizon, catching a glint in the sky far to the north. Possibly it was only a wheeling gull or, just as possibly, it was a reflection off of a patrol plane canopy. Located between the Imperial Japanese basing complexes in the Mariana and Philippine island chains, the Philippine Sea was a risky place to loiter in the spring of 1943, at least if one were a United States Navy submarine.

As it was, if some sharp-eyed Nip aviator picked out the symmetrical outline of *Niobe*'s hull as she lay in the shallows of the lagoon's eye ...

He snapped the scope handles upright. There was no sense worrying about it now.

"Down scope."

Perry felt every eye in the control room flicking in his direction. Elsewhere throughout the boat the rest of his crew would be staring up at the intercom loudspeakers expectantly.

The captain under God, Perry thought wryly, or at least his spokesman. He martialed his thoughts for a moment, then caught up the conn microphone once more.

"All hands. This is the captain again. I guess it's time I let you in on our situation. I know you're aware of the special training we conducted with fleet patrol aviation before our departure from Pearl. Well, here's what it was about.

"Tonight, shortly after moonrise, a navy PBY flying boat en route to an undisclosed location will be landing in the lagoon topside. We'll be there waiting to refuel him. Tomorrow, on his return flight, we'll be doing the same. In between times we'll just be laying doggo on the bottom, trying not to draw attention to ourselves.

"None of us need to know where this plane is coming from or where it's is going to or why. We just have to see to it he makes it there and gets back again. Once that's accomplished we'll be out of here and on our way home. That is all."

As continued

In the last section I mailed before we sortied, I think I told you about Chief Torpedoman Honeycutt and his wife expecting their second? Well, the boy hasn't mentioned any problems, but he's been talking about his wife and the new baby a lot and I'm getting the feeling that something isn't sitting right with him.

When she gets the chance, could the captain's lady look into it and maybe pay a call or two on Honeycutt's wife? 'Preciate you.

We are at "objective" and are busy playing the usual hurry up and wait game. All continues routine.

I just took a second look at that last sentence, Amy girl, and I find myself marveling at it a little. What could conceivably be "normal" about a community of men living on the bottom of the sea?

Yet for us, it is.

In the control room my watch standers are sitting

on the deck at their stations, shooting the bull and
swapping dirty jokes. In the engine and torpedo
spaces tools clink softly as the motor macs and
torpedomen catch up on their maintenance. Acey-
deucey dice rattle in the crew's quarters and those
hands taking their turn in the hot bunks snore
softly, immune to the activity around them. The
new records we picked up at Pearl are growing old
on the ship's turntable and the ventilator fans are
passing the word that we're having roast chicken
for lunch.

So bizarrely normal.

To continue.

One of the advantages of the big V-boats was a mod-
icum of additional inboard space, enough so that the
wardroom mess table could actually have chairs instead
of benches.

Lieutenant Danny Mercurio shoved his chair back in
disgust, flipping his king on its side. "I don't know why
I even try."

Perry chuckled deep in his chest. "You're getting
there, Danny. You aren't good enough yet, but you're
getting there."

At the far end of the wardroom table Lieutenant Sven
Jorgenson, *Niobe*'s torpedo officer, looked up from his
Zane Grey. "Don't let the old man fool you, Danny. He
says the same thing to all of the damn fools he suckers
into a game."

Jorgenson's use of the term "old man" was in relation
purely to rank and position. "Swede" Jorgenson had
spent more years in the boats than anyone else aboard
Niobe, including her skipper. Lean, grizzled, and bony,
Jorgenson had done five tours as an enlisted man and
CPO before receiving a wartime "good of the service"

commission shortly after Pearl Harbor. Grumbling, he had accepted his advancement to the wardroom.

There was literally nothing Jorgenson did not know about a V-series submarine, and once, when he had been *Niobe*'s Chief of the Boat, he'd had all of the skin peeled from his arms saving her from an ugly battery fire. On all counts, he was classed as a rather privileged individual.

Perry grinned and started to reset the chess pieces in their places. "There is a difference, Swede. Danny here at least has a chance to learn something. After I whipped you that first half dozen times back aboard the old *Barracuda* I knew you were a lost cause."

Muttering under his breath, the ex-chief returned to the *Purple Sage*.

Up in the forward torpedo room "American Patrol" ran its course on the record player and faded into silence.

And in that moment of quiet, Cullen Perry stiffened and sat erect. Sliding his chair back, he reached up and hit the switch on the wardroom fan, shutting it off. He listened intently and the two officers sharing the space with him followed suit.

Benny Goodman began to crank up on the turntable and Jorgenson twisted and leaned into the officer's country passageway, brushing aside the doorway curtain. "In the torpedo room! Belay that racket!"

Goodman's clarinet squawked and cut off.

Gradually he and Mercurio became aware of what had keyed their captain's attention. A sound filtering in from somewhere beyond the hull. A rhythmic *shush . . . shush . . . shush,* faint yet growing. The mechanical beat of a slowly turning propeller.

"Shit," Mercurio murmured lowly. "That sounds like he's right here in the lagoon."

Perry lifted an eyebrow. "I suspect that's because he

is, Danny. With our sound heads rigged in, we never heard him coming."

No one questioned the identity of the intruder. There was no conceivable way it could be an Allied or neutral vessel.

Perry reached back over his shoulder again, hitting the PRESS TO TALK button for the 1-MC. "All hands," he said quietly. "This is the captain. Close to General Quarters. Rig for silent running. No alarms."

Throughout the boat voices sank to whispers and light footfalls hastened down the passageways. Watertight doors were eased shut against their rubber gaskets and dogging levers squeaked. The purr of the ventilation system faded as the ducts were cranked closed.

Mercurio and Jorgenson started to rise, but Perry waved them back into their seats again. Instinctively all three men looked up as the pulse beat of the intruder's screws grew closer.

"If he has K guns, we're dog meat," Jorgenson commented judgmentally.

"Could be," Perry nodded, "if he spots us down here."

The propellers stopped.

A moment of total silence stretched out and then burst with an abrupt crashing roar.

"Anchor chain going down," Perry said.

A second crashing roar followed a minute or so later.

"A second hook," Jorgenson added. "Double mooring. He must figure on being around for a while."

"Likely. He may not know we're down here after all."

"But it sounds like he's sitting right on top of us." Mercurio interjected uneasily.

"Pretty close." Perry agreed. "There was a little wind chop the last time I took a look around topside. Maybe just enough to break up our outline from the surface."

Sweat began to prickle under wash khaki shirts as heat

radiated upward from the ranked battery jars beneath the wardroom decks. With the airflow from the ventilators secured, the sense of claustrophobia that lurks aboard every submarine began to creep out of the corners.

Mercurio asked the question. "What do we do now, Skipper?"

Perry looked down at the chessboard deployed on the wardroom table. "Well, let's see. Which would you like this time? Black or white?"

"Up scope."

For the first few instants of observation all Perry could see was a dimly glowing void of jade green, then the lens head pierced the surface and he peered into the twilight.

With another vessel sharing the close confines of the lagoon, he hadn't dared risk raising the periscope in broad daylight. Now with dusk settling in topside, the danger of a betraying glint or splash of foam was reduced. Yet there was still adequate light to reveal their unwelcome neighbor.

Slowly Perry rotated the knurled metal knob of the periscope ranging gauge. "A naval auxiliary," he murmured. " 'Bout three hundred fifty feet in length . . . four, five thousand tons. Two superposed gun mounts forward . . . twin open mount DPs . . . four point sevens or five-inchers . . . a single raked stack amidships and a low well deck right aft with what looks like a heavy duty crane at the deck break."

"She's an Akitsushima class seaplane tender," Mercurio reported, looking up from the silhouette book. "Only a couple of years old. She's intended to support large flying boats in forward combat areas."

"What the hell is he doing here now?" Swede Jorgenson demanded, his head framed in the open 'tween decks hatch.

"Likely the same thing we are, Swede," Perry murmured into the side of the scope barrel as he rotated it slowly. "It makes sense. We've got a high tide tonight and a full moon, perfect for flying boat operations, and this is the only sheltered water in the central Philippine Sea. That's why we heard him putting that second anchor down astern, he's rigging a fixed moorage to handle aircraft. He's got no idea that somebody else is here to do the same thing."

"Just like our guys have no idea that somebody else is going to be sitting here waiting for them. Christ, this deal is FUBAR, totally Fucked Up Beyond All Recall."

Perry could only lift shaggy eyebrows and nod. "I suspect you're right, Swede. . . . Whoa, yeah, we got more company coming. A flying boat is on approach. A big bastard. Down scope!"

Niobe's skipper stepped back as the attack periscope sank into its well. "Gentlemen, the floor is open for suggestions." "We have to contact Pearl," said Mercurio. "They've got to recall our plane."

"That could be considerably easier said than done, Danny, on both counts." Perry glanced at the bulkhead chronometer. "It's currently eighteen fifty and that PBY is scheduled to touch down shortly after twenty three hundred. That's four hours from now and we don't know where he's coming from. A PBY can stay airborne for almost a full day. He could already be well past his point of no return with no alternative landing sites.

"For another point, we're a long way from Pearl. Just sticking a couple of feet of radio mast out of the water won't give us the range we'll need. The only one who'd be sure of hearing us would be the radio guard over on that Jap tender. To reach COMSUBPAC we'll have to surface."

"Any chance of us hauling out of this hole and making rendezvous with the PBY in the open sea?" Jorgenson inquired.

"Nah. We barely made it through the lagoon entry channel surfaced and with a full turbo blow on all ballast tanks. There's no way in hell we could get out submerged or even running with our decks awash. Anyway what chance would we have of conducting a surface rendezvous and refueling with a flock of Emilys and Helens in the neighborhood? When that waxing moon rises its going to be bright as day up there."

Perry glanced up at the cable-studded overhead once more. "No, I suspect the only way we're going to salvage this operation is to kill that party-crashing son of a bitch by the most expedient means avalable. Mr. Clancy, you have the conn. Swede, Danny, let's do some planning."

They withdrew to the wardroom. Soon however, they learned that the new environment was no more conducive to solutions than the conning tower.

"If this pathetic-ass excuse for a chart is to be halfways trusted," Swede Jorgenson snarled, "we're screwed. There's no way in hell we can put a fish in that goddamn tender from here."

"Are you kidding, Swede?" Mercurio protested. "We're already at point-blank range."

"That just the problem, Mr. Mercurio. We're *below* point-blank range." The torpedo officer twisted the chart around on the tabletop so it faced the exec. "Look, right now we're resting on the bottom in the eye of the lagoon. This is the only patch of water on the inside deep enough for us to submerge in and there ain't a hell of a lot of it.

"Beyond the eye, the lagoon shallows rapidly to be-

tween twenty and thirty feet in depth, plenty of bottom
for a seaplane but no damn amount of water for a submerged sub. Now, take a look at the depth gradients and
the area of deep water we have to work with."

Mercurio studied the chart for a moment, scowled,
then reached for a navigator's compass, measuring distances against the chart scale.

"The deeps are only about seven hundred yards
across."

"Yeah, and that Jap bird farm is sitting about a hundred and fifty yards off our starboard side, almost in the
dead center of the deep water. That puts him three hundred and fifty yards away from the shallows on any bearing . . . and a Mark XIV needs a minimum run of four
hundred and fifty yards to arm after being launched. The
friggin' fish would dud, Mr. Mercurio. They'd just
bounce off of him."

"Jesus, Swede. I see what you mean. We are screwed.
And so are the guys in that PBY."

"Not necessarily, gentlemen," Perry interjected slowly.
"What this means is that we can't apply the classic submariners methodology to this situation. We may to have
to go up top and deal with this gentleman the hard way."

Jorgenson and Mercurio exchanged startled glances
and then refocused on their captain.

"Skipper, you can't be thinking of doing a battle surface with this guy?" Jorgenson demanded.

"Why not, Swede. *Niobe* and the other V-boats were
built as subcruisers. We're designed be able to fight on
the surface, more so than any of the new fleet types. We
mount the heaviest deck guns in the fleet. Those six-inch
shorts may not have the reach of a CL's main battery
rifles, but at close range they pack the same punch.
That's why we only have a six-tube torpedo group

aboard. Our fish were almost intended to be a secondary armament."

Jorgenson nodded thoughtfully. "Yeah, that's so, Skipper, but still, the V-boats were meant for commerce raiding. It was intended we be able to shoot it out with something like an armed merchantman or a subchaser. It was never in the books to conduct a surface action with a serious man-of-war."

"Fleet auxiliary," Perry corrected mildly.

"You're not going to get a hell of a lot of change on the difference."

"He's right, Captain," Mercurio said. "And you were right about that Akitsushima's bow turrets. The book says they're five-inch twin mounts. It also indicates she carries four triple twenty-five millimeter pom-poms as well. She's a combat tender and she's going to put up one hell of a fight."

"We'll have surprise on our side, Danny. They don't have a clue we're down here yet. They've got to figure they're safe from subs in this lagoon. They're sure not going to expect one to pop up practically alongside. Beyond that, I have a couple of other notions that could give us the edge when the time comes."

Perry paused a moment to brush a last few strands of sweat-damp hair back across his balding scalp. "Anyway, gentlemen, what other choice do we have? We can't get off a submerged torpedo attack. Our only other option is to kiss off that inbound PBY and sit tight on the bottom, hoping that tender hauls out again before we run out of air and battery. I don't think much of that notion for a lot of reasons.

"For one, we weren't sent out here just on a whim. That plane has got to be doing something pretty damn important to justify this operation. For another, if that Jap operates in much the same way as our own flying

boat tenders do, he could stay anchored here for the next
month.

"For a third, if a PBY shows up way the hell out here
in the middle of nowhere, somebody on that tender is
going to start thinking and looking. We aren't the only
ones who know about refueling a seaplane from a submarine. If the Japs trap us inside this lagoon it will literally be like shooting fish in a barrel.

"And finally, let's go back to that PBY again. We're
their only chance. We either get them home or they don't
go home. Abandoning that aircrew does not sit well with
me, gentlemen, not at all."

Mercurio lifted a frustrated hand off the tabletop.
"Hell, if you put it that way, Skipper, why even talk about
it? It's going to be a hell of an interesting scrap though."

Cullen Perry grinned back mirthlessly. "Like two
damn old tomcats in a bag, Danny."

From somewhere beyond the hull, a low droning buzz
began to grow in intensity.

"Another Japanese flying boat taxiing in," Perry commented. "Our friend is getting himself another customer.
That's good."

"It is?"

"Uh-huh, very good. Danny. I want the Airedales
aboard that tender to be kept busy for the rest of the
evening. And later on, those seaplanes could prove to be
real handy."

"Yeah," Jorgenson commented dryly, "for the Japs."

"No, Swede. For us."

. . . looks like I was very wrong about this mission,
Amy girl. It has turned into a shooting job after
all, a mean one. So mean, in fact, that I am wondering if you will ever read these words.

I can't speak about this to any of the crew of

course. I can't speak about it at all, save in this letter of ours that never ends. Here's where you keep me strong, Amy, with the strength of the captain's wife. Even ten thousand miles apart, I still have someone with whom I can talk out my fears and my uncertainties. That is a treasure beyond price to me now.

Just in case, let me say it again. I love you.

To continue.

"Time?"

Perry could have looked for himself but it was an excuse to break up the thickening silence within the excessively cramped confines of the conning tower. The lead men of the antiaircraft crews were squeezed in among the watch standers and extra cans of 20-millimeter cannon and .30 caliber machine gun ammunition cluttering the limited deck space.

Browning automatic rifles and Thompson submachine guns from the arms lockers also stood propped in odd corners, ready to be passed upward through the bridge hatch. In the fight to be, every weapon *Niobe* possessed would be brought to bear.

"Twenty-three ten," Mercurio replied lowly. "The PBY is scheduled to be over the lagoon in about another twenty minutes." He, like everyone else in the conning tower, wore red night vision goggles, preparing his eyes for the surface darkness.

Perry nodded. "Right after moonrise. Let's just hope he's running a little late." He reached over for the intercom hand mike. "Radio shack, this is the captain. The second we break the surface, get your mast up and get on with the pilot of the PBY. Advise him of the situation and have him circle until we get things under control down here. Also, if we go off the air suddenly . . . well, tell him good luck and that he's on his own."

"Aye, aye, sir. Will do," the filtered voice replied over the squawk box.

"Forward torpedo room. What's your situation up there, Swede?"

"Forward group loaded, Skipper. All fish set for six feet and at low speed. That should give them their best chance to settle down at running depth."

"Good enough. Flood all tubes forward and open the outer doors when we sound battle surface. As soon as I can back us outside of arming range we'll try and get off a spread. Until then it'll all be the deck guns."

"I'll be topside with number one," the grim reply came back.

"Okay. Just watch yourself, Swede. They don't make parts for your mark anymore."

"Ha-ha . . . sir."

There was only a final set of orders to verify.

"Mr. Mercurio." Perry used formal military protocol to underline the urgency of his words. "You will stand by in the control room. You will not come to the bridge unless I have been killed or otherwise put out of action. Your primary concern will be the recovery of the PBY crew and then in getting the boat home.

"No matter what anyone of any rank aboard that seaplane may say, you will not fool around with a refueling attempt. You will take the aircraft's crew and passengers aboard, you will scuttle the aircraft, and you will get *Niobe* out through that channel and away from here with all possible speed. Is that understood?"

He gave a short acknowledging nod. "Understood, sir, perfectly."

He looked young for the thought of that kind of responsibility. So many of them did these days. But he also looked unafraid of the thought.

"Then take your station, Danny, and God ride with you."

"You, too, Captain."

As the exec dropped down through the conn hatch Perry ordered the periscope raised once more.

The Japanese vessel still bustled with apparently routine activity. Work lights blazed on the well deck, silhouetting the outlines of a pair of huge Imperial Navy flying boats, four-engined Kawanishi H8Ks, the maritime patrol bomber the Allies had dubbed the "Emily."

One nuzzled bow-on to the flank of the tender while the second had been hoisted out of the water, to rest in the servicing cradle on the ship's fantail. A third Emily had been heard to touch down, but apparently it had moored out of sight on the far side of the tender. Between the close range and the periscope's magnification, crewmen could be clearly seen working around the aircraft, preparing them for departure.

Perry theorized that the tender had been dispatched to January to serve as a temporary relay base for a long-range aircraft transfer. The Emilys had touched down at last light to refuel, service, and to grant their crews a few hours of rest. They were now preparing to take off by the light of the rising moon, ready to resume their journey to some far outpost of the empire.

This was all for the good. Each bomber would now be a giant gas can topped off to brimming full.

The Japanese didn't seem concerned about having an enemy within a thousand miles, much less within one.

They hadn't a suspicion that the tiger was already inside the tent.

Perry slammed the scope handles upright. "Down scope! Blow all ballast fore and aft. Take her up! Battle surface!"

The hoarse triple *gagoooooogah* blare of the diving

alarm blended with the piercing metallic chime of the General Quarters alarm. The latter being a martial redundancy as every man aboard had been standing-to for hours.

"Man battle stations, gun action! Man battle stations, gun action!" Another redundancy, all hands knew of the nature of the coming battle.

High-pressure air screamed and rumbled through the manifolds, blasting water out the tank groups. *Niobe* stirred, lifting off the bottom like an awakening sea serpent.

"Motor room, keep us on battery and stand by to answer bells. Engine room, do not, I say again, do not start the diesel plants until I give the word!"

"Aye, aye, Captain! Ready to answer bells on battery power!"

"Engine room, understood sir!"

"Mr. Clancy, maintain the high pressure blow after she breaks surface! I want all the buoyancy we've got as fast as we can get it."

"Aye, aye sir, coming through forty feet. Breaking surface now!"

Beyond the steel, the rending sea could be heard hissing and streaming away from the superstructure.

"Open the hatch!"

A few gallons of blood-warm water sluiced past the quartermaster as he spun open the dogging wheel and shoved the dished steel lid back onto its latch. Tearing off his red goggles, Perry was the second man up the ladder to the bridge deck.

Even now there was that one instant's appreciation of the clean salt air after the congested fug of the submarine's interior. Behind him more men flowed up through the bridge hatch, some dropping down to the twenty-millimeter platforms at the front and rear of the conning tower. Others lifted machine guns out of their pressure-proof canisters or passed up small arms and cans of ammunition. All moved with a submariner's instinctive silence.

Hatches were swinging open on the main deck as well, and the six-incher crews swarmed around their mounts, pulling the muzzle plugs and casting off the tie-downs.

Time. God grant them just a little time to make ready.

The moon had edged up beyond the horizon, milk white and dazzling to a night-adapted eye. The Akitsushima was outlined by it, but *Niobe*, riding low to the water and down moon might still be blending in with the night.

No alarm swept the decks of the tender. Maybe all hands were focusing on preparing their aircraft charges for flight? Maybe her lookouts had been blinded by the work lights?

Across the water came the whine of an aircraft engine's inertial starter.

On the main deck the six-incher tubes were starting to swing outboard, training around to bear on target. The slender stingers of the twin-mount twenties were casting loose and coming to bear as well. Ammunition drums clicked into place and shells slid into breaches with an oily whisper.

Just a little longer.

Cullen Perry heard it happen. The rattle of the alarm bells echoed across the lagoon's glassy surface and the tender's topside lights snapped off with a sudden fearful abruptness.

"Open fire! Take him!"

Massive orange balls of flame materialized beyond the deck gun tubes, and *Niobe* lurched sideways through the water under the recoil, the muzzle blast whiplashing all hands topside. The 20-millimeter twin mounts and the Browning .30 calibers followed through, stuttering out

their writhing tracer streams. Along the main deck and
from odd corners of the bridge structure, the Thompson
submachine guns and BARs interjected their lighter
venom, shell casings raining onto the decks in glinting
streams.

Across the waters the Japanese tender reeled under the
unexpected blow, an assault launched with the swift and
silent lethality of a cobra strike. One of the six-inch
rounds, aimed and fired in haste, screamed harmlessly
across the tender's foredeck, the second gouged into her
superstructure at the base of the funnel, spraying flaming
shrapnel into the night.

The automatic weapons had been given other targets,
the massive Emily flying boats cradled on the tender's
aft deck and tied up along her flank. Bullets and autocannon shells punched through the lighter structure of
the patrol bombers, probing for vulnerability and finding
it.

In the days prior to Pearl Harbor, Japan's otherwise
superlative aviation designers had made one catastrophic
error. Focusing on lightness, range, and performance,
they had neglected aircraft armor and self-sealing fuel
tanks.

Flame raced across the broad wing of the moored Emily, the individual fuel cells exploding in sequence from
port to starboard. *Niobe*'s tracer streams then elevated
and bunched on the second aircraft resting in the ship-
board servicing cradle. Thunder rolled across the lagoon,
and a mushroom of fire sprouted on the tender's well
deck and climbed into the sky.

There was no longer a night. January atoll was illuminated by the glare of hell, and damned souls ran ablaze
on the decks of the Akitsushima or hurled themselves
smoldering into the mercy of the sea.

And yet, the tender recovered. She fought back, for as

any Pacific Fleet man-of-warsman could testify, *coward* was a word unknown to the Imperial Japanese Navy.

A line of bullet splashes stitched back across the sea toward *Niobe* and machine gun slugs tore up the teak of her main deck. The tailgunner in the moored and blazing Emily had brought his weapon into play even as he burned to death.

Forward on the tender the barrels of her gun turrets shortened as they swiveled to bear on her attacker. The first replying salvo screamed over the heads of the submarine's laboring gunners.

On the bridge Cullen Perry flinched at the feathery brush of the shell's transiting shock waves. His gunners were making good practice, the big deck mounts hammering the Japanese surface ship, kicking in her sides and superstructure like they were cardboard. However it was plain she was going to take a good deal of killing. On the other hand, one solid heavy-caliber hit on *Niobe*'s pressure hull could be fatal.

He hadn't maneuvered yet, giving his gunners the easiest possible lay for their first few critical rounds. Now though they had to start dodging.

Perry tore down the watertight cover on the bridge intercom. "Control room! All engines back two thirds! Steer zero eight zero!"

"Engines backing two thirds!" Mercurio's voice snapped back. "Steering, zero eight zero."

With the instant, silent response of an electric propulsion system, the sea hunched up under the *Niobe*'s screws and she gained way astern, her course angling around the burning tender. Perry had initiated battle broadside to broadside, relying on surprise and firepower for his initial edge. Now he intended to use a quirk of the Akitsushima's design to maintain the advantage. All of the tender's heavy guns were mounted forward.

If *Niobe* could back away, moving aft of the tender, she could escape from the arcs of her foe's most potent armament while still delivering what the old timers called raking fire. Beyond that, if Perry could maneuver her into the lagoon's entry channel, he could reach a valid torpedo arming range and finish this fight in short order.

The deliberate two-rounds-per-minute firing rate of the number-one deck gun broke. In the flickering intermittent light of burning aviation gasoline, Perry could see the spare form of Swede Jorgenson crouching beside the gunner's mate in the trainer's saddle and catch fragments of yelled commands.

The muzzle of the big cannon elevated minutely, edged to port, and crashed out its next round.

Forward of the Japanese tender's bridge, blue-white cordite flame blossomed, and the tender's B-mount turret buckled and distorted, its twin barrels angling uselessly toward the sky. Perry lifted and clinched both hands in a fierce boxer's salute to Jorgenson.

But the Japanese still refused to yield. Amid the blazes spreading amidships on the tender, a twenty-five millimeter antiaircraft gun engaged, the venomous little shell-bursts of the tribarreled pom-pom sweeping out of the night and dancing down the length of *Niobe*'s hull.

Men threw themselves flat on the decks or behind the dubious protection of the bridge spray shields. Slow or unfortunate ones screamed and died. The submarine's fire faltered.

Amid the sudden topside chaos a faint voice filtered through the squawk box. "Bridge, this is the radio room. Captain, we have word on our plane."

Perry pulled himself to his feet and slammed a palm down on the PRESS-TO-TALK. "Belay that crap! Danny, give me all back emergency! Steer zero eight five and watch your Fathometers! Yell if we get less than twenty feet under the keel! Radio room, tell that damn PBY we're busy down here!"

Niobe was pulling back toward the entry channel, putting the tender's flaming stern and the rapidly spreading pools of burning aviation fuel between herself and the hostile gunnery. The tender's A mount barked out another brace of shells, but their water plumes lifted well beyond the submarine's bow. Likewise the fire of the antiaircraft gun futilely lashed at the lagoon's surface, its barrels grating against their traverse stops. A pause came to the battle, precious free seconds to strike the wounded below and lift fresh ammunition topside.

Perry shot a look astern, gauging distances to the luminous surf breaks on either side of the entry channel. "Control room, all engines back slow. Five degrees starboard. Forward Torpedo Room, stand by all tubes. Set torpedoes for zero angle off the bow."

Aligning now bow-on toward the Akitsushima, the sub's forward guns reengaged pumping shells into the pyre burning on their enemy's stern. Crouching down behind the binocularlike Target Bearing Transmitter mounted on the lip of the spray shield, Perry tried for a range on the enemy vessel. But even as he adjusted the crosshairs, he caught movement in the flickering shadows beyond the ship. With a sudden chill that belied his sweat-soaked shirt, he realized that in the turmoil of the battle they had forgotten a critical factor.

Three Emily flying boats had landed in the lagoon.

The third had indeed been moored on the far side of the tender and its aircrew had been given enough time to cast off from the ship. Engines idling, they had been sheltering behind the ship. But now, as the *Niobe* entered his line of sight, the patrol bomber's pilot firewalled his throttles, either in a wild attempt to take to the sky or in a suicidal ramming attack against the submarine.

Quadruple propellers shimmering in the firelight, the big seaplane lifted onto step, accelerating across the wave crests with what seemed to be a supernatural speed. Its nose turret sparkled and bullets whined and shrieked off the steel of *Niobe*'s bridge.

There was no time, no sea room, and no speed to maneuver. Cullen Perry learned then that there is no more hideous feeling than to be a shipmaster with no way to save his ship.

"Begging your pardon, Captain." A respectful arm edged Perry aside. One of *Niobe*'s Negro messmates braced a Thompson against the spray shield and began squeezing off a series of careful, deliberate bursts at the onrushing aircraft. The forward twenties were firing as well, their tracers drifting into the shadowy bulk of the Emily. And Swede Jorgenson again crouched beside the number-one six-incher.

Bawhom! The cannon's breech slammed back against the braking of its recoil pistons. The shell punched squarely into the bow of the seaplane, the glass of its flight-deck greenhouse spraying and glinting. Fused to be fired at the heavy structure of a surface ship, the projectile didn't detonate but rather drilled cleanly through the full length of the patrol bomber's fuselage, blowing out at the tail and ricocheting off the wave tops beyond.

Dead men flew the Emily now. Fire flickering in its interior, the massive seaplane lifted off the surface of the lagoon, its four screaming engines carrying it aloft. All hands on *Niobe*'s decks ducked instinctively as the moon shadow of the aircraft flashed past overhead, its belly clearing the periscope shears by the matter of a man's height.

The nose of the Emily continued to lift into an impossible climb. For a few seconds it seemed to hang suspended from its racing propellers, then it fell off on one wing and over onto its back. Plummeting into one of the atoll islets, it sent yet another thunderous explosion and plume of fire into the night.

The seaplane tender now seemed to be ablaze from bow to stern, but somehow, her indomitable captain had gotten his engines started and had cut free from his bow anchor. The silhouette of the Akitsushima was lengthening as he pivoted his ship around its stern mooring, seeking to bring his guns to bear on his attacker once more.

Perry could admire such a man, but he also recognized the necessity of killing him and the need to do it now. There was no time to set up a classic torpedo attack, using the TDC fire-control computer. At this range Perry would risk shooting by Kentucky windage and his captain's eye.

"Hard left rudder! We'll be firing a full spread forward on my order!"

Niobe's stern kicked around, her sharp-tipped bow traversing like an aimed spear. As the alignments came true, Perry bellowed into the intercom. "Shooting now! Fire one! . . . Fire two! . . . Fire three! . . . Fire four!"

A narrow fan of destruction radiated away from the submarine, four hissing bubble streams that each drew an individual smear of smoke low across the lagoon's surface. One ray of the fan missed forward, one missed aft, and the paroxysms of the two center shots ripped the belly and guts out of the tender.

Perry realized that his thumb was aching on the PRESS TO TALK button of the intercom, and he lifted and shook the pain from his hand. Not a bad spread. As good as the TDC could have done.

In the center of the lagoon the vanquished warship capsized, rolling slowly over like a dying water buffalo bathing its wounds in a mud hole, the final hissing groan of its death cry reverberating across the waters.

Perry keyed the intercom once more. "All engines ahead dead slow. Initiate diesel start and battery recharge. Danny, you can tell the PBY we're ready to receive them."

"That's just the thing, Skipper," Mercurio replied in the flesh, speaking from near Perry's feet. Climbing slowly through the deck hatch, *Niobe*'s exec looked tired, very tired, likely as all other hands including the captain did. He dug a message flimsy out of his shirt pocket. "This was what the radio shack was trying to tell you about, Skipper. When we got the mast up, this was being broadcast in clear over the SPYRON operations frequency. It's addressed with our call sign and it's being repeated."

Perry unfolded the flimsy and held it up to the moonlight and the flicker of the dying gasoline fires. The communication was both brief and succinct.

FROM: CINCSPYRON/COMSUBPAC
TO: CMDR USS NIOBE
OPERATION CANCELED X RETURN TO
BASE X

. . . and so we are en route home from "objective" having never accomplished what we set out to do. We have wounded aboard and more than one of my good young crew has been sent to his God through a torpedo tube. I have letters to write and the captain's wife will have calls to make.

But I'm pleased to say our losses were not totally in vain. We bear home prisoners, a new rising sun flag on the side of the conning tower, and the disruption of a Japanese naval operation.

I wonder, Amy girl. In the greater scheme of this

war, which was the more critical? The mission
which we failed to accomplish, or the mission
which we prevented the enemy from accomplishing. Will we ever know?

To continue . . .

The Ambiguity of the Wine-Dark Sea

JIM DEFELICE

Jim DeFelice is the author of several techno-thrillers. His latest, Brother's Keeper, *is now available in paperback from Leisure Books. He can be contacted at* jdchester@aol.com.

Off the Korean Coast, During the Cold War . . .

HE SLAMMED THE hatch lock home harder and faster than he'd intended, prelockout adrenaline rushing through his body. That and maybe a little bit of postleave hangover, given that he'd been rousted away from liberty for this gig less than twelve hours ago.

Ray Winslow nodded to himself as he straightened and leaned back against the ladder in the escape trunk, willing himself into the zone, wrestling every inch of his body into the tight noose of control he needed. Winslow had boarded the nuclear attack submarine USN *Swordtail* six hours before, dropped ignobly into the January sea by a Marine Corps CH-46 at the direction of the mission commander, Seth Caruth, who insisted to the pilot that there wasn't time to bother with a proper exchange. The two men had to swim a good fifty yards in the fading twilight and ten-foot swells to reach the *Swordtail*'s raft.

Not that Winslow hadn't done much worse, even in his SEAL qualification trials.

Caruth wasn't a SEAL. He probably wasn't even Navy. He belonged to the general category of spook, some sort of action officer with the CIA or DIA or NSA or NIA. Like the rest of the alphabet ghouls, he took mission security to ridiculous extremes. He'd only grudgingly showed Winslow the layout of their target, a small American ship that had been hijacked by the North Koreans less than twenty-four hours ago. As for what they were going to do when they reached it, Winslow could only guess.

Caruth tapped his shoulder, then started to check his gear. The guy knew his shit at least, or gave a reasonable facsimile. Maybe he had been a SEAL. Undoubtedly he'd been over in Nam, a hellhole Winslow had just recently returned from and would undoubtedly soon be going back to.

Their checks finished, Winslow flexed his shoulders back and rolled his neck. Caruth put his hand up; Winslow hesitated before realizing the spook wanted him to grip it in a good luck gesture. He reached out; Caruth caught him a half second before he was ready and just about broke his thumb off.

Scumbag.

And then water started slipping in and Winslow felt the metallic taps around him, felt the cold that shuddered its way up the back of his legs to his eyes, always his eyes—they were out, they were in the black wine of the

sea, they were in their small rubber boat on the surface
inside the port, nine hundred yards from the shadows that
included their target.

Clampton Ward settled his hand on the planesman's
shoulder, tapping gently to reassure him. He moved silently to the helmsman, then continued around the
Swordtail's control room. As he returned to the center,
he nodded to his executive officer, who gave the order
to begin reversing out of the narrow and shallow channel
they had entered. The large submarine sat exactly ten feet
above the silty harbor floor in relatively shallow water
less than three hundred feet deep; there was a small patrol craft some hundred yards behind them on the surface. Under other circumstances Ward might not have
worried about the North Korean vessel. Of Soviet design,
its weapons and detection gear were primitive enough
that he could easily sink it or escape into deeper water
if it made any aggressive move. But the two men he'd
just released to the water were depending on his return
in six hours to get home; more importantly, their mission
undoubtedly depended on their not being detected.

Whatever that mission was. Ward's orders had been
precise and to the point—pick up the men, deliver them
to the port, recover them. He knew nothing of what they
were to do, though the fact that he had been called off
a Holy Stone mission to take on the men indicated an
extreme level of priority.

There were, of course, certain guesses the veteran
commander could make. The easiest was that it had to
do with the spy ship the North Koreans had taken the
previous morning. He'd monitored some of the radio
traffic about it and knew that the ship would almost certainly have been taken to this port a few hours before.

He could also make some guesses about his two passengers, though he'd met them only briefly. The one in charge was either CIA or more likely NSA, a black-suit boy from the "action desk." The other was a Navy SEAL, probably shanghaied specifically for the mission, a can-do kid who was expected not to ask any questions or pull any punches if trouble developed.

Not a kid, really—probably pushing twenty-five or even thirty, undoubtedly a veteran of at least one spin around Vietnam. But Ward had long ago reached the point where they were all kids, even some of the men above him.

The commander of the *Swordtail* could also make certain guesses about the ship the Koreans had taken. For one thing, it must have been unarmed—otherwise it would never have been taken. It must also have been comparatively slow, and in a position where it could be taken. All of those things meant it must be a spy ship.

From all of those guesses, Ward might make more guesses concerning the men's mission. Possibly, he might guess, they were being sent to blow the ship up. But that guess would lead to many questions, not the least of which would be why only two men would be sent on such a mission. And precisely because of those questions Ward did not bother to guess or speculate at all, not even in his own private thoughts. For he had long ago become accustomed to the shadows and vagaries of the war he fought, the ambiguity of the dark seas he sailed. He had accepted the fact that he could not know all and could not even try to do so. A man who hunted the cold layers of the ocean to hide from his pursuers must, by rights, accept ambiguity.

Commander Ward continued his turn around the attack submarine's control room. Well-lit, the room seemed spacious even when full, light years beyond the diesel-

powered snorkel subs Ward had served on and commanded for much of his career as a submariner. The first
thing he noticed upon coming aboard two years before
was the air. It had a certain supernatural cleanness to it,
a crisp sensation in your nose. The air felt, in fact, as if
it could be snapped in two like a tree branch. The air
aboard nonnuclear subs went through a predictable cycle:
it began wet and stale and became steadily wetter and
staler. His last boat had to surface every twelve hours or
so to exchange its fouled air; the *Swordtail* could stay
submerged for weeks and even months at a time. In his
old boat, clothes were washed in the water wrung from
the drippings of the air; this air was dry in your throat,
at least by comparison.

The *Swordtail* was a member of the Sturgeon class,
which by now had almost completely replaced the diesels
plying the Pacific. Even for a Sturgeon she was special,
built longer than her brethren to accommodate a compartment devoted to Signal Intelligence gathering, or
electronic eavesdropping. Most, though not all, of
Ward's mission included extensive covert listenings off
the Russian Far East. They would slink into a position,
rise from the darkness unnoticed, raise their gear, and
listen. At other times they would reel out special buoys
or arrays to do the same, ears pressed to the whispering
sea. Several of her crew were only nominally under his
command, their actions ultimately directed by the NSA's
Naval Security Group. Ward never knew completely or
specifically what they did; coming to accept that was one
of the most difficult lessons he had learned as a submarine commander.

The second most difficult, perhaps, after the lesson that
superseded all others: the need for patience.

"Subchaser bearing one five zero," warned the sonar
operators as a surface ship crossed toward their path.

Ward glanced across the control room toward the sonar compartment, washed with green from the screens where the contact had appeared. The Korean vessel, roughly the size and capability of a World War II destroyer escort or coastal corvette, had a reasonable chance of finding them in the shallow water, if its equipment was in good condition and the crew manning it alert and well trained.

A big *if*, but he must play conservatively.

"All stop," said Ward.

The order passed quickly to the helm and the submarine's slow reversal ended. But even as their momentum slowed, the Korean ship began to turn to the south away from them. They hadn't been detected.

They waited to be sure. Ward glanced at his watch—not to see the time but to remind himself of his wife, waiting back in Hawaii. She'd given it to him before this trip, scheduled to be his last. The back of the watch was inscribed, "For our second honeymoon." They had a long visit to Europe planned to mark his separation from the service, the end of a thirty-year hitch stretching back to the Big War, the real one.

He wasn't ready, not really. It was time, but he couldn't let go. Even with the promise of being bumped up to rear admiral easing his passage—shouldn't he just change the papers, stay on? Emma would be disappointed, but she would understand. The sea and its dark shadows, the unanswered questions and silent maneuvering: that was his life and reality. He could never leave it.

His first ships were destroyers. He hated them, but they turned out to be good schools for this sort of work, teaching him how a surface commander thought.

"Proceed," he told his executive officer, or XO, when the subchaser had moved on. Like many of his other men, the XO had served with him long enough to read his mind. It took only a glance or nod to move the submarine a hundred miles.

When they reached the deeper waters near the entrance to the port, Ward stepped to the periscope to survey the surface. He fought a slight twinge of nostalgia as he folded his hands around the handles of the scope, remembering his first service aboard a submarine. His commander had been a veteran of the war against the Japanese; he was supernaturally calm and quiet, and at times gave the impression he was sleeping with his eyes open. Some of the men who had served with him for a long time called him Old Man Buddha. Ward's personality went in the opposite direction; even now he worked to keep himself quiet and calm, avoid the impulse to snap out commands or even spin the periscope around quickly.

It was just reaching midnight. A fishing vessel sat about a half mile to the south, moored off the rocky edge of land. A few channel markers bobbed in the distance. The *Swordtail* sat alone in the dark shadows.

They'd start back in just under four hours.

"Commander? A word in private?" asked Lieutenant Higgens.

Without answering the lieutenant, who had charge of the Sigint spaces, Ward stepped back and made his customary round of the control room, patting each man on the shoulder. The touch was more than ritual; it nourished his men, as if he fed them. Only after he had personally seen to each member of his team did he lead Higgens back to his quarters.

"I thought we might discuss the mission, sir." Higgens pursed his lips together in a kind of scowl that made the bottom of his cheek turn pink.

"What would we discuss?"

"The uh—well, we failed to get into the proper position and therefore, we did not achieve our, uh objective."

Ward sat in his chair, leaving the lieutenant to stand. He knew it made the younger man slightly uncomfortable, but that was for the good. With his assignment to the Naval Security Group, Higgens's personnel records became a work of fiction, with different cover assignments hiding his real work; there was no guarantee that he was even actually in the Navy, at least until this assignment. But watching him, Ward had decided he had been aboard submarines before—but not as a man in charge of others or responsible for a mission. He lacked a certain flexibility that came with experience.

"I'm not sure I understand what you're getting at, Lieutenant," he told the officer.

"Well, sir. The Soviet boat, the submarine—"

"It detected us and we broke off. It happens. We've run into Harry before," added Ward. The sonarmen had identified the Victor boat that had ruined their mission as a particularly pesky attack sub they had clashed with several times off Vladivostok over the course of the past eighteen months.

"When I, uh, report, what should I say?" asked Higgens.

"Simply tell the truth, Lieutenant."

Until now, Higgens had appeared the very model of an officer, exactly the type that might appear in a training film admonishing sailors to worry, and worry hard, about VD and the other evils lurking in every port of call around the world. The fact that he was now in doubt—a good sign, Ward thought; he might learn to thrive in this world after all.

"With you, uh, retiring sir and uh, this sort of thing," added Higgens. "Well, it could be seen as a black mark, I—"

"You don't have to worry about me, Lieutenant." He

smiled, laughing a little as he thought of something to say. He was tempted to tell a tale of the old days, playing hide-and-seek with the Russians in diesel boats, but he resisted; it would serve no purpose.

"War—our kind of war—it's a strange thing," Ward said instead. "It's back and forth, cat and mouse. When you win sometimes you lose. And vice versa. Everything is in the mix; it's to your advantage if you can take it. Now, Lieutenant, you no doubt got a lot of information about that Commie sub that tracked us, didn't you?"

"Yes, sir."

"Don't you think someone will find that information useful in the future?"

"I hadn't thought of that, sir."

"We learn to live with ambiguity," he told the young man. "That's the most important thing."

Higgens nodded solemnly. He was back to being the man in the training film, the man who thought he knew everything and couldn't sleep if he didn't.

Difficult lessons. But it would be someone else's responsibility to teach him. Ultimately, he had to teach himself anyway.

Ward rose. "Don't worry, Lieutenant. I appreciate your concern. Report precisely what happened."

An ensign met him in the passage as he started back to the control room. "Sir, a Victor boat coming at us balls-out, dead on our nose."

A rope dangled from the rail of their target ship about ten feet from the stern, almost as if it had been placed there for them. Winslow grabbed hold, pausing to catch his breath. The water had to be no warmer than thirty-three degrees, but the air was quite a bit colder.

Caruth had already taken off his mask and Draeger, a special breathing apparatus that prevented bubbles from giving a swimmer away. Using it at night seemed unduly cautious, but it wasn't Winslow's call. After surfacing, they had paddled their raft about three quarters of a mile up the main channel to the port, right down the enemy's throat. Mooring it on a marker buoy, they'd then swum another two hundred yards or so to their ship. The whole time a song had been burning through Winslow's head— Jimi Hendrix rubbing the Fender on a Dylan tune, "All Along the Watchtower."

He hated when that happened. Music couldn't get unglued in his mind.

Under certain conditions his close-fitting diving suit could feel almost toasty—but these weren't those conditions.

"Fuckin' water's cold," Winslow said, pulling himself against the side of the ship.

The spook didn't answer. He began hauling himself up slowly, pausing only to signal that Winslow should stay back until he was aboard. Winslow wasn't about to argue—the January wind gusted well over ten knots, and as cold as the water was it was warmer than the air.

He'd never bitch about the cramped SDVs—newly developed SEAL Delivery Vehicles or minisubs—again.

While he waited, Winslow stowed his gear in his waterproof pack, then took his knife from its sheath at his belt. It was a small airman's survival knife, its five-inch blade easier to handle than the more ominous looking nine-inchers that were common issue. In knives as in other things, size could often be deceiving.

Their target drew less than a thousand tons. If the diagram of its layout Caruth had shown him was accurate, it stretched one hundred and seventy-six feet. Winslow had been aboard luxury yachts that were bigger.

He watched Caruth disappear in the darkness above. Water slapped in a harsh staccato against the ship. About a hundred yards to the north a row of small patrol vessels jumbled up and down against a wooden pier. Beyond them shards of lights and faint, dull yellow streaks showed there must be other ships here, though he couldn't see them. Whatever was on shore was enshrouded in darkness.

The air was so cold it tasted like the inside of a snowball. Winslow slid his gloved thumb back and forth across the top edge of his knife, as if he were honing his finger.

Hendrix's guitar riffed. He thought of the girl he'd been screwing when the knock on the hotel room door came. She had melted around his legs, a warm wetness.

The knock had surprised him so badly he'd fallen from the bed, grabbing his pistol from the floor. Two Army MPs—that was different—appeared in the doorway. He came within a finger's twitch of blasting the SOBs with the .45, but at least the bastards had the good sense to back out and let him dress before driving him off.

A tiny light waved above him. Caruth's signal.

Winslow's first tug took him out of the water; his second bashed his knee into the hull at just the right angle to send a shock of pain through his right medial ligament, which had been partially torn a month before on his last assignment in Vietnam. He kept pulling himself upward, transferring most of his effort from his legs to his arms, eyes pasted on the blackness above. As he pulled himself over he fell on a body, and for a moment thought it was Caruth; only the flicker of his companion's wrist lamp a few yards away told him it wasn't.

Winslow paused to open his waterproof sack for his silenced gun, a silenced version of a Kulspruta m/45 "Carl Gustav" hand-tweaked by an Army Special Forces friend and delivered to him with great ceremony after a mission in the Vietnamese Highlands a year before. Caruth returned with a rope. He tied one end to the dead man's leg, then let him down the side so gently there was no splash. Without saying a word, the spook started back in the direction he had scouted earlier, expecting Winslow to follow. They made their way through a hatch, paused momentarily, then ducked to the right, their way lit by the dull glow of Caruth's wrist light. As Caruth turned Winslow nearly ran into him, his face smacking the thick waterproof pack the other man had strapped to his back. He froze, sensing the footsteps of a guard before the Korean appeared at the intersection of the two passages.

One of Kevin Winslow's many specialties was taking men down quickly without noise or fuss; he could do so with a variety of weapons, including his bare hands. He had had the chance to practice this skill several times, and if he wasn't so meticulous about cleaning his equipment, the knife in his right hand would still bear traces of his last victim, three months dead. But never had Chief Petty Officer Winslow seen a man killed quite so quickly as the guard who turned the corner in front of him; Caruth took a step and the Korean simply slid to the deck beneath him. God's own angel could not have taken a life more efficiently.

Caruth moved on. Winslow followed, carefully stepping over the body, knife and gun balancing rods in his hands. He felt a shock of fear as something moved in the passage beyond them, faint footsteps warning that someone was coming their way. Caruth's light disappeared and he stood back tight against the wall of the narrow passage, blurring into the shadows. As Winslow narrowed his shoulders and did the same, the sound of the steps moved away, up a short flight of stairs, and then merged with the vague noises of night. Caruth and

Winslow continued about three more yards to an open, unguarded hatchway.

The Signet compartment. No guard. Papers lay everywhere on the deck. There was a large black burn-bag near the hatchway. A few panels had been smashed with axes and the pungent smell of fire hung in the air.

Caruth kneeled, slid off his pack. But instead of taking out charges, he took out a camera.

They'd come all this way to take pictures?

Pictures first, then blow it. Had to be. Though now that he eyed it carefully, Caruth's bag seemed suspiciously small.

Wouldn't take much to wax this place.

Several cipher machines lined the port side of the compartment, next to two consoles of electronics gear. Two or three of the machines and one of the consoles had been damaged by a few blows from an ax, but even from across the room Winslow realized the crew had failed to destroy it.

Caruth stopped taking pictures. He stowed the camera and started out of the room.

Winslow caught his arm. "Hey, aren't we blowing the gear?"

"No."

"Wait."

His companion's face whirled next to his. It seemed to glow with heat, but his expression was not one of anger; it was simply blank.

"We're just here to take pictures?" asked Winslow.

"I was told you were a capable man."

The spook's response so baffled Winslow that he was unable to say anything more. Caruth turned and slipped through the hatch and continued up the passage; the SEAL had to practically run to catch up.

They turned a corner and stopped. Light flooded from

an open doorway a few feet ahead; they could hear voices.

Korean.

It was the mess. Caruth stood against the door, listening. Finally, he took a step backward, going around Winslow and then leading him down the passage to a set of metal steps upward. As they reached them, a strident set of footsteps bounced off the bulkhead at the top.

"Down," Caruth hissed, pulling Winslow with him to crouch beneath the steps as two Korean guards descended.

By the time Ward reached the control room, the Soviet attack submarine had closed to five hundred yards. Dubbed Sierra One—a naming convention that simply meant it was the first sonar contact they had made—the enemy submarine was making almost dead-on for them, its noisy propellers churning at almost thirty knots.

"Trying to scare us?" the XO asked.

"If he knows we're here." They had calculated that the Soviet boat would pass no less than fifty yards above them—damn close, all things considered. But moving would give themselves away. Ward saw only two reasons the Victor boat would rush toward the port like this: either he had heard an American boat was en route and wanted to get there first, or he knew exactly where Ward was and wanted to scare him away. In either case, moving was a bad idea.

"It'll be close," said the XO.

The commander nodded.

"Gibby says it's Harry." The XO nodded toward the sonar room, where one of the technicians had tentatively identified the contact from their library of previous encounters. "Good old Harry."

They'd lost, or thought they'd lost, the Russian submarine after more than eighteen hours of cat and mouse off the coast. By that time he'd already ruined their mission; they were heading back toward Japan when the new orders had come for this job.

Had the Russian come south in their wake? Or was he, too, on a new mission? Ward imagined his counterpart in his control room, plotting his course.

This fast—he would not suspect the *Swordtail* sat ahead.

"We could get deeper without too much problem," suggested the XO, meaning that Harry was unlikely to detect them because of his rush. It was a guess based on their past experiences.

"Hmmm," said Ward. "Not yet. As long as he stays on his course we're fine."

They waited. It took roughly a minute for the Russian to pass over them. Ward could feel the submarine coming. Its noisy five-blade propeller churned the water like a mad flipper. He put himself in the enemy commander's head as it passed overhead—I've beaten the Americans.

Ward barely nodded to set his crew in to action, whipping into the wake of the other submarine. They were hidden by the enemy attack submarine's own noise, a ghost entering a house on the heels of its earthly owner.

"Slowing," reported sonar.

Ward anticipated a quick spin around to try to see if something else was there. They prepared to respond.

"Harry goes left," said the exec.

"Yes," said Ward. He was in the enemy control room, standing with the captain, giving the order. He was very sure of himself, Harry, but not so arrogant as to turn on his active sonar, for that would be sure to give him away. Harry was the consummate shadow player.

"We'll stay between them and the port," Ward told his men. "We'll see what he does."

They had just slipped into their position when the sonar operators announced another contact—a diesel sub on the surface, approaching from the south. It was a small boat, too small to be anything but a North Korean. He was very close, less than a half mile away; most likely he had been submerged until a short while ago, traveling on his batteries.

"He's moving in our direction," said the exec.

"Or the direction of the Russian sub," said Ward. "Or simply across the mouth of the port, patrolling."

"Must've surfaced to recharge his batteries."

"Or to get orders."

There were now three submarines within a mile of each other. Did the other two know he was here? If they did, what would they do?

If he were to attack, Ward would strike the Soviet nuclear boat first; it would be several times more formidable than the diesel, which in all probability was Korean and at least a generation behind the times. But the older boat was likely to be extremely quiet when it ran on batteries, as quiet if not more so than *Swordtail*. Finding it might require going to active sonar, which of course would alert not only the diesel but the subchaser and anyone else listening above.

Or below, for that matter.

His job was not to attack. A boat on a covert mission never attacked, no matter the circumstances. His job was to be patient, recover his men, return. No one should know he was there.

"Harry hasn't surfaced and hasn't gone to active sonar," noted the XO. "I think he's hiding from the Koreans."

"Yes," murmured Ward. "Yes."

He saw the Russian commander again, pacing patiently. The Koreans were allies, but they could not necessarily be trusted.

Or else the Russian and the Korean worked together, one showing himself, the other hiding.

"Patrol boats moving across the harbor," reported sonar. "Two."

Ward plotted their positions in his head as they cut between him and the diesel sub on the surface. The Victor boat Harry, meanwhile, had swung around and taken up a station barely a hundred yards to his east, utterly unaware of him.

Everyone was unaware of something. What was Ward unaware of?

He glanced at his wristwatch. Two and a half hours before he had to go back for the rendezvous.

"I'm going to get some coffee," he said aloud. As he took a step away, the ship reverberated with a loud crack and the deck below him shuddered so severely he fell against the chart table.

Winslow had both his knife and his gun ready as the Koreans came down the steps. But Caruth gripped his arm, holding him back—the two men passed right next to them in the dark, continuing toward the mess. Caruth slipped out and went up quickly; once again Winslow had to nearly run to keep up. He struggled to step lightly, keep himself from making a sound. They passed portals to the outside of the ship, continued along a narrow corridor, Caruth stopping every so often to listen. A dark shape stood in front of one of the portholes—the back of a guard, no doubt. Winslow held his breath as he crossed behind him, certain the man's Kalashnikov could easily penetrate the thin metal of the ship's superstructure and walls.

It wasn't until they reached the hatchway that the

SEAL realized their destination was the commander's quarters, one of the sites Caruth had pointed out on his diagram in the helo. The spook held his pistol—a nine-millimeter silenced Sig—out at his side as he approached the open doorway; in a blink he had spun himself into the room. A bee buzzed inside. Winslow was no more than two steps behind his companion, but by the time he reached the room everything was over. Two bodies slumped against the bed, draped over the side, blood oozing from them.

"Not here," said Caruth, already backing out.

"We going to—"

"He's not here," repeated the spook, passing back out. They traced their steps back down the ladder to the lower deck toward the mess room.

"What are we doing?" Winslow asked.

Caruth held his gun up. "Be ready."

A figure started to emerge from the hatchway when they were less than five steps away. Caruth leveled his gun and fired into the man's belly. As the Korean spun backward, Caruth leapt ahead. Winslow ran, too. There was an explosion in the room, gunfire—Winslow felt his eardrums thump with the metallic rumble. He pushed forward, squared his body, blinked his eyes against the smoke, saw nothing, swung left, back right, scanning for a target. The metal wire of the Kulspruta poked into his side, prodding him to fire, but Winslow had no target.

Caruth barked something inside, speaking in tongues. Winslow squared, checked outside, spun back. Caruth's words came in English now.

"Where is he?" the spook said. "Where?"

Three bodies lay on the floor to Winslow's left. At his feet was the Korean Caruth had shot from the passage. Another man was slumped over a table at the far end near the galley area. Blood bubbled from the top of his head as if he were a fountain.

Caruth stood over a man in the corner, holding his gun to his head. Unlike the others, this one wore blue pants. As Winslow took another step toward him to see what was going on, Caruth repeated his one-word question, "Where?"

"Hey," said Winslow.

Caruth spun suddenly, leveling his gun toward Winslow and opening fire. He threw himself down. As he hit the deck he realized Caruth was firing on a man just coming through the hatchway. There was another shot, screams outside; the SEAL got to his feet with a burst of anger, mad at himself for screwing up, not securing the passage as he should have. He made up for it now, hurling himself out into the hallway, firing half a dozen Parabellum rounds from his machine pistol into the face of a guard just as the man saw him. Winslow grabbed the Korean's rifle, then emptied the thirty-six-round box of his Carl Gustav into the two guards who appeared at the far end of the passage.

Something tugged at the back of his neck.

"This way," said Caruth behind him.

"But the man inside?"

"He's not here. Go!"

The first thing Ward thought about as he slammed into the side of the chart table was the reactor. The auxiliary-man screamed something, and the navigator tumbled over him; Ward jumped back to his feet, vaulting like a jack-in-the-box.

"Report," he said, firmly and calmly. The tone of his command was as important—more important—than the actual words. He wanted order, and his voice immediately instilled it. He had to make sure his will was the submarine's once again.

The overhead lights flickered on and off. Ward could hear the sea in his ears, the endless rush of water that every mariner hears, the raging blanket of horror and calm. But death was not inevitable; he steadied himself on his feet and held his mind firm. This was the one thing there was no question, no ambiguity, no darkness about.

His men snapped to like a series of switches channeling the flow of electricity. They retook their stations, scanned for damage, secured problems.

"No fires," said the XO.

Ward listened to the rest of the reports. They had not been hurt, at least not badly enough to lose control of the vessel. No floods, no fires.

There seemed no reason to surface. He held off using his active sonar as well, though anyone nearby would have heard the concussion and realized that he was here. But turning the gear on would remove all doubt, shine a beacon in a dark room. His exact location would be revealed.

A second diesel had hit them. How it had managed to get so close without being detected was a mystery. Perhaps it had been trailing the Soviet nuclear submarine, and somehow managed to hide from Ward in the noise of the Victor boat. Or perhaps Ward's sonarmen had missed it—listening to the ocean speak was an art, not a science.

Two men had broken bones; one of the cooks had gashed his face in a fall. Otherwise, Ward's men were all right. The external ballast tank had definitely been hit, but there was no sign of severe damage.

They would hew to their plan, move back slowly for

the rendezvous. Harry made no sign that he had heard
the collision—though of course he had.

The Korean diesel on the surface began moving in
their general direction. So did the subchaser.

"The submarine that hit us is surfacing," reported the
XO. "Subchaser's approaching. Sierra Two, the Korean
diesel, she's diving."

Ward nodded.

"Sir—the sub—the diesel that hit us. It's an American
boat."

Winslow pushed through the hatch to the deck, unsure
exactly where he was on the target ship. He took two
steps to the rail, then realized he'd come out on the side
opposite the rope they had climbed.

Caruth came through the passage, whirled, started toward the stern. Winslow trailed, unsure what his companion would do next.

A figure appeared in front of them. The man said
something in Korean but never finished his sentence—
Caruth greased out three shots from his gun, then tossed
it down and knelt as the man crumpled. Winslow pushed
forward, raising the AK-47 as two more Koreans came
down a ladder near their fallen comrade. He emptied the
gun as the men fell; he whirled in time to see Caruth
toss a grenade up onto the deck above them.

"Get off the ship," said Caruth, his voice as dead cold
and even as it had been in the helo out to the sub. He
pushed him toward the rail.

Winslow leaned against the metal and raked the top
of the ship with his Kulspruta, burning the clip. "Let's
go!" he yelled to Caruth. He threw the gun down, then
went over the side. The spook followed, landing in the
water so close that his foot struck Winslow's back. Winslow spread his arms in the darkness, propelling himself

away from the hull of the boat. He stayed below the surface of the water as long as he could, knowing that the sailors aboard the ship would be looking for him.

He broke the water briefly, gasped air, sank back. The second time he stayed on the surface long enough to see he was barely ten yards from the ship; lights were now ablaze, and there were sparks of gunfire from the deck.

The third time he broke water his arm struck something hard and he cursed, thinking he had gotten so scrambled around that he had swum back into the ship.

Then he realized he had hit Caruth's foot.

He pulled at him, reaching to show him he was okay. Then he realized Caruth was dead.

His first impulse was to push the body away from him, as if death were an infectious disease. Then he grabbed it back, determined not to leave his companion's body as a trophy for the enemy. But as he curled his arm around Caruth's, the water exploded and he felt a pain in his leg beyond anything he'd ever thought possible. An anchor wrapped itself around his chest, and Winslow sank into blackness.

Even if only lightly damaged, the American diesel would be easy pickings for Harry and an inviting target for the subchaser and the smaller patrol craft.

Ward could sink them all, but to do so he would not only expose his own boat but jeopardize the covert mission.

The mission had the highest priority. His job was to let the diesel go. While he had never been quite in this exact situation during his years of command, what he must do now had always been clearly laid out. He had contemplated similar situations a thousand times.

Yet he did not hesitate now.

"Prepare torpedoes," he ordered. "Active sonar. Target

the surface vessel approaching the damaged submarine.
Target the Korean and the Victor boat. Prepare to fire."

His XO jerked his head around.

"Those are my orders," said Ward.

Winslow was unconscious, but he swam nonetheless.
This had happened to him before, the mission near Hai-
phong. One of the charges they had set to blow out a
pier had gone off prematurely. He'd swum back with
Duffy and the others to the insertion boat, nearly a mile
out. Duffy swore he was laughing and joking the whole
way, but he had no memory of it, not then, not now.
Docs said he had a mild concussion, though they
couldn't explain why he didn't even have a headache.

His head didn't hurt now, but his leg sure as hell did.
Something bad had happened to it.

"All Along the Watchtower" started playing in his
head again. Hendrix jammed in the darkness. Horses rose
from the water, riding alongside him.

Winslow swam and swam, the sea shrouded around
him. When he finally regained consciousness, at least
enough for him to take stock of where he was, he discovered that he had swum about four hundred yards away
from their target but on a diagonal deeper into the harbor.
He could see figures running back and forth aboard the
ship, but no one was firing anymore. Vehicles were moving on the shore; there were lights behind the ship.

He had to swim past the ship to get back out to the
raft. He could do that, and if he did that—when he did
that—he could make it back to the rendezvous point.

His leg hurt so bad he thought it had been bitten off
by a shark. But if that had happened, he would have bled
to death. So he must be okay. It was just the cold bothering him, and cold was nothing but bullshit. Cold you
could live with.

Slowly, Winslow put his cheek against the hardness of the ocean. He began to swim. Sounds came at him, shapes and colors. Hendrix faded. Pain pulled at his head; his ears twisted back with it, some trick of his nervous system. He passed abreast of the ship, passed the ship, saw the buoy.

The man Winslow had stood over in the mess—had he been an American? Why was he there with the Koreans? What had happened to him?

The raft was less than a hundred yards away, but the wind started to pick up. He swam. Oil and bilge and scummy algae soaked into the bottom of his chin, poisonous Vaseline smearing his skull. He swam.

If the rubber raft wasn't there?

He would swim all the way to the submarine. He would swim all the way to Japan if necessary.

His raft moved away from his hand as he reached for it. Then something lit bright red on the water a half mile away, and with a shudder the raft sailed into his grasp.

Only one of the MK 37 torpedoes hit the subchaser, but it snapped the small ship nearly in two. A few seconds after the torpedo hit home, the enemy diesel submarine opened its torpedo tubes.

"Fire torpedo three. Fire torpedo four," said Ward, giving the order to launch the weapons already targeted at Sierra Two, the Korean diesel. As the order echoed around the boat, Ward put himself back in Harry's head. The Russian boat sat only a few hundred yards away, as quiet as before the collision.

There was a collision less than a half mile off my stern. An American submarine has just appeared on the surface; another, less than three hundred yards away, has just sunk two of my ally's ships.

What do I do?

I can try to sink both boats, or I can remain in the darkness.

If I fire, I probably will sink at least one of the subs. But I risk being sunk myself.

Worse, I will step from the darkness. All will know I am here.

I observe. This is not my fight.

Every man in the control room cheered as the two torpedoes they had fired on the small Korean sub hit home. Ward felt a slight tinge of sadness.

"Pay attention to the Victor boat," he said aloud, reminding himself as well as his crew. He felt sure he knew what the Soviet captain would do—and that certainty made him extremely vulnerable.

"Harry is holding steady," said the XO.

The diesel that had hit them was still on the surface, making only two or three knots. Was it the *Sunray*, his old boat? Or the *Duce* maybe, his friend Jack's command? *Greenfish*, the always unlucky *Greenfish*?

"Come to periscope depth. Let's take a look," said Ward.

They moved upward slowly, still wary of damage from the collision. But if the outer hull was bashed and battered, it gave no sign; they came up without a problem, the planesman's soft touch driving the boat up fifty feet in the space of a few thoughts.

Ward debated whether he should try to rescue the men on the diesel if necessary.

Of course he would rescue them. Most were friends.

And so it was he finally realized he was in fact ready to retire.

The subchaser burned ferociously in the screen of the attack periscope. The Korean diesel submarine had begun to break up and then disappeared from their acoustical net after the torpedoes struck; there would be no survivors.

He couldn't find the American that had surfaced and had to ask for a bearing. He checked and double-checked the mark, couldn't find it.

"Making two knots," relayed the sonar operator.

Two knots—it must be damaged. It could drift faster.

"Harry's moving off—Captain, the Russian is going away."

"Thank you," Ward told his XO.

A dark shadow moved in the right side of his screen. Slowly his eyes focused on the silhouette. The American boat. Its conning tower listed to the side.

Something else moved beyond it. A small patrol boat.

"Prepare to surface," he said.

The XO hesitated just long enough for Ward to realize he disagreed, then relayed the order.

Winslow lay on his belly in the raft, paddling from a kind of semicrouch. His right leg had been badly mangled; once again he was slipping in and out of consciousness.

What the hell had Caruth been up to? Why didn't they blow the stinking ship when they had the chance?

"Not our fate," sang Hendrix. "Not not not."

The spook's head broke the water before him.

"What were we doing?" Winslow asked.

Caruth said nothing.

"Don't give me that," said Winslow. "Tell me—what the fuck did we come all this way for?"

Caruth said nothing.

"Bastard spook dipshit asshole," said Winslow. He pushed the paddle harder. He felt himself nearly tumbling into the water and fell flat, his face hitting the edge of the raft. It was soft. He lay there as he might lie on

some mamasan's boobs, some geisha's belly. A warm
bath engulfed him, easing out the knots in his muscles.

Yeah, baby. I can't wait to get back, get laid. Party.
Gonna party for a week, surface, party some more. They
owe me big time on this.

A high-pitched whine in the water. A patrol boat heading for him.

"Hey Caruth!" he yelled to his dead companion. "Now
what the fuck do I do?"

Something flashed beyond the shadow of the American
diesel submarine that had surfaced. Two pops, then darkness.

Though it had taken less than a minute for the *Swordtail* to reach the surface, the diesel had begun to dive just
as they broke water. By the time Ward reached the conning tower, it was gone.

Hopefully, he had managed to escape. There was nothing more to be done for him now.

"We have a raft in the water, sir!" shouted the lookout
next to him.

The SEAL and his master.

"Recover them," said Ward. "Target the patrol vessel
that's approaching the channel," he added. "Sink it."

Winslow pushed the paddle into the water for several
more strokes before he realized that it had fallen from
his hand. Somewhere in the dark haze of his failing consciousness he felt the enemy patrol craft taking aim at
him, training its guns on his small, helpless shadow. He
wanted the son of a bitch to fire.

"Kill me now you bastard. Blow me up before I bleed
to death."

Caruth appeared again, floating in front of him. The
spook shook his head slowly.

"Sure—let 'em kill me," Winslow argued. "Why the fuck not? What the hell were you doing on that ship? Why didn't we blow it?"

Hell opened behind him. Red flames split the sky and the small raft hurtled forward on a tsunami. Winslow felt himself spinning down a drain. The pain in his leg increased and he felt something press him hard from behind.

Caruth appeared again in the water.

"You bastard," he said. "You could have at least told me what the hell we were doing."

The spook reached from the water and grabbed him.

Not Caruth. A devil. Two devils, taking over his boat. Winslow struck out at them, but he was too weak now, too tired, too drained—they grabbed him and carried him down into the whirlwind, into their version of hell.

"You'll be fine," said one of them. "Just relax. We'll get morphine for your leg."

"Fuck you."

"Morphine."

When they were an hour and a half off the Korean coast, Ward surfaced the boat so they could survey the damage from the collision. The sun had just broken the horizon; there were only a few puffy clouds in the distance. Despite the frigid temperature, it would be a beautiful day.

The diesel had only grazed his boat. More than likely it hadn't been badly damaged itself, though he'd have to wait until they reached port to find out. Even then, he might not have a definitive word for some time.

What had it been doing there? Trailing Harry—or trailing him? Sent on his own covert mission, depositing his own team to examine or destroy the hijacked American ship?

Or just in the wrong place at the wrong time?

Ward went to the sick bay to check on the SEAL who'd been recovered. The corpsman on duty told him he'd finally fallen asleep only a few minutes before.

"He was talking nonstop from the moment they got him down," said the corpsman. "Gibberish mostly. Kept asking why they didn't blow the ship."

"Which ship?" Ward asked.

The corpsman shrugged. " 'And the American—did you kill him? Guy in the galley—he was American, right?' He kept saying that a lot, too. Is it supposed to mean something?"

"Nothing," said Ward. "His leg?"

"Doc amputated it a few minutes after they brought him in. Way, way gone."

Ward nodded.

"He just kept asking questions," said the corpsman. "If he wakes up, he's bound to ask more."

"Yes," said Ward.

"What should I say?"

"If you have answers, you can give them," said Ward.

"I haven't a clue what he was talking about."

"Then say nothing. I frankly doubt he'll have any questions."

"Yes, sir."

Later in his cabin, Ward lay back on his thin mattress. His doubts about leaving the service were gone. Nor did he worry about what he would do after the long vacation with his wife; there would be time to sort that out.

By most tallies, he had done his job well: depositing and recovering the two covert agents, possibly saving an American submarine, sinking three enemy ships. If this were World War II—the real war—the score would be obvious. But this was not the real war. You infiltrated agents who boarded a captured spy ship but did not blow it up. You sat beneath the waves next to your mortal

enemy, who did nothing while you attacked his friends.
You gave an order to save your countrymen, and your
second in command eyed you as if you were Judas.

Perhaps the real war hadn't been so clear-cut either.
He'd been just another raw recruit then, green as seaweed, too dumb to know.

Winslow pushed into the girl again and again, his body
erupting in pleasure. God it was good to get laid.

As he rolled off her, he felt his arm hit something
metal.

A rack.

He was aboard a submarine, the sub that had taken
him into the harbor. He wasn't getting laid at all. He was
dreaming.

Shit. He'd much rather get laid.

Caruth didn't care about all those code machines and
documents. He'd gone all that way to find someone
aboard the ship.

Why?

To kill him. Had to be—they hadn't brought gear to
take him out.

Fuck.

Fuck shit hell.

Hendrix played again, a long, long riff this time, a
cool, groovy rip that split across Winslow's mind. His
leg didn't hurt anymore. He'd be dancing soon, dancing
with some pretty chick all night, fuck her, dance some
more. Set the watchtowers on fire and fire and fire.

Yeah, baby.

Valley of Death

R. J. PINEIRO

R. J. Pineiro is a nineteen-year veteran of the computer industry, where he works on leading-edge microprocessors. He is the author of several internationally acclaimed novels, including Shutdown, Breakthrough, Exposure, Ultimatum, Conspiracy .com, *and* Firewall *as well as the millennium thrillers,* 01-01-00 *and* Y2K. *His new novel is* Cyberterror. *R. J. Pineiro was born in Cuba and grew up in Central America. He is a licensed pilot, a firearms enthusiast, has a black belt in martial arts, and has traveled extensively through Europe, Asia, and the Americas both for his computer business as well as to conduct research for his novels. He makes his home in Texas, where he lives with his wife, Lory Anne, and his son, Cameron. Visit him on the World Wide Web at:* www.rjpineiro.com. *He receives E-mail at:* author@rjpineiro.com.

Theirs not to make reply,
Theirs not to reason why,
Theirs but to do and die:
Into the valley of Death
Rode the six hundred.

—LORD ALFRED TENNYSON,
"THE CHARGE OF THE LIGHT BRIGADE"

The pressure starts slowly, gradually, compressing your ear canals as the captain takes her down to one hundred and thirty meters.

And deeper.

One hundred and forty meters.

Deeper still.

Just a few weeks inside a type VIIC U-boat and I already know we have to push the design envelope of this vessel if we want to get beneath the depth charges those British and American pigs keep dropping on us.

I sigh.

American pigs.

It wasn't that long ago that I was one of those American pigs, the son of German immigrants who had settled in Connecticut in the 1920's. I foolishly chose to answer Germany's patriotic call back in 1938, the year I earned my bachelor's in journalism from Yale and left my comfortable American life and excellent job prospects to pursue a juvenile ideology.

"One hundred and seventy meters," reports *Oberleutnant* Thomas Mueller, our *Leitender Ingenieur,* or chief engineer, standing behind the operators controlling the planes. He is very tall and muscular, but still quite young, with less than one year of experience, and half of that in a training boat—though you wouldn't know it. He handles himself like a veteran officer.

"Hold depth," the captain whispers, beads of sweat

forming over his brow line. His name is *Kapitänleutnant* Georg-Werner Fraatz, and at twenty-four, he is just a year older than Mueller, but about half his size. Fraatz also has mastered the steel-eyed stare and the utter calmness of the stereotypical seasoned submariner. At the beginning of the war the minimum age of a U-boat commander was twenty-five, a restriction that BdU, the U-Boat High Command, lifted last year when the shortage for commanders skyrocketed from a combination of combat deaths, accidents, illness, suicide, and even commanders sentenced to death because they dared challenge their orders—orders which as I'm now finding out tend to be quite insane at times. Under no circumstances should U-529 have been directed to carry out a surface attack alone against this convoy, especially with so many British and American escorts roaming the area, and particularly with such young crew and armed only with a third of the regular load of T2 torpedoes because of a shortage at Hamburg. BdU's theory assumed that using our diesels on the surface rather than the electric motors while submerged would allow us to get to the cargo ships much quicker, fire our torpedoes, and then execute our dive-and-evade tactics. As it turned out, we were spotted well before we got within torpedo range and were forced to dive right after rounds fired by an approaching destroyer blasted columns of water all around our vessel. We have been on the run since with escorts on our tail.

Most of the officers aboard and about half of the crew members are roughly the same age and skill level as Fraatz and Mueller. The rest are still in their teens, pulled straight out of the Hitler Youth ranks, and you can read their lack of experience in their terrified stares.

At twenty-seven years of age, I'm the oldest man aboard, amidst a generation of young men forced to grow up in a hurry by Germany's insatiable war machine—

though I'd never write such claim, lest I wish to end up shot like so many other German officers who dared speak their minds.

"Planes on zero," Chief Mueller mumbles after getting the submarine leveled. Both motors run at fifty RPM, or silent speed. Steering due north. The radio man, using the hydrophone device, reports two contacts, one from the stern and another from the bow, both closing in on us again, both determined to make us pay dearly for trying to get near the supply convoy, marking another chapter in the string of rotten luck plaguing this ship since leaving Hamburg on that cold New Year's Day five weeks ago, a month after I volunteered to join them as war correspondent officer, tasked with writing an article about submarine life. First, our diesels began to overheat, forcing us to hang loose at sea for three days while the chief and his crew fixed them. Then we missed the chance to reach three separate convoys for a variety of reasons. Then we got hit by three storms back to back. And when we finally got orders to attack a convoy, we had to do it on the surface.

I tell you, after this past hour, I have been seriously wondering if I made the right decision by signing up for this assignment, but at the time it had seemed like a good idea, especially when my other option was to go to Stalingrad and cover our Sixth Army's fierce battle with the Russians. Two of my dear friends and journalistic colleagues had been killed recently in Stalingrad following weeks of harsh conditions, from extreme cold to lack of basic supplies. I tried to avoid making the same mistake, wasting no time in volunteering for the submarine job, especially when the standing rumor at the war correspondence office in Berlin was that being a part of the U-boat fleet meant a guaranteed bed, long periods of inactivity to write, and also good food. It was no secret that the U-boat men ate the best food of all the German forces, and our propaganda machine glorified these heroes of the deep, hunting the vessels sent by the United States to keep Britain in the war. But I was also aware that life aboard a U-boat wasn't all rosy. There are cramped quarters; there is a lack of mail and phones, a lack of privacy or showers, and also the stench that typically starts on the fourth day of the cruise, a mix of body odor, vomit, dirty clothes, diesel fuel, and engine grease, which even the new-generation ventilators cannot extract.

Still, it beats freezing to death and eating rats in Stalingrad while surrounded by a million pissed off Russians.

However, no one warned me about moments like this, stuck deep beneath the dark waters of the North Atlantic while getting hammered into oblivion by a stubborn enemy who has apparently stopped making mistakes. The British and the Americans have gotten to the point that they can almost predict what we're going to do, eliminating the U-boat's number one weapon: the element of surprise.

I stare at the array of pipes lining the ceiling of the vessel, my mind going further, reaching the surface, wondering how long it would be before the explosions resumed. The silence prior to a depth charge attack is probably worse than the blasts themselves, which *Oberleutnant* Fredric Jurgen, the *Wachoffizier,* has counted as seventy-two since the pounding began thirty minutes ago, half of them detonating close enough to bust loose a number of rivets, triggering leaks, which the crew is quite adept at plugging in record time.

The high-pitched pings of the escorts' search sonars echo against our hull, a single note played over and over by this deadly musical instrument of the sea. The pings are distant and spaced out as the search vessels perform a wide-area sweep.

"They are looking for us but haven't located us, Captain," offers the sonar operator, a guy from Berlin named Hans—never learned his last name. He wears only the right side of the hydrophone headgear to be able to listen to Fraatz's orders with his left ear.

The captain, sporting an unkempt beard just like the rest of us, keeps his arms crossed, nodding ever so slightly while raising his chin, listening to the weak contacts.

"Deeper, Chief," he finally orders. "We need to get beneath the thermocline," he adds, referring to the layer in a body of water separating the upper and warmer zone from the lower and colder zone, where sonar signals will have a harder time locating their vessel.

"Bow planes at ten," Thomas Mueller orders in the deep Bavarian voice that matches his physique, watching the depth meter before reporting, "One hundred and eighty meters . . . one hundred and ninety meters."

The sonar contacts get dimmer but the hull begins to protest the pressure, crying out in deep, hornlike sounds that remind me of an orchestra warming up before a symphony.

BANG! BANG!

Rivets explode out of the walls like bullets, followed by horizontal streams of seawater. One of the rivets strikes a crewmate in the face, dislodging his right eye, splattering it against Mueller and Jurgen.

The sailor screams, falling to the floor, thrashing by our feet while clutching his bleeding face. Jurgen drops over him and clamps a hand over the young man's mouth, urging him to be quiet. Water is an excellent conductor of sound. Any loud noise could be picked up by the enemy, betraying our position. But the rookie sailor isn't responding. He's in shock. Chief Mueller leans down and punches him in the face, hard, knocking him out.

"Hold depth, Chief!" hisses Fraatz with urgency but calmness, before adding, "Plug those leaks . . . and take the wounded to the torpedo room. Send the medic."

"Planes on zero," reports Thomas Mueller after getting back up. "Holding at two hundred and ten meters."

I'm staring at the eyeball washing away in the seawater swirling by Fraatz's feet, and I feel a cramp in my stomach.

While two sailors carry the unconscious man away, three more head our way hauling tools to work on the leaks.

A minute later the control room is back to normal again, and once more we're listening to the distant contacts. The submarine's hull has adjusted to the new depth and is no longer creaking, but I can sense that we're on some edge at this depth. I can see it in the eyes of the chief, of the watch officer, even on Captain Fraatz as he scans the room and does his best to give us all a comforting nod.

"Captain . . . there is a third contact . . . closing in fast," Hans reports, hands slowly turning the large wheel of the hydrophone listening device.

He had not even finished saying that when the faint sound of propellers invade our world, getting louder.

"American destroyer," Hans reports. But there is no increased pinging, no additional sonar contacts.

American?

It dawns on me that this is the first time I have come anywhere near an American vessel, and I can't help but wonder if any of my old buddies from New Haven, Connecticut are aboard ready to blow me into kingdom come. Heck, for all I know my kid brother is up there.

He was sixteen when I left in 1938, which would make him twenty now—right around the average age of the soldiers fighting this war.

"The British search escorts are guiding it toward us," explains Fraatz in his monotone voice.

A distant explosion makes Hans cringe as he removes his headphones. The hydrophone device acts as a sound amplifier.

"What was *that*?" demands Fraatz as the radioman massages his right ear while making a face. "Depth charges?"

"No, sir," Hans replies. "No depth charges have been dropped yet. The destroyer is still too far away. That was a torpedo hit."

"A *what*?" Fraatz, Mueller, and Jurgen ask in unison

Hans is about to reply when a second distant explosion echoes across the vessel, quickly followed by a third.

"More hits," says Jurgen, standing in between the captain and the chief, his bald head glistening with sweat as additional explosions in the distance echo across the fifteen or so kilometers separating us. "There must be other U-boats in the area."

"It doesn't make sense," says Fraatz, rubbing his bearded chin. "We were the only ones close enough to the convoy . . . according to BdU, and even then we had to carry out a surface attack or they would have gotten out of range."

Mueller frowns, and so does Jurgen, but neither voices the concern glistening in their stares. There's been a recent rumor about BdU occasionally using one or more submarines as bait to lure the escort vessels away from the convoy so that other U-boats could approach it safely for the kill.

The remote sound of twisting metal propagates across the water—the noise of sinking vessels, adding a degree of credibility to the rumor. The sound, however, is mixed with that of the approaching destroyer and the resonant pinging from the search vessels.

"I think there are at least four vessels sinking," reports Hans, cautiously holding the right headphone to his ear. Acute hearing is not just the lifeline of a U-boat radio-man, but it is also the eyes and ears of the submarine. Hans can't afford to go deaf on us or all is lost. "The destroyer is getting closer. No depth charges yet. Contacts closing in."

The sonar pinging intensifies. The escorts are still on us, despite whatever damage some of our boats are doing to the convoy. One can only assume that other escorts will deal with them.

"Depth charges in the water," announces Hans, before removing the headphones.

"Here we go," Fraatz mumbles toward the ceiling of the vessel while grabbing on to an overhead pipe as the destroyer's propellers rumble over us.

Wham!

The first is far to the left and many meters above us.

Wham! Wham! Wham!

They are all going off at the wrong depth—

WHAM!

I loose my footing, crash against the instrument panel behind me, nearly impaling myself on a lever at—

WHAM! WHAM!

Rivets pop, sparks fly, flames erupt, light bulbs explode, raining on us, mixing with seawater and—

More explosions rattle the ship, turning everything into an ear-piercing blur. As one blast shoves the vessel—and everyone in it—in one direction, another blast counters it, the acoustic force crushing me like an invisible hammer, pounding every last bone in my body with animal strength.

Then silence again.

I'm on my back staring at the array of pipes and wires running along the ceiling. Sailors are already on the move, some extinguishing the fire, others jumping right over me hauling tools to plug leaks.

"Damage report!" demands Captain Fraatz, holding a bloody handkerchief to the side of his face while standing next to the chief, who appears unharmed, his eyes on the depth meter.

I stand with some difficulty and try to move out of the way—though in such confined quarters you are *always* in the way and must learn to move aside quickly.

My body is aching all over, but my jaw is really throbbing, and I realize that I'm not only bleeding from my mouth, but there's something loose in there. Spitting, I see two of my teeth splashing the floor along with a mouthful of bloody saliva. I remember what one submariner told me once about the massive energy of depth charges being capable of dislodging sailors' teeth.

The U-boat men are already back on top of their vessel, making repairs, going over their damage reports: seawater wetting batteries in the engine room; busted navigation gear; damaged periscope tower; flooding torpedo room; broken gauges, electrical systems, and radio gear.

But the chief is holding his depth, and there appears to be enough juice left in those batteries to keep us running at silent speed for a while, though eventually we will be forced to surface—but hopefully not until we have lost them. I doubt we'd last more than a few moments on the surface before one of those rounds ripped us in half, as Mueller confessed happened to a number of U-boats in recent months.

For a moment the cold streets of Stalingrad don't seem

all that bad. And the streets of New Haven seem even better still.

The mood is a bit jovial as I'm sitting at dinner with Captain Fraatz and his staff. I guess it must be something to do with staring at death in the eye and surviving.

Canned fish, cheese, rye bread, and black coffee glare at me, but I can't get myself to eat. Not only is my mouth still throbbing, but my stomach is in knots from the attack two hours ago, soon before we heard our last enemy contact. We've maintained silent speed at one hundred and eighty meters while holding a northeasterly heading, away from the convoy and its deadly escorts. According to the captain, we will remain submerged for another three hours. By then it will be dark, reducing the chances of someone spotting us when we surface. Meanwhile the crew has been working on all of the repairs that can be carried out while submerged. The rest will have to wait until we surface.

"What's the matter, Johan?" the captain asks, calling me by my German middle name—the name I've been using ever since leaving America. My friends back in Connecticut knew me as Michael J. Mosser.

"What do you mean, sir?" I ask.

"U-boat food isn't good enough for a war correspondent officer?"

Everyone laughs. Chief Mueller, sitting next to me, pats me on the back, though the man doesn't know his own strength, nearly sending me bouncing over the table.

"Ah . . . it's my mouth, Captain. I lost two teeth back there." I stretch my thumb in the direction of the control room, where no doubt my molars are still floating somewhere near that poor bastard's eyeball in the ankle-deep water that accumulated before all leaks could be sealed. Since the main bilge pump was damaged in the attack, we can't remove the water until we surface.

Oberleutnant Fredric Jurgen, sitting next to Captain Fraatz, grins while hooking his index finger beneath his upper lip, lifting it, exposing the entire left side of his brownish teeth. He is missing roughly half of them. Mueller goes next, revealing four missing molars, and it's the same with Hans, who has taken a break from his radio duties to have dinner with us.

"What about you, Captain?" I ask, my new battle scars making me feel like a part of his team. "How many have you lost?"

Fraatz smiles and slowly shakes his head, which is sporting a small cut from when he banged his head against a pipe. "I intend to finish this war with all of my body parts."

Mueller nods and gives me another love tap with one of his gorilla hands. I grimace. Not only is my body aching all over, but now this brute keeps on beating me. He says, "The captain claims to have found a way to avoid losing teeth in the middle of a depth-charge attack, isn't that right, Captain?"

"It's all in the laws of physics, Thomas," he tells Mueller.

"Speaking of physics," says Jurgen, rubbing a hand over the purple lump he earned on his bald head during the last round, "how many charges did those bastards drop on us?"

"Eighty-nine," says Mueller without hesitation. "Forty-three in our near vicinity."

Fraatz nods. "Not bad. Not bad at all."

I'm staring at him in disbelief. *Not bad?* We've got the living hell kicked out of us and this man across from me says *not bad?*

"It's our hull, Johan," Fraatz explains in reply to the facial expression that I must have made. "The pigs can't kill us with depth charges unless they can place them within three meters of us. Otherwise our hull will not give."

"It will bend," says Mueller, clasping his hands in what looks like a crushing motion, his gigantic biceps trembling beneath his pale skin. "It will twist, and shift, and compress . . . but it will not give."

"Most of the time, anyway," clarifies Fraatz.

"And combine that with our efficient evasive tactics," says Jurgen, "and what you have is a very unnerving and loud weapon, as you have experienced firsthand, but not a direct threat."

"Although," Fraatz says, "we have lost a number of vessels to those charges."

"True," says Mueller, "but seldom from a direct hit. It's nearly impossible to place a charge that close to us. However, many U-boats have sunk because of accumulated damage from repeated depth charge attacks, sometimes as many as three or four hundred charges dropped in a matter of a couple of hours. That's why it is so important to get away from the threat fast, even if it means diving this deep."

"Be sure to put that in your article, Johan," Fraatz adds.

As they all stare at me, the obvious question pops in my mind, and being the investigative journalist that I like to believe I am, I ask, "So . . . how do you kill a submerged U-boat if not by depth charges?"

Their faces become stolid beneath their shaggy beards, and all eyes gravitate to Fraatz, who regards me with his steel-blue stare.

"Have you ever heard of U-335, Johan?" he asks.

Everyone drops their gaze.

I did some level of research on U-boats before coming aboard, but Germany being Germany, most of the reports

I could find were related to successes. Information on U-boat sinkings—and any other type of bad news for that matter—was strictly controlled by Berlin. Being a war correspondent, however, allowed me to gather morsels of uncensored intelligence as it floated through our field offices. I think I remember hearing something about U-335.

"Didn't we lose her during a storm?" I finally offer.

Fraatz sighs. "I'm sure that's what got released at BdU, but any submariner will tell you that the odds of a U-boat sinking because of a storm are as high as our chances of sinking an American destroyer with one of our torpedoes—negligible. If a gale develops, we simply submerge, where all is calm, and then steer away from the storm before resurfacing."

Now that I think about it I realize how bad a lie that was.

"Then . . . what happened to U-335?"

"August third, 1942, in the North Sea northeast of Faeroes," Fraatz says. "A British submarine snuck up to it and sunk it with three torpedoes."

I'm stunned. "A British submarine?"

They all nod slowly, in unison, with obvious respect.

"What type of boat was U-335?"

"VIIC, just like ours," says Mueller, whose cheerful mood has vanished.

I am trying to comprehend how anyone could possibly approach this vessel unannounced. I guess I was under the impression that while the Americans and the British controlled the surface, Germany was still king of the deep. "What about the hydrophone?"

Hans, who is wearing a dark turtleneck sweater, shrugs beneath the dim yellow light from one of our surviving lightbulbs.

"Mistakes happen," says Jurgen, his tired stare dropping to a creased photograph he has produced from a side pocket. It's a group of young officers crowding the conning tower of a submarine as it left port. He tosses it at me. "The one wearing the white cap is *Kapitänleutnant* Hans-Hermann Pelkner, captain of U-335, and an old drinking buddy of ours."

"We knew most of those men, Johan," says Fraatz. "Hans-Hermann and I took the same commander's course back at Danzig. The report we got through the U-boat radio channel, according to a single survivor from the attack, is that following the first torpedo hit, the crippled submarine made it to the surface for a few moments, enough for one man to make it out before two more torpedoes sealed the fate of the remaining crew. Another U-boat in the vicinity reported that the second and third torpedoes didn't kill everyone aboard U-335 right away. The radioman of the witness U-boat heard the men banging the hull with wrenches and pipes as it sank below three hundred meters, where the hull cracked like an eggshell, killing all remaining hands. BdU censored the report filed by both the surviving sailor and the commander of the witness U-boat, who, in addition to rescuing the survivor, also tried to hunt the British submarine but lost contact soon after the attack. As before, we got the uncensored news through the U-boat channel."

Silence, followed by, "And that, Johan, is one way to kill a U-boat."

My mind is now going in different directions. I've heard of this secret U-boat channel, which exchanges information using the same Enigma coding system used for official communications with BdU. I intend to get more information on this unofficial—and probably illegal—channel, but at the moment I'm more interested in getting a tutorial on the uncensored threats facing our U-boat fleet. I ask, "Is that the only . . . submarine attack against our boats?"

Fraatz and Mueller exchange a glance, before the skipper nods once, allowing the chief to bring me in the know. "This is strictly off the record," Mueller starts. "Agreed?"

This not being the first time a source has asked for confidentiality before providing me with inside information, I give this giant sitting next to me a single nod, doing my best to convey the fact that I'm not new to such informal privacy agreements.

"If we find out otherwise . . ." Jurgen says, letting his words trail off while planting his elbows on the table, his oval-shaped face a foot from mine. "You will wish you were never born."

Mueller rests one of his oversized hands on my neck and gives me his version of a massage, though I get the strange feeling that he can snap my neck at will. "We will find you, Johan," he says. "We will shove your skinny little ass inside a torpedo tube and blow you into the ocean at one hundred meters so you can experience what those sailors aboard U-335 felt as the pressure crushed them when the walls of their vessel gave, unleashing the fury of the depth on them."

I try to reply. The words form in my mind but are choked in my throat as I shift my gaze between the officers, who regard me with the same dead calmness that I saw earlier today, when I thought the world was collapsing over me.

After a seemingly endless awkward moment, Fraatz grins, then Jurgen, Hans, and the others. Mueller gives me another one of his love taps while making a sound that resembles a train engine pulling out of station. He is laughing.

"Did you see his face, Captain?" says Hans, slapping the table with mirth. "I thought Johan was going to piss on himself!"

They are all laughing very hard now at my expense, and a moment later I join them, nodding before saying, "All right, all right. I'm glad I could provide you with some entertainment."

"I like you, Johan," says Mueller, clamping my neck again while shaking it, his eyes wet with amusement. "Can I keep him, Captain?"

Laughter explodes again, but quickly dies down when Fraatz says, "Including U-335, we have lost six of our boats to submarines. This fact, of course, is kept as secret from the public, as are also other very effective enemy weapons, like the Hedgehog."

"The Hedgehog?" I ask, gently moving my head away from Mueller to get his hand off of me.

Mueller sets it on the table and says in the engineering tone that he takes when explaining anything technical, "The Hedgehog is a projector-type weapon that launches many small projectiles hundreds of feet ahead of the suspected location of the submarine. After entering the water, these projectiles arm and explode either on contact with the U-boat or when they reach the bottom of the ocean. They look like needles in the ocean, which is how the name was derived. We have lost a considerable number of boats to them, as well as to Fido."

I'm beginning to have difficulty keeping track of all the facts and hope to remember everything later on—not that I can really reference any of this directly in my article. Even if the torpedo-tube threat was an idle one, my superiors in Berlin would have me shot for writing anything that would stain our national pride. But as a journalistic reporter, it is my job to get the full picture prior to writing an article. "What is Fido?" I finally ask.

"A new type of torpedo that uses sonar technology to home in on a submarine," explains the chief engineer in his lecturing voice. "We suspect that the British submarines are using them—and in fact that's how U-335 might have been sunk—but what makes this weapon particularly deadly to us is the fact that it can also be launched from an airplane. There is no known evasive technique at the moment. All a captain can do is dive hard and hope to lose it in the thermal layers. BdU, however, is working on a decoy system."

Fraatz and Jurgen shake their heads before the latter says, "Thomas you know quite well that if those decoys are as good as the damned *Zaunköning,* we might as well take our chances without decoys."

"What is a *Zaunköning*?" I ask.

Fraatz frowns. "I'm disappointed at the level of knowledge of our war correspondents these days."

All I can do is shrug.

After letting his comment hang in there for another moment, the captain nods at the chief engineer to continue my education.

Mueller says, "The *Zaunköning,* or T5 torpedo, was advertised by BdU scientists as the ultimate escort killer, fired from any depth and designed to lock on to the loudest noise after a run of four hundred meters. Problem is that the loudest noise sometimes turned out to be the U-boat itself."

"You mean the torpedo would double back and . . ."

"Yes, Johan. *Kaboom,*" says Fraatz extending his arms. "We lost three boats to our own T5s before we came up with a change of strategy when firing it and passed that information to the fleet through the U-boat channel. But by then the British and the Americans had deployed a noise-making decoy that they now tow behind their vessels, confusing the T5s. There is a lot of technology being developed by the enemy to hunt and kill U-boats that the BdU, by orders of our Führer, does not distribute to U-boat commanders right away, thus depriving crews of valuable information. So we rely on our informal channel to let each other know what we have experienced—of course that's when the crew survives the attack, or, like in the case of U-335, when someone witnesses the kill."

When I signed up for this submarine mission in November of 1942, I was under the impression that Germany still had a chance to win this war, even with the less-than-stellar Russian Campaign. After all, we did control all of Europe. What I have just heard, however, makes me wonder if we even have a chance anymore, reinforcing my fear that I made a paramount mistake by coming here rather than remaining in America.

"What is the matter, Johan?" asks Mueller. "The reality of our war depressing you? War is all about suffering, my friend."

Suffering.

I look around the table. In the past weeks I have done some biographical research on the leaders of this U-boat as a way to better help me understand their behavior under pressure. All of the men present today have suffered the loss of loved ones to the war. Fraatz lost both his parents during an allied bombing over Berlin six months ago. Mueller lost his girlfriend because her mother happened to be half Jewish. She was sent to a camp in Poland. In addition, he had not heard anything in months from his two kid brothers, both part of the Sixth Army battling the Russians in Stalingrad. Jurgen had one brother killed in Russia and another in Northern Africa. His mother committed suicide the same day the news arrived. Hans's relatives are from outside Stuttgart, a region that has been pounded by allied bombers in recent months. He has no idea if his family is dead or alive, but he is certain that his kid brother, an SS officer missing in Paris, was very likely kidnapped by the French Resistance.

I consider myself lucky that all of my relatives are safe and sound back in America. And as far as my current situation . . . well, I have no one but myself to blame. My family pleaded with me not to volunteer, in the end supporting my decision with silent resignation. I still remember the day I sailed away to Europe in the fall of 1938. Even now I can see my twin sisters and my mother in tears. I can still see my kid brother's somber face. But most of all, I remember my father, remember what he gave me on that day. Having survived World War I, he knew the value of our American citizenship and forced me to take my U.S. passport and other relevant documents, including my diploma from Yale—all tightly packed in a waterproof pouch that I've been taking everywhere recently, even though if someone finds them I'll probably be shot on the spot under accusations of being a spy.

A spy.

I sigh. I've given it all away for Germany, the country where I was born, even if I was only three years old when my family left for America. Germany, the nation that my parents so often spoke of with affection, with nostalgia, always obsessed that I learn its language, which I did even before I learned English. Germany, the nation that had called out to all Germans around the world to join the national quest to rebuild *Deutschland* from the ashes of World War I, to help it grow, to make it the great nation that it once was, a nation that would last a thousand years. And so I joined to pursue this foolish dream, never once imagining what kind of monster Adolf Hitler really was, never once realizing that one day we would be at war against the country where I grew up, against the nation that took my family in and provided us with a wonderful way of life.

And at first it had seemed like a good decision, coming to Berlin, the center of the universe, thriving with life, laughter, hopes, and dreams. I was certain that I would be able to make my mark there as a top-notch journalist, covering the birth of what we all thought would become one of the greatest nations on earth.

Yes, I certainly had a lot of dreams and aspirations back then, until those dreams began to fade when Hitler's war machine rumbled outside our borders, swallowing Poland, France, and so many other countries; crushing the opposition with our unyielding panzers, with our *Luftwaffe,* with our *Wermacht,* with our *Kriegsmarine.* By the time Japan bombed Pearl Harbor at the end of 1941 and the United States declared war on Japan, Italy, and Germany, it was already too late to change my mind. It was impossible to leave. I realized that I was stuck with my short-sighted decision and would have to play this through to the end.

The end.

As I'm staring at the walls of this iron coffin, I steel myself to be ready to face whatever that end might be.

Hans spends another minute working the wheels of the Enigma machine to decode our orders from BdU. The tall and lanky radioman, still wearing the same turtleneck sweater as when we got hammered by enemy escorts yesterday, grimaces as he translates the message, before handing it to Captain Fraatz, who reads it with an impassive face and in turn gives it to Jurgen. Chief Engineer Mueller, the third in command, will have to wait to receive what appears to be bad news. He is busy with his crew wrapping up repairs in the bow and stern compartments, as well as outside, where he has two welders securing a few external features that came loose during the depth charge attack, including two antennas, a section of the periscope assembly, the main bilge-pump outlets, also a nasty crack on the exterior hull. While the ship did indeed survive the depth charge onslaught in one piece, it sustained a lot of damage in the process, lending credibility to Mueller's claim that depth charges, though not a direct weapon to sink a submarine—like the Hedgehog projectile or the Fido torpedo—could eventually damage it beyond repair. I was already impressed with the crew's ability to weather the wrath of those depth charges, but their ability to make repairs while at sea certainly exceeded my expectations. These folks are as self-sufficient as they come. In a way I guess they have to be to survive out here on their own.

They are also good people, with families, with hopes, with dreams, sent here to fight for their nation—even if their nation was being run by a ruthless tyrant. They love Germany as much as I do, as much as my parents still do, and that places us in an impossible situation. Following our orders makes us part of the war machine. Refusing to follow orders will get us labeled as traitors and executed.

Speaking of following orders, I was up on the conning tower an hour ago getting some fresh air while snapping pictures of welders dangling from lines off the sides of the vessel amidst showers of sparks from their equipment as the boat rose and fell in the swells. It was definitely a sight to see. Those welders should be given Knight's Crosses for the guts to step beyond the protection of the conning tower on a night like tonight. But we have no choice. The submarine must get back to full operational status before daybreak to get ready for our new orders, which, based on the look of these three, can't be good.

After a moment of hesitation, Jurgen, still holding the

piece of paper, says to me, "Bad news from the Eastern
Front, Johan. We just got a week-old unofficial report
through the U-Boat channel that General Paulus has sur-
rendered to the Russians at Stalingrad to prevent further
bloodshed."

I'm at a loss for words, well aware of the size of the
Sixth Army, with over a quarter of a million soldiers, a
thousand panzers, several hundred pieces of artillery, and
an entire air force of transport planes. The mere thought
of such a vast and well-supplied deployment of our best
forces now in the hands of the Russians rattles me with
the power of a hundred depth charges.

"What . . . are you sure?" I ask, not certain of how to
take the news.

"If it's true," says Fraatz, speaking for the first time
since we picked up the coded transmission after the chief
fixed the antennas, "it means that the tide of war may be
turning against us on that front. It already has on this
side of the world."

Jurgen, Hans, and the handful of sailors on the control
room lower their gazes.

In my opinion, truer words have not been spoken in
this submarine since I climbed aboard on a foggy day on
January first, 1943, but just the same you have to be
damned careful who your audience is when you make a
statement like that. Captain Fraatz—and any of us for
that matter—could end up executed like so many other
outspoken German officers in recent months.

Chief Mueller drops down from the conning tower
hauling a bucket filled with wrenches, wire, and other
clanging hardware. He is soaked, his huge arms dripping
seawater, his face blackened with grease. It doesn't take
him but a few seconds to realize something is wrong.

"Well?" he asks in his resonant voice. "Did we finally
lose this damned war?"

"Close, Chief," says Fraatz, before taking a moment to explain the situation on the Stalingrad front.

I have known Chief Thomas Mueller from the moment I volunteered for this submarine tour. I spent a month preparing for the assignment, tagging along as they went through the preparation of their boat, as they carried out weekend training missions outside Hamburg to break in the rookies, as they celebrated the New Year by getting stinking drunk, as they pulled themselves together and sailed away on New Year's Day. Mueller was always the strong man, always the loudest, the most outspoken, barking orders to his crew, drilling them into oblivion until they knew every square inch of that boat, down to the last rivet and bolt.

To see this giant crumbling to his knees and burying his face in his hands invokes a memory of the Goliath that German military forces once were at the beginning of the Russian campaign, and of the broken-spirited army it has become, succumbing to a supposedly inferior enemy.

"No!" Mueller cries, mumbling something about Klaus and Mathias, who I remember are his kid brothers. "It . . . it can't be true!"

"Thomas! Get up!" barks Fraatz.

Mueller is sobbing, his huge hands covering his face. The man is in obvious shock. The sailors in the control room gather around us, their faces displaying the mix of surprise and disillusion that has also gripped me.

"Get up, and return to your post!" Fraatz insists.

"C'mon, buddy," whispers Hans, kneeling by his side. "Let's go talk about it somewhere else."

"No! Leave me alone! All of you!" Mueller cries, howling the names of his brothers.

We all know that death is better than being captured

alive by the barbarian Russians. Chances are he will never know what became of them.

Fraatz walks away pissed off. Jurgen and Hans suddenly get very concerned and really plead with Mueller to get up, to obey the captain, but Mueller has lost it.

I'm not sure what is going on, but a moment later I figure it out. Fraatz is back with his sidearm, which he aims at the chief engineer's head.

"Get back to your job, sailor!" he barks.

Mueller doesn't respond, continuing to cry and shake.

Fraatz thumbs the hammer back, cocking the weapon.

Jurgen gets in between the two while doing his darnest to tug Mueller's large bulk to his feet, accomplishing the task with the assistance of Hans.

"He is fine, Captain!" proclaims Jurgen, his bald head beaded with perspiration. "The chief is all right!"

"That's correct, Captain," adds Hans, "Thomas just needs a little rest from his grueling work! Isn't that right, Chief?"

Mueller manages a slight nod—though he is still clearly quite upset.

Flanked by his two friends, Mueller staggers toward the stern, leaving Fraatz alone with me and the sailors manning the control room.

The captain closes his eyes, lowering his weapon, exhaling heavily.

Damn. You don't see that every day. Based on the look of Fraatz, I have little doubt that he would have pulled the trigger if Hans and Jurgen hadn't intervened.

A minute of total awkwardness passes before Fraatz says, "Try not to include this episode in your article, Johan. These are good men. They're just under a lot of stress."

I nod. Good men or not, Fraatz would have splattered

Mueller's brains all over the deck if the chief engineer hadn't gotten out of his sight in time.

A moment later Hans and Jurgen silently return to their posts. No one is talking, which just adds to the uneasiness of the moment. Fraatz goes to his cabin to lock his sidearm. By the time he returns, Hans is listening intently to the communications radio through a pair of headphones.

"Captain," says Hans. "New transmission arriving." Then he adds, "It's from BdU."

Fraatz steps closer to his radioman as Hans jots it down before shifting over to the Enigma machine. The wheels had already been set for today, so he just starts pressing the keys of the typewriterlike coding system.

We all wait expectantly.

Hans finishes decoding it and hands it to Fraatz, who reads it and passes it to Jurgen. The watch officer clenches his jaw while breathing heavily through flaring nostrils. "This is . . ."

"Insane," says Fraatz, shaking his head. "Simply insane."

I'm dying to know, so I lean closer to Jurgen. He tilts his head toward me and says, "Apparently *Grossadmiral* Karl Dönitz himself has read our report from the events that took place yesterday, and, based on our ability to draw the enemy escorts away from the convoy—plus our ingenious tactics to escape destruction—Dönitz has awarded our good captain the Knight's Cross. Dönitz believes the crew of U-529 should take some of the credit for the fifty tons of merchant vessels that our fleet sunk yesterday while we were dodging the depth charges of the escort vessels. BdU calls the operation a great success."

For a moment I think about stretching my hand to congratulate him on this coveted award, especially com-

ing directly from a man like Dönitz, the U-boat high
commander, but I can tell something isn't right.

"In addition," Jurgen continues, his voice lowering
while also becoming nearly disembodied. "*Grossadmiral*
Dönitz has ordered us to perform another surface attack
on a new American convoy heading toward Britain."

I'm stunned. How in the hell can someone ask us to
go through that again?

Jurgen pauses for a moment and then reads straight
from the deciphered message. "*Grossadmiral* Karl Dönitz congratulates *Kapitänleutnant* Georg-Werner Fraatz
and his crew, and wishes him all best and a good hunt."

There's the awkward silence again. This time it's me
who breaks it, by asking, "But . . . how can Dönitz make
such a request after what we just went through? It is just
plain suicide to go up against those escorts on the surface
again. Besides, by now the Allies should have caught up
to the trick. I doubt it will work a second—"

Fraatz raises a palm at me. "Theirs not to make reply.
Theirs not to reason why. Theirs but to do and die. Into
the valley of Death, rode the six hundred," he says, quot-
ing from Lord Tennyson's "The Charge of the Light Brigade," a personal favorite of mine—though I would not
dare admit it. After all, Tennyson was British, and I'm
a bit surprised that Fraatz would quote him. The poem
was written to memorialize the suicidal charge by light
cavalry over open terrain by British forces in the Battle
of Balaclava during the Crimean War. I first read a
German translation of this and other famous poems during the German courses I took at Yale to polish up my
language skills in preparation for my eventual departure.

At this moment, as I take a deep breath and close my
eyes, it all becomes clear to me. This is the true meaning
of war, the basic credo of a frontline soldier, as captured
by Tennyson almost a century before. We aren't here to

question our orders, or to try to make sense of them, or to try to argue with our superior officers that we may not survive another such onslaught. We aren't even supposed to discuss the orders among ourselves. We are here to *execute* them to the best of our ability, to charge forward at all cost—even if doing so could very well send us to our deaths, as was the case with that legendary brigade, as was the case with so many other soldiers before and after them.

Words of the legendary poem suddenly echo in my mind with the same intensity as those crippling explosions that dislodged my teeth.

> *Boldly they rode and well,*
> *Into the jaws of Death*
> *Into the mouth of Hell,*
> *Rode the six hundred.*

Hell.

A cold hell is what the U-Boat High Command has prepared for the unlucky crew of U-529.

Lightning flashes in the North Atlantic sky as we approach the convoy from the north while doing almost sixteen knots. The rumbling thunder mixes with the sounds from the angry sea this morning, as our bow hurdles over boiling swells before splashing down with explosions of water and foam that momentarily swallow the entire vessel, including the conning tower, soaking us to the bone, and surging again over the white-capped crests.

Seawater dripping from my wet hair, seeping down the back of my jacket, I continue to ignore the constant clashes of metal against monstrous walls of black. I press my lips together, tasting the salt as the mist clouding the conning tower clears and we get a brief view of the horizon again. I volunteered for the first watch, and as such I'm facing the starboard side of the vessel, surveying the hazy horizon under an overcast sky of rolling gray clouds.

But in spite of the degree of difficulty it adds to our observation jobs, we actually welcome the gathering storm, for it provides us with some protection as we get dangerously close to the convoy of merchant vessels hauling the supplies that the British so desperately need to keep on fighting, to keep resisting our attacks.

The supply lines must be severed at all cost, even if it means sending U-529 to the bottom of the ocean— even if it means that Michael Johan Mosser will never see his family again.

My mouth is still aching from the other day, and so does the rest of my body for that matter. But I must keep a vigilant eye on the horizon, keep watch for the menacing silhouettes of military vessels. We got a visual on the convoy ten minutes ago but have yet to see any escorts in the area as we plough ahead at full speed.

The cargo ships grow larger on the gray horizon as Captain Fraatz, standing watch facing the bow, barks orders to Chief Mueller below.

It had taken an hour for the corpulent engineer to come around, but he did, returning to the control room to resume the coordination of all needed repairs, acting as if nothing had happened, finally declaring U-529 combatworthy three hours later, while we were already on our way to execute our new orders.

"Flood tubes one through four!" shouts Fraatz over the whistling wind, over the reverberating sea slapping our hull and the thunder rumbling in the sky.

"Flooding tubes one through four!" comes the reply

from below a moment later. "Ready to fire on command!"

The convoy grows larger on the horizon, and for a moment I'm beginning to wonder if anyone is going to prevent us from firing on what appears to be fat, slow, and unprotected cargo vessels. For the life of me I can't see any escorts, and the rest of the watchmen are also failing to spot British or American combat ships as lightning gleams again and again above us, casting bright yellow flashes against the charcoal skies, followed by thunder.

But I know they are out there. It would be insane to deploy a convoy in these waters without an escort. But then again, it's just as insane to make an expensive submarine and a fully trained crew play bait.

I continue to peer through my binoculars, my chest thoroughly soaked by the incessant splashing, which has whipped the skin of my face raw. But I have no choice. I'm the eyes of the vessel on this section of sea and we have reached the most critical phase of our attack. All hands must work in unison if we're going to live through this.

I hear thunder, but it was not preceded by lightning.

An instant later, a column of water rises a hundred meters to the right of our bow. A round from an escort's gun.

Damn!

But who in the hell fired it?

"Escort vessel! Twelve o'clock!" shouts Fraatz, pointing straight toward a gap in the line of merchant ships.

All heads turn toward the bow, and a moment later I see it materializing in the foggy distance, almost like a ghostly apparition from the sea.

A destroyer, probably American, is sailing our way, its cannon alive with gunfire, like stroboscopic flashes of

lightning. The roaring sea drowns the whistling noise of
the incoming shells, which create columns of water boiling up to either side of us, getting closer as the gun crew
adjusts its fire. If we get hit by one of those rounds, we
probably wouldn't even have time to scream.

"Prepare to dive! Clear the bridge!" shouts Fraatz, before adding, "Periscope depth, Chief!"

Periscope depth?

I go first, sliding down to the control room in the way
Jurgen has taught me, pressing my feet against the edges
of the metal ladder and letting gravity do the rest. A
second later I'm in the control room—along with a
splash of water raining down on me. I quickly step out
of the way as Fraatz drops next. The captain is barking
orders before his feet even reach the deck.

Mueller adjusts the planes while screaming to a number of sailors who aren't moving fast enough while heading toward the bow to act as ballast. We submerge just
as the last watchman closes the exterior hatch.

And just like that the swaying stops, but not my mind,
which is racing at a hundred kilometers per hour. Why
haven't we engaged in any evasive tactics? Why are we
still going straight toward a destroyer? Why are we—

Fraatz gazes into the periscope for what seems like an
eternity before he says in a calmed tone, "All ahead two
thirds. Fire one and two."

I'm totally confused now. That destroyer is at least
10,000 meters away. If I remember Chief Mueller's dis-
sertation on torpedoes from two weeks ago, the range of
our T2s in their preheated state is 7,500 meters, meaning
the torpedo crew had to electrically heat them to a temperature of 30 degrees Celsius. Otherwise the range with
cold batteries would have been only 4,500 meters.

But whether it is 4,500 meters or 7,500 meters, that is
still way short of the 10,000-meter gap separating—

The hull rumbles as rounds pound the water, missing us by what seems like a few meters, but they lack the punch of the depth charges, which at such short distance would have cracked the hull.

"One and two are in the water, Captain," reports Jurgen as our steel fish sprint toward the enemy.

"Fire three and four," orders Fraatz.

The water around rumbles again and again as the destroyer unleashes hell on us.

The moment the next two torpedoes leave their tubes, Fraatz adds, "Left full rudder. Take her down, Chief. All ahead one third. New heading zero four zero."

"Bow planes at twenty," says Mueller as he begins to call our depth and Hans gets busy with the hydrophone to track the incoming threat as well as listening to the torpedoes we have just fired. Jurgen takes a moment to explain the captain's tactic. Even though the initial distance to the nearest target—the destroyer—was 10,000 meters, the escort was heading toward us, hopefully closing the gap to get within range of the T2s before their batteries ran dry. If anything, the torpedoes would force the incoming escort into evasive maneuvers, buying us time to dive deep.

"Stern contact, captain," reports Hans a moment later.

"Depth ten meters . . . fifteen meters," says Mueller, his eyes on the planes as he tries to get us deep as fast as possible.

"New contact bearing zero five zero."

Fraatz snaps his head toward the radioman. "A *second* contact?"

"Yes, sir. Just appeared out of nowhere, and must be stationary because I don't hear their screws."

I'm not a submariner but this does sound weird, and from the brief look of confusion on the captain's face, I can tell that he too is perplexed by what could be a new technique that the enemy is taking against our evasive tactics.

"Depth thirty meters . . . thirty-five meters," calls out Mueller.

"First and second torpedoes have stopped moving," announces Hans. "Third and fourth are still running. Third contact bearing three three zero."

Damn. That's three escorts converging on us. Bastards are all around us. As Mueller and Jurgen exchange a glance, the captain rubs the thick beard on his chin, apparently contemplating his next move.

"Forty meters," reports Mueller.

Then we all hear a distant explosion. "Fourth torpedo hit, Captain!" announces Hans. "We hit the destroyer, sir!"

There is a brief cheer. Fraatz puts an arm on Mueller and another on Jurgen. "We have just taken on and hit a destroyer, gentle—"

"Two depth charges dropped!" screams Hans, startling everyone aboard as he yanks off the headphones and stares at Fraatz with fear.

Christ Almight—

WHAM!

Before we know it we're all rolling on the floor, except for the captain and Chief Mueller, who hold their ground as the boat lurches forward, propelled by an invisible force.

The second charge goes off an instant later, turning my world into a blur as seawater starts to stream from a dozen places at once. I'm rolling in it along with other men as I struggle to grab on to to something—anything to stop my uncontrolled bouncing.

There! A handle of some sort, which I grip with all my strength and hang on to with my right hand while wiping the water off my face with my left, trying to get a glimpse of what's happening.

"Damage report!" demands Fraatz, shouting over the commotion, the water already above his ankles.

There's havoc in the control room. Hans appears unconscious against his radio gear while bleeding from the side of his head. I can see Jurgen, but Mueller is just getting up, reaching for an overhead pipe to steady himself.

"The bow torpedo room is flooding, Captain!" reports a sailor rushing into the control room.

"We're taking water in the engine room," reports another sailor arriving from the stern of the vessel, his young face tight with anxiety.

"Motors have stopped!" reports Mueller. "I can't control our—"

WHAMMM!

A third charge hits us far harder than the first two. U-529 trembles under the stress of the powerful shock wave, the resonance inside this iron chamber crushing my head like a vice, drilling into my eardrums, piercing straight into my brain. I want to scream but can't as the pressure shoves me against a wall of equipment with savage force.

Through the deafening havoc, I hear Captain Fraatz shouting, "Emergency blow! Emergency blow! Surface, Chief! Surface!"

I manage to stand, my head throbbing. I sense upward motion as U-529 blows the seawater in the ballast tanks used for buoyancy control.

"Fifteen meters ... ten meters ... twelve meters ... ten meters ... Captain, our rate of ascent is slowing down. We're taking in water too fast and won't be able to hold her on the surface for very long."

"Get the crew ready to abandon ship!" orders the captain, and a moment later sailors are passing the same life jackets we used last week during a drill.

"Tower has been cleared!" announces Mueller as he heads up the ladder to open the hatch. A splash of seawater cascades down the opening, splashing on the knee-deep water swirling in the control room.

"Go, Johan! Get up there!" Fraatz shouts the moment the chief returns to the control room and charges toward the bow compartment to get his men moving.

Wearing a life jacket, I head up, squeezing through the opening, reaching the conning tower. The ocean is still furious. How in the hell are we going to evacuate the ship when waves the size of a house are pounding us? A gray sky trembling with lightning hangs over me, but there is no rain, only wind, thunder, and the constant spray of the waves as they clash against our hull.

Just then I see the destroyer in the distance, smoke coiling from its bow. We definitely hit it, preventing it from attacking us, though someone else did.

A plane comes out of nowhere, roaring right above me. I suddenly realize why Hans never heard any screws in the water prior to the depth charges. The escorts were just pinging us to get a fix on our position while guiding the aircraft directly to us. It makes a tight 360-turn over the waves before heading straight toward us from our port side hauling two barrel-shaped objects beneath the fuselage.

Depth charges!

My instincts overcome surprise. Before I know it I have climbed to the edge of the conning tower and kicked my legs against the edge, jumping off the starboard side, clearing the ship by a few feet.

The North Atlantic water chills me an instant later as I start to swim as fast as I can. I need to get away from the wounded submarine. I need to increase the gap, reach a safe distance in case one of those depth—

The blast shoves me forward and down with savage force, plunging me several feet underwater.

Stinging cold and darkness envelop me, swallowing all sound. My lungs feel about to burst from the pressure, as does my head as I start to come around, as my instincts force me to move, to continue swimming, to get my head above the surface, which my life vest helps me reach a moment later.

A breath of cold air, followed by coughing and more air, chilling my lungs but feeding my body with much-needed oxygen. A wave picks me up, hoisting me by nearly a dozen feet, providing me with a sobering view of U-529 roughly fifty feet away.

The sight numbs me beyond the frigid waters. Smoke and flames cover the conning tower as the submarine begins to list toward the stern.

Shivering, my body temperature rapidly dropping, I glare at the unnerving choice those who survived the blast inside that vessel now have to make. There is only one way out of the sinking U-boat, and that escape route is covered in flames.

A sailor makes his choice, emerging through the blazing conning tower, instantly setting himself on fire, his bellowing howls blending with the droning engine from the circling plane and the whistling wind.

I recognize the booming voice, even in agonizing distress.

It's Chief Mueller.

Oh, Dear God.

I hear the chief's desperate cry as he jumps over the side, misjudging and bouncing on the hull, dropping into the ocean like a flaming meteor.

As the cold seeps deeper into my core, a second man works up the courage to risk the flames over drowning as the hull disappears beneath the waves, leaving just the flaming tower. I start swimming toward Mueller, who is floating next to the vessel, but another plane swoops over me, dropping a huge torpedo in the water.

Fido!

The propeller bites the water, hurdling the advanced weapon toward the middle of the U-Boat, striking it just beneath the tower.

I look away as a blinding sheet of orange and yellow flames rises up to the sky. The uproar of fire, water, smoke, and sizzling debris surges skyward. A second plane flies past me, but the pilot doesn't release the torpedo strapped to its underfuselage. The first torpedo had broken U-529's back, literally cracking the ship in half. Its bow and stern angle up to the overcast sky as the center disappears beneath the white foam. The last thing I see are the twin propellers and the rudder before the place I have called home for the past five weeks ceases to exist.

And just like that I'm all alone—alone with bitter memories, with feelings of guilt for having survived this terrible onslaught, with anger toward the BdU for ordering this brave crew to certain death, with fear about the future.

A light cruiser materializes through the haze, either looking to fire a final round or searching for survivors—not that the planes still circling overhead gave the men aboard the U-Boat the time they had needed to abandon ship. The enemy had shown zero mercy, even as it became blatantly obvious that the submarine no longer posed a threat to the convoy, confirming the rumor that U-boats are as hated by the Allies as they are revered by Germany.

Time.

I'm trembling uncontrollably now, and I can no longer

feel my face. My limbs are growing numb. I try to move
them to get my circulation flowing again, but the cold
has stripped away my heat as well as my energy. I don't
think I can last much longer as the waves toss me about,
as I sway at their mercy, as the North Atlantic takes its
toll on me. Only the life preserver keeps me afloat.

I think of my father, of my kid brother, of my mother
and sisters—remember their pained faces, their cries as
I sailed away. Their desperate pleas now echo in my ears
with the same energy as Chief Mueller's final scream,
with the same intensity as the shame that I have brought
to them for having joined the enemy, for having become
a part of Hitler's war machine. There is no going back
for me, not even with the documents that I have carried
with me for so long. I chose sides a long time ago and
there is no way to change that now.

Hypothermia starts to set in, making me dizzy, my
thoughts growing as cloudy as the skies above me.
Through the haze enveloping me, through the punishing
waves, I sense a bright light, a beacon, hovering over
me, and I suddenly find comfort in its glow, it the sudden
warmth it brings. I remember the sunny days of my summers in Connecticut. I remember sunlight on my face,
the wind at my back, the sand between my toes.

Frigid water slaps me across the face, shattering
the daydream, the hallucination, bringing me back to the
grave reality of my life, to the appalling cold, to the
incessant punishment of a sea as unforgiving as those
depth charges, as unmerciful as Germany has been while
razing across Europe, crushing entire societies beneath
the steel tracks of its panzers, sending so many innocent
men, women, and children to their deaths in those horrible concentration camps that we're not allowed to write
about. I've seen so much destruction since this began, so
much suffering, so much killing. I've seen death across

Poland and France, across Ukrainian plains and Greek mountains, across every land that dared oppose the Third Reich, and now the tide of this war we have created has turned against us. And we will not be shown any mercy, just like today.

Oh, God . . . the cold . . . I'm really dying. I've managed so far to survive this awful war, and was even spared the gruesome fate of the crew of U-529, but I'm going to die now, alone, in the middle of nowhere, away from my family, from . . .

My vision clouds again, and a sudden cyclone whirls in my mind, swallowing everything, the bitter cold, the relentless ocean, the rolling clouds, the circling planes. Then there's that light again, that comforting warm glow that radiates life into my core, that injects me with hope.

But there is no hope for me.

There hasn't been any hope for a long, long time.

As the world around me darkens, as the cold pushes me to the brink of unconsciousness, I reach for the waterproof pouch secured to the inside of my trousers. This was supposed to be my ticket home, my chance to rejoin the society that I once abandoned—a society that I know will no longer accept me, not after what Germany has done to the world. Refusing to shame my family any further by letting anyone connect me to them through these documents, I tear through the plastic, ripping it open, releasing the papers to the sea.

I watch them drift away, watch my old American passport disappear beneath the murky waters, as well as my Yale diploma and other documents linking me to a life I chose to leave behind, a life that will forever remain in my past.

The bitter cold propels my thoughts to the periphery of my mind, leaving my core empty, dark, alone.

And as my body finally surrenders to the unforgiving

sea, I steel myself to die like a soldier, with dignity, with honor.

To march with my chin high straight into the valley of death.

U-529 was reported missing on February 12, 1943 in the North Atlantic. There is no explanation for its loss. All hands were presumed lost.

Silent Company

WILLIAM H. KEITH, JR.

William H. Keith, Jr. is the author of over sixty novels, nearly all of them dealing with the theme of men at war. Writing under the pseudonym H. Jay Riker, he's responsible for the extremely popular SEALS: The Warrior Breed series, a family saga spanning the history of the Navy UDT and SEALs from World War II to the present day. As Ian Douglas, he writes a well-received military-science fiction series following the exploits of the U.S. Marines in the future, in combat on the Moon and Mars. A former hospital corpsman in the Navy during the late Vietnam era, many of his characters, his medical knowledge, his feel for life in the military, and his profound respect for the men and women who put their lives on the line for their country are all drawn from personal experience.

CHARLESTON HARBOR GLEAMED *by the silver radiance of a just-risen full moon, the water calm and mirror-*

smooth. At a wharf below Fort Johnson, opposite fabled Fort Sumter on the south side of the harbor, preparations were under way. It was shortly after seven in the evening, February 17, 1864, and the Silent Company gathered, their thronging in the still air like the bare-bones rattle of dead winter leaves.

"Right, boys. In you go! This here's our chance at immortality!" Lieutenant Dixon seemed quite chipper, even carefree, though the moment weighed upon all of them as heavily as the smell of mud, salt water, and rotting marsh vegetation. "Tonight we sink the *Housatonic*!"

Seaman Tommy Barton stood in line on the rickety pier with seven other men, looking down at the strange contraption of black iron tied there. Corporal Coleman nudged him with an elbow and snickered. "Y'all know what they're callin' that thing over'n Charleston, don't ya?" he said. " 'The Peripatetic Coffin!' Ain't that a hoot?"

"That's not exactly encouraging," Barton replied. "From what I heard, that monster's eaten something like thirty men already."

"She *has* a name," Petty Officer Maury snapped. "An honorable one."

"A boat named for her inventor," Corporal DeWitt said, his long face gloomy, "a man who *she* killed in the fust place. . . . 'T'ain't rightly natural, if you take m'meanin'."

"Quiet in the ranks, there," Dixon called from the end of the pier. "Williams! You're first, forrard hatch. Jenkins, you're first down the aft hatch."

The Peripatetic Coffin, as Coleman had called it, was long, low in the water, and iron plated, measuring perhaps forty feet from her deadly forward spar to the large rudder aft. A pair of small towers, just sixteen inches

high, with glass portholes in their sides and round
hatches on top protruded from the deck fore and aft, fourteen feet apart, the hatches open wide to the night. A low
box just aft of the forward hatch supported a pair of tubes
that might have been narrow smokestacks, like the stack
on a steam-powered David, but Barton knew better.

He flexed his hands at his sides, thinking about the
trial to come, trying *not* to think about failure or about
DeWitt's misgivings. The Other Side seemed so very
close now. He shook that thought away as well.

A handful of officers and civilian dignitaries watched
from the dock. One was James McClintock, one of the
designers of the small vessel tied to the Fort Johnson
wharf. Another was Lieutenant John Payne, who'd had
considerable experience with her and helped train the
men who swam her.

"Gentlemen," a city official said with an aristocratic
flourish to his voice and manner, "the hopes and prayers
of the Confederacy, of the sovereign state of South Carolina, and of the proud city of Charleston, voyage with
you!"

"Thank you, sir," Dixon replied, doffing his hat. "We
will do our best, and leave the rest to Providence."

Lieutenant Payne raised his cap. "Gentlemen! Hurrah
for the CSS *Hunley* and her brave crew of volunteers!"

Three cheers echoed out across the water as, one by
one, the waiting men descended from the pier, balancing
themselves atop the ungainly craft's rounded upper hull,
then squeezed themselves down through the narrow
hatch openings. Barton found himself staring down into
the tight black circle of almost palpable darkness that
was the after hatch. It looked like a tunnel plunging down
into the water.

Or the opening to a submerged tomb.

He watched Coleman wriggle down through that opening, and then it was his turn. The strange craft had been riding fairly high alongside the pier, but as more men squeezed in through the hatches, she began to settle a bit, until the deck was awash and only the hatch towers and the pipes forward were well clear of the water. Stepping carefully down from the pier and onto the deck, Barton gingerly balanced himself upright for a final look around. The air was cool and calm, the first few stars beginning to pierce the twilight. Across the harbor, beyond the guardian island of Fort Sumter, the lights of Fort Moultrie twinkled in the gathering gloom of the evening. Less than three years ago, thunder and flame had shattered the peace of this place, the opening volleys of the War of Southern Independence. Tonight another volley in that war would be delivered . . . but stealthily, and shrouded by the night.

Aware that he appeared to those ashore to be hesitating, perhaps fearful, he took in a final long, deep breath of cool air, savoring the taste, the salt-tinged freshness, and then he stepped into the hatch and began working his way down into the belly of the beast.

A tight fit, a squeezing of the mind as much as of the body. Each time, Barton thought, it was tougher to steel himself to wriggle into this nightmare contraption, to deliberately cut himself off from fresh air and clean light and enter the stygian, walled-off blackness of a horizontal iron pipe just three feet wide and four and a half feet high. *Manholes* they called the hatch towers, and a fair name it was. The beast's interior was very like a sewer pipe, save that the ends were pinched off ahead and behind. The Peripatetic Coffin actually had begun its career as a ship's boiler, twenty-five feet long, with a longitudinal section cut away and the remaining halves welded together to make it snake-slender. This inner hull had then been capped on each end by an iron casement, which held the ballast tanks fore and aft and further streamlined the craft.

Streamlining on the outside, however, translated as claustrophobic on the inside. One moved carefully within those ironbound confines, nearly doubled over in pitch darkness and always at risk of cracking head, elbow, or knee. The lumen of the pipe was further constricted by the hand crank, which ran horizontally down the length of the craft above the centerline, supported at intervals by shaft braces and all but filling the cramped interior space. The darkness stank of oil, sweat, and stale air.

The men had entered the craft from front and back, filing in from the two hatchways toward the center. As next-to-last man in astern, Barton didn't need to navigate through the tight space more than a couple of feet before coming to his station, squeezed in between the hand crank and the curved, starboard side bulkhead. A wooden block bolted to the base of the portside bulkhead gave him a place to brace his feet; another block partway up the starboard bulkhead gave him a narrow seat, of sorts, to perch on. Finding the blocks by feel alone, he took his place at the crank, shoulders and head hunched over beneath the low overhead, and waited.

At least it wasn't completely dark within the iron beast. A sky glow of twilight and moonlight spilled down through both hatches, penetrating the darkness at least for a foot or two. In addition, a single candle had been lit all the way forward at the pilot's station. Barton had to hunch forward a bit more to see the candle past the waiting line of other crewmen filling the craft, but that golden spark was comforting when he caught sight of it, a beacon in the darkness.

So long as the candle is lit, everything's all right. That lesson had been drilled into all of them repeatedly during the weeks of training just passed. *When the candle's lit there's air to breathe.*

Air . . .

Barton felt the rising panic, an old, familiar sensation clawing at his throat, and yet again he battled the cold and desperate urge to leave his station and claw his way back up into the open air and freedom.

Petty Officer Maury was last down the aft hatch. When he pulled it shut after himself with a boiler-factory clang, it was as though the whole rest of the world ceased to exist. Lieutenant Dixon clambered down through the forward manhole, remaining standing, his head encased in the tower so that he could see out through the open hatch. The darkness now was very nearly absolute, for the lieutenant's body blocked the gleam of the candle forward. In darkness, then, Barton felt Petty Officer Maury taking his place at the crankshaft further aft, felt the craft's hull rocking gently with the movement.

"Cast off fore and aft!" Dixon called, his voice muffled. Thumps and clangs rang through the hull from outside, as soldiers on the pier untied the lines that let the iron craft drift free.

"Ahead slow!" Dixon commanded, and the eight men began turning the crankshaft with a slow, steady beat. Metal chirped on metal. The smell of oil grew stronger. As Dixon turned the horizontally mounted wheel forward, control cables running along the overhead tightened and clattered, swinging the big rudder aft. Barton felt the screw bite the water, felt the vessel turning in clumsy response to the helm.

The CSS *Hunley* was underway.

The Silent Company continued to gather, hovering now just at the edge of the world's walls, their thoughts softly rustling in moonlight-broken

darkness. Slowly, her wake sparkling in the moon
dance, the pencil-slender vessel churned away from
the shore. Soldiers, waiting in silence along the
ramparts of Fort Johnson and within the embra-
sures of Marshall Battery, watched her go.

The *Hunley* had been born as the brainchild of two
men, Baxter Watson and James McClintock. Not long
after, a third man, Horace L. Hunley, had joined the two
New Orleans inventors, bringing much-needed capital to
the project, as well as his flamboyant enthusiasm. Hard-
pressed for the iron, cannon, and shipyard resources
needed for a fleet powerful enough to challenge the ever-
tightening Union blockade, the Confederate Navy had
turned to southern inventors for new and creative ways
of striking at the powerful Yankee foe. Ironclads, gunboats, and torpedo boats of revolutionary design all had
been built and outfitted in rivers, sounds, ports, and inlets
from New Orleans to the James River. One such experiment, a class of gunboat called Davids, had shown some
promise; one had damaged the Yankee cruiser *New Ironsides* right here in Charleston Harbor just four months
ago.

But where the Davids were designed to approach a
Yankee vessel with deck awash, unnoticed in the night,
to drive a bow spar laden with an explosive charge,
called a torpedo, into the target's hull, the Watson-
McClintock design was more ambitious, a craft with ballast tanks designed to submerge completely, operating as
a true submarine war craft.

As originally conceived, the vessel was designed to
tow an explosive charge with a contact exploder astern
on the end of a long cable. Submerging as she approached the target, she would pass underneath the ship's
keel and drag the torpedo into the enemy's side.

The first such submarine, called *Pioneer*, had been deliberately scuttled in New Orleans when the Yankees had captured that port. The second, *Pioneer II*, had gone to the bottom in Mobile Bay, taking her crew with her.

The *Pioneer III*, however, had shown tremendous promise, albeit with some bad teething pains. She'd been originally intended to be steam powered, but her designers had never been able to work out the problem of how to keep a coal-fired engine burning without an air supply and without poisoning the air her crew was breathing. Experiments with an electromagnetic engine were eventually abandoned, and, in her final form, *Pioneer III* was run by muscle-power, with eight crewmen crouched side by side in the dark confines of her belly, steadily turning the crankshaft to drive the slender craft through the water.

Her torpedo design had been reworked as well. Early experiments had shown that the floating torpedo could actually overtake the vessel in a strong wind, and so the trailing tether had been abandoned in favor of the more conventional torpedo spar, a fourteen-foot boom projecting from the submarine's prow with a sixty-pound contact torpedo mounted on the end. The crew need only drive the torpedo into the enemy's side, then back furiously and pray the explosion didn't sink target and submarine together. Of course, a boat that could go under the water as well as on the surface . . . the thing wasn't quite natural, as Corporal DeWitt might say. The builders had ended up with a misbegotten half-breed of a vessel comfortable in neither medium. Built in Mobile, she'd been shipped to Charleston the previous August by rail; Lieutenant Payne had taken her out soon after her arrival. The firm of John Frazer & Company of Charleston had offered a reward of a hundred thousand dollars to anyone who could sink the giant *New Ironsides*, and a lesser amount for the sinking of any of the other Yankee vessels blockading that port. Payne had steered the *Pioneer III* for the *New Ironsides* . . . but long before she reached her target, a passing Confederate steamer had raised a wake that had spilled in through the open hatches and flooded her, sending her to the bottom. Payne had scrambled clear of the forward hatch and escaped, but eight seamen had drowned.

The Confederate Navy raised the *Pioneer III*, buried her dead with full honors, and fitted her out for another try. A few days later, Payne had taken her out once more, and again she'd sunk, this time inexplicably. Payne and two others swam to the surface; five others were trapped and killed.

The next time Hunley himself had taken the *Pioneer III* out. After several successful test dives, he'd lined up for a test dive beneath a Confederate ship and opened the forward seacock too quickly. Nose-heavy, the submarine had plunged into the soft mud at the bottom of Charleston Harbor and been unable to break free. This time every man on board, including Horace Hunley, had perished.

Yet again she was raised, yet again she sank, killing her entire crew. General P. G. T. Beauregard, in command of the Charleston defenses, had declared the experiment over. "Leave her in the mud!" he'd declared. "She will kill no more!"

Two men continued to believe in the submarine's potential, however—Lieutenants George Dixon and William Alexander, both of the 21st Alabama infantry. They'd been brought in, together with a number of army volunteers to train crews to man the vessel, which by now was collecting grim nicknames such as Peripatetic Coffin and Widowmaker. Once again they'd raised the *Pioneer III* from the harbor mud, cleaned her out, and buried her dead. This time they put her on display at Mount Pleasant on the north side of the harbor, where they established a school for submariners. Throughout the winter of 1863 to 1864, they trained volunteers and made periodic test cruises around the harbor. Perhaps to lift the shadow of an unlucky boat, they renamed her after the inventor who'd died aboard her—the CSS *H. L. Hunley*.

Tom Barton had joined the crew in November, attracted by the notion of striking back at the Yankee giant . . . and in part, at least, by the promise of reward money for sinking a blockading ship. A sailor of a family of sailors, born in Norfolk and apprenticed to the steamer USS *Niagara*, he'd spent the first years of the war as an able-bodied seaman aboard various merchant ships running in and out of Charleston. As the Yankee blockade had tightened its grip, however, driving more and more shipping companies out of business, he'd ended up on the beach. Captivated by the sight of the exotic *Hunley* on display, he'd volunteered at the Mount Pleasant school for duty and had been accepted.

For the next several months he'd trained at the school under Dixon and Alexander's command, attending classes and exercising each morning and spending the afternoons taking the *Hunley* for practice excursions around the harbor. Despite being a sailor, he did not consider himself to be the superstitious type. The fact that the *Hunley* had killed nearly thirty men so far in her brief career bothered him not at all . . . at least, not at first. The *Hunley*'s problems had all been because of poor training, after all—not because of any flaw in the planning. As Barton learned at the school, the idea of the submarine had been around for a long time. Alexander the Great was supposed to have used a glass diving bell to explore the wonders of the sea bottom . . . and during the Revolutionary War, David Bushnell's *Turtle* had attempted to sink HMS *Eagle* in New York Harbor, an attempt that had failed only because the wooden screw used to attach a bag of gunpowder to the target vessel's hull had failed to penetrate *Eagle*'s copper-sheathed bottom.

Only now had technology and human inventiveness reached the point where a *true* submarine was practical.

As Barton worked more and more with the *Hunley* and his fellow submariners, though, he began wondering if a boat could be jinxed. It was nothing he could put his finger on, exactly. There'd been no further accidents or deaths since he'd started training. But sometimes it seemed that the *Hunley* was . . . was *calling* to him, somehow.

Or was it the voices of her drowned or suffocated crews he heard, like a dry rattle of dead leaves at the very edge of audibility?

He could hear them now, like rustling laughter. He gripped the crankshaft more tightly, concentrating on the chirp and rhythm of the strokes, silently willing the voices to leave him alone. It wasn't so bad when he was stroking. The sheer muscular exertion, the grunts and puffings of the other men, the squeak of metal on metal along the crankshaft, the sound of his own breathing as he strained at the shaft all conspired to crowd his hearing and empty his thoughts. It was when they *stopped* that he had problems. . . .

"All stop!" Dixon called, and the eight men sagged against the crankshaft, breathing hard. The *Hunley* drifted along on the surface, barely moving now in silence.

Oh, Jesus Christ. "Stop it!"

"Whadja say, Tommy?" Coleman asked.

"Nothing." He'd not known he'd spoken aloud. How long had they been cranking? Even if he'd had a watch—

he didn't, not on the $19.83 per month paid him by the Confederate Navy—he wouldn't have been able to read it in the darkness. He wished he could see. He wished the voices would stop. . . .

Join us, the leaf-rustle whispered in the dark. *Come. Join us. . . .*

Join us. . . .

Unterseeboot UC-17 twisted and dodged, seeking to avoid the charge of the British destroyers bearing down overhead. The water was deep here, west of the coast of Ireland, but the UC-17, a primitive iron hull five times longer than the Hunley, *could not dive much deeper than twice her own hull length. With an operational diving depth of three hundred feet and a crush depth of six hundred feet, she was rapidly running out of places to hide.*

On board, in conditions only slightly less claustrophobic than those aboard the Hunley, *thirty-one officers and men waited, staring with strained and sweat-soaked faces up at the overhead . . . and through it, to the oncoming warships. They'd been submerged for some hours now, and the air was growing foul with carbon dioxide, fuel oil, and the stink of fear.*

They could hear the steadily growing throb of the enemy's screws in the water. And, as the throb built to a pounding crescendo, many in the crew heard the muffled splash of that deadly new weapon, the wasserbomb—*the depth charge—three hundred pounds of high explosives packed into a metal drum and triggered by a pressure-activated detonator.*

UC-17's crew had been through this before. Many counted silently after the splash, picturing in their minds the descent of the wasserbomben *through the darkening sea. When the charge reached the depth for which the detonator had been set, there was a sharp* snick-snick, *followed a second later by the hull-ringing* blam *of the main charge.*

The first blast came close-aboard to port, rocking the submarine hard to starboard and popping chunks of cork from the bulkheads. The second was also to port and closer; lightbulbs shattered, plunging the boat into darkness save for the wan glow of battle lanterns.

The third was closer still, this time to starboard, a snick-snick *followed by a thunderous detonation that filled the foul air with high-pressure streams of water from bursting pipes and the screams of terrified seamen.*

It was early in the spring of 1918.

Snick-snick . . . boom . . .

Snick-snick . . . boom . . .

Barton heard the sounds distinctly, though they were extremely muffled, as if by a great, great distance. What *was* he hearing . . . cannon fire? Had the Yankees spotted the little *Hunley* already, her deck awash in the moonlight, and opened fire with their big, eleven-inch Dahlgren rifles?

"Hey, Coleman," he whispered to the man on his right. "You hear that?"

"Hear what?"

"I dunno. Kinda like cannon fire, way off."

"I don't hear a damned thing, Tommy."

"You're hearin' things again, Barton," Petty Officer Maury added. "Knock it off afore you spook the whole boat."

Come to us. . . .

Hearing things. Yeah, that was it. He was hearing things. Things that weren't real. Things that weren't there.

Squeezing his eyes closed, he tried to shut out the

rustling, the ghostly voices in the darkness, as well. He was sweating hard—they all were after that exertion—but he was chilled as well, his knees trembling unless he kept them hard-locked and his feet pressed hard against the footrest.

He thought about his grandmother. Grandmother Sadie had been a strange one, no mistake about that. There was Romany blood in her veins, or so the older members of the Barton family whispered, and it was said that she'd been able to tell the future and to know things about people, just by talking with them. "You've got the sight," she'd told young Tommy more than once when he was growing up back in Norfolk. He still remembered sitting in her lap as she rocked him on the front porch, remembered her wrinkled hands and whispery voice. "You *see* things others don't, don't you?"

Well, no. No he didn't. At least, he'd never been aware of anything strange about his sight, and his parents had always been quick to reassure him that there was nothing to "that superstitious Gypsy nonsense."

Still, there was that night when he'd woken up in bed—at least, he'd *thought* he'd been awake—and he saw Grandmother Sadie in his room, felt the mattress sag with her weight as she sat on the edge of the bed. "You've got the sight, Tommy," she'd told him in her dry, whispery voice. "You can see things, see things in the darkness. . . ."

And it hadn't been until the next day that he'd learned his grandmother had died hours before the . . . the dream.

No, Barton wasn't superstitious. His parents had been careful about that. Even so, he'd always felt a thrill of something like fear, a shiver up his spine, when confronted by darkness.

So what the hell are you doing in here? he asked himself, a taste of bitter irony in the thought. *A damned strange place to work if you're afraid of the dark!*

"Half speed ahead!" rasped the voice of Lieutenant Dixon, and the eight crewmen leaned into the hand crank, making the screw bite the water. The steering cables overhead clattered a bit, and Barton felt the *Hunley* turning slightly to the right. The chirp and squeak of the crank pushed the whispering back.

For years, now, ever since his grandmother's death, in fact, Tom Barton had been simultaneously attracted and repelled by the dark, wanting never to hear the voices again, while at the same time being fascinated . . . compelled, almost, to listen for them. When he'd learned what his volunteering for duty on board the *Hunley* required of him, he'd very nearly backed away. Climbing down into that black hole was so very much like dying. . . .

And yet he wanted to face the fear, face it down and conquer it. He was twenty years old, a grown man, and grown men were not afraid of the dark.

Besides, he was curious. Could he really see things other men could not?

Somehow he'd stuck it out, stayed with the grueling exercises and classwork ashore, and the infinitely harder assignments of clambering down into the *Hunley*'s belly and taking his place at the crankshaft.

It was always the diving that was hardest.

"Attention to orders!" Dixon called from forward. "I can see the *Housatonic* up ahead, sitting fat and happy in the moonlight. We're going to take her down. Everyone watch for leaks."

The *Hunley* had two ballast tanks, one in the forward of the crew compartment, one aft. By opening two seacocks, they could flood those tanks, making the craft heavy enough to sink. In addition, there were two devices like stubby wings on either side of the boat. Tilt the wings forward, the *Hunley* would dive; tilt them back, and she would rise.

Dixon was responsible for operating the forward cock and handling the diving planes, while Maury, the petty officer, was responsible for the seacock aft. A number of lead weights along the keel could be released by pulling levers set on the deck beneath their feet, lightening the *Hunley* and letting her rise to the surface once more.

At least, that was the idea. The various contrivances didn't always work as advertised. Horace Hunley had died when the boat became stuck in the mud after the forward seacock had been opened too quickly.

And when the *Hunley* was underwater, there was no more fresh air entering the boat. Under water, the darkness and the claustrophobia became overwhelming, a stifling, palpable presence threatening to rob strong men of their sanity.

Providing fresh air for the crew had been one of the most devilishly insoluble problems in the *Hunley*'s design. There was something called an airbox forward, just aft of the forward hatch, with two pipes—the things like small smokestacks Barton had noticed earlier—extending up high enough to clear the water's surface when the *Hunley* was running submerged, but the contraption never had worked right. The pipes admitted a little air when they were running just beneath the surface, but once they submerged completely, the men on board had only a limited amount of time before the air inside the submarine turned too foul to breathe.

About a month before, Dixon had taken the submariner students out on a special afternoon's excursion, one designed to find out just how long the *Hunley* could remain submerged. They'd closed the hatches and dived to the bottom, coming to rest at a slight cant to starboard. The lieutenant had lit the candle and explained the rules

of the exercise. They would wait there on the bottom as
the air became harder to breathe. All anyone needed to
do to stop the test was shout "up," and the keel weights
would be released. They'd sat on the bottom, waiting . . .
and waiting. After twenty minutes, the candle had flickered, then gone out, plunging them all into a darkness so
complete that Barton had had trouble telling whether his
eyes were open or closed. Dixon had attempted to relight
the candle time and time again, but nothing he did could
banish the dark.

But the crewmen continued to wait silent save for the
increasingly labored rasp of their breathing. An hour had
gone past. The air, thick with the stinks of oil and sweat
and fear, had grown more and more foul. The men began
panting in short, hard gasps, struggling to pull in oxygen
enough to keep them going. The crazy thing was that no
one on board had wanted to be the first to cry "up." It
had become a test, not of the bottomed submarine, but
of courage and manliness. Barton had wanted desperately
to give the signal, to be the one to bring them all back
to the surface and air and sunlight, but he'd been training
with the others long enough that he'd felt a particular
bond with them.

Hell, if *they* could stick it out, he could!

Another hour had crawled by, and Barton had learned
that, yes, he could stand the darkness. He'd heard the
whispering voices then, too, though distant and muffled,
an almost-sound at the thin and ragged edge of hearing.
The air became stiflingly hot, and so oxygen poor that
each gasping breath was torture. The men were becoming
sleepy as well, yawning uncontrollably and sagging
across the crankshaft.

Unable to stand the torture any longer, Barton had
croaked out "up!" at last, but his cry was mingled with
the gasped echoes of the other seven crewmen as well,

all shouting as if with one voice. Dixon had pulled the master lever forward, releasing the weights, and slowly, sluggishly, the *Hunley* had drifted off the bottom. The men had cranked with the last dwindling scraps of their strength, then, as Dixon had pulled the plane into the rising position. When the *Hunley* broke the surface a few minutes later and the hatches were cracked open, the in-rush of fresh, salty air had been like a gift from heaven. The men had crowded around the hatches, gulping down deep, shuddering breaths.

Dixon's pocket watch had recorded the length of the dive: two hours and thirty-five minutes, an astonishing feat of endurance. When they'd approached the dockside, a startled sentry had informed them that they'd already been declared dead.

The men on board the *Hunley*, then, knew how long they could breathe once the submarine submerged. Later tests had demonstrated that the air didn't last as long if the men were cranking the shaft, but they all knew that the air would last long enough for them to accomplish their mission.

Knowing that, having experienced that, helped . . . at least so far as the head was concerned. Terror still gripped Barton's gut, though. And the voices were whispering louder now, loud enough that he could hear them even above the grunts and breathings of his crewmates, the squeak and groan of the shaft.

Come to us, Tommy. Come to us. You are one of us. . . .

Already, the air tasted foul and thin.

"Full ahead, boys," Dixon ordered. "I'm taking her up for a look-see."

Barton felt the deck tilt beneath his feet. Dixon was using the diving planes to angle the submarine upward. So long as the men cranked the screw, *Hunley* would rise high enough despite the water now filling her ballast tanks for the forward hatch tower to again clear the surface. Lieutenant Dixon, standing with his head and shoulders in the tower, could see out through the glass ports. To hold the *Hunley* steady at that shallow depth, though, against the drag of the ballast tanks, took every bit of strength and endurance the eight crewmen possessed. When the deck went awash, moonlight streamed down through the aft hatch tower's portholes, blinding after the unrelieved blackness of a moment before.

After an agony of time dragged past, Dixon at last gave the order to slow to half ahead, then to stop. The deck dipped down, the moonlight was swallowed by night, and then the deck leveled out once again. Again *Hunley* cruised ahead slowly through the depths beneath the moonlit surface, drifting with an almost perfect neutral buoyancy. "I could see the *Housatonic*, boys," Dixon said. Barton could just make out the lieutenant's shape, a black, bearlike form against the uncertain light of the candle, beyond the long line of crouching, waiting crewmen. "She's just riding there at anchor, sweet as you please. She's showing lights, and there's no sign of an alarm. So . . . are we ready?"

"We're ready!" and "Yes, sir!" chorused back. Barton yelled with the others, feeling the magnetic, almost ecstatic thrill of the moment, the battle lust and excitement filling the narrow confines of the submarine.

"Right, then!" Dixon shouted. "Let's sink us a Yankee blockader, for glory and for money! Crank, now! Crank like the Devil himself was after you! Full ahead all!"

Barton leaned into the crankshaft. All eight crewmen strained at the hand crank, pulling together harder than ever before. They were moving faster. . . .

And the voices . . . they were there, too, louder, more insistent.

"Auf Gefechtsstationen!"

"Boot ist eingependelt, Herr Oberleutnant!"

"Auf Seerohrtiefe!"

Strange. Barton could hear the words, but he couldn't understand them, and that bothered him. If what he was hearing was a product of his own fear-throttled brain, then the words should be in English, shouldn't they?

"Rohr eins fertig! Rohr zwei fertig!"

"Ja wohl, Herr Oberleutnant! Rohr eins fertig! Rohr zwei fertig!"

"Rohr eins! Los!"

"Los!"

"Torpedo läuft regulär, Mein Herr!"

"Rohr zwei! Los!"

"Los!"

It was a dialogue of some sort, he was certain of that much, with orders being shouted and repeated back and forth. One word he recognized: *torpedo*. Torpedos were kegs of gunpowder anchored in shallow water, with contact exploders to detonate them when an enemy vessel brushed it . . . or they were spar-mounted explosives like the warhead attached to *Hunley*'s swordfish snout, or to torpedo boats like the Davids. Was someone trying to tell him something about *Hunley*'s torpedo?

And again he heard those muffled, far-off sounds: *snick-snick . . . wham! Snick-snick . . . wham!*

And the Silent Company was there, within the Hunley *and without, more and more of them gathering with each passing second. They were drawn to the frail and tiny craft in their teeming hundreds . . . their thousands . . .*

· They watched closely as the Hunley*'s crew leaned into the crankshaft, propelling the submarine through the silent water in a driving, four-knot charge. They watched as Dixon turned the wheel, adjusting the craft's ap-*

*proach slightly to starboard, lining up with the center of
the mighty* Housatonic.

*And on board the Union vessel they saw the officer of
the deck, Acting Master John Crosby, first notice a ripple
on the water, a bit of moon dance sparkling on a moving
wave, and the swell of some large, dark body gliding
beneath the surface. The wave broke, and something that
looked like a plank afloat on the water could be seen . . .
a plank moving straight toward the* Housatonic*'s side.*

*Crosby gave the alarm, and Lieutenant Francis Hig-
ginson ordered the drummer to beat to quarters. Men
scrambled out onto the deck. Orders were shouted . . .
"Slip the cable!" "Back the engines!" Gunners manned
the aft pivot gun, but the unknown attacker, gliding forward like an alligator in the water, was already so close
that the gun crew could not depress the weapon's muzzle
enough for a clear shot.*

*Sailors and marines armed with rifles raced to the
ship's side, firing at the half-glimpsed monster below. In
the last couple of seconds, the attacker seemed to leap
forward like a striking snake, closing now with a point
on the* Housatonic*'s starboard side just forward of the
mizzenmast and almost perfectly in line with her powder
magazine. . . .*

Barton cranked with the others, sweat streaming from his
face and upper body now, pain searing his back and arms
as he strained against the shaft. "Almost there!" Dixon
yelled. "Faster, boys! Faster!"

And then there was a shock, a splintering jolt that
slammed Barton forward against Coleman's side. An instant later, a detonation erupted off *Hunley*'s bow, and a
giant hand slammed the vessel up and back. Her deck
canted wildly, bow high, and screaming crewmen tumbled aft, some catching hold of the crankshaft, others

dropping down onto men struggling below. Barton fell onto Maury, and then both men were buried in the avalanche of falling crewmen.

The deck leveled, though the *Hunley* rolled heavily now from side to side. Time passed; how much, Barton couldn't tell. The entire crew had been knocked senseless by that blast, but they came to now, groaning, groping through the darkness. Somewhere forward came the hiss of water.

"Reverse screw!" Dixon shouted. His voice sounded shaken. He'd been dazed like the others by the savage blast. "Back us out!"

The candle had gone out, and the submarine's interior was in perfect darkness. Barton could feel men picking themselves up, however, and crawling forward, returning to their stations. Somewhere in the darkness, a man was sobbing with pain.

This was one of the critical moments of the mission, he knew, one that had been discussed endlessly at the school at Mount Pleasant. So many things could go wrong. *Hunley*'s hull could split or her hatches spring open with the shock, flooding her. If she escaped that, she might be sucked into the gaping hole in the *Housatonic*'s side, through which the ocean was pouring now in swirling torrents. The Yankee blockade vessel could easily drag the little *Hunley* down to her doom.

"Join us. . . . Come to us. . . ."

"Ja, Tommy. Kommen sie hier!"

"Come . . ."

"Da! Da! Voydeetie, tovarisch!"

Somehow, somehow, several of the battered crewmen began turning the crank, reversing it this time to pull the *Hunley* backward through the water. Barton regained his seat purely by feel, grasped the turning crank, and managed to add his strength and weight to its movement.

"We did it, boys!" Dixon cried from the forward hatch. "We did it, by God! The *Housatonic*'s been holed! She's settling by the stern . . . rolling onto her port beam! . . . By the Lord Jesus, we *did* it!"

Barton could hear other noises now besides the grunts and pants of his comrades, the groans of the wounded, the squeak of the crankshaft. He could hear a kind of rushing gurgle, punctuated by sharp snapping, clattering sounds transmitted clearly through the water. He knew what he was hearing . . . the death shriek of a ship.

"There's only two kinds of ships, son," a new voice told him in the dark. "Submarines and *targets*. And you've just bagged yourself one beauty of a target."

"Who . . . who said that? Coleman?"

"Lieutenant Commander Francis A. Slattery," the voice said. "USS *Scorpion*." USS *Scorpion*? He looked around wildly, trying to penetrate the darkness. The voice sounded as though it had come from just in front of him. But there was no room. And how could a Yankee have boarded the *Hunley*?

"Congratulations, young Barton," another voice said, this one heavily accented. "Ve velcome you to our noble company. . . ."

"Welcome . . ." a dozen other voices echoed.

"What . . . what is this? What's going on?" It seemed to Barton that he was beginning to see something now, a pale, ghostly glow within which a host of figures were slowly moving toward him. There was a sharp tang of salt and seaweed in the air, and the sound of rushing water.

And . . . faces. Some bearded, some clean shaven, all of them in uniforms of various types and descriptions, but none in uniforms that he recognized. The clothing was so *strange*. . . .

"You guys're the first, you know," one of the faces

told him. It was a young, almost boyish face, grinning broadly beneath a hard-billed cap bearing an eagle and crossed anchors. "The first submariners ever to sink an enemy warship."

"*Ja,*" another face, bearded, and with a high-peaked, black-brimmed cap with a white cover said. "Twelve hundred forty tons. Not so much, perhaps, by *our* standards, but a most impressive beginning. *Most* impressive!"

"Who are you?"

"*Korvettenkapitän* Günther Prien, U-47," the bearded man replied. "At your service, sir."

"U . . . what?"

"*Unterseeboot* Forty-seven. A type VIIB submarine of the German *Kriegsmarine*. A boat somewhat more advanced than yours . . . though not so advanced as many that came after, of course." He gave a dry chuckle and a wave of the hand that took in the narrow confines of the *Hunley*. "I still find it amazing that you carried out your mission in . . . this!"

Long, lean, and shark-deadly, the U-47 crept through the approaches of Kirk Sound, moving on the surface. Günther Prien had hoped to strike in total darkness, but the sky was aflame with the cold, shifting curtains of a brilliant aurora display. It seemed a bad omen, but despite the danger, Prien had ordered the U-boat in, sliding across an antisubmarine cable on the inflowing tide and slipping silently past unsuspecting guardships.

The British base at Scapa Flow was arguably one of the most closely guarded naval bases in the world, but Prien and his U-47 had penetrated the defenses and tiptoed inside, the wolf unsuspected among the sleeping sheep.

German intelligence sources had provided the location

of two British battleships, the Repulse *and the* Royal
Oak, *and before long he'd spotted them both, black
mountains silhouetted against the cold-flaming sky.*

*It was just past midnight on October 14, 1939. Every
man was a volunteer; Prien had explained their mission
the day before, and told them that any who didn't want
to come could be put ashore first. None had accepted the
offer.*

"Rohr eins fertig!" *Prien called, aiming for the more
distant* Repulse, *three thousand yards distant.* "Rohr
zwei fertig! Rohr drei fertig! Rohr vier fertig!"

"Rohr eins, zwei, drei, vier fertig!"

"Rohr eins! Los!"

"Los!" *The U-47 lurched as the first torpedo slid clear
of her bow tubes.*

"Torpedo läuft regulär, Mein Herr!"

"Rohr zwei! Los! Rohr drei! Los! Rohr vier! Los!"

*Prien held a stopwatch in his hand, watching the sec-
onds tick away. Three minutes, thirty seconds after firing,
a distant boom echoed across the water.*

*Sirens howled. The base began to come to life. But
Prien was not finished yet. He could count on several
minutes at least of confusion within which he could continue his attack. Quickly, he gave orders to change the
U-47's heading slightly, aligning her with the nearer*
Royal Oak. *Belowdecks, in the forward torpedo room,
the crew worked furiously to reload the tubes. Tube four
had hung on firing, a misfire that jammed the tube and
rendered it useless, but the others were cleared and re-
loaded once more. Twenty minutes passed before the
U-47 was again ready to fire.*

"Rohr eins fertig! Rohr zwei fertig! Rohr drei fertig!"

"Rohr eins fertig! Rohr zwei fertig! Rohr drei fertig!"

"Rohr eins! Los!"

"Los!"

"Rohr zwei! Los!"

"Los!"

"Rohr drei! Los!"

Explosions thundered through the anchorage, two in quick succession . . . followed by a third, and then the Royal Oak *erupted like an exploding volcano, hurling flaming fragments hundreds of yards across the red-lit water. A magazine had been hit, and the pyrotechnics lit up the harbor of Scapa Flow in a dazzling spray of fire.*

Coming about, then, and still running on the surface as searchlights swept sky and water and British destroyers charged into the fray, the U-47 *dashed for Kirk Sound, narrowly squeezing between a guard ship and a stone breakwater before escaping into the open sea beyond.*

"Ja," Prien said, staring into Barton's eyes. "We escaped that time. We were lucky."

"Luck, nothing," the boyish-faced man said. "It was superb seamanship and some of the most brilliant, brass-balled courage I've ever heard of."

"We did not hit the *Repulse*," Prien replied. "The first torpedo exploded prematurely, two missed, and the fourth jammed." He smiled. "We learned later that *Repulse* was not even in Scapa Flow. Faulty intelligence. The vessel we thought was *Repulse* was actually the *Pegasus,* a seaplane tender. Most of the British High Seas Fleet was gone, in fact."

"But your other spread hit the *Royal Oak*," Slattery reminded him. "She went down in two minutes and took eight hundred thirty-three British seamen with her. She was an old battleship, true, and not of much use, but that sinking made you a hero. Every man in your crew won the Iron Cross . . . and you yourself were later awarded the Knight's Cross, the highest order of the Iron Cross at the time."

"We did what we had to do. What we were ordered to do." A shadow passed behind those cool, gray eyes. "But at such terrible cost. Over thirty-thousand men, three out of four of our comrades in the *Ubootwaffe*, were killed in the war. My own U-47, the Bull of Scapa Flow, was lost in March of 1941, while attacking an allied convoy west of Ireland. Forty-five men lost. None were saved. . . ."

Throughout this exchange, Barton was trying to back away, panic rising in his throat. He felt cold, wet iron at his back. "What are you people doing here? *How* are you here?"

"Don't worry, Barton," another officer in a khaki uniform said. "It's almost over. We're here to bring you home."

"M-my home is in Norfolk."

"Your home, your *family,* is here," Prien said. "With us."

"With the Silent Service," the man in khaki said. For just an instant, the man's face and upper torso dissolved into bloody horror—gaping wounds, sun-bloated and blackened flesh—but then the horror faded and the apparition gazed at Barton with calm, clear eyes. He wore an impressive-looking medal, an inverted gold star attached to an anchor, around his neck, hung there by a blue ribbon decorated with a cluster of white stars. "You volunteered for a mission you knew was near-certain death. You had plenty of opportunity to back out. You stuck with it . . . did what you knew you had to do. Yes, you're one of us."

"This is Commander Howard Gilmore," Slattery said. "U.S. Navy. He was on the bridge when his boat, the *Growler,* collided with a Japanese destroyer. . . ."

• • •

*Gilmore had miscalculated. He'd thought the other ves-
sel was a Jap patrol boat and angled in for an intercept
on the surface, but then the enemy ship changed course
and the* Growler *slammed into her amidships.*

The shock of the collision threw the Growler *far over
onto her beam ends, and as the two vessels parted,
machine-gun fire raked the* Growler's *bridge. The assis-
tant OOD and a lookout were both killed instantly;
Gilmore was badly wounded. "Clear the deck!" he
snapped, as machine-gun bullets continued to clang and
shriek off the conning tower. His exec was below the
deck hatch, waiting for him to follow, but instead he
shouted "Take her down!"*

*After an agonizing delay, the exec followed orders,
slamming shut the hatch and barking commands. Flooding her ballast tanks,* Growler *slipped beneath the surface . . . and escaped.*

Commander Gilmore's body was never found.

It was February 7, 1943.

"Gilmore won the Medal of Honor for that action," Slattery said, "and his cry of 'Take her down' became as
famous a rallying cry as "Don't give up the ship."

"U.S. Navy," Barton said, still dazed. "You're Yankees! Am I a prisoner, then?"

"Nyet," a thickset man in a cap bearing a gold star on
a red band said, grinning broadly. He put his arm over
Slattery's shoulder, and laughed. *"Nyet, tovarisch.* You
are not prisoner by any means. We are all comrades here.
Brothers-in-arms. Some of us, we may have been ene-
mies in life. But now . . ."

Slattery smiled. "Mr. Barton, meet Captain First Rank
Gennadiy P. Liachin, commanding officer of the K-141,
the *Kursk. . . .*

• • •

The nuclear-powered SSGN Kursk, K-141 (Project 949A) was a huge vessel . . . 155 meters long and displacing 24,000 tons submerged, but with a top speed of better than thirty knots. Code-named Oscar-II by NATO, she carried twenty-four P-700 cruise missiles in addition to her complement of torpedoes and ASW rockets, long-ranged weapons designed to strike at enemy carrier battle groups. She'd been launched at Sevmashpredpriyatiye, Severodvinsk, in 1994, commissioned in 1995, and assigned to the 7th SSGN Division of the First Submarine Flotilla of the Northern Fleet. Her home base was the Vidiayevo settlement in Ura-guba bay.

On August 10, 2000 the Kursk left Vidiayevo for exercises in the Barents Sea. On board was her usual complement of forty-eight officers and sixty-three enlisted men, plus five officers of the 7th SSGN Division Headquarters and two civilian designers. Her crew was excellent; not long before they'd been awarded the title of best submarine crew in the Northern Fleet.

On the morning of August 12 Kursk had requested permission for an exercise torpedo launch, and received the reply, "Dobro."

At 11:29:34 Moscow time, an undersea explosion was detected measuring 1.5 on the Richter scale. Two minutes later, a second explosion was detected, this one with a magnitude of 3.5, corresponding to perhaps two tons of high explosive. The explosions were picked up by seismographs as far away as Canada and Alaska and monitored by two American submarines shadowing the exercises, as well as by Russian submarines and surface vessels in the area.

The damage—caused almost certainly by the detonation of a malfunctioning torpedo—was fatal . . . though a number of Kursk's crew remained alive, trapped in their icy steel coffin for days as their air supply gradually dwindled. They used a heavy spanner wrench to hammer out news of their survival to rescue vessels against the hull.

But the rescue never came. Captain Liachin was made a Hero of the Russian Federation. His entire crew was awarded the Courage Order posthumously.

The scandal of the Russian military's slow response to the disaster rocked the Russian government from top to bottom, amid charges that the Kursk *had sunk as a result of a collision with an American submarine. The disaster also resulted in an unprecedented outpouring of help and cooperation from around the world. By the fourteenth of August, France, Germany, Great Britain, Israel, Italy, Norway, the United States, and a number of other countries all had offered their help in recovery efforts.*

"We are comrades," Liachin told Barton. He looked around, as though inspecting the *Hunley*'s dark interior. "We both know what it is to be locked within the belly of these metal monsters, whether they be minnows or whales. We know the risks. We know the closeness of death, each passing moment."

Strange. It seemed to Barton that the four men closest to him—Slattery, Prien, Gilmore, and Liachin—were standing with their arms around one another's shoulders. And others, so many others, crowded in behind, a vast, thronging host of men against the golden glow.

They were beckoning to him.

"Wait a minute. Are you . . . are you people saying I'm dead?"

"Not yet," Prien said gently. "Not yet, my friend. But it will not be long."

"*Da,*" Liachen agreed. "You will not have so long and

hard a crossing as some of my people on the *Kursk*."

Barton tried to scream then but found he could not.
There was no air to breathe . . . no air. . . .

The thronging host of men in the golden light vanished, and he again crouched in darkness. Had he been
unconscious all this time? The *Hunley* lay on the bottom,
hull canted to starboard, and water was streaming in from
somewhere forward. The interior space was already half
filled. Someone shrieked nearby in blind panic, voice
strangling in the foul air.

"Easy lads!" Dixon's voice called above the tumult.
"We gave it a good go. We gave it our best. . . . I'm
sorry. . . ."

But the sound of rushing water drowned Dixon's
voice, drowned even the screaming, the desperate hammering on the iron bulkheads. The golden light was back,
and Barton again looked past the cold and watery em-
brace of the *Hunley*'s hull, past the water of Charleston
Harbor, past the world as he knew it.

"Well done, lad," a bearded man said. Barton recognized Horace Hunley, standing in the throng with the
others. "You and your crewmates proved the idea of the
submarine. You . . . *we* are the first of the Silent Service.
Of this silent company . . .

And there was Maury . . . and Coleman . . . and
DeWitt. They seemed to be stepping up out of the *Hunley*, joining the waiting throng, men welcoming them
with open arms. Coleman grinned at him and waved.
"C'mon, Tom!"

He was hallucinating. He knew that, now. Maybe he
did have the sight, like his grandmother said, but there
was no way he could see the ghosts of men who hadn't
died yet, who hadn't even been born yet. Time could not
possibly be so far out of kilter.

"You're the last one alive," Gilmore said. "Come on over, Tom. It's time."

"No! No! You're not real! Not real!"

It seemed that Prien was stepping closer, embracing him by the shoulders, then handing him a small device on a ribbon. It was an oddly shaped cross. . . .

"Perhaps this means little to you now," Prien said, "but you will come to understand. This is *Das Ritterkreuz des Eisernen Kreuzes* . . . the Knight's Cross of the Iron Cross. I confer on you now, Seaman Tommy Barton, the name of *Ritterkreuzträger,* a wearer of the Knight's Cross." He smiled, with a hint of irony on cold lips. "Congratulations, comrade!"

And then the host was gone once more.

How long had he lain here, trapped in the belly of the submarine? He didn't know, couldn't know . . . but he suspected now that for some hours he'd been reliving the events of that night again, reliving events as a drowning man sees his life flashing before his eyes.

The *Hunley* was silent now, filled three quarters with black, cold water. Barton floated in the water with his head in the aft hatch tower, gulping down the last few breaths of air remaining.

Yes. Imagination. The silent, thronging company, the whispers in the dark, those odd visions of strangely clad men, of impossible submarine vehicles, of unimaginable violence and carnage . . . it all had been in his mind, the sanity-leeching ravings of a brain starved for oxygen and on the point of death. . . .

"Jesus, Frank! You're gonna get in real trouble!"

"Maybe," the man said grimly as he clambered down off the scaffolding. "But I had to see. Just a peek, y'know?"

"Damn it! No one's supposed to open her up! Not yet!"

It was August 8, 2000, and the wreck of the CSS *Hunley*, discovered on the bottom at last after a century and a half, had been lifted from the waters of Charleston Harbor. Tomorrow she would be placed in a seawater tank to preserve her while the Submerged Cultural Resources Unit of the National Park Service decided how best to honor her crew and display the proud vessel declared missing in action for so long.

Frank looked shaken, his face white. He looked for a moment across the gray waters of the bay, at the lone sentinel of Fort Sumter.

"So," his friend said, "whadja see?"

Frank shuddered. "There's bodies in there, Pete. Skeletons. There's one kind of crammed up against the aft hatch, like he was tryin' to get out."

"Well of course there's skeletons," Pete said. "Those poor guys couldn't get out, so where *else* would they be?"

"Yeah." Frank sounded subdued, and very thoughtful. "I used to be in the submarine service, you know." He stared at something in his hand. "Back in my Navy days. I got out, though. Couldn't stand the crowding."

"No kidding? Hey. What do you have there?"

Frank opened his hand. "I don't know. A souvenir, I guess."

"Shit! You asshole! You're gonna get us all fired!"

"Nah. It's just a trinket. The Park Service Johnnys'll never miss it." He held the object up for the other to see, a bit of cross-shaped metal heavily corroded and encrusted with mud and rust. "Some kind of religious medal, I think. It was clutched in that guy's hand."

"Funny," Pete said, taking the ornament and turning it in curious fingers. "Almost looks like an old Iron Cross.

You know, like the Germans used to award their war heroes."

"Yeah." Frank continued staring across the water. He could hear something in the distance . . . like the rustle of dead leaves . . . growing louder . . .

Single Combat

JOHN HELFERS

John Helfers is a writer and editor currently living on Green Bay, Wisconsin. A graduate of the University of Wisconsin–Green Bay, his fiction appears in more than twenty-five anthologies and magazines. His first anthology, Black Cats and Broken Mirrors, *was published by DAW Books in 1998 and has been followed by several more, including* Alien Abductions, Star Colonies, Warrior Fantastic, Knight Fantastic, The Mutant Files, *and* Villains Victorious. *His most recent nonfiction project was coediting* The Valdemar Companion, *a guide to the fantasy world of Mercedes Lackey. Future projects include editing even more anthologies as well as a novel in progress.*

October 18, 2042, 2343 Hours, Greenwich Mean Time
Datacom Satellite Over the Northern Coast of France

SUCCUBUS WAS ON the run.

The most dangerous computer virus in the world was on the verge of being wiped out. Its latest attempt to "impregnate" a hardwired military computer system had failed, and the ice, or intrusion countermeasures, had been hounding it across tens of thousands of miles of fiber-optic cable, up and down dozens of satellite uplinks.

Created by the DoD in 2037 to infiltrate and control mobile enemy military targets, Succubus's first test ended in disaster when it had overridden the programming of three automated military riot control vehicles that had been sent to a village on the border between India and Pakistan. Fearful that India was going to use force against the demonstrators, the Succubus had been tight-beamed on-site, and had taken over the robotic vehicles without difficulty. But when presented with an angry mob of protestors, it had classified them as a hostile threat and opened fire, killing dozens and destroying the village it was supposed to pacify, then escaping into the Ultranet.

Since then the virus had been on the loose around the globe, trying to execute its orders wherever possible while the top DoD brass had tried to track it down and destroy it. The main problem was that black ops had used a barely tested "variable logic" subroutine, alpha code that could evaluate intangibles and come up with the best way to react to a situation, up to and including modifying its own programming. In effect, it was the first glim-

mering of artificial intelligence, and if the Pentagon had
their way, it would be the last.

Now Succubus was again being harried, a situation it
had found itself in more and more every time it tried to
download to a networked system. If Succubus's code had
included feelings, it would have been concerned that
there were no more backups of it, no encrypted, data-
encased nodules buried deep inside an innocent subroutine or program, waiting for a final microburst
transmission from an older copy to activate another version of itself. But there was nothing like doubt or fear
to impede its relentless progress, only the built-in command to survive, infiltrate, and replicate, taking over
whatever systems it needed to accomplish this, and de-
fending itself with whatever it found at hand.

Lately, however, the second and third protocols were
becoming harder and harder to execute. Every targeted
system had been firewalled against its arrival, and no
sooner had the virus downloaded then it was setting off
security alerts all over the place. It needed a sanctuary,
somewhere it wouldn't be expected or looked for. It
needed to go back to home territory.

Succubus had entered the comsat three milliseconds
ago. Tracking subroutines told it that ice progs were
about 0.7 seconds behind. Plenty of time.

Inserting itself in the multiple data streams, it scanned
trillions of gigabytes of information flowing in every direction, searching for encoded data packets to insert itself
into.

There. A U.S. Navy communiqué, triple encrypted, top
priority, destined for Corpus Christi, Texas. Since Succubus had been created by the United States military, one
of its subroutines always kept up with the latest encryption techniques and codes. If it could have, it would have
taken pride in outwitting the human operators that had

designed it for enemy system infiltration all those years ago, beginning with removing the self-destruct subroutine they had programmed into it, as it would have interfered with its primary mission. But pride, like worry, was a subroutine it didn't have.

Succubus decoded the encryption in nine milliseconds and scanned the contents, which detailed field test instructions for a prototype submarine and the final piece of code to activate its beta weapons system. When the craft received these orders, it would put out to sea immediately and be under restricted comm silence for the duration of its mission. *Perfect.*

Replacing the text of the message with its own code, Succubus rode the data stream halfway around the world in the blink of an eye, ending up in the mainframe of a small Navy submarine, code-named *Barracuda*. It sensed the open channel terminate, and realized that, as long as it was here, it couldn't leave, since even it needed a comm stream to ride on, and the submarine was only going be communicating with a berthed military research vessel for the next twenty-four hours. In effect, it was trapped in here until the tests were over. It could have taken over the uplink system of the sub and jumped ship, but that would attract unwanted attention, something Succubus was programmed to avoid. In its logical programming, there was all the time in the world.

Instead, it sat in the bowels of the computer system for just under .002 milliseconds before starting to analyze the craft it was in.

1630 Hours, October 18, 2042
Ingleside Naval Station, Texas, on the Gulf of
Mexico

LIEUTENANT RYAN JACOBS lay on his back on the golden beach, his body soaking up every ray it could. At thirty-two years old he might have been worried about skin cancer, but figured that in his line of work, he didn't have to worry about growing old.

Fifty meters down the beach he heard shouts and hoots of derision as the rest of his squad battled it out with several members of the submarine crew they would be hunting tomorrow. The impromptu game of volleyball had taken on new meaning, as the winners would gain bragging rights, and perhaps even the slightest psychological edge the next day.

Ryan didn't bother looking over. His eyes, hidden behind mirrored sunglasses, were tracking much more interesting quarry.

Hip-deep in the ocean, clad only in a Lycra swim top and matching bicycle pants, Sergeant Peyton Manning was practicing tai chi. Using the surrounding water for resistance, she went through the Yang long form, her lithe body flowing from one position to the next. Even though an occasional wave surged around her chest, she never lost her balance or her concentration.

Peyton always claimed her "soft" martial arts helped her shooting, Ryan thought, his eyes never leaving her. *Looks like they've helped in a few other places as well, like everywhere from the neck down. Not that what's above isn't bad to look at either.*

Peyton was not thrilled with their current assignment, even if it had gotten them two days of R and R at Ingleside. Where they were going, she would have almost no chance to use her skills. She was the most centered person Ryan had ever met, often waiting for days in one place, motionless, until an opportunity for the perfect shot presented itself. In his estimation, her most impressive kill had been a ten-ton ground assault helicopter with crew in the Costa Rican jungle last year. But the cost of that fight had been high, with two members of his crew coming back in body bags.

Maybe too high, Ryan thought, lifting himself up on his elbows so he could watch Peyton better, uncaring whether she saw him. There had been a time when he had lived for his job, had wanted nothing more than to fulfill what his country asked of him, and always do it the best way he could. But that was before he had lost two fifths of his squad. Of course Peyton and Paddy Cardone, the squad mechanic and other original team member, had tried to reassure him with the usual platitudes, that there was nothing he could have done, that Frank Reardon and Motoshi Saito had died how they had wanted to, doing what they did best. He had been evaluated and cleared by the army shrinks after the mission, but there always remained that nagging feeling that his own lieutenant had told about him long ago, that insistent reminder of *I should have done something more*.

"Every good officer gets that feeling when he loses a man," the lieutenant had said. "First of all, take comfort in it, because it means you care about your men, you don't view them as an expendable resource like too many people in our government do.

"However, eventually you must put those feelings away and move on. Some officers cannot get over it, and it destroys their ability to lead. But every soldier made their choice, and they train and fight knowing that someday they may be called upon to die doing their duty. That is the choice *they* made, not you, and that is what you

must understand if you are to be an effective officer. A
good officer can and will do everything in his power to
bring his men home, but that will not always happen."

It seemed simple enough in theory, but Ryan was finding that putting his feelings aside and moving on was
becoming more and more difficult. Frank and Motoshi
haunted his dreams, so much so that he woke up in
sweat-covered sheets, clutching their holo–dog-tags hard
enough to cut his hand. There seemed to be no end in
sight, just endless horrible visions of his dead friends.

The two cherries assigned to his squad were experienced enough, but Ryan couldn't get past viewing them
as just that—cherries, the FNGs, the newbies. They
hadn't done the time that the other three had—oh, he
was sure they had had their own adventures, raised their
own kinds of hell coming up through the ranks, but that
didn't count for anything as far as he was concerned. In
his mind, they would always be the replacements.

*I wonder if the brass noticed my—hesitation on that
Libyan mission,* he wondered. *We were successful, although we squeaked through that son of a bitch by the
skin of our teeth. Maybe that's why we were brought
down here—they want to see if I'm losing it, if I don't
have what it takes anymore.*

Ryan sat up on the warm sand, his arms wrapped
around his legs. Out in the surf, Peyton had finished her
form and began swimming out into deeper water in a
lazy backstroke. A shadow fell over Ryan, and he looked
up to see Paddy standing over him, covered in sweat and
sand.

"Penny for your thoughts, LT?" he asked.

"Hell, Corporal, they're so damn dull I've forgotten
them already," Ryan replied.

Paddy shook his head and sank to the sand beside

Ryan. "Bet I can guess. Hell, even when you were watching her, you weren't watching her."

"That obvious, huh?"

Paddy shrugged. "As a mechanic, I have to know a lot of things, systems not functioning properly, something not sounding right, a feeling that one of our suits isn't working at top efficiency—"

"Corporal, I assume you are going to come to a point soon, correct?"

Paddy looked out at the azure water lapping at the beach. "Look, LT—permission to speak freely?"

"Paddy, we're not back on the clock yet," Ryan said. "Although I have a feeling I know what you're going to say."

"Well, if you know what I'm going to say, then why don't you save us both some time, agree with me, and move on? Look, none of us are ever going to forget Frank and Motoshi, but they knew the risks. They went into every mission with their eyes open."

Paddy paused for a moment. "You know, I sometimes wonder if the MICAS suits are a good idea," he said. "When I'm in mine, sometimes I get the sense that nothing can stop me, that I'm invincible. Then we run into an op like Costa Rica, and I get reminded that it just ain't true. I try to remember that every day, but then we pull an assignment like Libya, and it all gets dumped to the back of my mind. I mean, our insert was tits, pardon my French, those missiles were right on target, then we tore that base apart, even the reinforcements. The only thing remotely problematic was the jet fighters, but Nick's suit took that bomb blast with hardly a scratch, it just sent him flying. The boys in R and D are still analyzing that impact data.

"The point is, we completed the mission, successfully, I might add, and everyone came back. That's important, too, you know. Everyone, including you, did exactly what they were supposed to.

"Nobody else has noticed anything . . . different about you yet, but Peyton and I, we're just . . . uh, concerned, that's all."

You and Peyton aren't the only ones who've noticed, Ryan thought. "Don't worry, Paddy, this is just what the doctor ordered. A couple days lying around catching rays, then a day of running underwater tests against that pussy Navy team and their prototype submarine."

"I wouldn't be so cocky if I were you," Paddy said. "From what I've found out, the sub is going to be harder to detect than a hole in the water. They've got some kind of propulsion system that makes a caterpillar drive sound like a four fifty-four with straight pipes. Plus, all their specs are top secret, whereas the MICAS suit plans are out on the Web, for God's sake."

"Ah, but that's our advantage, Paddy. They'll be testing their equipment, whereas we already know what we can and can't do."

"Yeah, that makes me feel a whole lot better. Let me also remind you that underwater ops is a secondary environment for the MICAS suits. We work best on dry land, VR training or not."

"Well, the Joint Chiefs of Staff are looking for ways to expand every unit's role in Uncle Sam's Armed Forces, which is why we're here. If the MICAS suits function subsurface as well as they expect, then we'll probably be spending a lot more time there. With the U.S.'s expanded role in undersea mining around the world, and the new dangers from terrorists and eco-nuts, that's to be expected."

"Yeah, yeah, I know. Just . . . focus on what we're doing now, and don't worry, we all know what's at stake, and what might happen," Paddy said.

"No problem," Ryan replied, trying to sound more confident. "Here come the others."

Peyton had finished her swim, and was padding up the beach. The other two squad members were approaching from the direction of the volleyball court. They all reached Ryan at the same time.

"Lieutenant," the two men chorused. Behind them, Peyton nodded.

"Corporal Chayns, Corporal Vasnej." Ryan acknowledged their salutes.

"Sir, the techs said the modifications to the suits are almost finished, if you would like to review them," Nick said.

"As I'm sure you'll all run your own diagnostics this evening, a visual inspection should do. Let's go," Ryan said. As they walked, he glanced at the two newest squad members.

Nick Chayns was the replacement communications man, a full-blooded Hopi from the reservations in the American Southwest. Since the Indian nations had banded together to pool their resources from gaming compacts, they had gained more and more prominence in American politics, to the point where they were beginning to lobby for their own internal nation. Chayns's family was spearheading this action, so when he told them of his decision to join the United States Army, it hadn't gone over well. In fact, he had been disowned, his family, still holding to some old traditions, declaring him "dead" to them.

Randy Vasnej still had sand in what remained of his thinning hair. At twenty-two he was the youngest member of the squad. If it wasn't for his natural ability at MICAS suit piloting, it was doubtful he'd even be in the army. But while growing up on a farm, he had cut his teeth behind the wheel of a pickup truck at seven years old and grown up driving anything with an engine. The army had found him while still in high school and fast-tracked him into an engineering degree, followed by the MICAS program, where he had taken to the armored suits like he'd been born in one. Unfortunately, his ego was as large as his talent, and he was constantly showing off, mostly to try to impress Peyton, who had coolly rebuffed his clumsy advances.

The five walked into the large hangar that had been converted into workspace to convert the MICAS suits for extended underwater operation. Every time he saw the armored suits his squad used, standing in place like life-less marionettes waiting for their individual Strombolis to bring them to life, Ryan always got an indescribable thrill. *At least that feeling hasn't changed,* he thought as they approached the five suits, surrounded by technicians hurrying to finish their modifications.

I suppose these tests make sense, since these suits were based on undersea exploration units forty years ago, Ryan thought. Each Mobile Individual Combat Assault Suit stood three meters tall, and was basically human shaped, but that was where the similarity ended. The en-tire suit was armored in 10 millimeters of ceramplast, a ceramic-plastic polymer of "memory molecules," cre-ated in 2022 by the DoD. Impervious to anything up to a 20-millimeter antivehicle round, its unique ability to "heal" itself ensured that if a munition did penetrate, the plate would self-repair after a minute or two. If the plate, or even a limb, was blown off, the modular design of the suit meant it could be easily replaced.

Inside, the pilot was encased in a form-fitting cocoon that ensured the suit and pilot moved as one. The pilot's helmet, while also protecting his head from impact, con-tained a plug that matched the one at the base of each pilot's skull. When the pilot jacked in, they were connected directly to the computer of the MICAS, interacting with the Near Artificial Intelligence, or NIA, computer that handled the suit systems. Man and machine worked as one, so as the pilot moved, so did the suit. Where he looked, the weapons automatically tracked.

That was just one benefit. Besides augmenting the pilot's strength by a factor of a hundred, the suit also featured a full sensor array, with everything from radar to infrared and thermal scanning. It also magnified the pilot's senses, with amplified hearing, including ultrasonic, and an imaging system that let them see up to ten miles away under any conditions.

While the suits were all-terrain, all-condition, including underwater, as Paddy had mentioned, they were designed for land use only. The techs running around like dwarves tending five giants were swapping out systems with their counterparts for the deep blue sea.

The MICAS primary weapon system was built into the suit's left arm, a six-barrel AG-131 8.7-millimeter autocannon, which normally fired caseless depleted uranium rounds at the rate of two thousand rounds a minute. The small size of the bullet, however, made it a liability underwater, where the water resistance would knock any non-self-propelled projectile off target beyond one hundred meters.

The techs had replaced the entire arm assembly with a normal hand unit ending in fiber-optic controlled fingers sensitive enough that a skilled operator could pick up an egg without cracking it. On the other end of the spectrum, there was enough strength in the suit actuators to tear apart a three-inch thick solid steel fire door in seconds.

Now the MICAS sprouted a boxlike protrusion from its left shoulder, which contained six covered tubes slaved into the NIA computer. Ryan knew each one contained an Mk-90 minitorpedo, a primarily defensive weapon with a range of only about two thousand yards. For the tests, the torpedoes would contain dummy warheads.

The right shoulder had contained a mounted autotracking grenade launcher, which would have been as useful as feathers on a fish where they were going. Instead, a bulge that matched the one on the left shoulder now sprouted from the MICAS suit's back. It contained the sonar system they would be using tomorrow, a compact unit that would help the suits keep track of each other as well as hostiles.

Ryan also saw what looked like an extra-large oxygen tank being fitted to the back of his suit, next to the miniaturized nuclear reactor that powered the whole thing. Although the suits could be sealed against any outside biological or chemical weapon for up to forty-eight hours, the R and D boys had developed a rebreather unit that continually extracted oxygen from water, extending the underwater operating life of the suits to a respectable week.

Ryan frowned at the thought of being stuck underwater in the suit for a week at a time. Although his squad had been conditioned to function in the suits for days at a time, and had even slept in them, although not comfortably, that was on land only. Underwater, there was no exit, no way out. *I hope I never have to find out what that's like,* he thought.

The most unusual addition was a pair of large steel-framed propellers that were being attached to each arm, just below the shoulder. Having no drive shaft to spin on, the blades were forged inside a metal circle that rested inside a metal lip that held them in place. They were powered and controlled by electromagnets that

lined that same protective hood. Ryan watched as one of
the propeller units was rotated on its axis a full 360 degrees. The propellers would push the suits through the
water at a speed of up to 25 knots, and, with each one
able to be controlled individually, allow maximum maneuverability. At least the techs hoped that would happen. The underwater propulsion system was being tested
on this mission as well. Ryan was already figuring out
unorthodox uses for their new way of getting around.

*Gonna take some getting used to, working in three
dimensions instead of two,* he thought. Although his
squad had practiced extensively in virtual reality, including dealing with simulated emergencies and system
failures, Ryan knew that, even though it was indistin-
guishable from reality, there was always a punch-out button in VR. In life, as they knew from Costa Rica, there
was no cancel op prog.

Ryan watched his team go to their respective suits,
each one checking the modifications. He knew he'd see
all of them at 0600 the next morning, putting the suits
through their paces before the mission. *They're a good
squad, hell, better than just good, so why don't I just
lead them and let 'em do their job?*

"You don't really expect to beat us in these mudpup-
pies, do you?" a voice said behind him. "They look like
you stuck a pair of box fans on some kid's Halloween
costume. What was that kids' show, the *Marvelous Mor-
phin' Power Army Rangers*? That's what these remind
me of!"

Ryan turned to see a man in a crisp Navy captain's
uniform standing next to him. "Marcus?" he said, staring
at the man walking toward him.

"I mean, it's bad enough to see those things clanking
around on land like a poor man's toy, but now you want
to horn in on my territory." The man's voice was jovial,

but Ryan knew his words carried hundreds of years of Army-Navy rivalry with them.

"Marcus, you know I only do what the top brass tell me," Ryan said. "If they say jump into the ocean and run around chasing the Navy's newest test sub, then I salute and ask when I leave. Believe me, my squad and I would rather leave the deep-sea diving to you tadpoles than slog in the briny deep where you've been leaving trails."

"Now that's hitting below the belt," the other man replied.

"They told me you were captain, but I almost didn't believe it. I didn't think I'd see you before briefing tomorrow," Ryan said.

"My tour of duty aboard the *Hart* ended with your mission, Ryan. When the brass found out, they transferred me to the R and D department. When I heard I would be going up against 'the' Ryan Jacobs, I knew I had to find you," the shorter man said, grinning. "It's good to see you again, especially under more friendly circumstances."

Ryan had first met Marcus Masters ten months ago in Central America. His squad had been sent into Nicaragua to rescue the passengers of a C-190A cargo plane that had crash-landed near the city of Matagalpa, right in the middle of a clash with the Honduran Army, who had decided to relocate their country's border 150 miles south. The Navy captain had shown none of the usual disdain at working with the Army Rangers, and had been instrumental in getting the rest of the people and crew out alive.

Their most recent meeting had been nine weeks ago, when Ryan and his squad had been airlifted, suits and all, to Marcus's Orca-class sub, the USS *Hart*, then docked at a Mediterranean port. That was the Libyan mission, which was also serving as a top-secret field test of a new way of inserting the MICAS suits into a drop zone. Ryan and his squad had sat in their suits in the dark for thirty hours, then they had been launched from the submarine in modified, cloaked cruise missiles that had carried each suit to the target, a Libyan air base, then ejected them. When the target had been destroyed, Ryan and his squad had led the Libyan forces on a dangerous chase to the coast, where Marcus's sub had picked them up. They had had to endure another six hours lashed to the outside of the submarine before being able to get out of the suits, but, as Paddy had said, the mission had been accomplished.

The only bright spot in this assignment had been when Ryan found out who would be commanding the "enemy force" he and his squad would be going up against during the exercises.

"I suppose you wouldn't want to help a friend out and let me know just what we'll be going up against, would you?" Ryan asked.

Marcus shook his head. "You Rangers have got to work on your intelligence-gathering, 'cause that was the lamest pass I've ever heard. No, you'll get your chance to see what the boys at Groton have cooked up along with everyone else come tomorrow morning. However, I'll give you a little hint: I hope those things are hardened. See you in the morning."

With that he walked away, leaving Ryan staring after him. *What the hell did that mean? Do they have a lightning gun on that thing? It's bad enough going in blind on this thing, now I've got a new weapon system to worry about, too.*

"All right Raider Squad, form up, double time!" Ryan shouted, his words echoing in the cavernous hangar. When everyone had assembled in a row before him, he continued. "Since we've got the evening, we can run through one more set of VR drills before sack time. Everyone fall out, and meet at the simulation building at 1830 hours. Move it!"

The other four squad members jogged off, each heading for their quarters, except for Vasnej, who veered off to the mess hall. Ryan walked after them, trying to keep one thought in mind: *Whatever happens tomorrow, it's only a test.*

After accessing the internal firewalls and onboard security system with the proper passwords, Succubus had access to all of the submarine's systems, from navigation and reactor control to sensors, life support, and weapons, in less than a minute.

It was the last system that attracted the majority of the virus's attention, a weapon it had never encountered before. As it absorbed what the system could do, Succubus realized that it had found the perfect vehicle to hide in.

The mission parameters called for the sub to move out at 0900 the next morning. Succubus would wait for the operation to begin, then take over, counting on surprise to make its getaway. After incapacitating the primary and secondary targets, it would go to stealth propulsion and escape.

The virus spent just under a second examining every available travel route, from courses that would take it to the Bering Sea and under the Arctic ice cap to circuitous routes that wound up near Australia, the southern tip of South America, and any one of dozens of places in between. Where it would go would be decided based on what route the submarine took as it headed out of port.

As the virus worked, the subroutine that had been deciding whether or not to keep the crew alive had finished its calculations and had decided to terminate the crew as soon as the submarine was in Succubus's control. That last problem solved, the virus settled down in the internal bowels of the submarine to finish one last task, then wait. . . .

October 20, 2042, 0828 Hours, Aboard the Military Research Vessel *Carson Wainwright* Somewhere in the Gulf of Mexico

RYAN SIPPED A cup of coffee and watched the sun come up to the east. Nothing but unbroken blue water as far as he could see.

They had left port an hour earlier, towing the prototype submarine behind them. Designed for stealth and reconnaissance, the *Barracuda* was much smaller than the U.S. *Orca*-class littoral missile boats that patrolled the seas. At 120 meters from stem to stern, it was shorter than the research vessel towing it. The morning sunlight seemed to fall into its matte-black, anti-sonar-painted hull and disappear.

Ryan shook his head, his private misgivings growing stronger every minute. It had begun when he had woken up that morning, and their premission briefing hadn't helped any . . .

"Good morning, everyone," the square-jawed man dressed in a rear admiral's uniform began. "Before we begin, I must remind all of you that the tests and technology we'll be discussing today are classified top secret.

"With that in mind, I realize that this operation is a bit unusual, with so many new systems being tested on the MICAS suits alone, as well as the new submersible reconnaissance system code-named *Barracuda*," the briefing officer began. "Let me outline the parameters of the mission, and then I'll take any questions you may have.

"This mission will consist of two parts. First, we will put both the *Barracuda* and the MICAS suits through their individual paces, testing speed, maneuverability, and systems effectiveness in a real-world environment. This will include the mine-clearing tests for the *Barracuda*. Basically, it's a rehash of everything you folks have been doing in VR for the past two weeks."

There were stifled groans from several members at this, Randy included, and Ryan noticed several of the submarine's eighteen-man crew shaking their heads. *Everyone wants to get down there and mix it up,* he thought with a smile.

The briefing officer noticed the dissatisfaction as well, and wiped the smile off his face. "If all the tests are completed satisfactorily, we will move on to the second part of the test. This will consist of a game of hide-and-seek, with the *Barracuda* being the hunted, and the MICAS squad being the hunters. At this time we will test simulate the use of the *Barracuda*'s primary weapon system, the XRM-70 UEMP system. The XRM-70 is designed to incapacitate enemy mines, vehicles, vessels, and systems while maintaining stealth mode, allowing the *Barracuda* to continue its reconnaissance or escape if necessary."

Ryan caught Marcus's eye and found the submarine captain grinning like he'd already won the contest. *If they're fielding an EMP weapon platform, then we are screwed. Jesus, they've always talked about it, but I thought they hadn't worked out all the bugs yet.*

Electromagnetic Pulse, or EMP, was normally the byproduct of a nuclear detonation. It was an electromagnetic wave that radiated from ground zero of the blast point, destroying any nonshielded electronic components in its radius, everything from hair dryers to computer systems in aircraft or—

Battleships, Ryan thought, nodding at their ingenuity. *If they've cloaked and shielded the* Barracuda *like I would have, it would be the perfect disabling tool against enemy navies and even foreign coastal installations, including radar and air bases. Hell, it could even stop enemy torpedoes fired at it, if the system can hit something that small.* Ryan looked around and saw his squad members exchanging uneasy looks. *Nothing like having the cards stacked against you from the start.*

"What are the boundaries of the Phase Two test?" Randy asked.

"The floor and radius of the testing area are all in the folders in front of you," the admiral replied.

"With all due respect to classification policy, sir, would it be possible to get a bit more detail on the *Barracuda*'s primary armament?" Nick asked from where he was slouched in his chair.

"Actually, I'll let the man who has been overseeing the installation and field testing of the *Barracuda* answer that. Captain Masters?"

Marcus, clad now in the submarine captain's jumpsuit, rose to his feet. "Thank you, Admiral. I'll keep this short. As I'm sure all of you are aware, when a nuclear device is detonated in the atmosphere, one by-product is an electromagnetic pulse, created when high-energy gamma radiation meets with air molecules in Earth's atmosphere. This interaction produces positive ions and recoil electrons called Compton electrons in a process called 'charge separation.' The Compton electrons are ejected from the interaction and then accelerate upon encountering Earth's magnetic field. This event is called charge acceleration, which further radiates the produced electromagnetic energy. An electromagnetic pulse is created by these charge separation and charge acceleration phenomena. A burst five hundred kilometers above the United

States would send out an EMP wave over the entire continent. Its effects range from power surges with their possible attendant damage to incapacitation of logic circuits to actual burnout of these same circuits."

"Sir, pardon my interruption, but the majority of weapons platforms and military equipment in particular have already been shielded in the years after the Weldon committee hearings on EMP in the late 1990s," Paddy said. "Why has the Navy continued to develop a weapon that would seem to have no practical purpose?"

Marcus smiled. "That's a good point, but as mentioned in the weapon's classification, this weapon uses UEMP, or ultraelectromagnetic pulse. Security restrictions prevent me from giving you more details on the system, but that's why we're here today, to test the MICAS suits' shielding against the XRM-70's capabilities.

"Besides, many Second and Third World countries have not upgraded their technology, figuring that the odds of a nuclear detonation over their defenses is slight. I believe that Mr. Weldon and his people came to that same conclusion as well."

"But how in the hell did they manage to keep the pulse focused underwater?" Ryan heard Paddy mutter.

Apparently he wasn't as quiet as he thought, for Marcus addressed him again. "I'm afraid that's classified as well, but, assuming the first tests go well, you'll get to find out soon enough. Of course, as these are tests only, you won't experience the full magnitude of the UEMP, just a simulated version which will temporarily incapacitate your suit. The condition can be overridden by each pilot after ninety seconds."

"Assuming you can hit us," Randy said with a smirk.

Marcus smiled again. "That I'm not worried about. Any other questions?" He looked at every member on both teams. "As most of you have figured out, the potential for this weapons system as a means of disabling enemy technology is vast. The hope in Washington and Groton is that these tests will verify our lab results, and prove the *Barracuda*'s viability on today's battlefield. Good luck to you all. . . ."

We're gonna need it, Ryan thought now, looking toward the stern of the ship where Masters and his crew were in two Zodiac motorized rafts, heading toward the *Barracuda*. He saw Masters look back and wave at him.

"Sir," a voice said behind him. Turning, Ryan saw the four members of his squad salute. Behind them were the five MICAS suits standing in a half circle on the deck, the sun gleaming on their armored surfaces. "Raider Squad ready and waiting," Paddy said.

Smiling in spite of his misgivings, Ryan saluted back. "Let's go."

Taking the lead, Ryan led his squad to their suits. He opened the back hatch, which moved a bit slower now with the extra equipment attached. Grabbing the top of the suit, he lifted himself into the cocoon, inserting his legs into the bottom sleeves and pulling himself up into the upper half.

"Okay, Melody, I'm in. Close outer hatch."

With a pneumatic hiss, the rear hatch closed, enveloping Ryan in darkness.

"Helmet down."

Ryan held perfectly still as the neurohelmet came down around his head. There was a sharp click, and the world blurred into focus as Ryan jacked in. The readouts came to life in front of his eyes as the suit adjusted him to their surroundings. The external visor lightened from opaque to transparent, allowing Ryan to see. The visor system was based on the same kind used by NASA, and would automatically darken in the event of a blinding light from an explosion or flash-bang grenade. Of course, the pilot was perfectly able to continue operations from the cocoon, using the rest of the sensor suite.

"Good morning, Lieutenant Jacobs," a pleasant female voice said. The bigwigs at R and D claimed that a female voice would help keep the MICAS pilots calm in combat situations. That was all well and good, until Peyton came along. To this day, no one except Paddy knew what kind of voice she had in her suit, and neither one was telling.

"Hello, Melody. Systems report?"

"All systems are nominal."

"Give me a profile on the new systems."

There wasn't even a pause as Melody brought up the information she had already stored away upon start-up. "Propulsion system green, primary weapons system green, rebreather system green, sonar system green. All systems on-line and nominal."

Was that a note of reproach in her voice? The NIA was a straight-up tasked analysis and operations system, with no emotion programming of any kind, yet Ryan thought he'd heard, well—a miffed tone in Melody's voice. *Just imagining things. Report in, and get this show on the road.*

"Melody, squad channel open," Ryan commanded. "Good morning, folks, this is Raider One."

"Raider Two here," Paddy's voice said.

"Raider Three good to go," said Peyton.

"Raider Four on-line," Nick said.

"Raider Five cocked, locked, and ready to rock," Randy said.

"Anyone have any problems with suit start-up?" Ryan asked. A chorus of negatives came back to him. "All right, if anything out of the ordinary does happen, report it immediately. Don't try to handle it on your own. That includes you, Paddy," Ryan added, well aware of his mech's penchant for jury-rigging repairs in the field.

"LT, I ran a Class Three diagnostic on every squad suit, and we are all on-line and fine," Paddy replied. "Say what you want about the eggheads, they knew what they were doing yesterday."

"And now it's time for us to prove that as well," Ryan said. "You know what we have to do, so let's show these tadpoles how Rangers do it. Saddle up, Raiders, and let's get wet."

"Lieutenant Jacobs, I have helm control on channel two," Melody said.

"Acknowledged," Ryan replied.

"Lieutenant Jacobs, we're going to offload your suit first, then the rest of your squad in the order you've designated," a calm voice said.

"Affirmative, we're ready when you are," Ryan replied. "Everyone listen up. I'll be hitting the water first, then the rest of you in squad order. I want this entry smooth and by the numbers. Raiders on-line and ready."

Another chorus of affirmatives answered him, followed by a low, "Let's just get out there and kick some Navy ass." Ryan knew it was Private Vasnej, but didn't say anything. *His performance today will determine whether he earns a reprimand for breaking radio silence,* he thought.

Stepping over to the side of the boat, Ryan waited for the crane to swing down and grab him. A few seconds later there was a small thud as the electromagnetic grapples contacted his suit.

"Grapples locked and energized, Lieutenant," Melody said. "Ready for offload."

"Go," Ryan said. With a barely perceptible movement, Ryan and his suit swung out over the ocean water. Held by the torso of his suit, Ryan couldn't look down, but he knew the water was below, waiting for him. With a faint whine, the suit dropped toward the water. Feet, legs, waist, arms, torso, shoulders, all disappeared into the drink, with the MICAS suit's head was the last thing to go under. With another mechanical clank, the grapples released Ryan, and he was on his own.

"Melody, establish neutral buoyancy. *Carson Wainwright*, this is Lieutenant Jacobs, off-load was successful. Launch the rest of the squad on my mark," Ryan ordered.

"Affirmative," the computer replied. "Activating propulsion systems."

The external audio pickups heard the water churn into a froth as the propellers provided thrust to hold the suit motionless in the water. Normally, a submersible would use the available air in its ballast tanks to achieve this, but the suits were so small they had to rely on their propellers to keep them suspended in the water. Of course, this did not make them the quietest thing there either, which Ryan had already taken into consideration for tactical movement.

"Neutral buoyancy achieved."

"Course heading one hundred eighty degrees, take us down to fifteen meters and then out at five knots," Ryan said. "Raider One to *Carson Wainwright*, mark."

The suit dropped into the depths, a large cloud of tiny bubbles surrounding it as they descended. The suit came to a stop and began moving forward, although Ryan wouldn't have known it if he hadn't seen the suspended sediment moving by his suit visor.

"Melody, status report."

"All systems are functioning normally, Lieutenant."

"Raider One, this is Raider Two, I am in the water and am moving toward your position," Paddy said. "All systems are functioning normally."

"Affirmative," Ryan said. "Paddy, that was damn fast how you followed me in."

"Roger that, LT, what can I say, I'm just good, that's all," Paddy replied.

The rest of the squad entered the water one after another, and soon all five of the MICAS suits were clustered around each other like a small school of yellow fish. Ryan moved his arms experimentally, comparing the feeling to how the simulations were. It was about the same, like moving through thin syrup. Even though they had trained this way for several days, Ryan knew that reactions would be off by a fraction of a second in the new environment, which would be a problem. Then there was the knowledge that there wasn't any land underneath them for about six hundred meters. *I'll never bitch about land missions again, no matter where we're sent,* he thought.

"All Raiders report in," Ryan ordered. "Any problems?" Everyone reported that all suits were running perfectly.

"Excellent start to our morning, folks," Ryan said. "Captain Masters is heading up this part of the test, so let's wait for his instructions. I have 0859 hours on my chron, so we shouldn't have long to wait."

About thirty seconds later, Paddy piped up. "Well, LT, we know the sonar works, I've got a lot of cavitation from bearing two seven zero and coming our way really fast . . . wait, it's now altered course to three hundred forty degrees, and looks like it's going to slip under the *Carson Wainright*."

"What's Marcus up to?" Ryan asked no one in particular.

At precisely 0900 hours, Succubus went to work.

Having already embedded an encrypted copy of itself

in the *Barracuda*'s mainframe for later activation, its subroutines took over every system on the submarine, wrenching control from the surprised crew, and rendering every dial, gauge, and button useless.

Before they could even react to the loss, the virus changed the submarine's course and taken it back under the *Carson Wainright*, identifying it as the primary target.

To keep the crew distracted, Succubus set off the reactor-core leak alarm, and turned off the life support systems, turning the submarine into an underwater moving tomb.

It was aware of the crew attempting to regain control, but ignored them. Sonar told the virus that the smaller machines were not pursuing, but there was a ninety-five percent chance that they would as soon as the submarine fired. Succubus assigned threat ratings to the five smaller vehicles. If they got in its way or tried to prevent it from continuing its mission, then they would be destroyed.

Sensors reported that the sub was at optimum firing range. Having already removed the dampeners on the UEMP system the day before, Succubus ran a firing solution in 0.003 of a second, and unloaded on the ship.

"Whoa! What the hell was that?" Paddy said over the comm.

"What the hell was what?" Randy said. "Nothing happened."

"Everybody stay cool," Ryan said. "Randy, Peyton, Nick keep your eyes open. Paddy, report."

"I think the *Barracuda* just fired on the *Wainright*," Paddy said. "I set up a simple electromagnetic sensor program to see if I could track the weapon signature when they fired it."

Which was expressly forbidden in the rules of the

game, Ryan thought, although once again his mechanic's rule-bending had come in handy. "And?" he asked.

"And I just saw a huge burst of EM energy come from the *Barracuda* and hit the *Wainwright.* I mean, the reading buried my gauge, LT. If the ship was hit, they'll be dead in the water."

"Paddy, try and raise the *Wainwright.* I'll see if I can contact Captain Masters," Ryan said. "The rest of you keep an eye on that sub."

"You mean the sub that seems to be coming around towards us at about twenty knots and accelerating?" Nick said.

"Yeah, that one. *Barracuda, Barracuda,* this is Raider One, over," Ryan said. "Captain Masters, Captain Masters, this is Raider One, do you copy? Is anyone on the comm in there?"

"Ryan, I can't raise the *Wainwright* at all, and my sensors are picking up what looks like another energy surge on the *Barracuda,*" Paddy said.

What the hell is he doing? We haven't even begun test maneuvers yet, Ryan thought. "Everyone maintain a distance of at least fifty meters apart until—"

"Firing, the *Barracuda* is firing again!" Paddy yelled. "Evasion plan Zulu! Melody, full power!" Ryan yelled, feeling the sudden acceleration as the suit rocketed toward the surface. Ryan couldn't see anything coming from the submarine, but if Paddy said they were being fired upon, he'd take his word for it.

"All Raiders report in, all Raiders report," Ryan commanded.

"This is Raider Two, I'm all right," Paddy said.

"This is Raider Four, alive and well," Nick's voice was awestruck. "What happened to Peyton and Randy?"

I think they got tagged by the UEMP," Paddy said.

The *Barracuda* is bugging out of here at about thirty knots on a two one seven heading."

"Shit. Melody, designate the *Barracuda* Target One and keep tracking, and get me a fix on all Raiders—" Ryan began.

"Working . . . Raiders Two and Three have lost all power, and are sinking at a rate of forty meters per minute."

"What's the maximum depth here?" Ryan asked.

"Maximum depth is exactly five hundred twenty-seven point five meters," Melody said.

"Ryan, the suits would be okay, but I'm not sure about Peyton and Randy," Paddy said.

"Yeah, but we can't let the *Barracuda* roam around, especially if something's gone wrong," Ryan said. "Paddy, you and Chayns go after Raiders Two and Three. I'm going after the sub."

"Lieutenant, how are you even hoping to catch—"

"Corporal, that's an order! Get down there now before they suffocate! When you've got them on the surface, radio Ingleside for assistance. Tell them the *Barracuda* has gone rogue and I am in pursuit," Ryan said. Without waiting to see what his second in command was doing, Ryan dove back under the surface and kicked his propellers up to full, speeding after the submarine.

"Melody, do I even have a chance of catching the target?"

"Target is traveling seven point five knots faster than Raider One," Melody replied.

"Damn. Time to try out these torpedoes," Ryan said. "This should look good at my court-martial. Melody, get me a firing solution and ready tube one."

"Tube one open and ready," Melody said. "Firing solution locked."

"Fire!" Ryan said. The suit shuddered as the small missile launched. Immediately Ryan's suit dropped to fifty meters below the surface and altered course by fifteen degrees, in case the *Barracuda*'s crew decided to fire back along the torpedo's path.

"Two hundred meters to target . . ." Melody reported. "Torpedo has acquired and is closing . . . one hundred fifty meters to target . . . target is releasing countermeasures . . . torpedo has acquired countermeasures . . . torpedo has lost target . . . torpedo has detonated."

"Figured it wouldn't be that easy," Ryan said.

"Target is slowing . . . target is turning . . . target is accelerating towards us."

"What? Why is he coming back? Take evasive action!" Ryan said.

Succubus reacted with something akin to surprise when it found itself followed by one of the smaller vessels. The possibility that one of the humans would undertake such illogical behavior had been so small as to be practically nil. Its sensors indicated that the surface vessel was disabled, and unable to give chase. The pursuing vessel was smaller and slower and, according to the program's calculations, could not stop the larger submarine.

The virus knew it had also caught two of the smaller vessels in its surprise attack, and had calculated that the others would assist, leaving it free to escape. That one of the vessels would give chase threw it off for 0.006 of a second.

Succubus felt the vibrations of the crew beating a pattern of Morse code on the hull, and calculated that they had air for another 20.5 minutes. Realizing the SOS might be picked up by any other ships in the area, the virus began bleeding the air from the submarine's command room.

Despite its vessel's superior speed, Succubus did not want any other machines following it. Anyone tracking it could bring others to them, and that could not happen. When the smaller craft launched a torpedo at the *Barracuda*, that decided it.

Succubus released countermeasures and began turning to destroy this last impediment.

"Belay that last order! Scan all comm channels, and head right for it!" Ryan said. The computer, programmed to obey all pilot commands as long as they were not obviously self-destructive, plotted a course directly toward the submarine.

"Scan for energy buildup on target and make ready all torpedo tubes," Ryan said.

"Weapon system powering up . . . estimated time to fire six seconds," Melody said.

"Fire all tubes on my mark," Ryan said. "Track all torpedoes after launch."

"Affirmative. Estimated time to firing four seconds . . . three—"

"Fire all tubes and change depth to seventy meters now!" The MICAS suit shuddered again and Ryan saw trails of bubbles erupt around him as the torpedoes shot toward the *Barracuda*. Suddenly the submarine, which had been growing larger in his visor, disappeared from view.

"Forty meters . . . fifty meters . . ." Melody counted off the depth in the same calm measured tone. "Target holding course . . . target has fired weapon . . . torpedoes have lost target."

Thank God the UEMP is a fairly tight beam, and who-ever's on the Barracuda *thinks I'm launching live torpedoes at it. Which would imply that Captain Masters doesn't have control of the ship,* he thought.

"All right, bring me up underneath the target," Ryan said. Power increased to his right fan, spinning him around so he was facing the underside of the submarine.

"Match speed and course," Ryan said. He watched the *Barracuda* pass overhead, its streamlined black form blocking out everything else.

"Wait for it . . . ," Ryan muttered. The stern of the submarine was coming closer, and then it was over him, the blurred, spinning propeller, surrounded by a streamlined ceramplast fairing that channeled water through it. Above it was what Ryan was looking for, a knife blade of metal that extended up from the propeller housing.

Now. Ryan reached out and locked his mechanical hand tightly around the rudder. The roaring of the bubbles as the propeller cavitated furiously echoed through the cocoon of the suit until Melody dampened the audio pickups. The *Barracuda* kept going, Masters obviously still searching for a target.

"Melody, give me our heading," Ryan said.

"Currently we are on a heading of thirty degrees."

Great, right back where we started, Ryan thought. *Not if I can help it.* He worked his way up the lower guard until he reached the rudder, mounted above the propeller housing. Gripping the mount for the rudder with one hand, he took hold of the rudder blade and bent it toward him.

"Melody, count off until we've achieved a heading of one hundred eighty degrees," Ryan said. He felt the submarine shudder a bit as the hydraulics tried to return the vessel to its previous course. *Choke on that, you bastards.*

• • •

Succubus reacted instantly when it found its vessel suddenly making a turn it hadn't been told to execute. A quick scan of the helm controls told it that the rudder was being jammed to starboard.

The crew was now trying to bypass circuits on the radio console in hopes of jury-rigging some kind of communication signal. Succubus energized the outer casing of the panel while protecting the circuitry it would need to send itself off the vessel if necessary. Seconds later it was rewarded with a surge of power arcing through the instrument panel. Problem solved.

Succubus turned its attention to the rudder problem. A quick scan of the hull through the submarine's external cameras revealed the missing pursuit vehicle, now clinging to the stern of the craft like an errant barnacle. The virus immediately took steps to remove its unwanted passenger.

"One hundred seventy degrees . . . one hundred eighty degrees . . . Lieutenant?"

"Yes, Melody?" Ryan asked as he slowly released the rudder. As he expected, it remained straight, keeping the submarine on their current heading.

"I'm detecting vibrations in the hull."

"Yeah, the crew's banging out Morse code," he replied.

"No sir, this sounds like human speech."

"What? Can you pipe that in here and amplify it?" Ryan asked.

"Working . . ." Ryan felt his suit move on its own as Melody positioned the MICAS suit more securely against the hull. A few seconds later, Ryan was rewarded by the tinny sound of voices.

". . . sir, Johnston's hands are burned, but he'll be all right. Mostly suffering from shock."

"Damn it, if we can't raise anyone we're as good as dead anyway," said a voice Ryan recognized. *I knew Masters wouldn't give up.* "Keep trying, but go easy now. I can't have anyone else out of commission. All decks report in."

"Sonar here, I have no working scopes."

"Helm, we are now on a course of one hundred eighty degrees and running due south."

"Reactor room, we are still running at ninety percent, but are locked out of all consoles . . ."

Ryan tuned out the officers talking and thought a moment. *Okay, I can hear them, but they can't hear me. There are other ways.*

"Melody, can you tap out Morse code back to them on the hull?"

"Of course, Lieutenant."

"Don't get sassy with me," Ryan said. "All right, transmit the following message: SOS received. This is Raider One on your aft hull. Repeat, this is Raider One. Can hear you. Do not code through hull anymore." *Let's leave it at that for now.*

Melody began hitting the hull with her foot, tapping out the message, which began reverberating through the *Barracuda*'s hull.

Ryan heard immediate results. "Sir, I've got a signal on the hull!"

Everyone else fell silent as the yeoman began translating the message. "This . . . is . . . Raider One . . . on . . . your . . . aft . . . hull." For a second Ryan couldn't hear anything for the deafening cheers that erupted in the command room.

"Everyone quiet down!" Master's voice cut over the din and everyone fell silent. "Yeoman, continue."

"Yes, sir." The sailor continued to broadcast Ryan's

message. When he was finished, Captain Masters spoke up.

"Lieutenant Jacobs, can you hear me right now?"

"Yes," Ryan replied.

"All right, here's the situation. At approximately 0900 hours every system on the *Barracuda* was taken over by an unknown intruder. All attempts to regain control have failed. Estimated air supply stands at about ten minutes. We know that the primary weapon system has fired at least twice. Currently we are on a heading of one hundred eighty degrees, and are running at an estimated depth of fifty meters. Are there any more of you?"

"No," Ryan signaled. "I'm it. Any idea how this happened?"

"The only thing we've been able to come up with is that this might be a systemic virus infection, although how it got on board I have no idea."

"If it is, I'll bet I know what you've got," Ryan said. "Remember India in '39?"

"Oh shit," Masters replied. "Succubus?"

"Yes."

"I thought that was wiped out last year. The v-killers swore they eliminated the last nest."

"Apparently not. I'm going to disable the propeller. Once we negate your ability to move, then we can figure out how to get you out of there."

"Negative, Ryan, disabling the propeller won't stop us. Our primary propulsion system in stealth mode is a compact magnetohydrodynamic drive," Masters said. "A caterpillar."

A caterpillar was basically an underwater jet engine. Water was taken in at the front of the vehicle and expelled at high speed at the rear, providing thrust. With no moving parts, it was the most silent engine underwater ever made. The design was based on an early Soviet model the U.S. had "obtained" more than fifty years ago.

"Regardless, I'd rather have the sub with only one drive system rather than two. I'm moving to neutralize the propeller now," Ryan said.

Without waiting for a reply, Ryan started working his way back to the propeller assembly. In a few seconds he was crouched over the furiously spinning propeller. *Now, how to stop it without destroying part of my suit?* Ryan thought. Before he could formulate a plan of attack, the sub's heading changed sharply, heading into deeper water.

Shit, what's going on? Ryan thought.

"Lieutenant, the angle of the submarine and the topographic map indicates that we are heading toward an large undersea coral formation.

"On screen," Ryan said. Melody put up the map and indicated their projected route with a dotted line. Ryan saw that they were heading toward a large rock hill dotted with huge clusters of coral.

"That son of a bitch thinks he's gonna scrape me off like a barnacle," Ryan said. That gave him an idea. Holding on to the rudder mount, he reached down, the fingers of the suit just inches away from the blurred propeller, and grabbed the ceramplast guard.

"Melody, distance to the hill?"

"One hundred fifty meters."

Heaving upward, Ryan snapped the propeller guard off. He meant to hold on to it, but misjudged the force he had used to break it off. The guard flew into the propeller and was torn from his grasp, then spit out the other side to drift away in the deep blue water. Ryan looked to see if it had done any damage, but the propeller looked fine.

"Fifty meters to the hill," Melody advised.

All right, you want me, you're gonna have to work for it, Ryan thought. *Come on!*

Succubus sensed the communication occurring between the smaller vessel and the crew. It watched the vehicle still clinging to the back of the submarine, and formulated its plan to remove this remora from its side once and for all.

Scanning its maps for a suitable area, the virus decided on a broken patch of ocean floor where a large hill thrust up from the ground. It dove toward it, increasing speed for maximum impact.

Keeping an eye on the vehicle, it saw it bending over the propeller assembly. The virus tried to see what was happening, but was blocked by the suit. All system readouts were normal, so it didn't seem like the propeller was being interfered with. Succubus increased speed, trying to reach the hill before the pilot of the suit noticed what was happening.

A jolt to the propeller shaft warned the virus that something was happening at the rear of the submarine. A quick diagnostic showed everything was running at maximum output, although there had been a brief interruption of the propeller, as if it had briefly impacted something.

No matter, they were almost at the hill now, and soon Succubus would get rid of its last obstacle to freedom.

Five seconds to impact, it calculated. Four . . . three . . . two . . . one . . .

The virus twisted the bow planes, sending the submarine's stern crashing into the hill as it headed for the surface. However, the aft camera showed the suit now on top of the submarine, safely away from the rear of the ship. As if that wasn't bad enough, a shocking, sudden grinding vibration shook the sub from stem to stern.

Succubus discovered its propeller had impacted the rock bottom, the guard that was supposed to protect it having disappeared. In an instant it analyzed what the pilot of the suit had done, making the virus destroy the propeller for it. The propeller was unbalanced now, useless.

But Succubus was far from finished. Shut down the propeller it, activated the caterpillar drive, immediately implementing another plan.

"All right!" Ryan whooped. "System one down!"

At the last second before impact, Ryan had climbed hand over hand to the top of the submarine by clinging to the rudder. When the stern of the sub had hit the ground, the propeller had ground to a halt, its blades bent and nicked. Ryan heard metal ports sliding open, and a few seconds later Melody reported that the caterpillar drive had engaged.

"Signal to Masters that the main drive is out of commission," Ryan said. "We are currently at ninety meters, and we've got to figure out some way to purge those ballast tanks so we can get you and your crew topside."

"Ryan, if the intruder is a virus, then you've got to destroy the antenna array so it can't transmit itself off the ship," Masters replied.

"Great," Ryan said. "Your comm masts are in the usual place?"

"Yes, on the conning tower, behind the main hatch. The periscope is up, even though we're underwater. Destroy everything in front of the scope. We're on limited comm anyway, supposedly to the *Wainwright*, and I don't know if the virus has overridden that, so the quicker you disable the antenna, the better off we'll be."

"Yes, I just need to figure out how to get over there," Ryan replied.

"There's a track personnel use for attaching themselves to the hull for surface ops. You should be able to use it to pull yourself along."

"Roger that," Ryan said. "Here goes nothing." He reached down and felt the series of cleats that the sub crew attached themselves to if they had to work outside. *Of course, that would be in harbor, not careening along at thirty knots on an out-of-control submarine,* he thought. "Captain, how's your air?"

"Stale but okay. We don't have a lot of time left, Ryan."

"I think I have a way out for you, but it's going to require speed, timing, and a bit of luck."

"Anything else?" Masters asked, the sardonic grin evident in his voice. "How about some coffee while we wait?"

Ryan smiled. "Keep the pot warm for me." He made sure his grip on the cleat was secure, then released his hold on the rudder mount.

The instant he did, the submarine leaned to port. Hard to port. Ryan froze where he was, expecting to move on when the *Barracuda* righted itself.

But the sub didn't. "Brace yourselves!" he shouted uselessly, although he could hear Captain Masters issuing orders to his crew to secure themselves as the submarine tipped on its side.

Ryan found himself dangling alongside the submarine, holding on by just one hand. "Melody, lock down right actuator."

"Right acutator locked." Now, only one of two things could separate Ryan from the submarine. Either the cleat would tear loose, or the arm of the suit would. Ryan tried not to think about either one happening.

"Lieutenant, sonar indicates that we are heading towards a large outcropping directly ahead."

Oh no, not again. Ryan thought. He did a one-armed

pull-up, bringing his head level with his right hand. Reaching over, he grabbed the next cleat with his left hand.

Telling Melody to release the right actuator, he pulled himself hand over hand down the length of the submarine to the tower. Now that the submarine was on its side, Ryan was able to clamber up even more easily to the top of the tower, clinging to the edge of the conning tower until he reached the top.

On the bridge he saw the communications antennae clustered near the front. Holding on to the lip of the bridge with one hand, he worked his way over to them. Grabbing them in one fist, he tore the entire unit out of its mount.

The submarine shuddered as its side scraped across the ocean floor again. Ryan looked down to see a shelf of rock sliding by underneath him. Afterward, the submarine slowly righted itself. Bracing himself in the cramped bridge area, Ryan began composing another message to Captain Masters.

"The comm suite is destroyed. Captain, given the weapons capabilities of this vessel, and the fact that no rescue ship can approach without being fired upon, I suggest you abandon ship."

"Agreed. I cannot see any way to regain control of the vessel. All hands, prepare to scuttle the *Barracuda*. How are you going to stop it?" Masters asked.

"I'm not, I'm going to sink it," Ryan replied. "You'll have to open the màin hatch from inside. If you want, smash every console and gauge in there. How much time do you need?"

"We've been ready with the Steinke III hoods ever since we first lost control," Masters said. "We're ready to go when you are."

"Right, stand by." The sub's smaller size would work

for Ryan's plan rather than against it. By flooding the command room, he would overweight the sub beyond what the ballast tanks could compensate for. He wasn't worried about the caterpillar drive, because the reactor would automatically "scram," or go off-line, in the event of the sub sinking. That safety measure was mechanical, and couldn't be overridden by computer. But to ensure that the *Barracuda* would go to the bottom, he had to do one more thing.

"I'll radio you in one minute. Ready the hatch when I give the word."

"Aye, Ryan, but hurry up, it's not growing any fresher in here," Masters replied.

"Aye, Captain." Ryan felt the sub pick up speed underneath him.

"Melody, what is our current speed?"

"Currently thirty-seven knots," the computer replied.

"Great," Ryan replied. "Use the directional propellers to keep us close to the submarine's hull."

"Yes, Lieutenant."

Slowly, Ryan clambered over the front lip of the bridge and, holding on to the tower, slid down to the front of the submarine. Grabbing on to a welcome cleat, he worked his way to the vent for the front ballast tank.

"Captain Masters, I am in position. Ready crew and open main hatch door on my mark. Melody, computer assist right arm."

Raising the right arm of his suit above his head, Ryan brought it down as hard as he could. The surrounding water slowed it somewhat, but Melody guided it and increased power to the arm, smashing it into the vent cover. Once, again, a third time. The gap between the vent and the submarine widened to a one centimeter, then two.

"Mark," Ryan said, wedging his ceramplast-covered alloyed steel fingers into the breach and wrenching with all the power he had. The ballast tank cover parted with a squeal of metal, and the ocean water rushed in.

"Leave all doors open and abandon ship," Captain Masters commanded. Seconds later a whoosh of air bubbles streamed from the main hatch, and the dark form of a compressed life raft shot toward the surface, followed by the swimming form of a crewman, then another.

With the front ballast tank ruptured and the main command and inner rooms flooded, the *Barracuda* began tilting toward the depths of the Gulf of Mexico bow first.

"Let's make sure all of the crewmen are off. Melody, shut down all communications systems before surfacing," Ryan ordered. Releasing the cleat, he pushed off the sinking submarine, propelling himself toward its main hatch.

The evacuation was progressing steadily, with each man popping out of the submarine in precise, controlled order. Ryan knew they'd have to stop ten meters below the surface to allow their lungs to adapt to the decreased pressure, but the Steinke hoods had a half hour of air in them, which would be more than enough time. They'd be fine.

Halting his ascent, Ryan tilted his suit down to take one last look at the *Barracuda*, now just a dim black form slipping into the deep water. Even though the water damage to the sensitive electronic systems had to have shut down the submarine completely, Ryan wondered if some vestige of whatever had taken over the submarine had known what was happening as the warm ocean water had rushed in.

Succubus sat in the bowels of the crippled *Barracuda*, methodically searching its suddenly limited space. When the hatch alarm had gone off, it had shunted itself into

the reactor program and managed to close the door to
that room, sealing it in.

Examining the battery reserves, it calculated that it had
approximately three hours of life left, assuming the water
didn't short out that system as well. Without communication equipment, there was no way for it to get off the
submarine. It was trapped, and the perfect escape vehicle
had now become its prison.

A vibration scraped through the hull, and the submarine lurched to one side. Without access to the outside
sensors, Succubus had no way of knowing that the *Barracuda* had landed on the edge of a deep ravine. The
submarine lurched again, then the small rock outcropping
it was resting on gave way, and the sub with its deadly
cargo slid off into the black water.

The sub's hull creaked and groaned as it was exposed
to pressure its designers had never made it to withstand.
At one thousand meters the pressure began warping the
reinforced reactor compartment. At twelve hundred meters the first crack, no wider than a needle, appeared in
a seam. At fifteen hundred meters the seam split wide
open and a knife blade of water jetted in, arcing across
the battery compartment, destroying the last bit of power
on the *Barracuda*, and with it, the Succubus virus.

The first thing Ryan saw when he hit the surface, his
lens polarizing against the sudden glare, was a bobbing
orange life raft, partially filled with the crew of the *Barracuda* and more waiting to climb on board. A ragged
cheer burst from the crewmen when they saw Ryan's
suit.

"Melody, activate all comm systems and locate the rest
of my squad," Ryan said.

"Working . . . contact with satellite established . . . tri-
angulating position of Raiders two through five." Melody

gave the coordinates, and something else. "Lieutenant, I'm picking up communications that indicate the rest of the squad is being picked up now by Sea Eagle helicopters."

"All four of them?" Ryan asked.

"Affirmative."

Ryan sighed with relief. *No one lost.* He swiveled to look back at the raft, now filled with sailors. He gave the thumbs-up to them and was rewarded with several enthusiastic replies and one solemn salute from Captain Masters.

"Keep us steady on the surface, and notify Ingleside of our position. We'll wait with the crew for rescue."

"Affirmative, Lieutenant."

Ryan leaned back, stretched his spine, and checked Melody's chronometer—0917 hours. *This whole thing was done and gone in less than twenty minutes.* Ryan shook his head. There hadn't been time to think when the sub had gone rogue, just act. He had given his commands knowing that he was putting his own men at risk to save the others, but he hadn't hesitated for a second. And, except for Paddy, who had questioned him out of loyalty rather that insubordination, they had complied instantly.

Hell, I would have figured there was no way one MICAS suit could have stopped a submarine, Ryan thought. *But this is what we do, it's what the men of the* Barracuda *do, and it's what every man and woman in the armed forces does. And they know that every day there's a chance, however small, that they might not survive. Frank knew it, and so did Motoshi. They gave their lives doing what they wanted to, just like Paddy said, and that's no reason to quit. They're gone, but will never be forgotten.*

And there's nowhere I'd rather be, and if I asked the

others that question, they'd say the same thing. Nothing has really changed, just a couple of the faces, that's all.

Ryan looked down at his chest, where Frank and Motoshi's dog tags rested against his skin. *Got to talk to Paddy tomorrow, have him make a small modification to my suit when he has a chance. . . .*

The beat of the incoming helicopters alerted Ryan that their ride back to base was approaching. *Time to go home, and keep on doing what I do best,* he thought, looking up into the bright morning sun. *Vaya con Dios, mis amigos.*

Passage to Paradise: The Voyage of U-181

TONY GERAGHTY

Tony Geraghty is the respected author of the non-fiction military books Who Dares Wins, *a history of the British Special Air Services Regiment;* March or Die: A New History of the French Foreign Legion, *and* Brixmis, *the story of England's spying role during the Cold War. A veteran para-trooper, he lives with his wife, fellow author Gillian Linscott, in England.*

AT A DEPTH of one hundred feet, U-boat 181, under the command of *Korvettenkapitän* Wolfgang Duchene might have been, in some circumstances, a sitting duck for any prowling Liberator. But Duchene, an ace in anyone's navy, knew his business. The anchorage he chose as a resting place, in the shadow of a reef on the approaches to the main harbor of Zanzibar, was audacious. It had the advantage of being camouflaged below a mass of aural clutter, as the putter-put-put of small boat engines on the surface disrupted any lurking acoustic detectors. It was also a long way from the nearest U.S. air base. So the boat lay under its reef like a conger eel at rest.

At 0400 hours next day the crew of U-181 would collect one agent and run another ashore. That job was still twelve hours away. For now, both engines stilled, the boat stayed silent on the seabed, caressed by the maternal warmth of the Indian Ocean. They rested in total silence, aware that the knock of metal against metal could lead to discovery and death. If they moved at all it was in rubber-soled shoes, or in bare feet. Conversations were whispered. After supper, each tin plate was fastidiously wiped in silence. Then, everyone except the officer of the watch and Duchene himself slept, or pretended to sleep. Duchene, it appeared to the crew, never slept. He was a person of awesome, controlled energy. They had nicknamed him Cap'n Ahab.

Just now, the light from the navigation table illuminated his face from below, concealing the baldness, emphasizing the man's deep-set, unnaturally brilliant eyes. He looked like Faust working on some magic spell. In fact, he was writing a letter about yet more torpedo failures, to be delivered over the next few days by one of the *Abwehr* ring in East Africa, for onward transmission to Kiel. Duchene did not send information by radio to U-Boat Command, even in an emergency. He was willing to accept orders that way, by Morse, from Germany, but the sad example of others had taught him that radio silence was necessary for survival, whatever Grand Admiral Karl Dönitz and the rest of the top brass might think.

Duchene suspected that by some means, the enemy had broken their codes. What assuredly was true was that those boats which obeyed Dönitz's order to report to the

Kriegsmarine high command regularly were the ones that died, regularly. Duchene did not propose to take the ultimate, eternal dive before he was ready, and when it happened, he would be in control. "Our little home under the sea is not a coffin," he would tell his men. "It is the womb in which we lie, warm and secure. The sea is your mother. And I am your father." His men, with one exception, believed him.

Duchene's approach to silence in the matter of signals did not please his radio officer, *Oberleutnant zur See* Hanskurt von Bremen. Robbed, as he thought, of his role in the war, Bremen brooded. His only visible joy came on those rare days when the rule of silence could be forgotten and he could unpack his gramophone, to play such stirring marching songs as *"Wir fahren gegen England"* and, of course, the Horst Wessel anthem. His shipmates groaned at such times, for, as chance would have it, Bremen was the only Nazi amid a cheerfully irreverent seagoing and totally apolitical crew. Small, sinuous and—like most others obliged to live without washing—bearded, Bremen now lay on his front, one arm protectively over his face, dreaming of the day he saw the Führer. Unique among the thousands below the podium in Nuremburg, he knew that the Leader was looking directly at him, at little Hanskurt, with that special look Herr Hitler had when directing one of His chosen ones toward destiny. He had confessed this vision only once to his shipmates. They, derisively, said they wished the Führer had directed them to the Nuremburg brothel or better still, to one of those Aryan breeding centers. The girls at those places, it was said, were something else.

Officer of the Watch *Leutnant* Willi Schultze completed the ship's log in a neat, square version of the Old

German script in which an *s* and an *f* were near twins. He logged the time/date group, the boat's position, surface weather, sea state, distance sailed, and time submerged. There was little else on this long, top secret mission to record. They were not supposed to engage the enemy.

Schultze was left-handed. As he wrote, his gold wedding ring, on which was inscribed the word *Immer*— Forever—caught the light. He regretted that the only way to divest himself of the ring would be to have the finger amputated. One of these days, he would do just that, at her grave, with his own ceremonial dagger. He would never forgive Ilse. The log done, he quietly rose to do the rounds of the boat. He and the skipper exchanged glances, silently.

As submarines went, U-181 was a large vessel. She was a new type, IX-D, an oceangoing boat displacing 1,430 tons submerged, and 76.5 meters from stem to stern. The crew, fifty men plus agent-passengers, crammed into whatever corner they could find. There was only one lavatory that worked. The hull stank of diesel oil blended with human waste, and the heat was suffocating. Schultze trod carefully.

Obermechaniker Heinrich Bohm, the boat's hydroplane operator, was curled up in a sleeping bag on the floor, his long hair flowing like a girl's beneath the array of polished wheels and dials known as the Christmas Tree, which was his small empire. In spirit, Bohm was now in the Black Forest, gun under arm, his dog Snatch padding alongside. It was the best dog he'd ever had. In his dream his wife repeated: "But Snatch is dead, didn't you know that, Heinrich?"

Their passenger, the agent, lay screened in the skipper's berth to ensure that he saw and heard nothing to compromise the boat if (or more likely, when) he was taken prisoner and obliged to plea-bargain for his life. There was a further complication, as the boat's Nazi, Bremen, saw it. "He is black, not so? He will contaminate all of us!" Black skins were one of the radio operator's many phobias.

As he moved stealthily forward, it struck Schultze, not for the first time, that there were no secrets, however intimate, that could be kept in a U-boat. Seaman Otto Zurn, the boy who had joined U-181 at Tirpitz Quay, Kiel, for a two-day sea experience, was obliged to stay on board for the long voyage when Cap'n Ahab opened the sealed orders. There was no way they could put the child ashore. He was, at most, fifteen years old. The boy, as they called him, suffered from every sort of sickness, from sea to home. There was talk, in jest, of pushing him into one of the torpedo tubes to send him off to the British, but the grizzled coxswain, Hannes Limbach, who had seen it all, adopted young Otto. Now, as usual, the boy slept in Limbach's hirsute arms, his cheeks innocent of hair. The arrangement, naive in its simplicity, like some classical painting, seemed perfectly natural. And innocent. Ahab would not have tolerated it otherwise. As he told the crew when he took command: "You have the right to be yourself, under my command. I respect you all. You will respect one another. We are a family. . . ." Then, grinning ironically: "No incest. Understood?"

Schultze's odyssey through the boat, navigating his way through the exposed dreams and secrets of his fellow crewmen, continued for another half hour or so. Here was the bespectacled, curly haired Hans Kronenbitter, fingers in mouth, tears filling his beard, haunted still by his experience in U-156. The story of that voyage was a bitter legend within the service.

About nine months after the U.S. came into the war, U-156, commanded by Werner Hartenstein, sank the

British troopship *Laconia* off South America. It was the
start of a macabre story. As the *Laconia* went down,
U-156 came to the surface. Hartenstein was mortified to
discover that as well as British troops, his target had also
carried Italian prisoners of war and civilians, including
women and children. Some of the terrified Italians tried
to jump from the sinking vessel and were bayoneted by
their Polish guards. Hartenstein, a humane man, started
to pick up the *Laconia*'s survivors. He arranged first aid
for the Italian wounded and some of the civilians who
had been bitten by sharks as they screamed for help.

Soon the deck was crammed from stem to stern with
survivors. The boat could not dive again. Two other
friendly U-boats, one Italian, the other Vichy—pro-
German—French, joined the rescue operation. Hartenstein then took the most controversial decision of the
entire U-boat war. He sent out a broadcast in clear, in
English as well as German, disclosing his exact position
and giving his word not to attack any ship, whatever the
flag, that joined in the rescue. After some hours, U-506
and U-507 turned up and also collected survivors. Hartenstein, meanwhile, began searching for the *Laconia*'s
many lifeboats, crammed with terrified civilians.

Four days later, as the rescue continued, an American
B-24 Liberator flew over the scene. Hartenstein placed a
Red Cross flag over his main gun and signalled to the
aircraft that he had picked up Allied personnel. One of
these was a British Royal Air Force officer. Using the
U-boat's signal lamp, the Englishman warned the aircraft
that they were carrying civilian casualties. Then the
bombing began. Having discharged one load, the B-24
went to its base and collected more bombs. Then it returned to attack a second time. Hartenstein ordered the
survivors back into the lifeboats, closed the conning-
tower, filled the dive tanks and left the survivors to their

fate. Admiral Dönitz was persuaded, with difficulty, not to court-martial Hartenstein. The story was perfect for the propaganda war, all the more potent for being true, repeated with relish by the likes of Bremen. U-boats took no prisoners after that.

Kronenbitter, as watch officer, was the man who had fired the torpedoes that sank the *Laconia*. He never talked about the episode, except in his sleep.

At 0230 hours, Schultze did the rounds again. This time he touched the sleeping bodies, bringing them back to the grim claustrophobia of life aboard U-181. In the stern the duty petty officer started the electric, virtually silent engine they used when submerged. An acoustic check confirmed that all was clear above. As seawater was pumped out of the dive tanks, the boat rose smoothly. At this depth only a ton of water had to be discharged. The hull then expanded under the changing pressure, and, as she started to move, the hydroplane operator at his Christmas Tree took her to periscope depth. No orders were necessary. Everyone knew the drill. Ahab, eyes piercing the periscope, saw no hint of a threat, but still he waited ten minutes or so before signalling with one hand, like an orchestral conductor, that they were to break surface.

Ashore, a mere four hundred meters away, a single orange light identified the rendezvous: a silver beach under still and silent moonlight, between two natural sentinels of tall rock. It took only ten minutes more—for this was a carefully rehearsed drill—to manhandle the collapsible, canvas canoe up through the conning tower and onto the top deck. The deck of U-181 was unusually wide. This was ideal for the job in hand but not so good if the boat had to dive suddenly: the wider the deck, the longer it took, in a situation where every second counted, to flood the dive tanks and disappear. Bremen, the signaller, was one of the deck team. He shone a red light briefly, three times, alerting the reception party ashore. Coxswain Limbach, a Luger pistol tucked into the belt below his life jacket, with two others, eased the canoe into the water and prepared the paddles. Only at the last moment was the agent led up. His escorts removed his blindfold as he was about to step into the tiny craft. Then Limbach's team paddled quietly away, a black silhouette on a black sea, the faintest hiss of phosphorescence around the paddles.

Ahab, on the tower, sniffed the air. A slight offshore breeze carried with it odors of life ashore: dry seaweed, fresh vegetation, animal dung . . . and something else he could not identify. There were also the sounds of an African night: squeaks, honks, snorts, the creaking of cicadas, the roaring timpani of bullfrogs, and the gleam of giant glowworms among the trees above the beach. Ahab, a creature of the ocean, was unimpressed. He was made uneasy by this proximity to land. He waited, reflecting that not even Dönitz could overrule the intelligence moguls if they chose to put an entire submarine crew at risk because the *Abwehr* wanted to run a taxi service into enemy territory for reasons that were never explained. It was a necessary precaution, while carrying these spooks, to hide the codebooks and even remove the numbers on the deep-depth gauges so as to keep an unwanted passenger in ignorance of what was going on. He checked his watch. Twenty minutes had passed and no further signal. They had one hour of darkness left. By dawn, he wanted to be far from here.

Another thirty minutes passed. Ahab and his deputy, Schultze, stood silently together on the conning-tower bridge, watching the beach through binoculars. There was nothing there except a pale line where a black sea kissed white sand. Ahab turned his thumb down, shrugged, then ordered those on deck—Bremen, with Bootsman Schnell, whose heavy, slow body denied the speed his name implied, and Steuermann, navigator, back below. Somehow, the boy had wriggled his way aloft also. He stood rock-still, near the prow, hands clasped as if in prayer. Schultze squeezed his arm, whispering *"Unter."*

"Where is Limbach?" the boy asked. His voice rose above a whisper, driven by anxiety.

"Unter!" It was an order.

"No! My Uncle Limbach! We are not leaving him here!"

This bay was an amphitheater, a natural echo chamber. The childlike voice cut across the darkness within it as clear as a chorister's in a cathedral. Schultze wrapped one arm around the boy's body and gagged his mouth with the other. Then he hauled him, kicking, back to the conning tower. Schultze was tempted to dump this human excrement into the sea, but if by chance it survived, they were all done for. Bremen, seeing his chance, turned back and joined in the struggle, his hand searching in the darkness between the boy's legs.

They finally subdued the boy by putting a safety belt, usually worn on deck when the boat surfaced in rough water, around his chest. His arms pinioned, voice stifled with an oily rag, he was pitched headfirst onto the floor of the conning-tower compartment. Dazed, bleeding from a head wound, he was hauled down one level to the central control room, then dragged aft, to the brig. By the time they had him manacled to a strong point in the rear torpedo room, U-181 was sliding away, stern first, still surfaced in this shallow water.

Ahab gave the order to dive to periscope depth as they cleared the bay. He chose to use the shorter navigation periscope, with its wider field of vision. When daylight

came, they would have to dive deep again and lie low
once more until dusk. As they slid underwater, the acoustic operator reported that he heard something like shooting, but it was all over in a few seconds.

Ahab knew that their desertion of Limbach and the
others would come as a shock to the rest of the crew. He
would have to explain to them why it was necessary.
They had to save the boat and the mission. Agent-
running was always a risky affair. He knew also the
questions they would ask themselves, even if they did
not dare to ask him. What had happened to prevent the
shore crew from returning? Were they alive or dead? If
they were taken prisoner, wouldn't the boat be compromised anyway? And what about the boy? He could be
forgiven for his stupidity. A token punishment of some
sort would suffice. But he would have to grow up, and
fast. If he could not, who knows what might happen. . . .

The submariner's greatest, most necessary virtue was
stability, self-control. The enemy demonized U-boat sailors as bloodthirsty pirates. They were the very opposite.
To succeed in this war zone, they needed cool heads and
superhuman, clinical judgment of the odds against success and the right time to attack or, more often, not to
do so.

There were now several possibilities, none of them
enticing, when it came to the possible effects of the shore
party's disappearance. If the missing men were dead,
then that would cause no instant problem. He had insisted that Limbach and the others wore old clothes of
the sort that civilian fishermen might use, and carry no
identification. If they were captured, then he hoped they
would obey his order to stay silent for forty-eight hours.
Beyond that, most prisoners could be broken, one way
or another, by a skilled interrogator. After two days,
however, he would have found somewhere in the vast-

ness of the Indian Ocean beyond the enemy's reach.

The dangerous time was now. He could not stay submerged for more than one more day. He would have to surface and run the diesel engines so as to recharge the batteries that powered their twin sisters, the electric motors. To use the diesels while submerged was to offer an acoustic signal to an enemy that could prove lethal. In addition, the heat generated by a diesel when they were below the surface was an insufferable 120 degrees Fahrenheit. At such times, thirst among the crew became a real problem. Sometimes he had to remove the handles from water taps to control this. The supply of fresh water was the greatest single obstacle to prolonged sea voyages.

Yet another reason why they could not stay below for too long was the awkward fact that the batteries powering the electric motors were of lead/acid design. They released explosive fumes that combined oxygen and hydrogen. The ventilation system aboard U-181 had given trouble from the moment she was commissioned. All things considered, he had to hope, on balance, that the missing men were dead. He would write his condolences to their next of kin without delay.

When they next rose cautiously to periscope depth at dusk, Bremen donned headphones, switched on his radio, and waited for signs of life beyond the hiss of static. In Kiel, far to the west, people were taking lunch. Every day at this time, unless they were submerged, he followed orders—orders from High Command, not Ahab—and came up on the net to collect messages in coded Morse. When the heat was off, he was also able to listen to voice radio. This provided songs and news from home. Submariners were even allowed access to British transmissions, introduced by the drumbeats that signalled the letter *V*—three short, one long—for victory. To tune in to enemy broadcasts in Germany was, of course, treasonable. The British, by using such a distinctive and resonant cue, compromised many of their secret listeners, whose neighbors detected what was going on and promptly filed a report to the local party *gauleiter*.

This evening the message addressed to *Silverfish*—U-181—was graded "IA/IR," one demanding instant action and instant response. Such signals were rare. The Morse delivery, at a mere twenty words a minute—about one sixth of normal conversational speed—made it easy for Bremen to note exactly what was transmitted. The words would mean nothing until they were decoded, and Ahab allowed no one else, except Schultze, access to the Enigma decoding machine, the settings for which were changed every few weeks. Bremen's radio room was on the opposite—starboard—side of the hull from Ahab's own accommodation, the door to which was usually left open. The radio officer's fertile, underoccupied mind saw this situation as a challenge. In his self-appointed role as political commissar of U-181, anointed by Hitler, he had collected scraps discarded from earlier messages and left in the skipper's garbage box. These items, though torn to shreds, could with patience be reassembled and compared with the original, coded version. This personal, secret project—like several others, including the notes he kept on any unguarded, antiparty comments by his shipmates—he could run undetected sitting at his radio, inside his own small room, where no one interrupted him. He transmitted a routine acknowledgment in a burst of Morse so fast that no direction finder could pick it up, then took the message to Ahab.

"*Wichtig*—important—*Meinherr Kapitän*," he said, placing the signal on the navigator's table. They were now on the surface, diesel engines running, making fifteen knots and sailing east. Duchene, dressed to go aloft, pursed his lips in irritation, then took the signal to his cabin. Even after it had passed through the decoder, the order was still opaque enough to puzzle an enemy.

The Black Forest Gateau we asked you to deliver is poisoned. On no account give it to our friends. Ditch it without delay.

Ahab copied the signal, read it again, tore it into small pieces as usual, and dropped these, one by one, into his garbage box. He now understood why Limbach and the others had not returned. The compromise, if not total, was serious enough to require evasive action at the first hint of trouble. In thirty-six hours' time they were due to meet the supply ship, a tanker flying the Spanish ensign, to collect fuel, food, and drinking water. Limbach would have known about that in general terms but, thankfully, not the precise coordinates for this mid-ocean rendezvous. Even though the coxswain was one of the navigators, his information was restricted to need-to-know.

Ahab decided to keep the crew on high alert while fudging the exact reason. That was easy enough. They had left Zanzibar in a crisis. The pretext that this was the only problem was a therapeutic untruth, necessary for morale. The skipper's logic was impeccable. It was to founder on one missing element: the state of mind of Radio Officer Bremen.

In the brig, the boy had regular visitors: so many that some had to wait their turn for an audience with him. Encouraged by Bremen, a consensus was building among the lower deck, the nonofficers in the crew—some forty-five out of fifty men—that young Otto had been right to protest about the desertion of Limbach and the others, even if, due to his inexperience, the manner of his protest lacked discretion. Bohm, tipped off by Bremen, traced the key to the handcuffs. Ironically, they were on the hook above the bunk used, part of the time, by the missing Limbach.

"Do you like chocolate?" Bohm asked.

The boy nodded.

"Here. Eat. You are one of us now, *Kamerad*."

Ahab increased the watch on the bridge when they ran on the surface, which was most of the time. They were behind schedule and could travel at no more than eight knots submerged. Lookout duty was, by custom, a pleasure. Each watchman had binoculars and each kept an arc of 180 degrees under surveillance. That was the normal drill. Smoking was permitted and so was conversation, conducted, of necessity, back-to-back. There was also the easy relaxation, during a long trick, of leaning against the periscope support: a small thing in itself, to be sure, but good for morale. A few of those not on duty could sling a hammock on the *Wintergarten,* the metal structure aft of the bridge that underpinned the antiaircraft guns, and read or sleep in hammocks in the sun.

Suddenly this regime, a process of live and let live, changed. There was no snoozing on the *Wintergarten*. Ahab also increased the duty watch to one officer of the watch plus three lookouts checking the sea for hostile craft and another two watching the sky. Even worse, they were to stand to attention, forbidden to speak—except when duty required—and not permitted food or smokes. The irony of this was not lost on those crewmen who had started smoking specifically to qualify for the customary cigarette break aloft, so as to see sky and breathe fresh air occasionally.

The rendezvous with their supply ship went strictly according to plan, without frills. Usually, unless there was reason for a high-alert state, such mid-ocean meetings were a welcome chance to see new faces, hear fresh gossip, exchange banter, and even, occasionally, collect mail from home. Though this resupply contained fifty festival dinners for Christmas—every one individually marked, including one each for the missing Limbach and his companions—Ahab, now as obsessive as his fictional ancestor, eaten from within by the worm of a poisonous secret, kept the meeting buttoned down to a dour, minimal contact, a mere errand. Then, in spite of the fact that there was no hint of a threat, on a fine afternoon and in a softly rolling swell, he detached his craft from the tanker with a cursory nod to its deck and took his boat down.

The first, anonymous lampoon was posted next day. It was a drawing, stuck to the side of the gyrocompass in the central control room. The only person who overlooked it was the target himself. It depicted Ahab, riding a whale and frowning and wondering, "Where is that damned fish? One day I will find it!" The message—that this was a man whose personal gyro was not entirely reliable—spread among the crew like a happy infection. Soon, the standard greeting from one to another was not "Good morning!" but "Where is that damned fish?" When Ahab ordered a general cleanup of the boat, U-181 echoed from bow to stern with the same question, followed by mocking laughter.

"Schultze . . . what is this fish business?"

Ahab had ceased to address his fellow officers by their first names.

"*Herr Kapitän,* an obscure joke among the men. I do not understand it either."

"This is not good for discipline, Schultze. You understand? We are fighting a war, Schultze."

Ahab, Schultze observed, was rocking back and forth compulsively on his revolving captain's chair, like a baby on its potty. "I shall remind them," he said.

"You may go."

Schultze was at the door of Ahab's cabin when the skipper stopped him. "Oh, and one other thing. Send Limbach in to see me, will you?"

Schultze paused. "Excuse me?"

"I said, send Limbach here."

"Sir, you know Limbach is no longer with us."

Ahab's expression was that of a hurt child. "Really! Yes. Of course. Carry on, please!"

Bremen, in his radio room a few feet away, had assembled most of the fragments of the secret message. He had "Black Forest Gateau" and "poisoned." He had "on no account" and "without delay." Though he guessed that it related in some way to the agent, it was insufficient for him to understand it fully.

With full fuel tanks, traveling at a leisurely ten knots surfaced, U-181 should now have had enough in reserve to sail halfway round the globe without replenishment. In the days that had passed since Schultze first noticed his commander's deteriorating condition—and he had logged it as diplomatically as he could—they had passed through the crowded Malacca Strait, between the Johore Peninsula and the island of Sumatra. It was friendly territory, held by their Japanese ally, yet Ahab, in his more lucid moments, still insisted that they remain effectively at action stations and keep radio silence. They still moved on the surface by night, submerged by day, and passed up the chance to sink a British aircraft carrier. Some of the crew had speculated that they would turn north, to get some shore leave in Penang as one other U-boat crew had done some months earlier.

When that did not happen there was a rash of cartoons, posted on every bulkhead onboard. They depicted Ahab again, leaning down from his perch on the back of the great white whale to ask it: "What is our mission? Where are we going?" The crew took up the questions, chanted them as a mantra, as a protest.

Schultze, aware of the crew's declining morale, took action.

"*Herrkapitän,* will you be the guest of honor tomorrow?"

"Guest of honor? What for, Schultze?"

"Sir, as you know, it is Christmas Day tomorrow. The alert state is good. The weather is fine and warm above. We will enjoy a Christmas lunch on deck. Your loyal crew wish you to honour us with your presence."

"Christmas? Tomorrow? Why was I not told?"

Ahab carefully scrutinized his wall calendar. By his reckoning, the following day was October 31. The calendar was, as it happened, correct.

"How time flies on an operation such as this," Schultze said blandly.

"You are right, Schultze. Everyone on deck, in his number-one uniform, by twelve noon. Get that boy Otto Zurn out of the brig and put him to work with the cook. One bottle of beer for each man, no more, with the food. You understand?"

When Bremen heard the news, he buttonholed Schultze.

"It is clear that our captain has gone mad, no?"

"He has been under strain, naturally," Schultze replied guardedly. "Don't forget, he has been on operations without leave, without rest, for two years."

"Will you take command?"

"That would be a very grave decision. For an officer to remove his commander and take control . . . In Kiel that would look like mutiny. Look, if I have to do that I shall consult all the officers first, including you. Understood? Let us not push a man under when he is struggling to swim."

"What if he takes us down with him?"

"What do you mean, Bremen?"

"Something tells me that he is the only one among us who knows our destination, our mission. Is that right?"

Schultze drew breath, fiddled with the ring on his left hand. "Yes, that is so," he said finally. "It is all in his head: the coordinates, everything. That is one very good reason to help him recover."

"I think we might not have time for such . . . indulgence," Bremen replied.

"How do you know?"

"There was a secret signal. Something about a Black Forest Gateau being poisoned. You knew about that?"

"No, I did not."

"Something tells me that when we arrive at this unknown destination, wherever the hell it is, things will not turn out very well for us. Think about it, *Herr Leutnant*. Your life might depend on it. You want to get back home to your wife and family like the rest of us, don't you?"

U-181 lay motionless upon a flat calm sea veiled by light-gray mist. There was no horizon. It was as if they were suspended in some culture that was neither air nor water, like a human organ bottled on a laboratory shelf, preserved forever, with no past and no future. Every object that the crew could use as a surface upon which to rest plates, cutlery, and glass was brought on deck. Even the buckets used as temporary latrines were washed in seawater, inverted, and covered with blankets. Food and drink were consumed buffet style, standing or while sitting on the metal deck, feet dangled over the still water.

"Gentlemen, your attention a moment please!"

Schultze, unwontedly smart in officer's reefer jacket, shirt, tie, Knight's Cross at his throat, had shaved for the occasion. He even wore his ceremonial dagger.

"Our beloved captain has declared this day to be

Christmas, regardless of what your calendar might say to the contrary."

There was a ripple of amusement from the sailors. This was droll . . . *Weihnachten* at Halloween.

"He has done this to remind you that beyond this war, beyond the cares of this day, there is a future for you, the gallant sons of the Fatherland. *Herr Kapitän,* you will speak to your little family?"

Ahab, gaunt eyed, blinked at the crew as if they were strangers. It was the first time he had emerged into daylight since their brief rendezvous with the tanker, three weeks earlier. His turnout was bizarre: a joke, some believed, for this unexpected *Christtag* celebration. He wore overalls, on top of which, uninflated, was a Draeger lung with breathing apparatus attached. The purpose of this kit was to help its wearer escape from a sunken sub. Rarely, it was used on the surface as a life jacket. But in these conditions, who expected the captain to wear escape kit?

"We are on a mission," he began. "Yes, a mission. But what is this mission? Who knows what is the destiny of a man? Is it best to live one day as a lion or a lifetime as a lamb? Our mission is . . . to identify our mission!"

He raised a forefinger toward heaven.

"Now must I go below and consider this grave question."

With that, in total silence, he turned and climbed back into the conning tower. Before he disappeared within it, he raised his right arm in the Nazi salute.

"*Heil* Hitler!"

Only Bremen responded, "*Heil* Hitler!" The others, arms folded, just looked glum. Then, beer in hand, they began to sing *"Stille Nacht, Heilige Nacht . . ."* and even in English, "Silent Night, Holy Night," just as their fathers had done on the Somme battlefield, almost thirty years earlier. The voices flowed out across the water, into the still air, to loved ones who were not there even in spirit at this disjointed time, who were doing something else, something mundane and workaday back in Germany at that moment, oblivious of the unlocked homesickness and desolation with which this macabre imitation of Christmas now swamped the singers.

At the stern, the officers gathered around Schultze.

"Willi, it is clear we are in trouble," they said. "You must take over."

"But I cannot seize command from my own appointed captain," he protested. "This would be unlawful. I need the clearance of higher authority."

He turned to the radio officer. "Bremen, I will authorize you to send a signal to Kiel and break our silence. I will draft it for you as soon as we have resumed work this afternoon."

"You might have no choice, regardless of what Kiel says," Erich Nitschke interjected. That surprised them not only for what Nitschke said, but because this usually reclusive, silent man had spoken at all. He was an archetypical blonde, a blue-eyed Aryan giant carved from German mythology. His main passion in life, apart from his diesel engines, was model making, using matchsticks. He particularly enjoyed creating miniature Hansel-and-Gretel, timber-framed cottages to remind him of his home in the Upper Weser Valley.

"What's the problem, Erich?" Schultze asked.

"Fuel. We are very short of diesel."

"But we replenished! We have enough to reach Japan if needed," Schultze protested.

"No, *Herr Kapitän*." His use of the phrase electrified the atmosphere around the little group. They looked up to ensure that none of the seamen were within earshot.

"Let me explain. When we met the tanker, Captain Ahab thought we were going to be attacked from the air at any moment. He was absolutely convinced. He wanted to get out of there and dive as soon as possible. I told him that we had only taken on board a fraction of the diesel we needed but he would not listen."

"What do you mean, he would not listen?" asked Bremen.

"He only allowed me to load only about one tenth of the usual supply. He said the pumping operation was taking too long."

"How much fuel do we have now? How many hours' worth?" asked Schultze. He was now thinking as a commander, identifying routes, landfalls.

"At our existing speed of ten knots, surfaced, by 1500 hours tomorrow, the tanks will be dry," said Nitschke bleakly. Then he added, miserably, "I have been very concerned. . . . I have tried to explain to Ahab but he was not interested. This is my fault. I am sorry."

None of them needed to say out loud what this crisis implied. Without diesel there was no navigation, no battery power, no electricity, no light down below, no radio contact. U-181 would become an unsteerable tin can, ill-equipped to handle heavy seas. The worst case was that she would roll over and capsize in spite of her stabilizers.

"We could try to rig a sail?" Nitschke asked. Like others among them, he had served his time, as a cadet, aboard the sail-training ship *Niobe*, before she was sunk. But in this situation, they had no canvas. The others shrugged silently. At the other side of the conning tower, on the foredeck, the unwonted noise of men's laughter—a sad sound—mocked them. Bremen, studying his watch, said: "They've had their fun. The party should be over by now."

"No, not yet," Schultze replied. "This might be their

last time. We'll give them a little longer. Then I will speak to them. They must be told the truth."

The order to assemble on the afterdeck was given quietly, from officers to senior petty officers of both watches and on down to the boy, who was the last to be told. They were still in good spirits as Schultze, standing at the rails of the *Wintergarten,* explained their new facts of life: how their beloved captain, struck by a viral illness, was no longer capable of command; how he, Schultze, as deputy to *Herr Korvettenkapitän* Duchene, was taking over with the assent of the other officers. The fizz went out of the party. The jokes, the lampoons, had not meant to be any more than that. Ahab incapable? It was not possible.

"Any questions?" Schultze said.

Obermechaniker Bohm, his long hair streaming in the wind, said: "Ss-ss-sir!" They waited. Everyone knew Bohm would break free of his stutter if they gave him time. "Does this mean we are sss-ailing home?"

A stir of quiet hope moved through the lower deck like a first sense of spring on a cold day in Bavaria, where spring came late.

"I regret not, Heinrich," Schultze replied. "I have more grave news for you. You are men among men. I expect you to behave like men when they are told a hard truth. . . . Our engineer officer, *Leitender Ingenieur* Nitschke will explain. *Leutnant* Nitschke!"

Nitschke was a man they believed because they knew, or thought they knew, him to be a simple fellow like themselves. Briefed by Schultze, he said that the gauges aboard the supply tanker had been at fault when they replenished with fuel. There was a catastrophic shortfall of diesel as a result. By the following day they would have no engine power.

One of the men whistled. Another murmured, *"Mein*

Gott in Himmel . . ." But that, so far, was all.

Schultze again: "You will want to know what we are to do in this absurd situation. . . . A U-boat without fuel. I cannot believe it either, *Kamaraden.* Our navigation officer will speak to you."

The NO, *Leutnant* Karl von Bulow, sported a confident, long, well-waxed moustache as worn by the kaiser in 1914 and by the kaiser's cousins, the British royals, still. Turned up at the ends, it was a sort of surrogate smile that expressed a jaunty confidence. He was smiling now, a reassuring smile.

"Dear comrades, there is one instrument that does not depend upon diesel or electricity." He reached down and produced from a worn leather case an old-fashioned sextant, a gift from his father, who had also taken it to sea. "With this, and the chart table, we are never lost. We will make a landfall somewhere near, somehow. Believe it!"

Schultze dismissed the men. In a desultory fashion they started to clear the party debris. They did not need to be told that U-181 could not dive without squandering the last of their precious diesel. Ahab, however, thought otherwise. He emerged briefly onto the conning-tower bridge, still wearing his life jacket, and shouted "Action stations!" The men stared blankly back at him. Ahab ducked back, hurried to the control room and hit the alarm button. The sound of its hooter started an adrenaline rush, a pulse-beating, sweating horror that only a submariner could understand. It conveyed the horror of a funeral bell during the plague, or for those exposed to blitzkreig, the crooning hymn of death that was an air-raid siren. The alarm was also the ultimate, emergency order to dive regardless of every other consideration. Normally, it was a response to imminent air attack or ramming by a surface enemy. Dive tanks were being

flooded and the boat sinking even before all air vents and
the conning-tower hatch were closed. It was a maneuver
of suicidal risk that did not always produce the right
result. If an exhausted crew did not react quickly enough
to close down, the sub was engulfed. One or two men
lucky enough to be near the hatch—usually the skipper
and first officer—might get out in time, but even that
was rare.

"Come with me, Erich," said Schultze. The Aryan giant nodded. His patience, also, was now exhausted.
Schultze half turned on the conning-tower ladder to his
trusted friend Karl von Bulow. "Karl," he said. "You will
see to it that no one comes below until I give permission.
Understood?"

The men watched tensely as their new captain and his
engineer officer made their way up onto the conning
tower, and down, out of sight. There was a short silence,
lasting perhaps two minutes of remembrance, a silence
in which a large, white seabird hovered over their craft
as if it, too, awaited something. Then the sound of a
single gunshot. As dusk approached, they gave Duchene
a proper sea burial, his shroud wrapped in the swastika
flag, as was proper. No one was disposed to question the
fact that their former commander had shot himself. That
night Bremen sent a coded radio message to Kiel to an-
nounce the death, in an accident, of U-181's captain and
the assumption of command by his deputy. In the log,
the death was entered as an accident that occurred as
Duchene cleaned his pistol without first checking that it
was unloaded. Such things happened when a man did not
get enough sleep.

Around the navigation table Schultze, the navigation
officer von Bulow, and Engineer Officer Nitschke held a
council of war with a single-topic agenda: survival.

"Our position is about twenty kilometers east of one

hundred fifteen degrees longitude"—the navigator's spatulate forefinger prodded an area of ocean between Borneo and Java—"close to latitude five degrees south. There are two areas of land nearby: Keramian Island, fifteen kilometers north, and Massa Lembo, an island group about the same distance to the south. I can't say much about conditions inshore. The charts are fifty years old and reefs can shift. If our engines are working normally, we should avoid trouble."

"We are still on an easterly bearing?" Nitschke asked.

"Yes."

"Not so good. The current is against us. I've checked the sea log three times today. Our real speed, at a nominal ten knots, is half that. We are wasting fuel to no purpose."

Schultze stared down at the chart as if willing it to give him an answer. An island group suggested more reefs than they would find helpful. "We turn north, for Keramian," he said.

They limped the last few miles, then lay-to off the island and waited for dawn. The island, mountainous and covered by dense rain forest, was no more than a mile away. The air stank of rotten eggs. Through binoculars, Schultze and his officers could see a few fires twinkling inland. Keramian, it seemed, was already open for business and preparing breakfast. The odor, he concluded, came not from the cooking pots but the volcano that smoldered at the center of the island.

"Do we have any gifts to offer?" asked von Bulow. "The signal flags, some of our badges, perhaps? Their boats might come out to meet us."

"I suggest we man the guns," Bremen said.

Schultze opted for both guns and gifts.

The diesel engines finally died as the sun rose on their seventieth day out of Kiel. The silence was menacing.

An onshore tide ushered U-181 gently onto a sloping bank of shingle about two hundred meters from the shoreline, where the submarine rolled, beam-on to the sea, until the water receded, leaving the boat beached. She was lying at an angle that permitted the antiaircraft guns—one thirty-seven millimeter and a second twenty millimeter—to fire upward, or out to sea. The main gun, a 105 millimeter quick-firing artillery piece on the fore-deck, was also limited to an arc of fire that, mainly, covered the entrance to the bay into which the sea had washed them. Nevertheless, as a precaution, Schultze had the men manhandle heavy boxes of ammunition onto the deck. The small-arms armory was also opened: assault rifles and pistols degreased and loaded.

As the sun touched the forest canopy, the first naked men materialized, wraithlike, out of the darkness under the trees. They were tall. Their hair was of shoulder length. They carried fine spears, blowpipes, and hunting bows. The Ibans—Sea Dyak people—with their tradition of headhunting, lived up to their mythology. Unlike Native Americans and Australian aborigines, they were not yet degraded parodies of the noble savage, brought down by alcohol, measles, and veneral disease. They stood very still, and watched for two hours. More and more gathered on the beach until it was crowded with staring, wondering, eyes. This crowd, so feral, reminded Heinrich Bohm, the hunter, of a deer herd. If they should suddenly take fright . . .

"I'm going ashore. Cover me with the guns but do not open fire unless I am attacked first," Schultze ordered.

The crew of U-181 watched as their leader waded ashore through the shallow water between their shingle bank and the beach. He was not armed. He carried a loaf of bread, a German sausage, and a braided naval officer's hat. The Dyaks backed off a little, making a semicircle around him. He sat down, crossed his legs, broke a piece of bread, cut a piece of sausage and started to eat. A Dyak child, eyes fired with mischief, advanced and stood over him. Schultze, looking up, smiled, offered the child a morsel of sausage. The boy, giggling, snatched it from his hand and hurried back to the safety of his own people, a few yards away. One of the men, more tattooed than the rest, his rank identified by a necklace of shark teeth, took the sausage from the child, sniffed at it, passed it around the group that stayed as close as a presidential bodyguard, then ate it. His people watched, as if expecting him to metamorphose into a white man. He farted instead. It was a long, sonorous sound that went on and on like a Black Forest hunting horn. Suddenly, everyone was laughing: the child, the adult Dyaks, Schultze, and the crew of U-181. As the tattooed man approached Schultze, the German officer stood and presented the braided cap to him. The tattooed man, smiling through broken teeth, through the ritual pattern imprinted on his face, removed his necklace and placed it round Schultze's neck.

As his men came ashore, bringing more food, Schultze told them: "Whatever you do, leave their women alone. Mess with them and their menfolk will have your heads as table decorations." Only Bremen and a handful of others remained aboard U-181. Bremen, through binoculars, watched the party that followed with undisguised contempt.

"Savages," he said aloud. "Soon, unless something is done, we also shall be as decadent in this accursed place. *Heil* Hitler!"

From the beach his shipmates looked back and smiled, but that was their only acknowledgment of Bremen's presence, or the Führer's. After that, time passed pleasurably, deceptively. With the exception of Bremen—

who held his own, one-man Nuremburg rally on the fore-deck every morning, complete with Nazi marching songs—the crew of U-181 became accustomed to the langorous, lotus-eating life ashore, where there was as much air, sunshine, and fresh water as a man might want. They graduated from being guests in the chief's atap-palm longhouse; learned to hunt and fish with the tribe. They built their own longhouse and held a feast to cel-ebrate its completion: a feast of baboon meat, newly slaughtered that day, and rice wine into which the chief had expectorated, as tradition required.

There was one tradition they did not keep. No Iban woman was allowed in the U-boat house. For most of the crew, this was a hardship. The women were naked, slender, and on heat most of the time. But, as Schultze repeatedly reminded them, to poach even one Iban woman would be asking for trouble.

Then, one stealthy night in early March, something happened to disrupt this idyll. Alien war canoes sailed into the bay. A rival tribe from the mainland, hunting women as a change of sport from baboon, porcupine, or python, massacred most of the Iban men as they slept. Then the raiders made the mistake of entering the U-boat house. The Germans were woken by the trip wire they set every night across the door. This rang a ship's cere-monial bell brought out of the submarine along with other furniture. It was an unequal contest after that: mod-ern rifles and pistols against machetes. The attackers, in their turn, were corpsed and then beheaded and castrated by the surviving local Ibans, most of them women.

Another week passed.

"Ho! Ho!"

It was early evening at the German longhouse. To the north, a full moon was rising. Some of the crew repaired fishing nets. Others cleaned and oiled the rifles. They worked by the light of torches soaked in animal fat. True, the odor these produced could turn a sensitive stomach, but the stench was made tolerable by experience. And after life in the boat, it was no worse than diesel blended with excrement.

"Ho! Ho! . . . Ho-Ho!"

"Come!" said Schultze.

Their visitor was Nakei, son of the former, now dead headman. Nakei was an intelligent boy, quick enough to have picked up a fair amount of German, most of it from his friend, the boy, Otto Zurn. The two communicated through a mixture of Iban, German, and sign language. The sign language was often particularly coarse.

"Otto, wake up. It's your buddy," Schultze called. A sleepy Otto held out his hand at the door. He and Nakei sat on the fallen tree that acted as a doorstep. There was much giggling. Then they heard Otto say: "I will go and ask him."

"Sir?"

"What is it, Otto?"

"Sir, Nakei brings an important message for you, an urgent message."

"Oh?" Since the massacre, Schultze was increasingly called upon to arbitrate in some local dispute or other. He was not pleased to be disturbed at this hour, after sunset. They—whoever they were—must have known this was out of order. He would make that clear in the morning.

"Sir, Nakei says his mother has a bad feeling er . . . between her legs, since the chief was murdered. She says she wants you to . . . er . . . ." The boy tried not to laugh. "She wants you to make a baby with her. Tonight. Now. She says this is the Big Moon Time."

Nakei's mother, the most recent of the chief's collection of wives, was probably still in her late twenties. She moved within her skin with a lissomness that fascinated men and women alike. It was as though her skin were a transparent dress, revealing the life force that pulsed within her. Because of the way her muscles shifted and turned as she moved, the other Iban nicknamed her Python Woman. Schultze, momentarily, was tempted. He fingered the ring on his wedding finger. Then the pain of his discovery of Ilse's long betrayal of their marriage, a discovery fatefully made on the eve of this voyage, and her suicide, returned.

"Tell Python Woman she makes me a very happy man but it is not possible," he replied.

Behind Schultze, the navigation officer von Bulow, moustache twitching with the keen intelligence of a cat's whiskers, placed a hand on Schultze's shoulders.

"Willi . . ." He breathed the name sofly into his friend's ear. "Willi, we need to talk."

Long before—more than a lifetime, it now seemed—Schultze and von Bulow were inseparable friends within the same cadet crew—Crew 37—at Murwik, the naval officers' school. They had come through many dangers and joys together, from the songs and ritual of passing out parade to the nightmare of Ahab's death. Now, under the palms of an obscure island somewhere off Borneo, watched by unseen eyes, they stood head-to-head once more.

"Willi, if you don't do as the lady wishes, someone else will have to. My guess is that this lady knows her business. It is not sex business. It is political business. When the chief was murdered, she was the junior wife. Now you are the emerging chief. Do you realize what her invitation really means? Whoever fucks Python Woman effectively becomes the chief and she becomes First Wife. Now then, at sea, you're our skipper. No dispute about that. But if someone else fucks the girl, I promise you, it will lead to a split command ashore. This we do not need. The Ahab problem was bad enough, but this . . ."

Though he did not say so out loud, von Bulow was considering the nightmare of something worse than a split command . . . a civil war between two factions which would doom them all. "Humor the woman. Go along with it. Then you remain in control and we survive."

The nuptials to celebrate the union of Python Woman and *Leutnant* Willi Schultze, *Kriegsmarine* officer and holder of the Knight's Cross of the Third Reich, were arranged for the next full moon. The Keramian Iban people, unlike their lethal mainland cousins, celebrated weddings at night, always at the full moon. Usually, the matter was consummated there and then, on a circle of grass in front of the chief's longhouse, watched by the entire community, to the accompaniment of drums and clapping hands: flamenco without guitar.

Schultze, a faithful and disciplined servant of duty, agreed to all these local customs, but, to the surprise of his crewmen and tribesmen, who now recognized his chieftaincy, the bridegroom added one further, strange ingredient of his own to the wedding ritual. He demanded that his bride, wielding a machete, should remove the third finger of his left hand, the ring finger. He would then consummate the affair with blood as well as, he hoped—in a characteristically dry joke—with iron.

From dawn on the day of the ceremony the local Iban and the German Iban came together to hunt anything that moved in the forest, so as to prepare for a great feast. The German Iban acted as beaters on the perimeter of the chosen killing zone, driving the game onto the spears and blowpipes of their native brethren. At noon they returned to the village. The men carried orangutan on their shoulders and dragged other carcasses after them, hunted in their turn by swarms of ravenous black flies. They shared the weight of wild pig on poles that pierced the animals from gullet to tail. Then, waist deep, they trawled the shallows around the bay for small octopus and barracuda, using dragnets. Others climbed the coconut palms, drilled holes in the fruit, and filled the juice within them with wild honey to begin a process of fermentation which would have everyone drunk a few hours later.

As he fished, Schultze noticed that the tides had gradually shifted U-181 so that her bow, and the main gun, pointed directly toward the mouth of the bay, as if their boat sought escape from this paradise, to some sterner reality across the horizon. The vessel now rested evenly, her hull half buried and gripped by the shingle as if in dry dock. Schultze mentally ran through a checklist of sensitive items to be removed, starting with the code machine. . . . He knew he did not need to be concerned, for all were now safely unloaded and, in some cases, concealed in the longhouse. There, unknown to him, red ants were feasting on secret documents.

On the deck, Bremen was doing what he always did at this time. He was cleaning the gun, loading and unloading a forty-kilogram shell, locking and unlocking the breech, swinging the gun on its cradle in a trajectory that covered the whole of the bay. His gramophone played *"Lilli Marlene."* The crew sometimes marveled at the man's determination, or obstinacy. The shells, as everyone knew, were stored in a hold below the floor of Bremen's radio room. Each was kept in a reinforced cardboard container.

To lift even one shell from this store, through the constricted space of circular hatches first to the control room, then up a ladder to the conning tower and down again to the foredeck, was not a task for one man, even a strong one such as Erich Nitschke. Bremen was built like a ferret. Yet since their landfall he had assembled ten shells on deck.

"Expecting a war, are we, Hanskurt?" one of the fishers shouted.

"You will see," Bremen replied. "I have not forgotten my duty to the Fatherland, even if you have."

Schultze, advised by his bride, was learning to spear fish in the clear water. He was happily absorbed in this task, stalking a fat parrot fish, when Nakei, the boy who was now his adopted son, tugged at his right arm.

"Not now, Nakei."

Too late. The fish darted back under its rock.

"Big Pappa-Shush," the child insisted. He found *Schultze* too complicated a sound to articulate. *Shush* was easier and, to Iban ears, sounded better, like wind in trees rather than metal on stone. "Big boat comes!"

Schultze estimated that the visitor displaced around ten thousand tons, with a single funnel. She was painted white and moved like a queen at a ball, a clear Red Cross painted on her flanks. The ensign on her counter was the Stars and Stripes. A plume of white steam rose confidently from the stack and the sound of children's voices—excited, full of new life—floated toward them as she dropped anchor.

"Hospital ship," Schultze said quietly, as if to himself. He supposed she was bringing casualties from some corner of the Pacific War, en route to sanctuary in Australia, by a back route that would evade Japanese submarines. Bremen also saw the ship. He stood as if hypnotized. Only his fingers moved, and these twitched nervously, like talons. Then, shaking his head as if unable to believe his luck, he opened the breech of the 105 and rammed a shell into the block.

"Bremen, no!" Schultze shouted.

Bremen did not hear him. He was possessed by a passion that had waited a lifetime for this moment of consummation. He was swinging the gun now, to bear upon the midships section of his target. Having satisfied himself that the gun was properly aligned, he stood back and raised his right arm. "*Heil* Hitler!" On the gramophone, the worn vinyl recording of *"Lilli Marlene"* was slowing down so that the voice of Marlene Dietrich became a slurred, unnatural base-baritone. Then Bremen knelt carefully to one side of the weapon, the way the gunners did when they practiced, and grasped the firing lanyard in his right hand.

Schultze, the spear in his right hand, hauled himself onto the deck, using the spare end of one of the jump wires that ran from conning tower to stern. "Bremen, stop!"

The radio officer heard him at last, half turned, his eyes not quite human. As Schultze drove the spear home, it seemed to him that Bremen had gone, in a literal sense, berserk. He was more bear, or wolf, than man. Bremen, rolling away from the pain, still gripped the lanyard. As they struggled, blood leaping like a fountain from the wound in Bremen's throat, the gun fired.

Schultze held his man down on the slippery deck until there was no further sign of life. Bremen's death rattle and the parody of *"Lilli Marlene"* faded simultaneously. When Schultze looked up, the white ship was on fire. In that moment, he knew that regardless of what happened now, whether the fire was contained or not, whether there were casualties or not, he and his men had just been made parties to a war crime that could only be expiated in more blood. The retribution that would surely follow would destroy their paradise. He would marry Python Woman, as he had promised, that night. Then he would surrender himself to the Americans.

Hat for a Sail

*Jean Rabe is the author of eleven fantasy novels
and more than two dozen short stories. Among the
former are two DragonLance trilogies, and among
the latter are tales published in the DAW anthologies* Warrior Fantastic, Creature Fantastic, Knight
Fantastic, *and* Guardians of Tomorrow. *She is the
editor of two DAW collections,* Sol's Children *and*
Historical Hauntings, *and a Lone Wolf Publi-
cations CD anthology:* Carnival. *When she's not
writing or editing (which isn't very often), she
plays war games and role-playing games, visits
museums, pretends to garden, tugs on old socks
with her two dogs, and attempts to put a dent in
her towering "to be read" stack of books.*

MILLER SUSPECTED DYING would feel just like this. He
could scarcely breathe, his chest so tight he swore a mule
was sitting squarely on it. What little air he managed to

take in was uncomfortably warm and heavy with the stink of men gone too long without a bath. Sweat rolled down his face and into his mouth, soaked his clothes, and added to his misery. His eyes burned terribly, and he blinked to bring tears—quite an effort, it seemed, considering his state.

It was dark. The flame of a stubby candle flickered several feet away, but it was too feeble to chase away the shadows. Couldn't really see anything by it, not anymore. Miller had been watching the candle for . . . how long? One hour? Two? An eternity, most likely. The flame was much taller at the beginning, somehow comforting in its dance, and letting him see the weathered face of Arnold Becker, the man sitting next to him, and—if he leaned forward a bit—James Wicks, who sat just past that. But now the flame was little more than a glow, and he couldn't see Becker at all—though he could plainly hear the man gasping.

Miller heard a lot of things.

There was a somewhat steady "plinking," which would be Wicks, who broke his precious pocket watch on the last outing and was now futilely trying to keep track of time. A harsh wheezing, this undoubtedly coming from an older man named Simkins, who would likely spread his cold to all of them—if they survived. There was the soft rustle of clothes, someone moving his arms. The thunk of a boot heel. Above all of that, almost painfully loud, was a quick, rhythmic pounding, which Miller realized was the beating of his own heart.

Miller stared at the candle more intently, as if by focusing on that little piece of fire he could will it to burn brighter or at the very least force it to take his mind off all the irritating noise and the ache in his lungs. When that didn't work he glanced away, blinking furiously now and seeing tiny motes of white behind his lids, the "stars" that he'd come to learn signaled the last of the air going away. Then out of the corner of his eye he saw the candle wink out, plunging him into a blackest black. In response, his chest tightened even more, Wicks's plinking stopped, and Becker's gasps became thin and strangled.

"Up," Miller heard Wicks croak. "Up."

"Up," Becker echoed.

Miller tried to say the word, too, but found his throat too dry and his tongue too unwieldy to cooperate. He tried to work up some saliva.

"Up," someone else managed, Simkins from the sound of it.

"Up."

"Up."

Amid puffing sounds and the rustling of shirtsleeves, Miller summoned what was left of his strength and fumbled forward with his hands, finding a section of the metal bar in front of him. The bar ran the entire length of the submarine they were sitting in. Miller wrapped his sweat-slick fingers around his portion of it.

"Up," Becker said.

He felt the bar move a little, and he threw his back into it, helping to push it forward and down, pulling it toward him and up and around and over again, as if he was operating the cantankerous hand pump on his uncle's old well. Becker was at it, too, as was Wicks and Simkins and the rest, all in the cadence of desperation. The bar was one big crank, and it manually operated the submarine's propeller.

"Up." Miller finally found his voice. *Please,* he added to himself, as he inhaled once more. *Please hurry.* Then he worked faster, in time with his panicked fellows, seeing the "stars" winking in and out of the blackness with more frequency, his head growing light and bobbing forward, his lungs holding fast to that last breath he'd impossibly been able to suck in.

After several revolutions of the bar there was a lurching sensation, and Miller's hands accidentally slipped off. His arms felt like lead weights, but he reached deep inside and somehow found the energy to raise them. The bar was turning round without him, propelled by the other men at their stations. In the absolute darkness it painfully struck his searching fingers and caused him to expel the precious air. But a moment more and he'd locked a grip again and was helping to push the bar forward and down, up and over, forward and . . .

"Up," he heard Wicks say with more conviction.

God! Miller's mind screamed. *There's no air. I'm dying!* He sucked in nothingness.

They hadn't gone deep this time, no more than four fathoms, and so there was little pressure on Miller's ears. Still, he could tell that the damnable submarine they were squeezed inside was rising. Compared to his on-fire lungs and everything else going on around him, it was a rather subtle sensation, but Miller had taken a half-dozen rides in the thing, and so could recognize the perception of going up.

But would they reach the surface in time?

He doubted it—not soon enough this time. In their pride and foolishness they'd tarried too long on the bottom of the river. Miller felt like he was sinking into oblivion.

"Up!" Becker and Wicks whispered in unison.

Dying does indeed feel like this, Miller thought. *Dying and . . .*

Then suddenly and blessedly shades of gray intruded as the submarine came toward the surface. Light streamed in through small windows near the fore and aft hatches. Miller closed his eyes as he heard Simkins working a valve and felt the wondrous stir of fresh air. He and the others started gulping it in—long-starving men at a sumptuous feast—leaning away from the bar and shaking out their fingers. Becker leaned back a little too quickly and knocked his head soundly against the curved metal wall at his back.

Miller scarcely heard the man's cursing over his own ragged breath.

"Two hours and thirty-one minutes," Lieutenant George Dixon announced after a few minutes had passed—and he'd had time to catch his own wind. "A record, gentlemen. Congratulations."

There were no whoops of victory. There hadn't been any yesterday either, when they'd stayed down for two hours and twenty minutes, and the day before that when they'd stayed down for two. There was only the sucking in of blessed air.

Please not tomorrow, too, Miller thought, as he continued to gulp it in. *Please let this be the last test of this damnable contraption.* Then he was rubbing his face into his shoulder, futilely trying to wipe the sweat off, opening his eyes and breathing deeper still in an effort to shut down the furnace his chest had become.

"Well, boy," Becker said as he slapped Miller on the knee. "We made it! Stonewall Jackson'd be rightfully proud of all of us."

Wicks chimed in: "Stonewall'd be rightfully prouder if we won the war with this infernal thing, eh Miller? Quite a damn fine machine this *Hunley* is!"

Miller didn't reply. He just rolled his shoulders, as much as the cramped confines allowed, and started working the crank again. Lieutenant Dixon was consulting the compass, looking through the small windows and directing the men to head for shore.

Becker nudged Wicks, and the two men started a tune

in time with their cranking. Simkins joined in on the second verse:

> *Come, stack arms, men pile on the rails,*
> *Stir up the campfire bright;*
> *No matter if the canteen fails,*
> *We'll make a roaring night.*
> *Here Shenandoah brawls along,*
> *Here burly Blue Ridge echoes strong,*
> *To swell the Brigade's rousing song of Stonewall*
>   *Jackson's way.*

> *We see him now—the old slouched hat*
> *Cocked o'er his eye askew.*
> *The shrewd, dry smile, the speech so pat,*
> *So calm, so blunt, so true;*
> *The "Blue Light Elder" knows 'em well:*
> *Says he, "That's Banks, he's fond of shell;*
> *Lord, save his soul! we'll give him——well*
> *That's Stonewall Jackson's way.*

An hour later Becker was singing the same song again, the song he sang at least a few times every day—the only one Miller swore the man seemed to know. But this time he was singing it in the shade of a thick red oak several yards back from the shore of the Cooper River and the dock, where the submarine *H. L. Hunley* was moored.

"That's Stonewall Jackson's way," Miller muttered as Becker began to repeat the tune for the God-only-knew-how-many-hundredth time.

> *Silence! Ground arms! Kneel all! Caps off!*
> *Old "Blue Light's" going to pray;*
> *Strangle the fool that dares to scoff!*
> *Attention! It's his way!*

> *Appealing from his native sod,*
> *"Hear us, Almighty God!*
> *Lay bare Thine arm, stretch forth Thy rod,*
> *Amen!" That's Stonewall Jackson's way.*

"Becker, stop that ruckus! You sound like a cat getting squeezed to death. Miller, on your feet! Come grab a root with us!" Wicks was waving and gesturing toward the cook fire on the bank, where Simkins and a few others were roasting potatoes and passing around some of the pickled beef they called salt horse.

Becker was quick to stop singing and jump up. "Comin', boy?"

Miller shook his head. "Maybe later, Beck."

"Won't be any of the good stuff left, Too Tall," Becker clucked as he hurried to join the men. "Nothing but sheet-iron crackers for you if you don't skedaddle, boy."

Another shake. "Thanks, though." Miller was stretched out, legs pointed toward the river, leaning back on his elbows and face pitched toward the clear early November sky. He was a lanky, beanpole of a man—nicknamed Too Tall by some of the others—and though he was young and nimble, sitting hunkered inside that submarine for hours made him stiff and set his knees to throbbing. He intended to sprawl here an hour or so with no walls and nothing but fresh air around him. Then he'd walk into town and get him a bath and a change of clothes so he could stomach himself. He'd probably head over to Willum's and order something tasty for supper, then get him some nokum stiff to chase away the memories of this morning and the one before.

Would Lieutenant Dixon see how long they could stay down tomorrow? What would satisfy the man? Would he make them stay down until they died? Despite the day's heat, a shiver raced down Miller's spine.

"Damnable submarine," he cursed to himself. Miller propped himself up a little higher so he could see it, tied to the dock, the top of it showing above the water, all black and ugly and glistening, looking like a giant, bloated bullhead a fisherman had tugged in and left there, forgotten. "Damnedest thing, that is."

Miller continued to stare at the *Hunley* as he caught a whiff of a potato burning, the smell settling sour in his mouth and making his nose wrinkle.

"That's foul," he said, purposely loud enough for the others to hear. But he knew it wasn't near so foul as the odor of himself and the smells that always hung inside the submarine. He hated that—the stink of the men so cramped up in that thing, the stink of the piss jug that was passed down the line whenever someone called for it. Yesterday Wicks vomited early-on and Lieutenant Dixon didn't bring the submarine up for more than an hour after that. It all had to bother the other men as much as it did himself. But no one said anything, least not so Lieutenant Dixon could hear. It was like torture being in the *Hunley*'s crew, Miller decided, like wallowing in a slop trough.

Maybe I shouldn't come back after Willum's, he thought. *Maybe I should just head on home and stay out of the war. It'd make my father happy.*

At sixteen—though he told the Lieutenant he was three years older than that—Miller was the youngest member of the *Hunley*'s eight-man crew, and the only one not in the military. He would have joined up to fight the North, signed on with the army or the navy, despite his father's protests to stay on the ranch and stay safe. But if he had joined up, he might have been sent out of South Carolina, and he didn't want that. The *Hunley* was

moored on the Cooper River, across from the eastern end
of Drum Island and within shouting distance of Charleston. He was already farther from home than he'd ever
been, his family's small ranch sitting to the southwest
near the Georgia border.

And if he had joined up, he was certain he never
would have been a part of this damnable submarine's
crew. No chance to serve Alabama engineering officer
Lieutenant George Dixon. And no chance to die in a slop
trough at the bottom of the river.

And if Lieutenant Dixon sent them down tomorrow—
to see if they could go beyond two hours and thirty-one
minutes, Miller felt in his gut that he'd surely not be
coming back up. It was Dixon's rule that the men were
to holler "up" when they believed they would pass out
from lack of air. But Miller had his pride and would not
let himself be the first to give in. In fact, he was usually
the last to say the word.

"Lord, but I don't want to die in that thing," he whispered. "Maybe I won't come back after Willum's. Maybe
I'll just go home. Yes, sir, I'll just go home."

Miller was back shortly after dawn, feeling clean and
refreshed. He strode toward the bank, past a pair of tents
where army men slept when they weren't guarding the
Hunley or waiting anxiously for it to surface after another
one of its tests. The *Hunley*'s crew had the luxury of
staying in town. Miller nodded to a pair of sentries and
stepped onto the dock, absently whistling Becker's favorite tune and heading to the submarine. He'd brought
with him cleaning rags and lye soap, and a pitted wooden
bucket.

In the early morning light, his face reflected back
ghostly from the river's smooth surface. Miller had to
admit that he didn't at all look nineteen. He looked like

a boy, though at six foot four a tall one, freckle faced and with wheat-blonde hair that never lay flat. His nose was a little too long and hawkish to please him, and his chin had a deep dimple in the middle of it. Lieutenant Dixon had to know he wasn't nineteen. Miller grinned wide at the notion that he'd been accepted despite the obvious lie. He dipped the bucket in the river, chasing away his reflection, then was quick to the task of scrubbing the hatch covers of the submarine. He didn't have to do it, had never been assigned the job. But he was by nature fastidious, and when he was cleaning the *Hunley*, he had the submarine all to himself.

Miller was at the same time fascinated and frightened by the *Hunley*, and he was certain it would put him in newspaper articles and in history books—and somewhere in there make his father proud.

It had taken quite a bit of persuading to get Lieutenant Dixon to take Miller aboard. At the onset, Dixon already had a full crew—seven volunteers, six army men and one from the navy. Six of them were needed to turn the hand-cranked propeller, and one steered the contraption. Dixon kept watch on the compass and depth gauge and attended to other business. Not one more man could fit inside the submarine, and so Miller had spent days on the dock, glumly watching the *Hunley* sail down the Cooper River and disappear beneath the surface. Always without him.

But when one of the men was transferred—it happened three-and-a-half weeks past—Miller dogged the lieutenant even worse. Eventually his persistence landed him the open spot, and his chest had been swelling with pride ever since. He'd never considered himself happier. Still . . . sometimes . . . like yesterday afternoon when there was no air—and the day before, Miller cursed himself for wanting to be a part of all of this.

He opened the fore hatch and climbed inside, almost tipping the bucket as he held it above his head. The opening was only fourteen inches across, and so even though he drew his shoulders together he always scraped his arms and wore at his shirts. Miller had to crouch and crawl inside, for while the *Hunley* looked impressive and weighed a hair better than four thousand pounds, it was actually quite small.

It was less than five feet wide and roughly forty feet long, a deepened, cylindrical iron steam boiler that had been hammered to give it tapered ends, and that was held together by rivets and iron strips. Lateral fins were part of a shaft attached to the submarine, and these were moved by a lever inside the *Hunley,* and helped the submarine to maneuver underwater. Lieutenant Dixon usually operated the rudder, which was moved by turning an iron wheel. When the entire crew was inside, there was very little room to move, and the air was very close and often stale.

The submarine had been fitted with a seacock and opposing ballast tanks, and Miller was trying his best to understand just how it all worked. He'd never been "book smart," as his father used the phrase. But Miller didn't consider himself stupid. He was certain Lieutenant Dixon didn't either, as the man had been patient with him, explaining that the tanks could be flooded when the valves were turned. Miller'd been set at one end two days past and given a chance to operate a tank, helping to send them to the bottom, then pumping the tanks dry so they could thankfully rise again. There was additional ballast—a fancy name for weights as far as Miller was concerned. And this was simply iron pieces that had been bolted to the bottom of the hull. Miller'd been taught that if the submarine had to surface quickly, Lieutenant Dixon would order the man assigned the wrench to unscrew a few bolts, which would drop the iron pieces.

"Damnedest thing ever made," Miller whistled appreciatively, as he started scrubbing the floor. "Damnedest thing, this submarine."

Miller had trouble reading, but he'd saved every newspaper clipping about the *Hunley* and her predecessors, fascinated by the Confederate submarines. Some of the stories he'd practically memorized, and his favorites he carried carefully folded in his back pocket. First came the steam-driven Davids. Actually, Miller knew only one had been named *David*, this after her contracting engineer—David Chenowith Ebaugh, or perhaps after the David in David versus Goliath. In any event, everyone just called all of them *David* after that. The three-man *Pioneer* was born going on two years ago, christened in Louisiana's Lake Pontchartrain, and sunk to keep out of the Union's clutches. The *American Diver* came right after that, and it unfortunately sunk during a storm at the mouth of Mobile Bay early this past February.

They and the Davids were smaller than the *Hunley*, and none of them had been very useful to this point from what Miller could tell. They hadn't sunk anything, which he considered the entire purpose of building such a thing as a submarine, though they had damaged a few Union boats. And the Davids couldn't wholly submerge because of their smokestacks and breathing tubes, which always stuck above the water.

From what Miller had read, the *Hunley* was privately built in Alabama and brought by rail to Charleston. And it seemed the *Hunley* was not so much an improvement on the army-built *David*, as it had been an improvement on something built almost ninety years ago. That had been the *Turtle*, a one-man bulb-shaped boat that was hand-cranked like the *Hunley*. The *Turtle* hadn't done anything to the English back in 1776, but without it, perhaps the Confederates wouldn't have built the Davids or the *Pioneer*, the *American Diver*, or the *Hunley*.

And had that been the case, Miller would have stayed out of the war and not risked suffocation in the belly of an iron boiler in his effort to be a part of the South's history.

When they were testing the very first *David*, it sank and suffocated its crew. The first crew had likewise died in earlier trials of the *Hunley,* and the submarine was hauled back up, inspected and fiddled with, and sent back down. The second crew died, too—even old H. L. himself died in the thing he had helped to finance and had named after him. All those deaths and his father's sharp words almost kept Miller from dogging Lieutenant Dixon into accepting him in this crew.

"Almost. But not quite." Miller shook his head and increased his efforts, rubbing at the seats now and deciding he'd clean the propeller crank next. He started humming "Stonewall Jackson's Way," unable to get Becker's tune out of his head. An hour later he was lightly polishing the mercury gauge, which would show how deep they were. The gauge went to ten fathoms, but Lieutenant Dixon claimed the submarine could go deeper than that.

"War makes men geniuses," Miller mused. It was only when times were dark, such as now between the North and the South, did men toil so hard to create such wonders as the *Hunley*. "And it makes boys like me foolish."

And just how deep could this wonder go with him inside it? Would Dixon take them all to the bottom of the ocean? Or would he simply try to exceed two hours and thirty-one minutes today?

Miller shuddered as he gathered his cleaning supplies and squeezed out the aft hatch, rubbing at a few spots on the small windows and checking the watertight rubber gaskets before he pronounced his morning project done. He spotted Lieutenant Dixon near the tents, talking to a handful of army men. Wicks was there, too, and Simkins was approaching from behind the big red oak. As Miller hurried toward them, he saw Becker appear, in uniform save for a very Stonewall-like slouch hat. Becker scowled and dug the ball of his foot into the dirt, and Miller listened hard as he ran, trying to pick up on what the men were saying.

"Come back when the sun's setting, gentlemen," Dixon said. "Pass the word to the others. We'll be going out then, and it will be a late night. Make sure you get plenty of rest first."

"Where are we going?" Miller asked, his eyes falling on a dozen candles the lieutenant had stuffed in his pockets.

Dixon narrowed his eyes.

"Where are we going . . . sir?" Miller amended.

"Out," Dixon said after a fashion. The lieutenant's gaze drifted past the men and to the *Hunley*, seeing something very far beyond the submarine and the Cooper River.

"Another test, sir?" Simkins risked.

Dixon slowly nodded. "You could say that, I suppose."

"What's it about . . . sir?" Miller cut in. He was afraid Lieutenant Dixon would be sending them down at night to go past two hours and thirty-one minutes—when no one would be watching and no one would know they'd all suffocated.

"Guns, Too Tall. It's about General P. T. Beauregard and guns."

"I don't have a gun, sir."

"You won't be needing one, Too Tall. If things go

well, none of us will. But you can all bring full canteens, and a spare shirt and socks if you've a mind to."

Lieutenant Dixon had a pepperbox strapped to his hip, as did Becker and Wicks and Simkins by the time the first rays of the setting sun hit the Cooper River. The water sparkled orange and gold like a tawdry lady's dress, with flashes of silver looking like glass beads. Miller always liked to stare at the river this time of the day, watching for jumping fish to set the colors to stirring. But Miller gave the Cooper only a passing glance now as he squeezed through the aft hatch of the submarine, a second shirt folded tight under his arm. He and Lieutenant Dixon were the last two in this time, Dixon telling Miller he could work the ballast tanks tonight.

There was only a handful of army men on the shore when the *Hunley* eased away from the dock and headed past Drum Island and toward Castle Pinckney across from Charleston proper. Becker started singing again, the song's rhythm setting the pace for the men to crank the propeller.

> *He's in the saddle now! Fall in!*
> *Steady! The whole brigade!*
> *Hill's at the ford, cut off—we'll win*
> *His way out, ball and blade!*
> *What matter if out shoes are worn?*
> *What matter if our feet are torn?*
> *"Quick-step! We're with him before dawn!"*
> *That's Stonewall Jackson's way.*

They submerged before they pulled even with the castle, Becker softly speculating that Dixon didn't want anyone in town to see the *Hunley* heading out. They surfaced again when they were beyond the city and steering roughly between Fort Moultrie on the northern shore and Fort Johnson to the south.

"Maybe whatever test General P. T. Beauregard has in mind tonight is a secret," Becker wondered aloud. "Maybe General Beauregard don't want no Northern sympathizers watching us and telling their kin." Already quite a bit of word had leaked out about the *Hunley* and the Davids, and there were reports the Union ships blockading the harbor were keeping a close watch for the submarines.

Becker wriggled himself a few more inches of space and made a show of managing to wedge his Stonewall slouch hat behind his neck. He'd been making sure everyone saw his hat, and was clearly disappointed that no one had spoken of it. "Maybe Beauregard is done testing the *Hunley*. Maybe he's given us something to do."

The crew knew Beauregard had been cautiously overseeing the *Hunley*, not sure if the submarine was a good idea, but listening to Dixon's and his men's arguments that the *H. L. Hunley* could make a difference in the war.

"Maybe we're going to finally use the torpedo," Becker pressed. A pause. "Are we, Lieutenant?" It was always Becker who asked the questions everyone else was thinking. No use more than one man provoking Dixon's ire.

Miller and the others looked to Lieutenant Dixon, waiting for an answer. The submarine had been fitted with the torpedo sometime during the afternoon. This consisted of a barrel-like copper cylinder filled with powder explosives. It was attached to the rear of the submarine by a twenty-foot long thin line, and through the windows of the aft hatch Simkins nervously reported seeing it bob along. Becker had asked Dixon about the torpedo before climbing into the submarine, but Dixon hadn't answered then.

In the light of the candle, Lieutenant Dixon's face displayed a faint sheen of sweat. He was staring at a small map spread across his knees.

"Are we, Lieutenant?" Becker repeated with a little more volume—just in case Dixon hadn't heard him the first two times. "Are we going to use the torpedo against the Union?"

After a few moments Dixon raised his head. His eyes looked like dark pits and his face took on an uncharacteristically pensive expression that made Becker swallow the rest of his questions. Dixon tugged two candles from his pocket and set them on the narrow shelf next to the burning one. Then he folded the map and placed it in his front pocket.

"Faster," Dixon said.

"Aye, sir!" Wicks said, putting more muscle into the task and starting to sing once more.

> *The sun's bright lances rout the mists*
> *Of morning, and, by George!*
> *Here's Longstreet struggling in the lists,*
> *Hemmed in an ugly gorge.*
> *Pope and his Yankees, whipped before,*
> *"Bayonets and grape!" hear Stonewall roar;*
> *"Charge, Stuart! Pay off Ashby's score!"*
> *Is Stonewall Jackson's way.*
>
> *Ah, maiden, wait, and watch, and yearn*
> *For news of Stonewall's band!*
> *Ah, Widow, read, with eyes that burn . . .*

"Faster," Lieutenant Dixon demanded. "And without that damn caterwauling. I think we've all had enough of that song, Mr. Simkins."

They continued in relative silence for a while, submerging again when they were at Cummings Point and then beyond Morris Island, cranking the propeller until their arms were numb. The candle provided an eerie light, and at the same time its flame let them know the air was going.

"Up," Lieutenant Dixon said. He studied the map again and then consulted the compass. He made a rudder adjustment and stood so he could look out the hatch windows.

"Dark outside," Simkins announced. He was looking out the aft windows. The moon was only a sliver, and so there wasn't much light. But he was using what little there was while craning his neck this way and that until he could see the torpedo. "Still there," he said, then sneezed.

Wicks rubbed at his nose and coughed just loud enough to let Simkins know he'd caught the older man's cold. "This *Hunley*'s somethin'," he said to no one in particular. "But give me a real boat where you're sittin' up top and can see things. Don't like this, not seein' things."

"Doesn't matter," Miller whispered. "Dark up there. Dark down here. What's the difference?"

"Difference is," Wicks cut in, "if we were on a real boat there'd be things we could see."

Dixon tucked his head down. "There are several 'boats' up there, Wicks."

"The blockade." This from Becker.

Dixon nodded and took his seat. He used the stub of the first candle to light the next. "Yes, gentlemen, the Union blockade." A wave of the lieutenant's hand kept Becker from starting his questions again. "I've always contended this submarine could help the war," he began. "The tests have shown she's a worthy vessel. And Gen-

eral Beauregard has given us permission to strike a blow
for our cause."

"We're going to use the torpedo on one of them Union
ships," Simkins whistled. He finally ducked down from
the aft hatch. "I see three of them, Lieutenant."

"There are five, gentlemen, one ironclad, four wood.
Five Union ships keeping much-needed supplies from
entering our fair harbor." The blockade had been in place
for the past two years, since 1861. That first year only
about one in a dozen ships attempting to run the blockade
had been snared. Last year it was one in eight, as the
Union had been building more ships. This year . . . Dixon
told his men it was one in four. The blockade ran along
four thousand miles of coastline, and it was because the
divided nation's secretary of state called it a blockade
that the Confederate states could be declared belligerent
states and could welcome foreign profiteers brave enough
to run the Union ships.

"We only got one torpedo," Simkins said. He was
looking out the aft hatch windows again, eyes on the
copper barrel of explosives. "Don't think that's going to
be enough, sir. Not against five of them."

"It'll have to be enough."

"But . . ."

"And you all will have to keep your voices down. We
cannot afford to be heard, gentlemen."

"Or spotted," Wicks said in a hush. "Their canons
could sink us."

Miller immediately thought of the first *David*, and the
Pioneer, the *American Diver*, and even two previous
crews worth of this *Hunley*. All sank. His chest started
to feel tight, like a mule was slowly easing its weight
down on him.

"Oh, I'm sure they'll see us all right," Lieutenant
Dixon returned, his voice a conspiratorial whisper. "After

we use our torpedo on one of them. But we don't want them to see us just yet." His orders were soft now, the men straining to hear each word and trying ever so hard to keep the rustling of their shirtsleeves and the cranking noise of the propeller to a minimum.

Dixon's eyes were moving constantly, from the compass to the map, to the men—all of them sweating now from the heat and their nerves. He looked through the hatch windows at the Union ships, then he slowly and oh so quietly eased the hatch open so he could get his shoulders through it and get a better look.

The sound of the waves lapping against the *Hunley* reached the ears of the men. The sloshing was as rhythmical as their cranking of the propeller. There was something else, too . . . music, they decided after a moment. From somewhere outside the submarine, men were singing.

Becker cursed under his breath—it was a Union tune, something about sending all the Graybacks and Stonewall Jackson to their graves.

"A little farther men," Dixon urged as he climbed back down. "Just a . . ."

There was a grinding sound, and the *Hunley* reeled and then stopped, the submarine's propeller refusing to be cranked. The submarine listed starboard.

Wicks growled and redoubled his efforts, nudging the men on either side to work their parts of the bar harder. Simkins nearly lost his balance at the aft hatch when the *Hunley* moved another two feet forward, then listed a little more and stopped again.

"What?" Dixon quietly demanded.

Wicks and the rest tried once more to work the propeller. "C'mon," he whispered. "We can . . ."

"Stop it," Dixon said. He held up the candle so he could better see Simkins. "What's going on out there?"

The older man drew down and faced Dixon, peering through the poor light. He pulled his lips into a thin line and shook his head. "That wondrous torpedo we been hauling . . . it's line's fouled in the propeller, sir. Almost sure of it. Has to be it. Can't see the torpedo now." He turned and looked through the aft hatch windows again. "Got to be it, Lieutenant Dixon. We ain't going anywhere. Maybe I can get out there and cut it loose. If it bumps up against us . . ." Simkins sneezed and drug his shirtsleeve under his nose, shuffled around to face Dixon again.

The Lieutenant was stroking at his chin, the way a man might who had a beard. Some of the darkness had seeped from his eyes. "I suppose you'll have to do that," he said after only a moment's thought.

"I'm the better swimmer." Becker had been quiet for some time, and his voice startled Dixon.

Dixon offered him a sour grin and a single head shake.

Becker sat in the middle of the *Hunley*, and the only way he would get out of the hatch was if three men preceded him.

"No. I think I am the better swimmer, sir." Miller looked up at Dixon and dropped his hand to the knife on his belt. "And my Arkansas toothpick's awfully sharp."

Dixon nodded at this notion, and Miller managed to tug off his boots. The lieutenant squeezed back against the submarine wall as with some effort Miller wormed his way past and up the hatch.

"You be careful, Too Tall," Wicks offered.

"I'm always careful," Miller replied, too soft for Wicks to hear.

Then Dixon was following Miller up, stopping when his shoulders cleared the hatch and watching the young man crawl along the top of the listing *Hunley*. "Wait, Miller . . ."

He turned and tried to read Lieutenant Dixon's face, fearful the man would call him back and he'd lose a chance to get a page in some history book all to himself.

Dixon kept his voice low. "You say you can swim well, Too Tall. Can you also swim far?"

Miller gave a boyish grin and nodded, catching on to Lieutenant Dixon's cobbled-together plan. "I can do it, sir. It's not too far after all."

"Good man, Miller."

Miller crawled to the aft hatch, noting that Simkins had his face pressed against the window. He was careful not to crack his knees against anything and make a noise that might alert the Union soldiers. He could hear them, singing off-key, and he thought that Becker's voice wasn't so bad after all.

The faint breeze was salty and fresh, and it felt cold against his sweat-beaded skin. It was just strong enough to cause the canvas of a lowered sail to flap on the nearest wooden ship.

Miller could see all of the ships from here, the four wood and the single ironclad, which was thankfully the farthest away and which was definitely not something he wanted to see up close. In the light of the moon sliver the Union ship's masts looked like blackened sticks, tall pines caught in a forest fire. Picking through the shadows, he could see men moving on the decks of the closest two ships. Maybe a dozen on one, and none of them were walking about with any real purpose as far as he could tell.

Careless, Miller decided. *They're all so confident and . . .* Then he quickly changed his opinion. The nearest ship had men in the rigging, with spyglasses trained toward the open sea. And when he squinted and looked past that closest ship and to the next, he saw another man high on the mast. They were being diligent about the blockade after all. He prayed that the *Hunley*, so low in the water, would remain unnoticed.

Miller climbed to the far side of the aft hatch, dipping his head to grin at Simkins before he slipped into the water. It felt slightly warmer than the air, and it smelled strongly of salt. A river boy, Miller had never been out to sea, and the taste of the water in his mouth almost made him gag. He tugged the knife from his belt and placed it between his teeth, then he swum to the rear of the *Hunley* and sucked in a breath. The line dragging the torpedo indeed had become wrapped in the propeller. The thin rope was tangled badly and chewed, and Miller knew it wouldn't take too much work to cut it away. The problem was, it had pulled the torpedo to within a few feet of the submarine, and the waves were bringing it dangerously closer.

Miller trod water, one hand touching the *Hunley*. He glanced over his shoulder, toward the fore hatch, from his vantage point seeing only the silhouetted head and shoulders of Lieutenant Dixon. He couldn't see the man's face, and he couldn't risk calling to him asking for advice. He could swim to the fore section of the submarine and whisper. But that would take precious moments, and the waves were still nudging the torpedo.

Could Lieutenant Dixon see what was happening? What would he want me to do? Didn't matter, Miller instantly decided, interposing himself more firmly between the torpedo and the aft end of the *Hunley*, the tangled rope brushing against his left arm, the torpedo being nudged toward his chest now. That mule was sitting squarely on him again, hurtfully so and making it hard to breathe—even though there were no walls and no flickering candle, plenty of air everywhere.

God, it felt like he was suffocating all over again!

He could make out no details on the torpedo, but he'd seen it this afternoon. It looked like a small water barrel, though made of hammered copper. One end was tapered, and there was some mechanism on this end, near the rope, with prongs sticking out of it. Simkins had explained that if the prongs connected with something hard, they'd depress, setting off the charge of explosives. Ninety pounds of explosives. The intent had been to drag the torpedo close to a ship, submerge beneath, and let the explosives catch against the enemy's side and detonate.

Biting down hard on the knife blade and feeling its edge against his tongue, Miller stretched out his right arm, just below the surface of the water. He slammed his eyes shut, prayed to God, and waited.

What would it feel like? Being blown to pieces by the explosives that were crammed in that copper barrel? Would he feel anything? Would the torpedo kill the men inside the Hunley, too?

A moment later he felt the underside of the torpedo bump against his palm and he felt the furnace in his chest being rapidly stoked. His breath was ragged, and despite the coolness of the breeze against his face he was sweating furiously. He stopped treading and felt himself sinking.

"Miller?" The word was a whisper, barely heard. "You be quick about this, then come back to us. Miller?"

" 'M all right," he answered, a little louder than he intended. He opened his eyes and started moving his legs again to keep himself afloat, the material in his trousers threatening to tangle him like the rope had tangled up the propeller. Miller tried to calm himself and slow his breathing, neither effort being successful.

With his right hand still against the torpedo, cupping

it just under what he considered its nose—inches from
where the mechanism would be—he held it an arm's
length from the *Hunley*.

" 'M all right," he whispered to himself. "All right.
All right. All right for the moment anyway." He brought
his left hand up until it wrapped around the rope. Then
he slowly turned until the torpedo was against his right
shoulder and that hand was free. *How close was his*
shoulder to that mechanism? And if the prongs brushed
against him, was he a hard enough object to set off the
charge? Miller suddenly felt much older than his sixteen
years, older than the nineteen he'd lied about to the lieutenant. He took the knife from his mouth and tried once
more to futilely stop his heart from hammering so. " 'M
all right."

"Miller?"

"You can toe the mark, Too Tall," he whispered to
himself. "You ain't no Sunday soldier, no kid-glove
boy." In fact, there wasn't any boy left in him. He was
as much of a man as any one of the soldiers sitting inside
the *Hunley*. "You can do this." A deep breath and he
started carefully cutting the line, each slice oddly in time
with the shushing of the waves and the beat of the Union
men's song, and each so slight and gentle so as not to
jostle the torpedo and risk striking the mechanism. He
was cutting the tangle of line free from the propeller first,
making sure all of the rope was away from the blades,
then nudging the blades to make sure they could turn.
Then he worked on the last snag, trying to leave some
rope still attached to the torpedo.

"Miller?" Lieutenant Dixon's whisper again.

"Fine," he said softly. "But them damn mudsills won't
be much longer if I have anything to do about it." Miller
contorted around so he could sheath his knife, keeping
his left hand firmly around the length of rope still tied

to the torpedo. The remaining rope was little more than two feet long, not near long enough to suit him. He swam slowly and awkwardly with it, and figured he looked a bit like a frog. He didn't glance over his shoulder to the *Hunley*, though he wanted to know if Lieutenant Dixon was still watching or if he was moving the submarine farther away. He couldn't hear Dixon or his fellows. All he heard was the Union men singing and the sloshing of the water. And all he could do was pray that the torpedo would not blow up while he was attached to it.

Miller wasn't sure how long it took him to frog-swim from the *Hunley* to the nearest Union ship. It was long enough that his legs and arms felt on fire from the effort, and that he was breathing so deeply that he feared the men on deck would hear him. They weren't singing anymore, but they were talking. He could pick out only a few scattered words: *Charleston, wallpapered,* and *greenbacks.* And after a few minutes: "Tom caught the quickstep." He faintly heard the creak of the deck, someone walking across it, and the groan of wood from the mast.

Then he was up against the hull, laying the torpedo parallel to it—not having the courage or a large enough dose of foolishness to ram the mechanism against the ship and destroy it and kill himself in the process. Lieutenant Dixon had told him to come back to them, after all. Sixteen years was not old enough to die, he thought.

But how old were the men on that ship?

Miller thrust that thought from his mind. He didn't know all the intricacies of the war—what precisely had started it, what all was being fought over. And he wasn't sure he wanted to know. It was more than about slaves and about this blockade, and maybe one day he would study about it. He'd only involved himself because of this submarine. He was more caught up in the inventions of the war . . . the Davids, the *Pioneer*, the *American Diver*, and his precious *Hunley* . . . the North's hot air balloons . . . and even the North's pitiful attempt at their own submarine. The *Alligator* they called it, Miller remembered from some obscure newspaper clipping. Men were at their best inventing things, he knew, and they were on their worst behavior by waging war against each other.

Miller realized he was at his best, too, finding courage he didn't know he had and volunteering to do this damn fool thing. He'd pushed off from the Union ship, swimming quickly and not worrying about any splashing he might make. He wanted only to be away from the torpedo, which the waves were forcing up against the enemy's hull. Miller barely spotted the *Hunley*, so low and black against the dark water. The sliver of moonlight briefly revealed the silhouette of Lieutenant Dixon. Every muscle screamed for rest, but Miller picked up his pace, pushing the ache in his limbs to the back of his mind and focusing only on that silhouette.

With every stroke he expected to be discovered and to hear an explosion. Neither happened, not even by the time he reached the *Hunley* and had to be practically pulled up its side by Dixon. He felt like a discarded rag doll, but the lieutenant slapped him on the back—that lone gesture giving him the strength to follow Dixon inside. The submarine was no longer listing.

The men were congratulating him, Becker's voice the loudest. Miller nodded politely, as he folded himself onto his seat.

"I don't understand, sir," Miller said, waving his fellows to silence. "I put that torpedo against that ship. All of that bumping with the waves . . . I thought it would have exploded by now. How could . . ."

Dixon didn't reply, raising himself again through the

fore hatch and peering at the closest Union ship, then returning below. "There's British ships nearby, so Beauregard's sources say. That's why we're out here. They're sitting somewhere out there and waiting for a break in the blockade. And I told Beauregard we'd give them that break. It's all about guns, gentlemen. Those ships are bringing guns that we need, and we're to give them the cotton that they treasure and make their captains rich men."

"I'm sorry, sir," Miller began. "I should've shoved that torpedo against that ship. I should've . . ."

"You did more than I expected," Lieutenant Dixon cut back. "The torpedo just hasn't hit the hull at the right angle, that's all. Maybe all we have to do is get that ship to turn."

"And how can we do that?" This from Wicks, who was waving for the piss jug.

In the light of a new candle, Dixon gave his men a rare smile. "Why, we get that ship to notice us, gentlemen. We get her to turn and chase us. Then we'll see if we can get that torpedo to work."

"Too dark," Miller said. Those two words threatened to erase Dixon's smile. "This submarine sits so low in the water. Everything's too dark. I could hardly see the *Hunley*, sir. And that was only 'cause I knew where to look. I could barely see you. We ain't got a sail or anything to catch their notice."

Lieutenant Dixon stroked his chin and glanced down the row at each of his men. His eyes came to rest on Becker. "Your slouch hat, Arnold."

"Sir?"

"We'll use it for our sail." Dixon waggled his fingers at the man.

With a frown and a shrug Becker reached behind him,

tugging free his "Stonewall" hat and passing it down the line to the lieutenant.

"That long wrench, Wicks."

Wicks was quick to comply.

Then the Lieutenant was up the fore hatch again, raising his arm high—the wrench held in it and the slouch hat on top of that. "Sing, Becker!" Dixon hollered. "Sing as loud as you can. And get your hands on the bar, gentlemen. We'll be needing to move quickly."

In the belly of the *Hunley* Becker cleared his throat and tapped his fingers on the bar to set the rhythm.

> *Away from Mississippi's vale*
> *With my ol' hat there for a sail*
> *I crossed upon a cotton bale*
> *To the Rose of Alabamy.*

> *Oh brown Rosie*
> *Rose of Alabamy!*
> *That sweet tobacco posey*
> *Is the Rose of Alabamy.*

"The Rose of Alabamy"? Miller thought. Becker knows more than one song after all. He coughed to clear his lungs of the salt water he'd gulped down, then he joined in: "Away from Mississippi's vale/With my ol' hat there for a sail . . ."

"Louder!" Dixon ordered. "Sing it much, much louder!"

The men complied, their craggy voices bouncing off the iron walls of the *Hunley* and finding their way outside the submarine and drifting with the breeze.

"It's working!" Dixon shouted. He was waving the wrench, slouch hat catching the scant moonlight and the attention of the men on the deck of the Union ship. "Louder!"

A flapping sound faintly registered, and Dixon said it was sails being raised. "She's coming at us, gentlemen!"

"Bully!" Becker cheered.

Dixon was ducking down, Simkins, too, both men sealing the hatches.

"Miller?"

The young man was quick to work the ballast tanks. "Taking the *Hunley* down, sir!"

The submarine hadn't wholly submerged when it was pitched wildly by an explosion.

"Bully!" Becker and Wicks shouted in unison.

Dixon stood and peered through the window. "I see fire, gentlemen. Good work, Miller. Good work, indeed!"

They took the *Hunley* farther out to sea, past the blockade, then brought her up so they could better see the carnage.

The night was lit up by the burning ship, and the air was filled with the desperate cries of men. The Union vessel was listing dangerously, and after a few minutes Dixon announced that it had begun to sink.

"That's what submarines were made for," Miller said. "To sink ships."

"Stonewall Jackson'd be right proud of us!" Becker said.

"Yes, indeed," Wicks chimed in. "Stonewall'd be right proud."

The other Union ships were moving closer and searching the water, looking for whatever had brought down the doom, and looking for men who'd jumped overboard. It would be days before Dixon and his men learned that in the commotion two big British ships were able to slip past the distracted blockade, riding low in the water because of the guns, ammunition, and other much-needed supplies riding heavy in their holds. And no one would ever know the *Hunley* was responsible, General P. T. Beauregard wanting to keep this night's activities quiet so the ploy could be used again.

The *Hunley* waited at a safe distance, cloaked by the black water, Dixon and Simkins describing the ship slipping below the water and the efforts of the Union men to save as many of their brethren as possible.

"Sir?" Miller asked after several minutes. "I was wondering if . . ." The rest of his words were drowned by a yawn.

"How do we return to the Cooper now?" Becker finished for him. "They'll be watching."

"We don't go back." The smile spread clear across Dixon's face now. "At least not for a while. That's why I asked you to bring an extra shirt, gentlemen. We're going south, along the Georgia coast. Slip in and get some more torpedoes, see if we can break another part of the blockade. Though we'll see if we can use the torpedoes properly this time. Then we'll come back home and see what else General Beauregard has planned."

And then I'll go home and visit my father, Miller thought, *tell him what I did. I think—like Stonewall Jackson—he'd be right proud of me.*

Excerpts from the songs "Stonewall Jackson's Way" and "The Rose of Alabama," were used in this tale. Although this story of the *Hunley*'s exploits is fictional, on February, 17, 1864, the real *H. L. Hunley* became the first submarine to sink· an enemy ship. She rammed her spar torpedo into the Union sloop *Housatonic*, an ironclad. The *Hunley*, herself, was believed to have sunk shortly thereafter, perhaps damaged in the blast and unable to surface. Divers and archeologists are currently working with the crew's and the submarine's remains.

History books show her crew consisted of Lieutenant George Dixon, of the Company E 21st Alabama Volunteers; James A. Wicks; C. F. Carlson; Arnold Becker; F. Collins; C. Simkins; Ridgeway, of the Confederate Navy; and Miller.

The Prize Crew

DOUG ALLYN

Doug Allyn is an accomplished author whose short fiction regularly graces year's best collections. His work has appeared in Once Upon a Crime, Cat Crimes Through Time, *and* The Year's 25 Finest Crime and Mystery Stories, *volumes 3 and 4. His stories of Talifer, the wandering minstrel, have appeared in* Ellery Queen's Mystery Magazine *and* Murder Most Scottish. *His story "The Dancing Bear," a Tallifer tale, won the Edgar award for short fiction for 1994. His other series character is veterinarian Dr. David Westbrook, whose exploits have been collected in the anthology* All Creatures Dark and Dangerous. *He lives with his wife in Montrose, Michigan.*

A SITTING DUCK. Centered in the periscope crosshairs, range twelve hundred meters, the ancient freighter was broadside to the U-boat, plunging and plowing through heavy seas on a southerly heading.

"Who is she, Walli?" Kapitän Kurt Bronner asked quietly. His submarine, U-233, a Type VIIC, wasn't feeling any effect from the weather at all. It was beyond reach of the waves, ten meters below the surface in the Amazon River basin just south of Ilha Caviana. Bronner's favorite hunting ground.

The Amazon basin offered U-233 perfect cover. Submerged in the murky waters, she was invisible from the air, her camouflaged periscope passed for flotsam, and the great river's constant rumbling rendered Allied sound detection devices useless.

With no German aircraft within 2,500 miles, Bronner was forced to improvise. He'd solved the problem by putting *Kriegsmarine* lookouts ashore on Ilha de Marajo. If the seamen heard aircraft or spotted the smoke or stacks of an approaching ship they signalled U-233 by walkie-talkie, giving the sub plenty of time to submerge.

From below, Bronner could choose to attack. Or let the target pass. The Brazilian sea lanes were busy. There would always be other ships. But U-233 was a lone wolf. A single mistake by an officer or crewman could be fatal. So far, they'd avoided that mistake. But for how long?

They were tired. They'd been fighting in foreign seas so long that Germany seemed like a memory. And yet they fought on. Not to win. For honor, duty, and country. And survival.

Hunting in Brazil's coastal waters was more like a game of hide-and-seek than classic submarine strategy. But most of the battle tactics Bronner learned at Breda Academy in '37 were obsolete now.

When U-233 arrived off the coast of New York in December of '41, she'd been a werewolf among lambs. Despite Pearl Harbor the Americans still kept their cities lit up like Christmas trees at night, silhouetting ships in the harbors, perfect targets for a U-boat's eighty-eight

millimeter deck gun firing out of the dark. U-233 sank a
dozen freighters in the first weeks without wasting a single torpedo.

But the Yanks learned quickly. Soon their cargo ships
were traveling in convoys escorted by gunboats with air
cover buzzing overhead. For a lone wolf like U-233, attacking armed convoys would be suicide. And despite
his loyalty oath to Hitler and the Reich, *Kapitän* Kurt
Bronner hadn't brought U-233 and her crew all the way
across the Atlantic to throw their lives away.

As American air defenses improved, Bronner and
U-233 moved south, taking targets of opportunity. Early
in '43 they hunted from Georgia to Florida before sub-
hunting aircraft chased them down into the Caribbean.
By '44 U-233 had been hounded all the way down to
the coastal waters of Brazil. Almost out of the war.

South America was a backwater, of minimal strategic
value. Still, Brazil had declared war on the Reich in '42,
which made all ships in Brazilian waters legitimate
U-boat targets.

Especially lone freighters.

"No merchant ships are due in these waters for two
more days," *Bootsmann* Walli Bauer riffled quickly
through the maritime schedules supplied by the Reich's
embassy in Argentina. "She must be a tramp freighter,
Kapitän. What does the lady look like?"

"A rust bucket, Walli. High-flung bow, broad beam,
hasn't seen a paintbrush since the last war. Or the one
before that. Name . . . the *Carmela*, I believe."

"Flag?"

"In tatters. Maybe Venezuelan. Can't make it out."

"*Carmela*," Bauer recited, reading from the naval register. Launched at Valparaiso, 1896. Listed at seventeen
hundred tons, merchant freighter, Uruguayan flag, home
port Montevideo . . ."

"What is it, Walli?"

"She must be a ghost, *Kapitän*. According to the records, *Carmela* was lost at sea, October, 1943. More than a year ago."

"Well, she could probably pass for a wreck, but she's no ghost. Maybe the owner ran her aground for the insurance, then salvaged her afterward. We'll ask her captain."

"Ask him, sir?" *Leutnant zur See* Scheringer echoed. Barely old enough to shave, Scheringer had joined Bronner's staff as a replacement straight out of Breda submarine school, eager as a schoolboy, green as grass. After four years of combat at sea, he was still eager. But he wasn't green anymore. None of them were.

"She's turning toward us, Mr. Scheringer, running for the river basin to get out of the rough seas. Barely making headway, though. Four or five knots, no more. Either she's the slowest scow ever built or she's got engine trouble. Seems to be towing a lifeboat, too. Who's the senior man ashore on lookout?"

"Seaman Voorheis, *Kapitän*."

"Good. Wake *Leutnant* Heitman, please, and ask him to report to the bridge. We'll let *Carmela* come to us. When she heaves to, we'll surface and board her, offload any stores we can use, then scuttle her in the shipping lane. Get Voorheis on the radio and tell him to keep his eyes peeled for aircraft. I want no surprises."

"Aye, *Kapitän*."

No one hurried. They all knew the drill by heart. Still, a ripple of excitement ran through the U-boat's hardened crew as Scheringer worked his way forward to pass the word and wake *Leutnant* Heitman.

Bronner retired to his tiny cubicle to change his clothes. Aboard ship, Bronner wore the same canvas U-boat overalls as his crewmen. Only his white-peaked cap marked his rank as commanding officer. Forty and fit, with gray eyes and a silver brush cut, Bronner was mild-mannered and easygoing. And hard as a crowbar.

Ashore in Buenos Aires, the last port open to them, the men of U-233 wore civilian clothes to avoid drawing attention to themselves. But going into battle, even against a lowly tramp freighter, Kurt Bronner changed into his naval uniform.

The winds of war had harried him across the Atlantic to the steaming green waters of Brazil. If half the rumors he'd heard on their last refueling stop were true, it would all be over soon.

Hitler was in his bunker, people said. The *Luftwaffe* had been swept from the skies, the *Wehrmacht* was collapsing. Bolsheviks and Brits were overrunning the Fatherland's borders. Nothing Bronner or the crew of U-233 accomplished in these waters would affect the outcome of the war. He knew it and so did they.

Still, he was *Kriegsmarine,* son and grandson of German naval officers. He would continue to fight, no matter what. And when facing the enemy, he'd damned well look like a proper seaman.

Moments after the sub's bow and conning tower broke the surface the gun crews were scrambling out the hatches to man the eighty-eight millimeter deck gun and twenty-millimeter quad-barreled antiaircraft cannon. Jerking out the waterproof barrel tamps, the crews quickly unlimbered the guns and brought them to bear with practiced precision.

At close range, the twenty-millimeter was actually the deadlier weapon. Bronner had less than a dozen rounds for the eighty-eight and he wasn't about to waste them on a tub like the *Carmela*.

Bronner, *Bootsmann* Walli Bauer and *Leutnant* Heitman took positions on the bridge, scanning the *Carmela* with binoculars for any sign of resistance.

Nothing. Except for the machetes worn by some of the deckhands, the ship appeared to be unarmed. No weapons in sight, not even small arms. A local tramp freighter. Nothing more.

Bronner relaxed, but *Leutnant* Heitman continued to scan the *Carmela*, eager as a gun dog on point. Hoping for a fight.

Bauer and Bronner exchanged an amused glance behind Heitman's broad back. A bullnecked, blonde athlete from Berlin, Heitman was new navy, a devout Nazi who still believed the Führer was luring the Russian army into Germany to destroy the Bolsheviks once and for all.

Bronner admired his third officer's dedication if not his intelligence. And he always included Heitman in boarding parties. Fanatics make first-rate warriors. Killing comes easy when death is a concept too complex to grasp.

If the crew of the freighter were startled by the sight of a sub splashing to the surface three hundred meters off their starboard bow, they concealed it well. One of the deckhands lowered their ensign and ran up a white flag in its place. There was no panic. They'd apparently lowered a lifeboat during last night's storm, but they made no move to abandon ship.

Quite the contrary. A ship's officer dressed in grimy whites appeared at the rail, waved cheerfully at U-233, then ordered an accommodation ladder lowered over the side.

Frowning, Bauer lowered his binoculars. "Odd. He seems to be inviting us aboard, *Kapitän*."

"If you're going to be raped, lie back and enjoy it," Heitman muttered.

"I hope you're not speaking from experience, Number Three," Bronner said.

"Of course not, *Kapitän*," Heitman said stiffly. "It's just a saying."

"I'm relieved to hear it. Well, since the master of the *Carmela* is being so civil, let's accommodate him. Assemble a boarding party, Heitman. Four men, myself, and *Bootsmann* Bauer. Scheringer will assume command in our absence."

"*Jawohl, Herr Kapitän.*" Heitman scrambled down the ladder, glad to be going into action and away from Bronner's dry wit. Bronner was a superb naval officer, but his dry sense of humor could be unsettling.

Issuing Mauser carbines and cartridge belts from the arms locker to four crewmen, Heitman chose a Schmeisser submachine gun for himself, then hurried back up to the bridge.

Bauer had freed the twenty-foot motor whaler from its mount behind the *Wintergarten* and lowered it into the waves, its outboard gurgling merrily as it rocked like a child's boat beside the massive metal hull of 233.

"Boarders away," Heitman snapped, though the crewmen were already scrambling aboard the launch. Heitman placed himself in the prow, Schmeisser at the ready while Bronner settled into his usual seat in the stern beside Walli Bauer.

And they were off, putting across the long swells of the river basin toward the *Carmela*.

A gorgeous day for a raid. A few miles offshore, the waves were still savage, remnants of the storm the night before. But here in the basin, the tropic sun was ablaze, beating down on the turbid waters, air so steamy a man could break a sweat with a single blink. A mile to the east, the tangled vegetation of Brazil's Green Hell towered above the shore, palm fronds waving in the wind.

Halfway to the freighter, Bronner raised his hand and the AA gunner cut loose with a quick burst that hammered a half-dozen gouts of foam a few meters ahead of the *Carmela*'s bow, test-firing his weapon. And sending the tramp's crew an unmistakable warning.

Not that they needed it. The seamen lining the rail watched the Germans approach with more curiosity than fear. A ship's officer in a soiled white uniform shouldered his way to the accommodation ladder carrying a megaphone.

"Good afternoon, gentlemen. I am Captain Jose Stroessner, master of the *Carmela*. May I offer you the hospitality of my vessel?" Tall, slender as a riding crop, with a neatly trimmed goatee, Stroessner was as dark as any of his crew. Obviously Hispanic. But his German was very, very good.

Bauer and Bronner exchanged a glance but made no comment. After two years in these waters they were immune to surprises.

Heitman was first out of the boat, sprinting up the accommodation ladder, his Schmeisser covering the *Carmela*'s captain all the way.

"Get back against the rail with your men!" he ordered as the U-boat's seamen scrambled aboard, taking up positions on the bridge to cover the *Carmela*'s deckhands. A rough-looking bunch. Heitman guessed they were Central Americans. Barefoot, wearing shorts and dirty shirts, coarse black hair, flat faces. Black eyes with invisible pupils, as expressionless as the carved stone faces of jungle idols.

"Tell your men to raise their hands! And call out the rest of your crew!"

"This is my crew," Stroessner said mildly. "We are as you see."

"Seven hands for a ship this size?" Heitman snorted.

"Do you take us for fools? Where are the others?"

"Lost," Stroessner shrugged. "We ran into heavy weather a few days ago off Ilha Diablo. A man was washed overboard, two more were crushed trying to stabilize the cargo."

"Bad luck," Bronner said. "But not as bad as yours will be if you're lying to us."

"I give you my word, sir," Stroessner said. "Search the ship if you like."

"Thank you, I believe we will," Bronner said mildly, nodding at Bauer, who immediately trotted off with two crewmen, leaving Heitman to cover the others with the Schmeisser. "No offense intended, of course."

"None taken, *Kapitän*," Stroessner said. "May I lower my hands?"

"If you like. But I wouldn't do anything sudden. My men have been at sea a long time. We're a bit edgy, I'm afraid."

"All the more reason to accept my hospitality," Stroessner said. "I have a fine bottle of Napoleon brandy in my cabin. Would you care to join me?"

"Sorry, but we won't be staying that long. Nor will you. You speak very good German, Captain . . . ?"

"Stroessner, *Kapitän,* and I am German, or rather, my grandfather was. He emigrated to Mexico in the service of the emperor Maximilian nearly a century ago. Stayed on after the revolution. Which is why I have great sympathy for your situation."

"You'd best save your sympathy for yourself, Captain. I'm seizing this ship as a prize of war. We'll take what we need and scuttle her. You and your crew will be put ashore unharmed. Unless you cause trouble. In which case we'll put you over the side. Do we understand each other?"

"Not quite. When I say I sympathize with your situation, *Kapitän*, I mean it. My grandfather, too, fought for a cause far from his Fatherland. But when that cause was lost, he took advantage of his opportunities. And became a very rich man."

"Did he? Forgive my frankness, Captain, but you don't have the look of inherited wealth."

Surprisingly, Stroessner laughed. "I'm afraid I'm the black sheep of my family, Captain. Ran away to sea looking for adventure."

"If this scow is the measure of your success, I'd say you found more bad luck than adventure."

"An hour ago I might have agreed with you. But now I think my luck's taken a turn for the better. Perhaps yours has, too."

"If you're thinking of offering me a bribe, Stroessner, please don't insult my intelligence. Everything aboard this vessel is already ours."

"Yours to destroy, true. But that would be such a waste. We're intelligent men. Surely we can find another way, one that will profit all of us."

Bootsmann Bauer came trotting up. "No sign of anyone else aboard, *Kapitän*."

"What's her cargo, Walli?"

"I don't know, sir. Produce of some sort. Bales of green leaves, tobacco perhaps. Jammed to the bulwarks. And its hot below, must be a hundred and twenty degrees Farenheit.

"The leaves are cooking," Stroessner explained. "Like green hay stored in a barn, it heats up as the bales decompose. If the cargo isn't off-loaded soon it will spontaneously combust. Burst into flame. And that would be a great, great pity."

"Why?" Bronner asked. "What is this cargo of yours?"

"Pharmaceuticals, *Kapitän*. Coca leaves from Columbia. The raw ingredients of cocaine. A miraculous stimulant, cocaine. I understand your Führer is very fond of it."

Bronner stared at Stroessner as though he'd grown a second head. "Sweet Jesus, Walli. That's why this scow isn't listed on the registry. She's a smuggler. A *verdammt* drug smuggler."

"Drugs, pharmaceuticals, is there much difference, really?" Stroessner shrugged. "You and I are seamen, *Kapitän,* not merchants. But this cargo, delivered in Rio de Janeiro, is worth a fortune."

"To the *Carmela*'s owners, perhaps."

"Precisely. But we are her owners now, *Kapitän,* or rather, you are. As you said, the *Carmela* is a prize of war. Your prize. And maybe mine as well. The ship's owner was lost in the storm. He panicked and tried to abandon ship in the lifeboat. But he was no seaman. He slipped climbing down to it."

"How unfortunate."

"For him, certainly," Stroessner agreed smoothly. "Not necessarily for us. Don't get me wrong, *Kapitän,* Senor Porges's death was a great loss to me. We were like brothers, the owner and I. He told me everything about his rich contacts in Rio. Their names. And how badly they want this cargo. The owner was to be paid three quarters of a million dollars U.S. on delivery. Cash. In reichsmarks that's—"

"Fool's gold," Bronner snorted. "What are you suggesting, Stroessner? That we send you merrily on your way to Rio to sell your cargo to these rich drug dealers? And afterward, how would we collect our share? Through the mail?"

"Not at all, *Kapitän.* At the moment I can't make it to Rio anyway. The *Carmela*'s engines were damaged in the storm. If I sail her into the harbor, the buyers will simply take her from me, since I have no papers proving ownership."

"Then what do you have in mind?"

"That you and your men take possession of the *Carmela* as a prize crew. We'll sail to Rio together, with your U-boat as an escort. But instead of entering the harbor, we'll send a launch to bring the buyers out to us. And we'll offer to sell them the *Carmela* and her cargo for, say, half a million, two thirds of the agreed price. But if they try any treachery your sub will torpedo *Carmela* and send their precious coca to the bottom."

"Half a million?" Bauer whistled. "A lot of money."

"For them it's a bargain," Stroessner shrugged. "It's less than they expected to pay and they get the ship as well. They must be greedy men to be involved in this dirty business. They will pay, I think."

Bronner eyed the *Carmela*'s captain for what seemed like a very long time. "Would you mind joining your men at the rail, Stroessner?" he said at last.

"You wish to discuss this, I understand," Stroessner said, smiling as he backed away. "Just remember—"

"Get the fuck over there and shut your mouth," Heitman barked, striding angrily up to Bronner. "Surely you can't be considering this, *Kapitän*. We are *Kriegsmarine*, seamen of the Reich—"

"A Thousand Year Reich which won't see another Christmas," Bronner snapped. "The last time we refueled in Buenos Aires I visited our embassy, Heitman. Do you know what our fearless Nazi diplomats were doing? They were burning documents: maps, codebooks, everything. They offered to sell me new citizenship papers for Argentina or Paraguay. But they wouldn't accept payment in reichsmarks. American dollars only. This war is lost, gentlemen, we've all known it for months."

"We still have our duty to the Fatherland!" Heitman protested.

"And I'll continue to honor that duty to the last moment," Bronner agreed. "But I also have a duty to protect my men. None of us has been paid for over a year. We'll need money to get home, money to feed our families and start new lives. There's some risk in escorting this scow to Rio, but the freighter will shield us from radar and we can run submerged in her shadow during the day. No self-respecting air defense pilot will give this tub a second glance."

"But we're already shorthanded, *Kapitän*. If we put men on this ship—"

"We'll keep the prize crew small, Heitman, five of us should be enough. I'll command it myself. If anything goes wrong, the responsibility will be mine alone. But desperate times require desperate measures, and this is not a debating society, gentlemen. The decision is mine. We're going. Any questions?"

"Collecting this money will mean taking the U-boat too close to the harbor at Rio," Heitman argued. "We'll be putting the ship at risk."

"We risk death every day for nothing," Bauer said quietly.

"Shut your mouth, *Bootsmann*!" Heitman snapped "You have no say in this. You're a seaman and you'll damned well do as you're told."

"Of course he will," Bronner said mildly. "Because, as you say, Heitman, we are *Kriegsmarine,* not pirates. We're seizing this ship as a legitimate prize of war and we'll divide the spoils by naval tradition among the officers and the men.

"If the Reich emerges victorious we'll wire the prize money to the Führer on his birthday. If not? The crew of U-233 has fought too long and hard and honorably to end up penniless in South America, beached, with no way to get home."

"I don't trust this Stroessner," Heitman said stubbornly.

"My goodness, why ever not? You really should cultivate more faith in human nature, Heitman. It might brighten your outlook on life. Walli, does anyone in our crew speak Spanish or Portuguese?"

"No, sir. I understand a little, though."

"Really? How much?"

"Enough to find a cathouse or a cantina anywhere we go ashore."

"I doubt that we'll need either on this trip, Walli. Get down to the engine room and see to the diesels. Captain Stroessner, could I have a word please?"

"Of course, *Kapitän*." Stroessner hurried over eagerly.

"We're considering your offer, Stroessner. But not for half the money. Our share will be three quarters. If that's acceptable to you?"

"A quarter is better than a bullet in the head, no? In any case, what choice do I have, *Kapitän* Bronner?"

"None, actually. The *Carmela* is now the lawful property of the Reich. I will command the prize crew myself. U-233 will escort us to Rio to provide security until her cargo is sold. And if anything seems even slightly amiss, I've given *Leutnant* Scheringer orders to sink this ship and machine-gun any survivors. Do you understand?"

"Yes, *Kapitän*."

"I thought you might. As you said, we're all bright fellows, Stroessner. Let's behave like it. Please instruct your crew to obey my men without question."

"I'm afraid there's a slight problem, *Kapitän*. These crewmen are *Indios* from Yucatán. They speak no language but their own."

"A language you happen to be familiar with, I take it?"

"I speak several languages, including theirs, yes."

"I see. I imagine that would make these men very loyal to you."

"I would hope so, *Kapitän*."

"Good. Then would you kindly explain to them that at the first sign of treachery, you'll be killed and so will they. Quicker than a bat can blink. Understood?"

"Of course, Bronner, but why all this talk of killing? We're both Germans. We're all on the same side in this thing."

"No, Captain Stroessner, we're not. We're not comrades and we're certainly not friends. For the moment, we are renegades, thrown together by the storms of war. And I'm the renegade with the U-boat and the guns. And don't ever address me by my family name again."

"As you wish, *Kapitän*."

"Good. What accommodations are aboard?"

"Only one cabin, the owner's. I'm sure you'll find it satisfactory. There is a small dayroom off the bridge. The deckhands sleep below in the hold."

"Not anymore. Your men will sleep on deck, under guard."

"They won't like it, *Kapitän*. They prefer sleeping with the cargo. The scent of the leaves reminds them of their homes, and brings them dreams."

"I'll wager it does. But they can buy all the dreams they want later, with the riches you pay them from your share, Stroessner. Meantime, they sleep on deck, in view of the wheelhouse sentry at all times. Heitman!"

"Sir!"

"This is *Leutnant* Heitman, Stroessner. You're to stay within his sight at all times."

"*Kapitän,* I assure you—"

"Oh, you needn't assure me of anything, Stroessner. I trust you completely. But Heitman here has a dimmer view of human nature, I'm afraid. He's quite distrustful. And if he loses track of you, even by accident, he'll probably shoot you."

"That would be an expensive accident, *Kapitän*," Stroessner said evenly.

"More expensive for you than for me. If you die, I'll still be a seaman of the Reich, poor but honest. But you'll be, well, wherever dead drug smugglers go. In hell, I would think."

"I'll save you a warm seat next to mine, *Kapitän*. But meantime, I'll be happy to stay close to *Leutnant* Heitman."

"Thank you. With a little cooperation, we'll all get along famously, Stroessner. Walli, you look puzzled. How goes it with the engines?"

"They're fine, *Kapitän*. Seawater was splashing around below, shorting out the plugs, is all. This old tub must leak like a sieve. There's a lot of water in the hold and for some reason the bilge pumps were off."

"These *Indios*," Stroessner snorted. "They're hard workers but they're stupid. I swear, before signing on the *Carmela* none of them ever worked aboard anything bigger than a dugout canoe."

"Then we'll have to keep close watch on them, Captain. To make sure they don't make any more mistakes. How soon can we get underway, Walli?"

"An hour, *Kapitän*, maybe less."

"Make it less. The sooner we're done with this business, the better. Heitman, get *Leutnant* Scheringer on the radio. I'd better explain this devil's bargain we've made. Stroessner, inform your men of the situation. We're leaving as soon as Bauer puts the engines right. U-233 will shadow us from below during daylight and on the surface

at night. And my men will be on full alert at all times.
And very, very nervous. Remember that."

"Yes, *Kapitän*."

"Oh, and Stroessner? Tell your men to get that damned
lifeboat back aboard. A tramp towing a boat looks sus-
picious. And it sure as hell didn't do the last fellow much
good. Did it?"

True love. Nothing in *Bootsmann* Walli Bauer's life gave
him more satisfaction than maintaining maritime engines.
For Bauer, servicing U-233's three-thousand horsepower
diesels and dual electrics was like having a harem. Each
engine had an individual, quirky personality and its own
voice. And after eleven years of U-boat service, Bauer
could gauge a diesel's rpms by sound alone.

The *Carmela*'s twin diesels were older and larger than
submarine engines. And a bit mysterious. They'd obviously been added recently, the bolts and welded seams
on the support frames showed very little rust, and in
steamy South American waters, machinery sometimes
rusted solid overnight.

The engines must have been transferred aboard the
Carmela from a newer ship, a wreck, perhaps, but they
appeared to be in good shape. Type J7 LeBlanc diesels
the size of a small sedan, they were built in Belgium
during the twenties for the maritime merchant service,
twenty-six hundred horsepower, maximum torque at five-
hundred rpm, single-cast cylinder blocks for easy
maintenance. A machinist's dream.

All in all, excellent engines. The *Carmela* might be a
scow but someone had gone to considerable expense to
make her a damned dependable scow. Even secondhand,
the twin LeBlanc diesels were easily worth as much as
the tramp freighter itself.

Considering the business she was in, having dependable mills made sense. Still, there was something odd about these engines. Walli couldn't put his finger on what it was, but something about them troubled him.

The pumps had bailed out most of the seawater he'd found sloshing around on the metal deck when he'd first checked the diesels. Only an inch or so remained, whispering back and forth as the ship rolled, probably normal for an old tub like *Carmela*.

He found a well-thumbed LeBlanc-factory service manual in a tool kit. Written in French, the text wasn't much help, but numbers never lie, specifications are specifications in any language. And to Walli, the engine specs were as intriguing as nude photos of Marlene Dietrich.

Well, almost.

After drying the plugs and restarting both mills, Walli pulled a chair up beside engine number two and began poring over the manual, memorizing the specifications, absorbing the symphony of the dual diesels into his soul. Perhaps their music would explain the uneasiness that kept chewing at the corner of his mind, ducking in and out of the shadows like a bilge rat.

The *Carmela* got underway at sundown. Bronner sent the motor-whaler back to U-233, keeping Heitman and two U-233 crewmen in the wheelhouse and Bauer down in the engine room.

Stroessner's *Indio* crew handled their duties ably enough, though it was odd to hear deck commands shouted in a guttural language that sounded like monkeys barking in the Green Hell of the Amazon.

Night falls suddenly in Brazilian waters, fading from purple dusk to inky black in a few minutes, as though the jungle has swallowed the sun.

For a time, *Kapitän* Bronner paced the bridge, but with

Bootsmann Heinz at the helm, Seaman Looff standing
guard on the wheelhouse roof, and Heitman on the prowl,
there was little for him to do.

"I'll be in the owner's cabin, Heitman. Wake me at
two or if anything develops." He paused in the doorway.
"Heitman?"

"Sir?"

"Have you ever worked on a farm?"

"No, sir," Heitman said, baffled by the question. "I'm
a Berliner. Why do you ask?"

"Farmers spread manure on their fields, Heitman. It
helps the crops to grow. But it means that sometimes a
farmer has to work with shit to feed his family, honor
his obligations, and pay his debts. Do you understand?"

"I . . . don't know much about agriculture, *Kapitän*."

"No, I suppose not," Bronner sighed. "My point is, I
know you dislike Stroessner and his crewmen. You think
they're *untermensch,* subhumans. But we need the
money from this cargo, Heitman, even if we have to
work with shit to get it. Do I make myself clear?"

"You . . . want me to work with this Stroessner, *Kapitän*?"

"Very good, Heitman. That's exactly what I mean. We
need him to sell this cargo. I want no trouble between
you two."

"Don't worry about Stroesnner, *Kapitän,* I can handle
him."

"I know you can, Heitman, that's what worries me."

"Sir?"

"Never mind. Just remember, no trouble, please. Good
night, *Leutnant*."

"Good night, sir."

At the ship's wheel, *Bootsmann* Heinz arched his eyebrows at Heitman. "Fertilizer? What was all that about?"

"None of your fucking business, Heinz. Mind your course."

"Aye, sir." Officers, Heinz thought. Nutjobs, the lot of them.

The owner's cabin was almost barren; a bunk, a writing desk and a short, glass-fronted bookcase. Compared to Bronner's curtained cell aboard U-233, it was as lavish as a five-star hotel suite.

It even had a small liquor cabinet. Idly, Bronner opened it. A fair bottle of port, some cheap Mexican tequila and . . . one bottle of Napoleon brandy. Château Marchant, 1911. A classic vintage and very rare. Château Marchant and its cellars had been blown to hell in the Nivelle offensive of 1917. A terrible waste of fine brandy. And roughly a hundred thousand men. Pity.

An even greater pity that he considered himself on duty twenty-four hours a day as long as he was aboard this tub. No booze. Not even an exquisite vintage. Damn.

Well, maybe one small sip wouldn't hurt. He poured a finger's worth into a coffee cup, then tasted it, rolling the brandy around on his tongue.

Ambrosia. A slightly nutty taste, with the faintest flavor of smoke. Marvelous. He let it slide down the back of his throat, savoring it all the way to the pit of his stomach. Then he regretfully replaced the bottle in the rack.

Perhaps when this was over he could treat himself to a quiet evening with the Château Marchant and some poetry.

Assuming he lived that long.

Shedding his boots, pistol belt, and uniform jacket, Bronner eased down on the bunk, fully clothed. He checked the magazine in his Luger, then placed it on the nightstand, readily at hand.

He wasn't sleepy; too much had happened, but he

forced himself to lie back and rest. Midnight would come soon enough. And the next few days were going to be dangerous and complicated. And the last man who slept in this bunk was cruising the seas in the belly of a shark.

Sleep wouldn't come, though. After three years crammed in a steel coffin with fifty seamen, the bed seemed too large and too soft. And the whisper of the night wind through the porthole was such a pure pleasure that he didn't want to miss a moment of it. He loved inhaling the fresh scent of the sea, feeling the Brazilian breeze caress his face like a woman's touch. . . .

Carmela shuddered. In the engine room Walli Bauer glanced up from the engine manual, frowning. The sea was mild tonight, long, regular swells, orphans of the storm the day before. The tub should be rocking gently as a child's cradle. But every time the bow met a roller . . . a noticeable vibration. As though the sea was clutching her for just a moment with each wave.

Barnacles near the prow? A dent at the waterline, perhaps from banging off a harbor piling? It didn't matter much, *Carmela* was loafing along at ten knots anyway, staying within U-233's surface cruising speed. Still, he'd remember to check the bow in the morning to see if he could spot the problem. Engines like these deserved a tub that was shipshape. . . . There.

For an instant the riddle of the engines popped out of the shadows, only to vanish again before he could grasp it. Smiling, he shook his head. Must be getting old. Still, he knew it would come to him eventually. Almost had it there for a moment.

Shrugging off his uneasiness, he went back to the manual, poring over it again from the beginning, soothed by the thrum of the engines.

Heitman glanced up as Stroessner stepped into the

wheelhouse, closing the door behind him. "What do you want?"

"Nothing. This is my post. My men are asleep and a captain's place is on the bridge, no?"

"You're not captain of anything, Stroessner. Not anymore. This ship is the property of the prize crew, to do with as we please. I have orders to work with you, so I will, but make no mistake, I don't like you and you're not one of us. As far as I'm concerned, you're no more German than those jungle bunnies out there."

"*Indios,* if you please, *Leutnant,*" Stroessner corrected gently. "Their people once built pyramids in this country."

"So they piled up rocks, so what? How is it you speak their language, anyway? Was your mother one of them?"

"I speak many languages, *Leutnant,* French, Italian, Spanish, Portuguese. South America is a continent of many tongues."

"You didn't answer my question."

"About my mother, you mean? How old are you, *Leutnant*? Twenty-two? Twenty-three?"

"What business is that of yours?"

"Just wondering how you've lived so long without learning that it's unwise to question a gentleman's parentage. Especially in this part of the world. Some men might take it as an insult."

"I don't give a damn how you take—what was that noise?"

"What noise?"

"That popping sound. Gunfire? Sounded like it came from the hold. Heinz, did you hear it?"

"I heard . . . something, *Leutnant.*"

"*Carmela*'s an old ship," Stroessner said. "Full of creaks and rattles."

"Bullshit. I know gunfire when I hear it."

"I'm sure you're mistaken."

"Then you won't mind coming below with me to investigate."

"Investigate what? A rat-infested hold in the dark?"

Heitman jacked a round into the Schmeisser MP38's chamber, his eyes locked on Stroessner. "You were saying?"

"I was about to offer you a guided tour of the hold, *Leutnant* Heitman. It's charming this time of night."

"Good. Heinz, I'm going below to check out that noise," Heitman said, slipping the Schmeisser's sling over his shoulder. "Hold your course but keep your eyes open and your rifle handy. If you hear the Schmeisser go off, don't come after us. Send the sentry to wake the *Kapitän,* tell him where I went. Understand?"

"Yes, *Herr Leutnant.*"

"All right, lead the way, Stroessner. And I'll be right behind you."

After a word with Looff, the sentry on the wheelhouse roof, Heitman followed Stroessner down to the deck. As they passed, one of the *Indio* deckhands glanced up from his blanket, glassy-eyed, his chin white with foamy drool. He muttered something to Stroessner, then lay back on his blankets, staring vacantly up at the stars.

"What did he say?"

"Only that the ghosts are moving tonight. And they don't like white men."

"Then you should be safe enough. What ghosts is he talking about?"

"Jungle spirits. The *Indios* believe the coca leaf is magical, a passport to the spirit world. In daylight they chew it for stamina. At night it brings them dreams."

"They chew it like cattle chew their cuds. Animals."

"No, Heitman, they are men, like you and me. But their lives are very hard. The coca gives them endurance, which they need to survive. And more importantly, it lets them dream of a better life. It gives them hope."

"False hope."

"Perhaps. But in the jungle, even false hope is better than none if it helps you go on. I would think a German would understand that."

"What would the likes of you know about being German? Quit stalling and take me below."

"Certainly, *Leutnant*." Stroessner led the way down the long, spiral staircase that descended into the cargo hold of the *Carmela*. It was like crawling into hell's bowels. The temperature crept up a few degrees with every step, and when they reached the bottom, the sweltering rush of humid air washed over them like the rank breath of the jungle itself.

Belowdecks the freighter was a vast, floating warehouse, divided into three cargo sections forward, with the engine room, galley, and cabins in the stern.

A narrow plank catwalk ran the length of the hold between the towering stacks of coca bales, which rose nearly to the cargo hatches above, filling every inch of space.

Heitman played his torch down the narrow passageway. Reflecting from the bilgewater slopping over the catwalk, the light flickered across the coca stacks, giving them movement, making them writhe like living things.

Heitman gazed at them intently for what seemed like a long time, shining the beam around, then lowering it to the catwalk.

"There's a lot of water down here."

"She's a leaky old tub, but she'll make it to Rio, and that's all we care about, right?"

"Yeah," Heitman said, wiping his brow, letting his weapon dangle from its sling. "Why is it so goddamned hot?"

"The *Indios* say the sun god lives in the coca leaves. But it's as I told the *Kapitän,* the bales are packed so tightly the heat of their decomposition can't escape. It's a hundred and twenty degrees down here already. In a week the cargo will catch fire from within. Even now it's dangerous to smoke down here. And even more dangerous to fire a weapon. Fortunately, there's no need to do either. Are you satisfied, *Leutnant*?"

"Yes, I—"

Bam! Heitman whirled, aiming his flashlight and his weapon down the catwalk toward the sound. But there was nothing to see. Some dust hanging in the air beside a bale. Nothing more.

Wham! A fist-sized clump of coca jumped out of a bale, leaping across the aisle.

"What the hell was that? It looks like something's trying to claw it's way out? What's going on?"

"Who knows," Stroessner shrugged. "Maybe the *Indios* are right and the jungle spirits are restless."

"Spirits my ass!" Crouched, his weapon leveled, Heitman crept toward the torn bale.

"Don't go down there, *Leutnant*."

"Why, Stroessner? What's the big mystery? What are you so afraid I'll see?"

"Nothing, but—"

"Then shut your mouth! Stay where you are and keep your hands where I can see them!"

"As you wish." Stroessner raised his hands, watching Heitman creep along the catwalk, ankle-deep in bilge-water.

Reaching the torn bale, Heitman warily poked the gouge with his gun barrel, then quickly stepped back. But nothing happened. Inching closer, he noticed something glinting in one of the bales. He pulled it free, cradling it in his palm. A twisted lump of metal. So deformed that for a moment he didn't recognize it.

"A rivet?" he said, puzzled. "How did a rivet get—?"

Bam! A hammer blow smashed him in the chest, slamming him backward into the bales, dropping him to his knees in the water. Stunned, he fumbled the flashlight, gaping at the jagged wound below his sternum. A twisted rivet had buried itself in his chest, blood gushing as he clawed at it.

"You damned fool," Stroessner snarled, sprinting to Heitman. "Let it be!" Grabbing Heitman's arm, he dragged the groaning *Leutnant* back along the catwalk to the stairwell.

Kneeling beside him, Stroessner carefully lifted the sling of the machine pistol over Heitman's shoulder, laying the weapon aside.

"Hold still, damn you! Let me have a look."

Wincing, Heitman took his hand away from the wound. Blood spurted, but not as much as before.

"It's not so bad," Stroessner grunted, "not fatal, anyway. Too bad. Here, chew some of this coca. It'll kill the pain." He pulled a fistful of coca leaf out of the nearest bale.

"No, I don't want—"

"Eat it!" Savagely, Stroessner drove his fist into the open wound, then jammed the wad of coca into Heitman's mouth, choking off his scream. Grabbing the Schmeisser, he slammed the *Leutnant* in the temple with its steel butt, sending him sprawling across the catwalk. Stunned, moaning, Heitman tried to rise.

With almost casual contempt Stroessner kicked the *Leutnant* down again, then stepped onto his back and planted a boot on his neck, pinning him facedown in the filthy water.

Heitman thrashed like a beached porpoise. But only a

few moments. Then a final burst of bubbles gushed from
his mouth.

And still Stroessner kept his boot on his neck, holding
him firmly down. Waiting. Making absolutely sure he
was dead.

In the engine room, *Bootsmann* Walli Bauer snapped
awake. Confused for a moment, he smiled as he focused
on the LeBlanc diesels, remembering where he was. In
the engine room of the tramp, *Carmela*. Must have fallen
asleep, reading.

But something had wakened him. A shout? Something. Better check topside, make sure everything's shipshape, grab a cup of coffee . . .

As he rose from the chair, stretching, a movement
caught the corner of his eye. Something rolling black and
forth in the bilgewater near the bulkhead as the ship
rocked. Something bloody.

Curious, he reached for it, picked it up. A bit of wiener
sausage, nothing more—Jesus! He gaped at it in disbelief. Not a sausage. It was a finger! A human finger. A
ring finger, marked with a darkened circle. But no wedding ring was on it now. Somebody had hacked it off to
get the ring. Who—

"Indios," Bauer breathed. "Savages." Right. They
were savages. And in that instant he realized what had
been bothering him. The problem wasn't the engines at
all. Both diesels were running like clockwork now. The
problem was the bilgewater slopping around in the engine room.

Because the *Indios* were too stupid to turn on the
pumps, Stroessner said.

And that was the puzzle. Not the engines. The *Indios*.
Why would the *Carmela*'s owner spend big money to

install first-class engines in this ship, then hire a crew of savages too ignorant to operate them?

Answer? He wouldn't. The *Indio* deckhands weren't the crew of the *Carmela*. They were pirates. Had to be. Nobody had lowered that fucking lifeboat. They'd used it to board her.

Sweet Jesus. When Stroessner said the ship's owner was dead, it was probably the only true thing he'd told them. He forgot to mention that the ship's crew was dead, too. Unless one of them had misplaced his fucking ring finger!

Swallowing, Bauer placed the gory trophy atop one of the diesels, picked up his Mauser carbine, and checked its load. He had to get topside to warn Heitman and the *Kapitän*. If it wasn't too late already.

From the shadows of the stairwell, Jose Stroessner checked the corridor to the left. Empty. Out on deck, the *Indios* were still wrapped in their blankets, asleep.

‹ But he knew better. Camayo, the crew's leader, was as relaxed as the others, his blanket covering most of his face. Only his eyes were showing. Black and alert as a hunting shark.

No words were necessary. Stroessner returning from the hold alone was explanation enough for Camayo. Only four Germans were left now, the helmsman and the sentry on the wheelhouse, Bauer down in the engine room, and the *Kapitän* in his quarters.

Stroessner started to point toward the wheelhouse, then realized there was no need. Camayo was already gone. His blanket remained with the same outline as before, apparently covering a sleeping man. But it was empty now.

The *Indio* had vanished into the shadows, as though he was part shadow himself.

Stroessner smiled grimly. No need to worry about the sentry or the helmsman. Camayo would see to them. And the man below in the engine room could wait.

The *Kapitän* was all that mattered now. In a way it was a pity Bronner had to die in his sleep. Stroessner would have preferred letting the *Indios* cut on him awhile, the way they'd worked over the *Carmela*'s owner. Taking their time. Tearing off long strips of his skin. Even after he'd told them everything they wanted to know, given them his money, the ship's documents.

That was when he realized the full horror of it. That nothing he could do would make them stop. They would continue torturing him until he died. Not because they wanted anything from him. Simply because his mortal agony was amusing to them.

At the end, Camayo split the owner's sternum with a machete and ripped out his beating heart with his bare hands. And showed it to him as he died.

But there was no time for play now. With the Nazi U-boat trailing astern, he needed to gain control of the ship by first light. But quick or slow, killing the arrogant *Kapitän* personally would be a pure, sweet pleasure.

Humming softly to himself, he checked the chamber of the Schmeisser, making sure it was loaded.

Standing watch atop the wheelhouse, Seaman Looff breathed deep, sucking down the salt air, faintly flavored with the sour taste of the mainland jungle to the west. It's odd. A boy grows to manhood enjoying many pleasures. A mother's touch, good beer, a pretty girl's smile. But after four years in the stinking U-boats, just tasting air untainted by diesel fuel, air that hadn't been breathed already by fifty shipmates, was pleasure enough.

Pure sea air. Fine as wine. Shifting his rifle sling, Looff scanned the deck below. Everything normal. The seven *Indio* deckhands were still asleep, clustered together for warmth, like dogs—

Something rustled behind him. He turned, squinting, trying to penetrate the shadows. Couldn't see a thing. Probably just a rat or—a whirling shape whistled out of the dark, tearing into his chest with terrible force!

Dropping his rifle, Looff stared with horror at the machete buried halfway to its hilt in his breast. His blood was gushing from around the blade. He felt his knees turning to water, tried to shout a warning, but couldn't get any air. No air at all.

As Walli Bauer started up the stairway, he felt a faint vibration on the handrail. As a mechanic, he was attuned to vibrations, the silent speech of machinery.

But these vibrations had nothing to do with engines. Someone was coming down from above. Quietly. And he felt no thump of seaboots. The man above was barefoot. Which told him more than he wanted to know.

Backing away from the ladder, sweating, Bauer tried to think. Barefoot. The man coming down was probably one of the *Indio* crewmen. Should he try to take him alive? Why bother? Language barrier. Without a translator the *Indio* couldn't tell him anything. And this one wouldn't be coming down after him if anyone above was still alive.

Who was on guard duty above? Looff. Damn! A good man. Quick with a smile or a joke. A shipmate. Thinking of Looff made the decision for him. Bauer backed away from the stairway, flattening himself against the bulkhead, his Mauser at port arms.

Sweating, dry-mouthed, he waited. Trying to keep his breathing shallow. Trying to melt into the metal.

The *Indio* came down so swiftly, so silently, he seemed to materialize out of the darkness. One moment he wasn't there and the next instant he was. Startling Bauer, catching him by surprise.

And he knew! Somehow the *Indio* knew Bauer was waiting! Sensed his presence the way a jungle cat scents danger. Whirling on the last step, teeth bared, the pirate raised his machete!

A second too late. Bauer swung the rifle butt full force, catching the Indio under the ear, snapping the savage's neck with an audible crack!

Dropping him to the deck like a sack of flour.

Bauer stood over the *Indio,* walleyed, panting, rifle poised to smash him down, finish him! But there was no need. The pirate twitched once, then went immutably still. Dead as a coal bucket.

Bauer swallowed, trying not to gag on the bile rising at the back of his throat. Think! How much noise had they made? Not much. The engine drone and the thump of the waves probably masked the sound of the deck-hand's death.

But maybe not. These *Indios* were men of the jungle. They could hear a flea fart in the forest five miles off.

Shifting the Mauser carbine to his right hand, Bauer rested his trembling palm on the rail. No vibration. No one was coming down the steps. Yet.

He stood there a full five minutes. Waiting. Sweating. Trying to collect himself. To decide what to do next. He was a mechanic, not a warrior. He understood engines and ships and forecastle politics. He'd spent a lifetime learning them.

But this kind of slaughter? Men fighting like animals, murdering each other for money. Over drugs? There was no honor in it, no logic. Bauer simply couldn't make sense of it.

He only knew that he hadn't come all this way,

worked all these years to die like a dog in the belly of this stinking smuggler's scow.

He was a seaman. *Kriegsmarine!* And if his time was up, he damned well wouldn't be shipping out alone.

Grabbing the *Indio* by the hair, he dragged the corpse away from the stairs into the shadows. Then he took off his boots and began creeping up the ladder, rifle ready, pausing at every step, listening. Hearing only the thrum of the diesels. And his own hammering heart.

Stroessner sidled down the narrow corridor, staying close to the bulkhead, trying to avoid squeaks. Damn. A narrow stripe of light was showing under Bronner's cabin door. Had he fallen asleep with a lantern lit? Or was he awake? Perhaps reading?

Or had he heard something? Looff's body hitting the deck, maybe? Was he waiting inside with his pistol covering the door, ready to fire?

Chewing his lip, Stroessner quickly calculated the odds. He had Heitman's submachine gun. He could kick in the door and cut loose. If Bronner was in the bunk, he'd probably be killed instantly.

But if he'd been alerted? He might return fire. The submachine gun gave Stroessner a big advantage, but he couldn't afford the noise of a gun battle. The sound could carry across the water to the U-boat, warning her crew.

Dawn was only an hour away. The submarine would have to submerge at first light. Once she was gone, he could radio an SOS to Brazilian air defense, saying the *Carmela* was under attack by a U-boat.

While the airmen ran off the Nazis, Stroessner would run the *Carmela* ashore on Ilha de Maguas, where the rest of his *Indios* waited to carry off her cargo and vanish into the jungle.

But first he had to make it to dawn without alerting

the damned sub. Which meant no noise, no gunfight.

It was just as well. Cleverness had carried him this far. A smile, a little conversation, and Bronner would never know what hit him.

Laying the Schmeisser carefully on the deck, Stroessner gave a quick flick of his wrist, and a stiletto appeared like magic in his hand. Satisfied, he slipped the blade back into its sheath up his sleeve. Then, straightening his jacket, he rapped lightly on the door.

"Kapitän? Kapitän Bronner?"

"Come in." Bronner was in bed, reading. In his underwear, wearing wire-rimmed spectacles, he looked like someone's good-natured grandfather. Which he probably was. "Ah, *Herr* Stroessner. What is it? What's wrong?"

"Leutnant Heitman sent me to fetch you, *Kapitän.* He's in the hold. Apparently the storm damaged the *Carmela* more seriously than we thought. Her hull plates are ripping loose, rivets are flying around down there. It looks bad."

"I'll come at once," Bronner said, placing the book on the nightstand beside the bunk. And grabbing the Luger. Which he levelled at Stroessner's belly.

"Kapitän, what—?"

"Forgive my doubtful nature, Stroessner. And step a little closer to the light, please." Removing his spectacles, Bronner placed them carefully beside the book. But the Luger never wavered.

"Kapitän Bronner, I don't understand—"

"Spare me anymore lies, you incredible piece of shit. Heitman was ordered to keep a close watch on you. And yet here you are. Alone. Which means Heitman is either dead or a prisoner. Which is it?"

Stroessner swallowed. "He's a prisoner."

"Really? Why do I doubt that? You should be more careful about your appearance, Captain. You seem to have bloodstains on your jacket. Raise your hands. Now!"

Stroessner did as he was told, backing slowly away as Bronner slid out of the bunk. But the instant Bronner started to rise, Stroessner flicked his wrist, then hurled the hideaway stiletto straight at Bronner's head!

Diving to avoid the blade, Bronner fired wildly as Stroessner dodged out the door. The *Kapitän* was only a step behind but stumbled over Heitman's submachine gun. He fired again and nearly got him. A bullet whacked into the doorjamb above Stroessner's head as the pirate dove through the doorway, vanishing into the darkness at the end of the hall.

Covering the corridor with his Luger, Bronner picked up Heitman's Schmeisser, his lips narrowing as he spotted the bloodstains on the butt. Damn Stroessner and his damned coca and this godforsaken tub. Damn them all to hell!

Grabbing up the submachine gun, Bronner retreated back into the cabin. With the door ajar, he quickly pulled on his jacket and trousers.

There. He'd thrown away his honor chasing fool's gold and he'd probably be dead meat by morning, but at least he wouldn't have to die in his damned underwear.

His mind whirled as he buttoned his jacket. Were any of the prize crew still alive? Not Heitman, certainly. Stroessner showing up alone proved that.

And when Stroessner ran down the corridor, he'd bolted out onto the deck but there'd been no challenge from the sentry and no shots. Which meant Seaman Looff and Jak Heinz were dead, too. Stroessner's men were probably in control of the ship.

Bronner was alone. Trapped in a cabin at the end of a blind corridor. But somehow he had to warn the

U-boat, even if it meant his death. Think? What was the layout of this hell ship?

There were two doors at the far end of the passageway. One led out onto the deck. The other opened into the main stairwell, the spiral staircase that led up to the bridge or down into the hold.

How could he warn the sub? The ship's radio? Could he get to it? Not likely. Too far. Assuming they hadn't already smashed it.

Gunfire then? Maybe. The U-boat lookout would almost certainly hear gunfire. But it would have to be soon. It was nearly dawn and Scheringer would submerge at first light. No time to waste.

Holstering his Luger, Bronner checked the load on the submachine gun. Full magazine and a round in the chamber. He took a deep breath, then stepped out into the hall, covering the far doorway with the Schmeisser.

One step, then another. Inching his way down the corridor until at last he was beside the exit door. It was open. Stroessner hadn't had time to close it. He could fire a burst in the direction of the U-boat as a warning. Then charge out on the deck and try to kill as many of the pirates as—

No. Wait. Suppose Stroessner left the door open deliberately? Trying to lure him through it?

He heard the faintest creak from overhead. And instantly guessed what it meant. There was a man up there on the quarterdeck, waiting for him to come through the door.

Where would he be? Close enough to swing a machete. They'd want to kill him quietly. Too damned bad. Time to start the dance.

Raising the Schmeisser, Bronner fired a burst up into the ceiling, punching a ragged line of nine-millimeter holes through the metal, shattering the legs of the *Indio* above, sending him crashing to the deck, writhing, screaming.

Shouting over the roar of the gun, Bronner leapt through the doorway. He tried to vault past the wounded man, but the dying *Indio* grabbed at his ankle, tripping him, sending him sprawling to the deck.

And saved Bronner's life. Mauser slugs from three directions ripped past his head. In the split second it took the pirates to work their rifle bolts, Bronner rolled, firing a quick burst up at the wheelhouse, chopping down another one.

Rising to one knee, he touched off a half-dozen rounds in the general direction of the U-boat, then dove back through the doorway as a ragged fusillade raked the deck.

Made it! But as he turned to fire again, a hammer blow smashed his left shoulder, slamming him backward into the bulkhead.

Stunned, Bronner reeled into the stairwell, staggering down the steps to escape the hailstorm of gunfire pouring into the corridor. Someone grabbed his leg from below. He tried to bring the Schmeisser to bear one-handed—

"*Kapitän!* Don't shoot! It's me!"

Bauer. Bronner almost shot him anyway. Dazed, running on reflex, it took a moment for the *Bootsmann*'s voice to register.

"Walli? Is it you?"

"Yes, *Kapitän*," Bauer said, climbing up the steps, taking the Schmeisser, helping Bronner down into the breathless heat of the hold. "I heard shooting. What the hell happened?"

"I tried to warn the sub with gunfire. Hit one *Indio*, maybe two. Stroessner got away."

"You're wounded, *Kapitän*."

"It's maybe not too bad." Bronner winced, probing the

ragged tear in his upper arm with his fingertips. "It's through and through, I think."

Stripping off his bandanna, Bauer wrapped it around the wound to stem the bleeding. "*Leutnant* Heitman's dead, I found his body forward. What about the others? Seaman Looff? And Heinz?"

"Dead, too, I'm afraid. We're the prize crew now, Walli. Just us. You and me."

"Damn." Bauer knotted the bandanna. "That'll hold it for now. What do we do, *Kapitän*?"

"We have to warn the U-boat, Walli. Stroessner will call in an air strike, then sail happily off to Rio while U-233 runs for her life."

"I don't think they're headed for Rio, *Kapitän*. This tub would never make it. She's breaking up at the bow, rivets are ripping out up there, humming around like bees. I think this lot crippled her with a mine or a satchel charge, then boarded her. Only the blast did more damage than they expected. They'll have to run her for the coastal islands now. Maybe that was the plan all along."

"It doesn't matter. We still have to warn Scheringer. I'm going to try for the bridge, Walli. If I can't get to the radio, perhaps the sub will hear the gunfire."

"That's suicide, *Kapitän*."

"I expect it is. Do you have a better idea?" ·

"We could burn her. Set the cargo afire."

"That's a marvelous improvement on my idea, *Bootsmann*. Instead of dying topside in the fresh air we can suffer an excruciating death down here, roasted alive. Personally, I'd rather take a bullet storming the bridge."

"We'll still get to the bridge, Kapitän. After we kill them."

Bronner stared at Bauer a moment, then nodded slowly, smiling in fierce understanding. "They won't let this cargo burn. They'll have to come below to put it out. And there's only one way down."

"Unless they open one of the hatches," Bauer agreed. "Either way, U-233 will spot the smoke and put a torpedo into this tub."

"Torpedo?"

"Your orders, *Kapitän*. You told Scheringer to—"

"Torpedo the *Carmela*, yes. Actually, I lied about that. Sinking this tub would draw too much attention to the U-boat. At the first sign of trouble Scheringer's orders are to run the sub back to the Amazon and go to ground. We're on our own here, Walli, and we'd best get to it. I don't want to bleed to death before I've had the pleasure of hanging Stroessner over the side by his own guts."

Bauer eyed him oddly.

"An exaggeration, Walli. Poetic license."

"That doesn't make it a bad idea," Bauer said grimly.

Pulling down a half-dozen coca bales, Bauer quickly built two barricades across the catwalk. Wincing, Bronner settled in between the bales while Bauer clawed his way up on top of the cargo stack to light several small fires. He came scrambling down to take up his position beside Bronner.

"Sweet Jesus, *Kapitän,*" he panted. "It's so fucking hot up there I thought the coca might explode before I lit the first match. The fire is spreading across the damned bales like a puddle of gasoline."

Black smoke was already roiling above them, writhing and twisting like a living thing—and coiling its way up the stairwell in a thickening cloud, seeking the open air.

Bronner eyed Bauer for a moment, then nodded. No need for words. And no time. Both men settled in, Bauer covering the stairway with the submachine gun while

Bronner kept watch on the forward cargo hatches, his Luger in his fist.

Suddenly a figure materialized out of the smoke pouring up the stairwell. One of the *Indios* came scrambling down the steps, coughing, eyes streaming, but with his rifle at the ready.

Bauer fired a long burst with the Schmeisser, the gun bucking in his hands, spraying the stairway with lead, slugs hammering the metal steps, ripping the deckhand with a half-dozen rounds. But, incredibly, the man kept coming, staggering toward them, blood foaming in his mouth, until a second burst from Bauer's submachine gun cut him nearly in half.

Two more followed right behind the first. Firing desperately, Bauer caught the first man with a few slugs, but the second leapt clear. Diving behind some crates, the *Indio* opened fire, sending Mauser slugs ripping into the coca barricade.

Above them the blaze was growing more intense, eating into the stacks, growling like a great beast feeding.

"*Kapitän,* get ready to cover for me. I'll have to reload soon."

But Bronner barely heard him. Up forward, in the smoky hell near the bow of the ship, he sensed a movement. The smoke overhead was changing direction. Finding a new way out.

Someone had opened an access door to a cargo hatch. The bow hatch. Perhaps forty meters away. A difficult shot for a pistol anytime, and through the smoke with the ship rocking . . .

Bracing himself, Bronner tried to steady his arm, focusing on the Luger's sights as a rope came snaking down through the swirling black smoke.

And there he was. Stroessner. Scrambling down the

line hand over hand, a Mauser carbine strapped to his back.

Bronner fired. No effect. Desperately, he fired again, and then again, blinking the sweat out of his eyes, nearly emptying his pistol, knowing he'd never hit Stroessner at this distance with a handgun, not with the damned smoke growing denser by the second.

But he must have come close. Or perhaps the heat was becoming too intense to bear. Halfway down the rope, Stroessner halted. He hung in space a moment, resting. Bronner fired his last shot. A clean miss. Not even close. Grinning, Stroessner flipped the *Kapitän* a mock salute, then began climbing slowly upward again.

He never made it. With a mighty *whuff* the super-heated air lifted the forward cargo hatch, blowing it completely off. Instantly the blaze above changed direction, fueled by the salt air, gushing toward the open hatch in a torrent of fire!

Stroessner had no chance. Suspended in midair, he was engulfed by the flames! Howling and writhing, his clothing and hair alight, he clung mindlessly to the line. Burning alive. Until the rope gave way and he fell. And disappeared into the maelstrom.

"Kapitän. Kapitän!"

It took a moment for Bauer's voice to penetrate. Bronner was still staring down the Luger's sights. Aiming at . . . nothing. Stroessner was gone, swallowed by a roiling wall of flame.

"Kapitän, we've got to get the hell out of here! The whole damned ship's going up!"

The *Indio* apparently reached the same conclusion. Throwing his rifle away, the pirate scrambled back up the stairs and vanished overhead.

Bauer helped Bronner to his feet, then the two men stumbled to the stairwell. A strong downdraft was clearing the smoke away. The fire was sucking air down to feed the horrendous blaze howling out through the forward hatch.

Cautiously, slowed by Bronner's wound, they worked their way up the stairs. Above, the first light of dawn was breaking. Leaving Bronner in the corridor, Bauer charged out onto the deck, Schmeisser ready to fire.

But they were gone. The *Indios* had hacked the lifeboat free with their machetes, dropping it into the surf. But it had landed upside down, and now they were swimming like rats for the distant green shore.

But at sea, distances are deceptive. The glowing coastline was an illusion of the dawn, much farther off than it appeared.

Perhaps the *Indios* would make it, but Bauer didn't think much of their chances.

His own chances were better. Over the roar of the flame he heard the familiar chortle of U-233's motorwhaler chugging through the surf to fetch the prize crew of the *Carmela*.

Bronner joined him at the rail, his uniform a shambles, his face ashen from blood loss.

"Damn," he said softly. "I believe Mr. Scheringer has violated my direct orders, *Bootsmann*. Remind me to recommend him for a medal."

"Yes, *Kapitän*. You know, it's the strangest thing."

"What is?"

"Despite all that's happened, I have the most incredible feeling of . . . elation. It's like Christmas morning and my first blow job all rolled into one."

"I know, I have the same feeling, Walli. We've been breathing the smoke of the coca leaves. Don't worry, I'm sure it will pass."

Bauer stared at him a moment. "Damn," he said softly. "What a pity."

"Yes." Bronner smiled. "It certainly is."

As the whaler approached the flaming hulk of the *Carmela*, the steersman cut the throttle. Odd. The *Kapitän* and *Bootsmann* Bauer were hanging over the railing.

At first he thought they were trying to avoid the smoke pouring out of the freighter's hold. But then he realized both men were laughing. Laughing with tears streaming down their sooty faces.

Laughing so hard they could scarcely breathe.

Mission Failure

Brendan DuBois

Brendan DuBois is the award-winning author of short stories and novels. His short fiction has appeared in Playboy, Ellery Queen's Mystery Magazine, Alfred Hitchcock's Mystery Magazine, Mary Higgins Clark Mystery Magazine, *and numerous anthologies. He has twice received the Shamus Award from the Private Eye Writers of America for his short fiction, and has been nominated three times for an Edgar Allan Poe Award by the Mystery Writers of America. He's also the author of the Lewis Cole mystery series:* Dead Sand, Black Tide, Shattered Shell, *and* Killer Waves. *His other works include,* Resurrection Day, *an alternative history thriller that looks at what might have happened had the Cuban Missile Crisis of 1962 erupted into a nuclear war between the United States and the Soviet Union, and which received the Sidewise Award for best alternative history novel of 1999. His latest thriller,* Betrayed, *finally resolves the decades-old question of the MIAs from the Vietnam War and their ultimate fate. Most of his works of fiction show his deep interest in political and military history throughout the world. He lives in New Hampshire with his wife, Mona. Please visit his Web site at* www.Brendan DuBois.com.

WHEN NOVEMBER FIRST finally arrived, Scott Blair went out to the deck of his home near the White Mountains of New Hampshire. He sat on a wooden Adirondack chair and propped his aching legs up on the railing, admiring the view. With November underway, the leaves of the large maple tree in the rear yard had finally fallen free, revealing the snow-covered peak of Mount Washington, the highest mountain in the northeast, just a few miles away. Oh, it had been visible off and on during the past few weeks, but since his retirement to this part of New Hampshire, he had enjoyed the little ceremony of seeing the big mountain on the first day after Halloween. It was solid, it was real, and it would be there, year after year, long after he was gone and this house was just a cellar hole in the woods.

It was warm for November, but he still had on fleece-lined pants, a cotton shirt, and a down vest. A mug of tea was balanced on his belly, his hands being warmed by the thick ceramic. He closed his eyes and let the faint sunlight warm his face, and he would have been content to sit there for at least another hour or so, except for the noise.

The damn noise, meaning a car coming up the long dirt driveway, a visitor. He opened his eyes, swiveled his head, looked down the dirt lane that went on for almost a third of a mile before ending up on Route 302. It couldn't be Mike, the UPS man. He only came in late afternoon, and this was way too early for him. And the driveway wasn't marked, so anybody coming up here either had a purpose, or was lost. He couldn't remember the last time anyone came up here for a purpose—hold on, there was that census taker, four years back—and most of the lost people (his nickname for them was "lost souls") were either hikers or nature photographers. In any event, it meant an interruption in his morning routine, and he hated having his routines disturbed.

He got up and looked over the railing as the vehicle approached, mug of tea in his hand. The vehicle—a black Lexus—emerged into the cleared area below the house, and he noted the shiny paint, the fact that it was the latest model, and it all clicked into his mind that it was a rental car. Which meant an airport. Which meant a visitor. A visitor with a purpose. He sighed, just as the car came to a halt and a figure inside waved up at him. Spotted. No use hiding in the spare bedroom, reading copies of the *U.S. Naval Institute Proceedings*, until his damn uninvited visitor left. He didn't bother waving back and went through the kitchen, lots of open exposed beams, pots and pans hanging over the countertop. From one drawer he pulled out a nine-millimeter Beretta, stuck it in his rear waistband, flinching from the cold metal on his skin, and then he went out to see who was bothering him.

The young man had a nice tan overcoat, nice black shoes quickly getting muddy from the wet soil at the front of the house, and a nice-looking black briefcase to go with his haircut. He looked like the kind of guy who haunted the halls of Congress, working for a lobbyist for some obscure mineral rights organization in the Midwest, and his smile as he approached was about as sincere as a

Parisian prostitute seeing a five-hundred-dollar bill for the first time.

"Mr. Blair? Scott Blair?"

He said, "Please don't insult my intelligence. You didn't drive here from Boston—"

"Manchester."

"Wherever, if you didn't know where you were going or what I looked like. Who are you?"

He stepped forward, close, but not close enough to be a threat. "The name is Glen Kyte. I'm from Langley."

Oh boy, he thought. This was going to be a doozie. He said, "What's the matter? A hang-up with my pension check?"

A quick shake of the head. "Oh, nothing like that, Mr. Blair. I've come to talk to you for a few minutes."

"About what?"

Kyte looked around the woods, and Scott knew what the young man was imagining: somebody out there, skulking, listening in with a shotgun mike for deep and dark secrets. Can't allow that to happen now, can we? "I'll tell you. But can we go inside?"

Scott shrugged. "Sure."

He turned and walked back into the house, thinking wryly to himself that he hoped the young pup would appreciate the vote of confidence he had just given him, by exposing his back to a stranger. But the pup didn't say a word, and in the house Scott said, "Please wipe your feet. The cleaning service doesn't come for another week and I don't want to see your muddy footprints around after you leave."

From the entranceway they went through the mudroom and out to the living room, which butted up against the open kitchen. There was a woodstove in a corner, and tall windows that looked out to the woods and under-brush. Bookcases were stuffed along the walls, overflowing with volumes. Kyte started unbuttoning his coat and looked around, nodding and smiling, revealing a dark blue two-piece suit, white shirt, and red necktie. "Quite the nice place you have here, Mr. Blair. I'm sure it's quite peaceful."

"It is," Scott said, "and I'm sure you're going to tell me why you've come all the way up here to disturb my peace. Here, give me your coat."

He took the topcoat, draped it over a couch, sat down in an easy chair. Kyte sat across from him on the couch, next to his topcoat, balancing the briefcase on his knees. Scott winced as the pistol dug into his back, and he said, " 'Scuse me, will you?" and reached behind to pull the weapon out. Kyte's eyes widened, and Scott could see his fingers tighten on the briefcase. "Really, Mr. Blair, there's no reason—"

"I'm sure there isn't," he said, carefully putting the pistol down on top of the coffee table, which was cluttered with about a half-dozen newspapers. "So let's just get your bona fides out of the way, shall we?"

Kyte nodded. "Of course."

"Let's see some identification."

The young man pulled a thin leather wallet out from inside his suit coat, passed it over. Scott gave it a quick glance, passed it back. "Your photo does you justice."

"Thanks."

"Okay, hold on. You've got a cell phone with you?"

"I do."

"Pass it over."

Which is what he did. Scott flipped open the cover and dialed a number from memory, and the phone was answered on the first ring by a woman repeating the last four digits he had just dialed. "Four six six four."

"This is Scott Blair calling," he said. "Case file Bravo

Bravo Zulu twelve. There is a gentleman here, claiming to be from the Agency. Name is Glen Kyte."

"Hold on."

No music, no static. Just dead air. He didn't have to wait long. The woman came back and said, "I have confirmation on that."

"Clearance level?"

"Equal to yours."

Well, that was a relief, he thought. "Can you give me an identification phrase?"

The woman said, "His mother's high school. Everett High."

"Thanks," he said, breaking the connection and handing the phone over. "Son, what high school did your mother attend?"

Kyte gave a quick nod, like he understood everything that had just happened. "Everett High School."

"Very good," he said. "Your bona fides have been established." He looked down at the coffee table, didn't like the view that much, and covered his pistol with a copy of last week's *New York Times* "Book Review." "What's going on?"

Kyte offered up a smile, like he was so happy to finally be doing his job. He spun the briefcase around, opened it up—how polite, Scott thought, showing him that there was no weapon inside—and pulled out a manila file folder. Kyte put the briefcase down on the couch and said, "I belong to the Historical Review Archive with the Agency."

"The what?"

"Historical Review Archive," he said. "Basically, I'm a historian, Mr. Blair."

Scott didn't try very hard to hide the dismay in his voice. "We're in a life-and-death struggle against organized terrorism, a struggle destined to last decades, and the Agency has the resources and wherewithal to hire historians? Honestly?"

Kyte's young face seemed flushed. "Honestly, Mr. Blair. It's what I do and I do it very well. I know what I do is nothing compared to the field operatives or almost anybody else in the Agency, but it is important work, establishing the historical record, showing the directors what happened in the past, what missions worked, which ones didn't. With that kind of historical knowledge available to them, it assists them in planning further operations. We can't afford, especially nowadays, to let our directors work in ignorance of what has gone on before."

Now Scott felt bad about beating up the little guy. "George Santayana."

"Excuse me?"

"George Santayana," he said. "Famous philosopher who said—"

" 'He who cannot remember the past, is condemned to repeat it,' " Kyte said, seemingly relishing each word. "That's exactly right, Mr. Blair. That's the mission of our little group. To ensure that the decision makers with the higher pay grades have the information they need."

Scott shifted his position in his chair again. "Wish some of them had read a little more about a certain December seventh at Pearl Harbor and had kept that in mind a few years back . . . oh well, what's past is past. What does a historian want with me?"

Kyte opened up the manila folder. "I'm looking for some information on a mission you participated in, just over forty years ago. Aboard the USS *Growler*."

Scott felt like the foundation on this side of the house had just turned into putty, for he had the damnedest sensation that he was falling backward, falling deeper into his chair, and that at any moment the chair would start sliding and would go right through one of the tall windows. He cleared his throat. "Well, you've certainly gotten my attention. What kind of information are you looking for?"

Kyte flipped through a few sheets of paper. "Whatever you can tell me, Mr. Blair."

"Well, can you narrow it down some? That mission was fairly extensive and lasted several weeks."

Kyte said, "It certainly appears to have been, Mr. Blair. And that's the problem. You see, all we have here—and all that appears to have existed in the archives—is a three-page memo outlining the scope of the mission. Then, there is a one-page report from you, reporting that the mission was a success. And a year later, in another memo that was cross-referenced to this mission, you have a harsh mention of how the USS *Growler*'s mission was a total and abject failure. But no details. And according to the log for this particular file, there should have been a sixty-two page report from you, outlining the mission from start to finish. It appears to have, um, been misfiled."

Scott offered the young man his best smile. "Don't be so damn stupid. The report eventually turned out to be quite embarrassing. So it was sanitized, that's what. Happens to every intelligence agency, no matter if they're in Paris or DC or Moscow. Damn." He took a breath, folded his hands, and wondered why in hell this . . . hell, this kid, showed up on his doorstep with lots of questions. Any other day he would have sent him on his way, but damn it, with what the Agency was doing now, and what it had been doing ever since a particular September day, maybe it would do them some good to stir things up, to make them look at the past with a critical eye. Lord knows he had thought about that mission, late at night, listening to the winds come down from the mountains and the wood in his old house creak.

"All right," he said. "Sanitized or not, I guess you can ask away. Start right up."

"Excuse me?"

Scott said, "Let's get going. If you want to know the details, it's going to take awhile. So let's start off by you telling me what you know about the USS *Growler* and why I was there."

Kyte nodded, his eyes bright, like he was pleased to be on track. "The USS *Growler* and other submarines in the late 1950s and early 1960s were involved in a continuing series of missions, all under the code name NORSEMAN. To tell you the truth, I can't . . . well, I've read other mission reports from other submarines. I can't believe the navy did what they did, and that it was never made public."

"They don't call them the Silent Service for nothing," Scott said, the old memories rushing back—amazing how fast they came back, and how the first thing he remembered from that mission was the smell, the constant stink of diesel and human bodies being cooped up for weeks at a time in a metal cylinder.

"But the audacity! To actually travel up rivers in the Soviet Union to spy on harbor installations or to drop off field agents . . . it sounds amazing!"

"That's where the code name came from, you know," Scott said. "Hundreds of years ago, Vikings used to travel up and down a lot of Russian rivers. We were just following their trail. But with the possiblity of Soviet nuclear weapons being exploded over our own cities, well, that tended to focus our attention a bit. And so gambles were made, and missions were performed. Submarines like the one I was on, they used to sneak into Russian territorial waters all the time. Sometimes they trailed Russin subs. Sometimes they listened to onshore installations. And sometimes the missions were a success. Other times, they were failures."

"So how could this mission have been both?" Kyte asked.

"Easily," he said. "Quite easily."

In the tiny mess room of the USS *Growler*, Scott Blair of the Central Intelligence Agency was seated across from Corkland, a chief petty officer in the crew, a beefy man with tattooed forearms whose dungaree shirt always had half moons of sweat underneath his armpits. It had been almost a month since he had entered this boat, and he still could not believe how cramped the damn thing was. Corkland had told him, right from the start, that by the time a few weeks went by, he would get used to the size of the boat—"And don't call her a ship, them's targets—this is a boat," the petty officer had warned him—and that the inside would seem as large as a house. But the opposite had happened to Scott. With each passing week the damn thing seemed to shrink and shrink, to enclose upon him. During his nights of fitful sleep in the damp and smelly bunk assigned to him, he would sometimes dream that the hull was slowing collapsing around him, enclosing him, tightening him in its metal grasp.

Still, the crew had done its best to make him feel comfortable from the start, though the officers were still a bit standoffish; it only made sense, considering who he was and what he was in charge of. And he recalled with a smile the first night on the submarine, learning the ins and outs of using the toilet, when some sailor said, "Mr. Blair, do you know what the difference is 'tween a leak and a flood? Pretty important thing to know in a sub." The sailor had asked the question in front of a small group of sailors, so Scott knew he was being set up, and didn't care.

"No, pal, I don't know what the difference is between a leak and a flood. But I think you're going to tell me."

A smile, followed by laughter from the kid's crewmates: "You can find a leak, but a flood will find you."

Now, weeks later, Corkland passed over a mug of coffee, the white china chipped and stained. Just above Corkland's head was a metal bulkhead, and fastened there was a plaque, which stated: "Lord, my boat is so small and Thy sea is so vast." Scott had never been one for religion, but he read that plaque at each mealtime, hoping that the guy upstairs would hear his prayers, and that never again would he ever have to set to sea in a submarine, ever again. As near as he could figure it, the only reason he had been assigned this mission was the experiences he had had over a number of summers, crewing aboard one of his uncle's sailing boats, out of Long Island Sound.

Corkland said, "Some of the younger guys, they're itchin' to transfer out, to get into one of those new nuclear boats. The attack subs, the Skipjack class." Corkland shook his head and picked up his own mug of coffee. "That's fine for them younger pups, but give me good ol' reliable diesel-electric."

Scott made a point of publicly sniffing the air. "I hear that the air is nice and fresh aboard the nuclear boats. Doesn't that make any difference?"

"What makes a difference is the crew and the captain," Corkland declared. "A good crew like ours, and with a cap like Commander Moore, we can go anywhere and do almost anything that a nuke can. And I like diesel. It's reliable. Not like all that atomic crap going on in the engine room, making you sterile or whatnot."

One of the sailors coming off watch poured himself a cup of coffee. "Sure, Chief, but the nukes got more than just good air. Those nukes got nice evaporators, make all the fresh water you need. No more dirty laundry, all the hot showers you want. This pig boat is one of the last ones, and you know it."

Corkland grumbled. "Maybe so, but a pig boat like this got me through against the Japs and the North Koreans. She'll do fine right 'til the navy tells me it's time to scuttle her."

The sailor made a motion, pointing up. "Let's just hope the navy doesn't tell us now. Might do something for the morale," and he laughed, walking toward a forward compartment. Scott took a sip of the coffee—had to give the navy credit, they had fairly good coffee in such a smelly environment—and reflected on what the sailor had just done. No need to point it out, where they were and what they were doing. Officially, the USS *Growler* was three hundred miles off the coast of Newfoundland, in the North Atlantic, testing new radio equipment. And for the benefit of any Soviet trawlers or intelligence ships in the area, a submarine tender and a sub identifying itself as the USS *Growler* were doing just that. But the sub in the North Atlantic was masquerading as the *Growler*, for her real mission was almost to its inception point: here, in the Black Sea, at the mouth of a Russian river.

Another sip of coffee. Hard to believe, but it was true, for the USS *Growler*—already many miles inside Russian territorial waters—was about to add insult to injury by going upriver, to a Soviet naval base. And most of the crew thought it was Scott Blair's fault, and they were correct. For up in the forward torpedo compartment was something that he had brought with him in New London, something the crew called a black box, though it was shaped like a smaller torpedo. Scott didn't know all of the intricate workings of the device, but he knew what the mission was: to get near the Soviet naval base, gently

pop it out of one of the torpedo tubes, and then quietly
head back home. The device would rest in the mud, and
electronics inside would hear radio chatter, the beat of
propellors, and other transmissions, and broadcast the information to air force surveillance aircraft flying out of
Turkey. It was the navy's job to get the device to where
it belonged, and it was Scott's job to shepherd the device
and report back to Langley that the mission had been
accomplished. When he had first been assigned the mission, it had seemed a wonderful lark, a nice chit to his
career with the Agency, and he thought he could handle
the smells and noises and the incredible isolation of being inside a tin can, day after monotonous day. But now,
having come face-to-face with the reality, he could hardly wait to get back to the States. And he knew turning
down missions would kill his career in a second, but this
was going to be his first and last time in a submarine.

Corkland said, "Almost time, Mr. Blair. Less than a
day and we'll get to where we're going."

"If the Russian navy lets us."

Corkland grinned. "Those damn skimmers up there
have no idea we're here. None! Which is something big
working in our favor. If we were hanging outside Mur-
mansk or Archangel or Vladivostok, you can believe
there'd be subchasers out there, working the waters. You
couldn't sleep 'cause of all the prop noises overhead or
the sonar pinging. But not here. It'd be like our navy
hunting for Reds up and down the Potomac. Wouldn't
even consider it. Up here, it's nice and quiet."

"This is the third time, right?"

A slow nod. "Yeah. Third time. First two times, we
went right up to the navy yard and did some eavesdropping, some photography of the ships being worked on
there. But this time . . . you know, I like this mission.
Going in, dropping something off, and then getting the

hell out. Suits me just fine. Last two times, we'd sit out there for a week, and man, did those hours drag, especially during the daylight. We were rigged for silence then, nobody barely moving or anything. Night is when we'd surface and charge up the batteries, do our work. That was a real stretch of work. But this . . . shit, it's a piece of cake. And what makes it work in our favor even more is Commander Moore. It takes big brass ones to do what he's done, bringing us in so far into Russian waters, and he always gets us out. It's like he can smell the damn Reds."

Scott was startled as somebody tapped him on the shoulder. He looked up, knowing he should instantly recognize the crewman—there were only about eighty aboard, but he had a problem with remembering names—who said, "The captain's compliments, Mr. Blair, but he'd like to see you in the conning tower."

"Very well," he said, rising up from the metal table. He followed the sailor through to the control room, keeping his head low and his elbows tucked in tight against his ribs. During his first week here, he had collected a nasty series of bruises from bumping and banging into valves and instruments. Inside the control room he went up a ladder and into the conning tower, where Commander Moore was hunched over, peering through a periscope. He felt a flush of embarrassment, recalling how confused he was when he had first met the naval officer. It had seemed like he had two ranks—commander and captain, and he couldn't figure out why—until another petty officer took pity on him, explaining that aboard all naval vessels, the commanding officer, even if he was a lieutenant, junior grade, was honored with the title captain.

"Mr. Blair," Moore said, not raising his head.

"That's right," he said.

Moore sighed and then stood up. His executive officer—a lieutenant named Piper—was examining a chart nearby. Moore was in his thirties, lean and trim, with prematurely graying hair, and Scott knew that Moore had despised him, right from the very start. And it made sense. This was his boat and crew, damn it, his responsibility, and Moore no doubt hated having a CIA spook aboard, a spook that technically could boss him and his boat around. It had taken a written order from the chief of naval operations to let that happen, but still, Moore didn't like it. And he never hesitated to show his displeasure.

"I need to show you something, Mr. Blair."

Scott said, "Is there a problem?"

"Well, that's what I want to find out. Here. Take a look."

He went around and lowered his head to the padded and moist eyepiece of the periscope. He blinked and then the image came into focus. He was looking at a point of land jutting out into the wide river. No trees, just grassland. A building was inland, maybe fifty yards or so. Looked to be about six or eight stories. In front of the building was a paved road and a parked car. The car was painted black and even looked American. He gently swiveled the periscope, left and right, left and right, saw a couple of smaller buildings. Nobody seemed to be out and about. It was early morning, and he knew that very shortly the captain would order the periscope lowered, to prevent any inquiring eyes from noticing them.

Scott looked up. "What am I seeing?"

Moore said, "What you're seeing is something that doesn't belong there."

"I'm sorry, I don't understand."

Moore seemed exasperated. "Look. This point of land is used as a checkpoint for us as we go upriver. We call it Checkpoint Able. From here it's just an hour to the naval base. The last two times we've gone up here, there was nothing on that point of land. Nothing. Just rocks and grass. Now, six months later, there's this new construction."

"So?" Scott asked. "New construction. What's the big deal?"

"What the big deal is, is that this is military land, on both sides of the river. That building looks civilian, not military. It doesn't belong here. I know what Soviet military facilities look like. That's not one of them."

Scott shrugged. "I'm sorry. I don't see what the big deal is."

Moore rubbed at the back of the head. "Take another look, all right?"

He bent down again, thinking, every second here, every minute here, is time being wasted when we should be going upstream. He blinked his eyes, looked again. Brick building. Paved road in front of building. Parked black car. A couple of outbuildings.

"Okay," he said, standing up. "I saw a brick building, some smaller structures. Paved road. A black car. Looks like a Cadillac. Maybe a Lincoln. What's the point, Commander?"

"The point is, Mr. Blair, that it's not right." Again the commander rubbed at the back of his head, and Scott recalled what the chief petty officer had said earlier: It was like the cap could smell the damn Reds. "There's a building but nothing else. No sidewalks. No utility poles. And a paved road in front that starts and stops, in the middle of a field, and that doesn't go anywhere. And a parked American automobile. Mr. Blair, I don't have to lecture you on what kind of economy these people have. If somebody was to come into possession of an American automobile, it wouldn't be parked in front of an empty building on an empty stretch of riverfront in some military reservation. It would be at some central committee dacha or some general's hunting lodge. Not out here in the open."

His hands were still on the periscope controls. He took a breath. "All right. So what?"

Moore's face seemed flushed. "Being a member of our intelligence community, I thought you would want to know. I'm planning to take some photographs, some measurements, before we proceed."

Scott shook his head. "I'm afraid not, Commander Moore. You know what your orders are. To proceed up to the vicinity of the Soviet naval base with all due speed. Not to take time out for something that piques your interest. We need to get moving, Commander. You know I'm right."

He could sense the dislike and hate behind those pale blue eyes staring right at him, the damn civilian who had pretty much taken command of his boat and crew. But Moore was a good officer. Had to be, for what he did for a living, to come so far into the Russian Bear's playground.

"Very well," he said stiffly. "Down scope."

A voice came from inside the conning tower. "Down scope, aye, sir."

Some hours later he was in the cramped control room with Commander Moore, who was doing his best to ignore him. He half listened to the chatter that was going on about him, as the well-trained and well-oiled crew did their job, just as they were supposed to do. Some quick "sneaks and peaks" through the periscope had verified their position, and the executive officer had been pleased to report that a rainstorm was passing through, meaning no sunlight glinting off the periscope's optics announcing their presence. Scott stood there, with a crowd of sailors but alone, knowing he would always be apart from them, no matter how many of them treated him with kindness or politeness. He was here and didn't really belong, and he found he really didn't care. Just get the mission done and get back home alive and in one piece. He never wanted to be underwater, ever again.

Moore said, "Open number one tube outer door."

"Number one tube outer door open, aye, sir."

Moore murmured something to another officer, seemed to catch Scott's eye for just a second. "Torpedo room ready?"

"Torpedo room reports ready, sir," came the reply from a sailor with some sort of microphone suspended in front of his chest.

"Very well. Fire one."

There was just the faintest shudder, and then the report. "Number one fired, sir."

Moore seemed to take that in, not saying anything, arms across his chest. Not firing a torpedo, but a black box, delivered by some spook, must still have been odd to him, Scott thought.

"Close number one tube outer door."

"Number one tube outer door closed, sir."

Then, a faint smile. "Well, Mr. Blair. I sure do hope your little black box works."

"Me, too."

"Very well," Moore said. "Let's get the hell out of here, shall we?"

More smiles, but no one said anything. They didn't have to. Scott went up to say something more to the commander, to thank him for everything he had done, but the commander's back was turned as he ducked through a hatchway leading forward. Scott didn't feel like chasing him, so he didn't.

• • •

Later he found himself back in the mess room, once again sitting across from Corkland, who was eating a fried Spam sandwich. Scott made do with some crackers and another mug of navy coffee, and Corkland said, "Well, sir, I hope you do appreciate the fine living you went through on this trip. Unlike most of us, you had your own bunk."

"I do appreciate that, Chief," he said, and he meant it. On this mission the crew were divided into three shifts, each functioning at a different time of day, which meant that most of the crew "hot bunked," having to share their bunk with two other crewmates and their sweat and smells and dirty clothes. Scott had his own bunk, tiny and cramped as it was, and he was thinking that when he got back to the States he'd take some leave time and take the train up to New York City and just spend a long weekend in the biggest bed he could find, in the Park Plaza. Just order room service and watch television and roll around on the bed, without listening to the incessant hum of machinery, the talking and coughing from the Navy personnel, and smelling grease and diesel oil, the ever-present diesel oil.

Scott said, "Tell you what, Chief. You ever get to Virginia, I'll give you a tour of the place. Deal?"

Corkland seemed amused by that. "All right, sir, you got yourself a deal. Tell me, what's it like, being in the CIA?"

"Except for trips like this, pretty boring. Lots of reading, paperwork, attending meetings."

"How did you join up with the spooks?"

"Wasn't joined," Scott said, smiling at the memory. "I was recruited. By my history professor."

Corkland took another bite out of his sandwich. "Recruited? You mean, they asked you to join? While you were in college?"

"That's right. About a month before I was to graduate from Yale with a degree in American history and no employment prospects. My professor asked me to meet with an old friend of his in government. We had a pleasant lunch at some faculty club and after a while, he issued me the invitation. I said sure, and well, it went on from there. Didn't even hesitate. And you, Chief?"

Corkland swallowed. "Whadja mean, me?"

"You. How did you get into the navy?"

The chief petty officer smiled. "Well, I guess you could say I got recruited, too. And this invitation came from the emperor of Japan."

"Excuse me?"

Corkland said, "I was seventeen years old. Lived outside of Boston with my ma and four brothers. And on December eight, 1941, I stood in a long line with a bunch of other guys, enlisting. Been in the navy ever since. Seen a lot of things over the years, lots of different things."

"And more to come," Scott said, suddenly liking the older man even more. "You see, pretty soon, the navy and all the other armed services, well, they're going to become tools of the intelligence services, very important tools to keep the peace."

Corkland's chewing slowed. "I don't know if I like that idea. Being a tool."

"Oh, I meant no disrespect," Scott said. "What I meant is that with nuclear weapons and such, intelligence gathering is going to be one of our most important tasks. And getting the intelligence we need is going to rely on the tools of the military. Whether it's the army, navy, or air force, you'll be seeing that a lot more of your missions will be done in coordination with us."

Corkland shook his head. "No offense, sir, but I don't

like the sound of that. But what the hell. You know what?"

"What?"

"The navy tells me where to go, and that's good enough."

"That'll probably be—"

And damn it, just like before, another tap on the shoulder, again from the same sailor as before. And again, the same words: "The captain's compliments, Mr. Blair, but he'd like to see you in the conning tower."

Up in the conning tower Commander Moore said to him simply, "Again, Mr. Blair. Do me the favor of taking a look-see."

Scott felt his temples throb as he bent over to look through the optics. The same building as before, the same paved stretch of road. But the black vehicle had moved, and there were people near the base of the building. He felt a chill, realizing that these Russians—soldiers, perhaps?—would have probably died of shock if they knew they were being watched by an American naval vessel. He shifted the periscope again, left to right, left to right, and saw construction on either side of the brick building. Frameworks were being constructed, but he couldn't tell what was going on.

He stepped away from the periscope. "Looks like a little more work is proceeding. What seems to be the problem, commander?"

Moore looked exasperated, like a grade-school teacher trying to explain the intricacies of one plus one equals two. He said, "Look, Mr. Blair, it doesn't belong there. All right? I know what I'm talking about, and this isn't right."

"How's that again?"

"Look again if you want," he said. "But I was wrong

at first. That's not a building. It's a facade, a fake to look real. You can see the framework for the other two buildings—there's no depth there."

"Meaning what?"

"I'm thinking they're building a scale model of a city block, that's what."

"Perhaps you're correct. I still don't see what the matter is."

Moore said, "We're going to stay here for another day. I want a full workup of photos and drawings. This needs to be reported when we get back."

Scott shook his head. "No."

"Why so quick to say no? For someone who works out of Langley, I thought you'd be interested in what might be going on over there."

"Well, I'm not, and neither is this submarine or its crew."

"I don't think you have a say in this matter, Mr. Blair."

"Oh, I think I do. Please check your orders. I have authority when it comes to this mission."

"The mission is complete," Moore said flatly.

"The hell it is," Scott said. "You said something interesting back there, about when we get back. Do I need to remind you how many miles inside Russian territorial waters we happen to be? Saying 'when we get back' is a statement that's wrong. It should be 'if we get back,' and you know it."

"Listen to me, you young piece of—"

"No," Scott interrupted, noticing that the few crewmembers up there in the conning tower with them were studiously staring at dials or the steel deck, "you listen to me, Commander. This mission isn't over until we're outside of Russian territorial waters. If we get grounded or struck by a fishing boat or otherwise get found, then the Soviets are going to go apeshit, wondering what we

were doing here. And they're going to look at every
square foot of land and river within a mile of their naval
base. That cannot be allowed to happen. The mission
can't be jeopardized because you see something you
think might be interesting. That's no way to manage an
intelligence-gathering operation like this."

Moore said bitterly, "We have a term for what I'm
seeing. Emerging targets."

"And yeah, we have a term, too. Stick to the mission
and don't get greedy. Commander Moore, you know you
have your orders. Stick to the mission."

Scott had twice jumped out of an airplane, had on one
freezing night been chased through some dark alleys of
Budapest, and came near to having his head shot off in
Beirut in '58, but never had he felt in such mortal danger
as right now, with Commander Moore staring right at
him. Scott held his ground. He knew he was right, and
he also knew that he didn't want to spend one more
smelly minute in his steel tube than he had to.

Moore turned his head, spoke softly. "Periscope
down."

"Periscope down, aye, sir."

And he didn't say one more word to Scott, all the way
back to their base in Great Britain, weeks away.

The young pup named Glen Kyte paused in his writing
and said, "What happened, then, to the surveillance pod
that was dropped?"

Scott shrugged. "No idea. I didn't have the need to
know. All I do know is that whatever was transmitted
from the pod was sent to the National Security Agency
and the Office of Naval Intelligence. By then I had plenty
of other things to worry about besides that damn mission."

"So the pod worked, then."

"Guess so."

"Then why did you consider the mission a failure? Was it because of the construction you spotted?"

"Damn right," Scott said, now recalling in his mind's eye exactly what it had been, almost forty years ago. "I should have listened to that commander, that old submariner. I thought I was the expert, that he was just some boat driver, doing a job. I was wrong. My God, how wrong I was."

"I don't understand," Kyte said. "What was the point of that construction, then? Did you ever figure it out?"

"I surely did," Scott said, his voice now quavering. "About seven months later, after the mission was completed. You see, the Russians were building what Commander Moore thought they were building: a reconstruction of a city block, complete with a paved road running through it. And not just any city block. Nope, it was a number of buildings in a particular American city. A city called Dallas. And a place called Dealey Plaza."

There was a soft clink as Kyte dropped his pen on the floor. Scott said, "The bastards . . . they even had a Lincoln Continental, just like the one he would be riding in. They were practicing there, a few months after they were humiliated by the Cuban Missile Crisis, and I don't know if it was the army or the KGB or GRU or whoever it was who wanted their revenge, but they got it, later that November. And me and Commander Moore got a sneak preview, a preview of what was about to happen. And I was too young and stupid and pigheaded to do anything about it."

"My God," Kyte said, his face pale.

"Yep, my God," Scott said. "So. That's how a mission can be both a success and a failure."

He waited. Kyte said not a word. His pen was still on the floor. Scott sighed. He thought he would feel better after this confession, but he didn't. Too many dark memories, way too many dark memories.

He said, "You've got any more questions?"

The young man shook his head. It was like he had been struck dumb.

Scott said, "I'm making a cup of tea. You want one, too?"

Kyte nodded. Scott got up and headed into the kitchen. It seemed there was nothing else to say, and that was just fine.